MUR
COOKBOOK NOOK

The Secret, Book & Scone Society

"Adams launches an intriguing new mystery series, headed by four spirited amateur sleuths and touched with a hint of magical realism, which celebrates the power of books and women's friendships. Adams's many fans, readers of Sarah Addison Allen, and anyone who loves novels that revolve around books will savor this tasty treat."
—*Library Journal* (starred review), Pick of the Month

"Adams kicks off a new series featuring strong women, a touch of romance and mysticism, and both the cunning present-day mystery and the slowly revealed secrets of the intriguing heroines' pasts."
—*Kirkus Reviews*

"This affecting series launch from Adams provides all the best elements of a traditional mystery. . . . Well-drawn characters complement a plot with an intriguing twist or two."
—*Publishers Weekly*

"Adams's new series blends magical realism, smart women, and small-town quirks to create a cozy mystery that doubles as a love letter to books. Readers will fall in love with Nora's bookstore therapy and Hester's comfort scones. Not to mention Estella, June, hunky Jed the paramedic, and Nora's tiny house-slash-converted-train-caboose . . . a book that mystery fans—and avid readers—won't want to put down until they have savored every last crumb."
—*RT Book Reviews*

Books by Ellery Adams:

Book Retreat Mysteries:

Murder in the Mystery Suite

Murder in the Paperback Parlor

Murder in the Secret Garden

Murder in the Locked Library

Murder in the Reading Room

Murder in the Storybook Cottage

Murder in the Cookbook Nook

The Secret, Book & Scone Society Mysteries:

The Secret, Book & Scone Society

The Whispered Word

The Book of Candlelight

Ink and Shadows

MURDER IN THE COOKBOOK NOOK

ELLERY ADAMS

KENSINGTON
PUBLISHING CORP.

www.kensingtonbooks.com

KENSINGTON BOOKS are published by

Kensington Publishing Corp.
119 West 40th Street
New York, NY 10018

All Kensington titles, imprints, and distributed lines are available at special quantity discounts for bulk purchases for sales promotion, premiums, fund-raising, educational, or institutional use.

Special book excerpts or customized printings can also be created to fit specific needs. For details, write or phone the office of the Kensington Sales Manager: Attn.: Sales Department. Kensington Publishing Corp., 119 West 40th Street, New York, NY 10018. Phone: 1-800-221-2647.

Kensington and the K logo Reg. U.S. Pat. & TM Off.

First Printing: May 2021
ISBN-13: 978-1-4967-2946-0
ISBN-10: 1-4967-2946-3

ISBN-13: 978-1-4967-2947-7 (eBook)
ISBN-10: 1-4967-2947-1 (eBook)

10 9 8 7 6 5 4 3 2 1

Printed in the United States of America

Even the most avid technocrat must occasionally escape from virtual space, and what better place to do it than the kitchen, with all its dangerous knives and delicious aromas?

—Ruth Reichl

From morning till night, sounds drift from the kitchen, most of them familiar and comforting. . . . On days when warmth is the most important need of the human heart, the kitchen is the place you can find it.

—E. B. White

Village of Storyton

Welcome to Storyton Hall

OUR STAFF IS HERE TO SERVE YOU
Resort Manager—Jane Steward
Butler—Mr. Butterworth
Head Librarian—Mr. Sinclair
Head Chauffeur—Mr. Sterling
Head of Recreation—Mr. Lachlan
Head of Housekeeping—Mrs. Templeton
Head Cook—Mrs. Hubbard
Spa Manager—Tammie Kota

SELECT MERCHANTS OF STORYTON VILLAGE
Run for Cover Bookshop—Eloise Alcott
Daily Bread Café—Edwin Alcott
Cheshire Cat Pub—Bob and Betty Carmichael
Canvas Creamery—Phoebe Doyle
La Grande Dame Clothing Boutique—Mabel Wimberly
Tresses Hair Salon—Violet Osborne
Pickled Pig Market—the Hogg brothers
Geppetto's Toy Shop—Barnaby Nicholas
Hilltop Stables—Sam Nolan
Potter's Shed—Tom Green
Storyton Outfitters—Phil and Sandi Hughes
The Old Curiosity Antique Shop—Roger Bachman

PERSONS INVOLVED IN THE POSH PALATE COMPETITION

Chef Michel

Chef Saffron

Chef Pierce

Chef Alondra

Chef August

Chef Lindsay

Judges—Levi Anjou and Coco Kennedy

Host—Mia Mallett

Assistant to Ms. Mallett—Bentley Fiore

Director—Tyler Scott

CHILDREN'S BOOK CONFERENCE ATTENDEES OF NOTE

Birdie Bloom

Nia Curry

Gunnar Humphries

Sasha Long

Reggie Novak

Todd and Tris Petty

Gloria Ramirez

THE GOLDEN BOOKMARK WINNERS

Max Gilbert

Alika Gilbert

Fern Gilbert

Peter Gilbert

MISCELLANEOUS VISITORS

Zoey (Mrs. Templeton's niece)

Malcolm Marcus (book dealer)

Dr. Brandon Parks (Gloria Ramirez's fiancé)

Chapter 1

Jane Steward, single mother to twin boys and manager of Storyton Hall, the renowned resort for bibliophiles, saw no cars on the narrow bridge she and her sons needed to cross as they headed home from the village.

Glancing over her shoulder, Jane adjusted her bike helmet and shouted, "The coast is clear! Catch me if you can!"

Her sons, Fitzgerald and Hemingway, responded with ear-piercing war cries that would have made Genghis Khan proud. They'd slowed down to polish off their ice cream cones, giving their mother a sizeable lead, and now pedaled like mad to catch her.

Jane was halfway across the bridge when the twins— known to all as Fitz and Hem—began singing "London Bridge Is Falling Down."

With the school year finishing three weeks ago, the boys were officially rising fifth graders and therefore, too old for nursery rhymes. It wasn't a lack of maturity, but a recent devotion to all things British that inspired the song about the famous London landmark.

The twins had become Anglophiles back in February

when Jane's beau, Edwin Alcott, had given her a very thoughtful and generous valentine: a literary tour of London. Edwin had included the boys in the invitation, a gesture that elevated him even higher in Jane's esteem.

The trip had been scheduled for the beginning of June, and Fitz and Hem spent the months leading up to their departure researching British customs. And while Jane admired their enthusiasm, she could have done without their British accents or their obsession with certain British terms. They were particularly fond of "loo," "lift," "telly," "biscuits," "cuppa," and "crisps." By April, Jane was tired of her sons describing everything from food to books to television shows as dodgy, mental, or brilliant.

Hours after landing at Heathrow, the twins had talked Jane and Edwin into a tour of London Bridge. Jane had listened to the guide's disturbing tales of human sacrifice and the immurement of prisoners within the foundations without batting an eye. Unlike the other tourists, she knew that all old places had secrets, and it would take more than a whisper of skeletons to upset the heir of Storyton Hall.

Somewhere behind Jane, Hem now bellowed, "Take the keys and lock her up!"

"On death and darkness will she sup!" Fitz cried merrily.

Together, the boys finished the verse by shrieking, "My fair female bag of bones!"

Seeing as the current version of the classic nursery rhyme omitted much of the landmark's grim history, Fitz and Hem had decided to rewrite it. Over a dinner of roast beef and Yorkshire pudding the evening after the tour, they'd shared their new and improved "London Bridge Is Falling Down."

Edwin had applauded their efforts, calling their work clever and creative, but Jane had leaned over and whispered, "Don't encourage them. They're like the Vikings. Show the slightest weakness, and before you know it, they've taken all of your treasure."

"Then it's a good thing my treasure is right here," Edwin had said, squeezing Jane's hand.

But on this glorious summer afternoon, Jane felt like a warrior as she raced past Storyton Outfitters. She maintained a decent speed on the treacherous Broken Arm Bend and, feeling invincible, prepared to face the hill.

Crouching low over her handlebars, she pumped her legs even harder, trying to gain momentum before the road began its sharp rise. With the warm breeze caressing her flushed cheeks and her strawberry-blond ponytail streaming out behind her like a comet's tail, Jane felt unstoppable.

The feeling was short-lived.

She was still on the lower part of the hill when the twins caught her. Hem's front tire practically kissed Jane's rear tire, and Fitz was poised to overtake her as soon as the shoulder widened.

"Are you tired, Mom?"

"We can hear you panting."

Jane scowled. She *was* panting. It was a blisteringly hot day, the air was thick with humidity, and Jane was out of shape.

A guest had once told her that British food was awful, but Jane disagreed with this assessment. She'd eaten plenty of lovely food in England. After she and the twins had indulged in fish and chips, bangers and mash, Welsh rarebit, and ploughman's lunch, Edwin had taken charge of their restaurant picks.

In addition to running a restaurant in Storyton, Edwin was also a food writer. He'd traveled the world for years and knew exactly which dishes to order at which restaurants.

Based on his recommendations, Jane dined like a queen in London. She ate amazing sushi, sumptuous savory pies, truffled egg toast, Peking duck, a flat-iron steak she chopped with her own cleaver, bao buns, and the best Indian cuisine she'd ever tasted. She also feasted on delectable desserts that included, but weren't limited to, puddings, pastries, gelato, pies, biscuits, teacakes, and scones.

Her delight in British cuisine was easily measured. Two days after returning stateside, she'd stepped on the scale and let out a squeak of dismay. The offending device was now under her bed—banished until further notice.

"I'm not panting," she protested as she tried to focus on pedaling and not on the pair of pants she could no longer zip. "I'm opening my lungs to get more oxygen in."

"You're panting like Lassie," said Fitz.

"Or Fang," Hem said in an English accent. "Hey, Fitz, do you think Mom could beat Hagrid up this hill?"

The twins laughed.

Jane wanted to sprint up the rest of the hill like a racehorse out of the starting gate, but her pace was more like a snail's than a thoroughbred's.

When she finally reached the top, she steered her bike into a patch of scraggly grass and waved for the boys to go ahead.

Instead of speeding off, they both stopped.

"Are you okay, Mom?" Fitz asked with genuine concern.

Jane waved again. "Just . . . catching . . . my . . . breath."

"You should be careful," Hem said with devilish glee. "Queen Anne wasn't much older than you when she died."

Fitz peered into the basket attached to Jane's handlebars. "Did you pack your smelling salts?"

Jane glowered at her sons. "I'm not . . . too tired . . . to think of extra chores for you two."

Suddenly, Hem's smile vanished, and he pointed at the woods. "Is that smoke?"

The sun's glare bounced off the road, so Jane shielded her eyes with her hand and followed her son's gaze.

He was right. A ribbon of smoke rose above the tree-tops.

"Mom? Is it coming from our woods?" Fitz asked.

"But we're under a fire restriction," Hem interjected before Jane could respond. "No campfires allowed. Mr. Lachlan told us to look for guests breaking the rules."

As Jane watched the smoke, a darker curl joined the pale gray coil. The fire was growing stronger.

"Should we ride over there?"

"Yes," said Jane. "If there's a wildfire, even a small one, use the phone in the archery hut to call 911. Got it?"

The twins said, "Got it," and sped off.

Knowing they'd reach the source of the smoke much quicker than she could, Jane stayed where she was and called Butterworth. A former member of Her Majesty's Secret Service, the butler of Storyton Hall was also an expert in marksmanship, reading body language, and remaining calm during a crisis. A bit of smoke wasn't a crisis, but when it came to the safety of Storyton Hall guests, Jane always erred on the side of caution.

"Good afternoon, Miss Jane." Butterworth's voice was as deep and constant as a mountain.

"The boys and I are on our way back from the village," Jane said. "We just crested the hill and saw smoke rising over the trees. I think it's coming from the archery fields. Has anyone heard from the film crew in the past hour?"

Butterworth replied, "Mr. Lachlan was scheduled to walk over after his falconry lesson, but I'll drive there posthaste and report back to you."

Jane thanked him, pocketed her phone, and followed after the twins.

She would have made better time if she didn't keep glancing skyward, but she couldn't help it. The smoke was no longer shaped like ribbons or curls. It had grown thicker, billowing over the treetops like dragon's breath.

Jane pedaled harder. The muscles in her legs ached. Her lungs burned. Sweat ran down her cheeks and dampened her shirt. The path was made of packed dirt, and her front tire flung dust onto her ankles and calves. The woods were quiet until the howl of sirens rent the air. Minutes later, two fire engines turned onto the service road leading to Storyton Hall's grounds, and Jane's imagination went wild.

The tent's on fire. The filming will be canceled before it can begin. I'll have to return the check to the production company. And it was such a nice *check.*

Apart from the money, Jane didn't want to disappoint the guests who'd booked rooms months in advance for the privilege of watching some of the greatest chefs in America in action.

Everything had been running smoothly until today. Last week, a construction crew had raised the tent and hooked up the appliances. After the set designer and her team had finished staging the interior, the director and film crew had flown in from LA. The six chefs had arrived at Storyton Hall last night, and the judges had checked in this morning. The international trendsetter, taste guru, social media influencer, foodie, and celebrity host of *Posh Palate with Mia Mallett*, would make her grand entrance this evening.

After several lengthy email exchanges with Mia's assistant, a young woman named Bentley, Jane came to understand that Mia Mallett's public image was meticulously curated and zealously guarded. Known as The Girl with the

Midas Touch, Mia was a twenty-seven-year-old billionaire and social media darling. If she endorsed a product, her millions of fans would immediately buy it.

As the manager of a five-star resort, Jane had met her fair share of actors, politicians, writers, musicians, and media sensations, but none had made requests quite like Mia Mallett's. To guarantee her boss's privacy, Bentley had booked the entire third floor of the East Wing. Only Jane, select Storyton Hall staff members, and Mia's entourage were allowed to step foot on the floor while Ms. Mallett was in residence.

How will I fill those empty rooms if Mia checks out after a single night?

Jane pushed the thought aside. There was no sense in catastrophizing. All she could do was find out what was burning, and if the fire would affect tomorrow's filming.

"Don't be the tent," Jane chanted as she rode on.

Her phone was mounted to her handlebars. When it rang, she pressed the speaker button and kept pedaling.

"The fire's in the archery field," Butterworth said. "Chief Aroneo has the situation well in hand, and the flames should be extinguished shortly. A gentleman from the temporary power supply company is talking to the chief. From what I understand, this is an electrical fire."

Butterworth sounded so calm that Jane's panic instantly subsided. "What kind of damage are we looking at?"

"The fire was restricted to the grass. It didn't have the chance to reach the tent, but the smoke and ash have severely discolored one side."

"Is the director there?"

Butterworth grunted in disapproval. "Mr. Scott is using his bullhorn to shout orders contradictory to those the chief is issuing. If I don't intervene, the firefighters may turn their hoses on him. If they do, I won't lift a finger to intervene."

"We knew this reality show would be a challenge, but I expected to only see flames when the chefs flambéed food," Jane said. "Please take charge until I get there."

After five more minutes of exertion, Jane emerged from the shady forest into a clearing filled with smoke, noise, and sunbaked spectators.

Jane leaned her bike against a pine tree and jogged over to where Butterworth stood. Though the butler was in his mid-fifties, he was tall and powerfully built. Most people found his physical presence and gargoyle stare intimidating, but Mr. Scott was clearly the exception.

Even though Butterworth's muscular chest was firmly pressed over the bell of Mr. Scott's bullhorn, the director didn't seem to realize that he was seconds away from having his legs swept out from under him.

"How am I supposed to tell people what to do?" he whined. "I'm in charge, man!"

Butterworth was as unmovable as a boulder. "As I said, sir, Chief Aroneo is in charge. You will surrender your bullhorn until he and his firefighters have given the all-clear."

Jane pasted on her most winsome smile and approached the two men. "Thank you, Butterworth. I've got it from here." Turning to the director, she said, "I almost missed all the drama, and you haven't even started filming yet."

Butterworth retreated to a polite distance, bullhorn in hand, while Mr. Scott took in Jane's sweaty face and dirty clothes. "Ms. Steward? Whoa. I didn't recognize you, well, looking like that." After raking his eyes over her once more, he pointed at the tent. "It's been a helluva day."

"How is it inside?"

The director chewed his lip. "Fine. But my opening shot

is ruined. I wanted that *Little House on the Prairie* vibe. A picnic blanket here. A horse grazing there. A kid flying a kite. But I can't work with burned grass. I'm filming a cooking competition, not *Apocalypse Now*."

Since Jane had never seen the famous war film, she focused on the television show that would introduce Storyton Hall to hundreds of thousands of potential guests. "Maybe the burned grass could be a metaphor for cooking. Fire can transform food into something magical, right? When we were kids, putting a marshmallow on a stick and holding it over an open flame was one of the best things about summer. And adults love watching a chef prepare crêpes suzette. But too much fire, and that nice cut of Wagyu beef will taste like an old boot."

Scott touched his hair, which rose high over his forehead like a cresting wave. "That won't work for the opener, but I could use it when one of the chefs has a kitchen disaster."

Jane cupped his elbow and gently steered him toward the tent. "Does that happen often?"

"We hope so. With every episode." Scott grinned. "Drama makes for good television. If drama doesn't happen naturally, we create it. Things like this fire rarely happen on set. Too bad I wasn't filming. But I could always start another fire."

As they rounded the corner of the huge tent to face a patch of black and sizzling ground, Jane said, "Don't do that, Mr. Scott."

"I'm just kidding. And call me Ty. By the time this show wraps, we'll be good friends." He flashed her a bright Hollywood smile that Jane didn't find the least bit charming. Though she and the director were both in their late thirties, Ty looked younger than Jane. The skin on his face was smooth, his body was trim, and his hair—the color of a new penny—gleamed in the sun. The sleeves of his oxford shirt were rolled up to the elbow, exposing tan forearms and a gold Rolex. Designer sunglasses dangled from his breast pocket. He moved and spoke with the ease of a person who's never known true hardship.

We're not going to be friends, Jane thought. Aloud, she said, "Protocol requires that I stick with Mr. Scott. If I can help, let me know. I'm going to speak to Chief Aroneo."

Putting his hands on his hips, Scott frowned at the stained tent and the smoking field. "Wait! You *can* help. Find me a company that can lay sod. *Today*. I want green grass for my opening shot. Cool?"

Jane bristled. She wasn't this man's lackey. "My first priority is to speak with the chief. After that, I need to clear my guests from the area. Don't you have an assistant to handle phone calls?"

Ty Scott waved in the direction of the manor house. "Everyone's busy. We start shooting tomorrow, remember? What about that grumpy butler? Can he help?"

Feeling wicked, Jane smiled and said, "You're free to ask him."

Leaving Tyler Scott to Butterworth's mercy, Jane looked for Chief Aroneo and spotted him talking to a man in coveralls. The man was red-faced with fury. He pointed from the burned grass to the tent and then jabbed himself in the chest. The chief held out his hands to show that he was listening before accompanying the man inside the tent.

Jane glanced around, expecting her sons to be among the spectators. When she didn't see two boys or two bikes, she assumed they'd gone home. She slipped into the tent.

Though she'd been inside before, Jane was still amazed by how much work had gone into creating this set. Storyton

Hall used upscale tents for outdoor weddings all the time, but they didn't have kitchen appliances, sinks with running water, granite countertops, or butcher block chopping stations. And that was just the cooking stations. The perimeter was lined with antique country furniture. Dry sinks, cupboards, pie safes, and hutches filled with stoneware, copper pans, milk glass vases, mason jars, and vintage kitchen scales. Other cabinets featured sets of jadeite, Lenox, Blue Willow, and Royal Albert dishes.

The ground had been leveled before the tent was erected so that a temporary floor could be installed. Between the floor, lighting, appliances, and décor, the tent was an interesting blend of an upscale restaurant kitchen and the kitchen in a country home.

Tomorrow, bucketloads of fresh flowers would augment that home kitchen feel.

"They'll be everywhere," the set designer had told Jane. "In vases. On top of cupboards. In baskets. It's how we'll get that outdoorsy summer vibe inside the tent."

"Are the flowers coming from the Potter's Shed?" Jane had asked. She wanted the local businesses to profit from the show along with Storyton Hall.

The set designer had consulted her clipboard. "Yes. Sunflowers, bachelor's buttons, coneflowers, and Queen Anne's Lace. But if Mia wanted Venus flytraps, she'd find a way to get them. Things tend to appear at the snap of her fingers."

"I wish she could snap her fingers and erase this fire," Jane muttered as she approached Chief Aroneo and the angry man in the coveralls.

The men were standing at one of the cooking stations, their backs to Jane. A large sheet of paper was spread across the counter and the man in the coveralls was tracing something with his finger.

"I've been doing this job for twenty years, Chief. I know how to avoid an overload. There's no way I plugged all that juice into one generator. None of my guys did either."

"How can you be so sure?" the chief asked. "Things seem pretty chaotic around here."

The man shrugged. "It's always this way around TV and movie people. Lots of yelling. Lots of freaking out over nothing. We ignore most of what they ask for because it goes against every safety protocol in the book. Scott wanted so many lights in this tent that the butter would have melted as soon as it came out of the fridge. I tell him what he wants to hear, but I stick to the contract." He tapped the paper. "The contract called for these lines. That's max capacity for the transformer."

"So who added an extra line?"

The man rolled up the paper. "Not me or my guys. Twenty years and not one fire, Chief. Maybe somebody wanted a fire, but it wasn't us."

"What's going on?"

Startled, the men spun around to face Jane.

"Please," she added. "I need to know if the fire was deliberate."

Jane saw the answer in the chief's face before he said a word. After glancing at the other man, he said, "I'll open an investigation, but considering all the people who've traipsed over this field lately, I don't expect to find much."

Someone called for the chief on his radio, and he excused himself and exited the tent. The man in the coveralls was staring intently at his cell phone when he suddenly went rigid.

"Just like I said," he mumbled. "It wasn't me or my guys."

Moving closer to the man, Jane introduced herself. "This is my resort, and I'm responsible for everyone here, so I'd like to know what caused that fire."

The man nodded. "I'm Jeff with Ashley Power Solutions. Our company provides temporary power for movies and TV shows. I'm in charge of this job. How much do you know about electrical systems?"

"Nothing."

Jeff showed her the image on his phone screen. "Pretend this box with all the wires and circuits is the brain of our system. These bigger cables have to plug in here. These skinny wires plug in here. And so on. All the wires have to be coated. Everything has to be clean and kept out of the weather. No water can get inside. Okay. See this red wire?" He tapped a red wire in a nest of black wires. "It shouldn't be there. Way too much juice went into the brain at this spot. That's where the fire started. See how black the board is around that wire? But there's more."

Though Jane didn't like where this was headed, she had to hear the man out. "Go on."

"Somebody helped create the overload by making sure the brain got wet. We haven't had a drop of rain since we've been here, but when the chief takes a closer look at this box, he'll see what I'm seeing. Wrong wire in the wrong place plus liquid. That's a recipe for an electrical fire."

"But aren't these boxes locked? To avoid tampering?"

Jeff looked aggrieved. "Once everything's up and running, yeah. But we were still tweaking things to make Mr. Scott happy. Anyone could have walked by, swapped a wire, and left a chunk of ice on top to melt into the box. I'm sorry to say this, but somebody has it out for this show."

After Jeff left the tent, Jane sent a text to Butterworth.

Fire wasn't an accident. Someone wants to sabotage filming. Since attempted arson failed, what's next?

Staring at her screen, Jane cursed her own stupidity. She knew better than to tempt the fates by wondering what else could go wrong.

Besides, she already knew the answer.

It was everything. Everything could go wrong. And that's when people got hurt.

Pushing her damp hair off her forehead, Jane glanced around the empty tent. "I'd like a summer without violence. A nice, easy summer filled with weddings, barbecues, and beach reads. Can I have one of those?"

The stain on the tent wall, which crawled from floor to ceiling like some multi-limbed shadow creature from a child's nightmare, felt like a sign that her wish had little chance of coming true.

Chapter 2

After freshening up at home, Jane called a meeting with Butterworth, Sterling, Sinclair, and Lachlan. These men were all department heads. More importantly, they were Fins.

The Fins were established a century ago in England by Walter Egerton Steward, Storyton Hall's original owner. Walter required protection for both his family and the secret library hidden inside his manor house, so he hired a small group of men with specialized combat training to serve as his personal guard. Because the Fins were named after the stabilizing device used on arrows, every Fin had an arrow tattooed over his heart.

Despite the presence of these skilled fighters, threats against Walter Steward persisted. Thieves came from every direction, hoping to steal Steward's treasure, and Walter was forced to make a drastic decision. He dismantled his estate and shipped it overseas. Brick by brick, a slightly modified version of Storyton Hall was built in a picturesque, isolated valley in Western Virginia. The location was ideal because very few people could approach the manor house undetected.

A village sprung up around the estate, and all its residents were fiercely loyal to the Stewards. For many years, Walter and his family lived in peace. After Walter's death, his Fins stayed on and vowed to protect the next generation of Stewards.

As the current Guardian of Storyton Hall, Jane had her own Fins. To her, they were much more than bodyguards and department heads. They were family. Butterworth, Sinclair, and Sterling had been surrogate fathers to Jane, and she loved them with her whole heart.

Landon Lachlan was a relatively new addition. When he'd first come to Storyton, his rugged good looks and shy demeanor had caused a stir among the single women. But none of them had ever stood a chance of capturing his heart. Landon Lachlan had fallen for Jane's best friend, Eloise Alcott, the moment he'd laid eyes on her.

The couple was getting married in August, and Jane planned to host a bridal shower for Eloise soon after the cooking competition wrapped. And though she was the Guardian of Storyton Hall, Jane would much rather be at home, finalizing the party menu and reading Jasmine Guillory's *The Wedding Party* than discussing arson.

"I spoke with Chief Aroneo," Lachlan said, interrupting Jane's rosy visions of a novel in one hand and a glass of iced coffee in the other. "An arsonist caused that fire. Unfortunately, no one saw anything and there are no leads, which means our chances of catching this person are slim."

This was deflating news. With a hotel full of strangers, identifying the saboteur would be incredibly difficult.

"We need to find out if Mr. Scott, Ms. Mallett, or any of the competing chefs have enemies," Jane said. "Serious enemies. Let's assume the arsonist meant to burn down the tent. That would have delayed filming and cost the studio lots of money. Was this the arsonist's goal? Or do they have another objective?"

"And will they strike again?" Lachlan added.

"Monitoring activity around that tent will be a challenge," said Sterling. The head chauffeur was also in charge of Storyton Hall's surveillance system. "When my drivers aren't working, I'll ask them to change into plainclothes and mingle with the guests. They can keep their eyes and ears open and report any suspicious behavior to me."

Sinclair, Storyton's head librarian, smoothed a wrinkle on the lapel of his tailored seersucker suit, adjusted his pink bowtie, and said, "It wouldn't hurt to let certain members of Mrs. Hubbard's staff play a similar role. I imagine she'd be amenable to the idea."

Jane laughed. "Amenable? She'd be over the moon. I'll talk to her as soon as we're done rolling out the red carpet for Mia Mallett. Sterling? What's her ETA?"

"Her train arrived at four thirty. During the thirty minutes it took the porters to unload her luggage, Ms. Mallett posed for photographs around the station. Ms. Mallett and her staff were then loaded into cars around five. I've been informed that she plans to stop just outside our main gates to have more photos taken. After that, she'll start a live feed, inviting her followers to share in her first glimpse of Storyton Hall."

"Just imagine." Jane sighed dreamily. "Mia Mallett is going to introduce Storyton Hall to three *million* followers. All the people watching that video will pass through our massive iron gates, hear the gravel crunch under the tires of a Rolls-Royce Silver Wraith, and see the Blue Ridge Mountains rising over our tree-covered hills. They might even spot a red-tailed hawk circling in the sky. But when

Mia's driver eases around that final bend and Storyton Hall comes into view, they'll forget about the mountains and the sky. They'll be entranced by a man-made marvel."

Unable to resist, Sinclair picked up the narrative. "Ms. Mallett will let out a soft gasp. Though she's seen architectural splendors like the Taj Mahal and Buckingham Palace, Storyton Hall is enchantingly unique. She is the jewel of this valley's crown, a queen dressed in a gown of stone and brick. Ms. Mallett's viewers will notice her clock tower first, soaring into the sky like an obelisk. Next, they'll see how the mansion's wings stretch out to the sides like two arms opening for an embrace. Golden light shines from every tall window. And on the other side of the carved entry doors, a bear of a man waits with champagne flutes balanced on a silver tray."

Butterworth flicked a disdainful glance in Sinclair's direction. "Your use of zoomorphism is unamusing."

Sinclair grinned at his longtime friend and colleague. "Come now, Mr. Butterworth. It was meant as a compliment. The bear is a noble creature. In addition to being one of the most intelligent animals, the bear is known for its strength, protectiveness, and devotion to family."

Butterworth was about to respond when Sterling's phone buzzed. "Time to get the bubbly ready, Paddington Bear," he said. "Ms. Mallett is at the gates."

"Really? How do I look?" Jane leaped to her feet and smoothed imaginary wrinkles from her clothes. "Why am I nervous? Is it because I can't speak in hashtags?"

Sterling smiled at her. "Don't worry about that. You'll make this young lady feel at home. It's what you do. You make all your guests feel welcome."

Butterworth also got to his feet. After giving his blue livery coat a sharp tug, he arched a brow at Jane. "And you're quite positive that Ms. Mallett will abide by our technology restrictions?"

"Yes. She signed an agreement stating that her staff would only use cell phones and tablets in the privacy of their rooms or during filming and prescheduled photo shoots. Mia has requested shoots in the kitchen, the Ian Fleming Lounge, Milton's Gardens, and the Great Gatsby Ballroom."

"No reading rooms? What about the Henry James Library?" Sinclair was affronted. "I was under the impression that Ms. Mallett chose Storyton Hall because this season has a literary theme?"

Jane shrugged. "I'm not privy to any details about the show. All I know is that Mia wanted to film at a *posh* country estate, and that she fell in love with the photos she saw on our website. According to her assistant, the library and reading rooms will be used to film chef interviews."

"I've studied Ms. Mallett's social media accounts. She doesn't use her celebrity status to promote literature or literacy. Perhaps that will change after her stay," said Sinclair.

Jane brightened at the thought. "Yes! She's sure to realize that Storyton Hall is more than a picturesque mansion. Once she sees that it's a respite for readers, she might grab a book and have someone photograph her doing what the rest of our guests do." Recalling some of Mia's posts, which featured designer clothes, makeup tutorials, and lush photographs of food, Jane's face fell. "But can I convince a twenty-seven-year-old billionaire that books are the secret to a happy and fulfilling life?"

"There's only one way to find out," said Lachlan, opening the conference room door with a flourish.

Jane walked to the center of the lobby and took up her

customary position in front of the round walnut hall table holding a magnificent floral arrangement comprised of birds-of-paradise, ginger lilies, Santana roses, Bells-of-Ireland, and protea.

A bellhop opened the front door and Mia's staff filed in. After accepting glasses of champagne from Butterworth, two of the three twentysomethings began assessing the lobby's décor.

"It has a vintage Versailles vibe," said a young woman with short rose-gold hair. A baby-faced man in a straw fedora with a floral band flicked his wrist in dismissal. "Nah. If *Downton Abbey* and *The Crown* were Americans, this would be their summer house. Like the Hamptons, but in Virginia. Instead of water, you get mountains."

The woman nodded. "I see that. I can also see Mia coming down that staircase in her gold Versace. Now *that's* Leo DiCaprio Great Gatsby level glam."

They turned to face each other, and in perfect unison, cried, "Straight fire!"

Laughing, the pair wandered off to examine another part of the lobby.

Jane said hello to the third staff member. Like her colleagues, she wore stylish clothes and a full face of makeup. After telling Jane that she was responsible for Mia's wardrobe, she hurried away to check on the luggage.

Finally, Mia Mallett walked through the doorway.

She was a very slim, diminutive young woman with teardrop-shaped brown eyes, radiant skin, and dark brown hair that cascaded over her shoulders in soft waves. She wore a sleeveless white jumpsuit and stiletto sandals.

As Butterworth bent to offer her champagne, Jane pictured Roald Dahl's Big Friendly Giant and the sweet little girl Sophie.

Mia Mallett might have been small in stature, but her smile was wide and winsome. After thanking Butterworth for the champagne, she asked if she should take off her shoes.

"These heels are super pointy, and I don't want to damage your floors."

How considerate, Jane thought as she moved forward to welcome her famous guest.

"Ms. Steward!" Mia shook Jane's hand with enthusiasm. "Wow, has anyone ever told you that you look like Evan Rachel Wood? You have the same creamy complexion and model-perfect posture. Thanks for hosting us. This place is *amazing*." She gazed around the lobby, taking in the crystal chandeliers, the grandfather clock, the plush sofas and chairs, and the grand staircase.

"Would you like to see your rooms?" Jane asked.

Mia tapped her handbag, a massive Hermès tote that probably cost more than the contents of Jane's house. "Actually, I was hoping I could pop by the kitchens. I'll be super quick. I have something for Mrs. Hubbard, and I'm dying to give it to her."

A guest bearing gifts? This is a first.

"Of course. Right this way." Jane started walking, but when she realized that Mia's entourage was scurrying over to join them, she stopped and looked to Mia for help.

Mia winked at Jane and turned to her staff. "I have a personal thing now. Why don't you get our space situated? And when I come up, we can grab drinks in that fab Ian Fleming Lounge. Cool?"

Her staff members murmured in congenial agreement and headed for the front desk.

When they were out of earshot, Mia released a soft sigh. "They're great, and I couldn't manage without them, but it's a drag having to ask for me time. I miss the days when I could choose an outfit or cook a meal without wondering about how many likes I'd get. That's why it's been *so* nice to talk to Mrs. Hubbard. She helped me remember what I love about food. Not just the cooking part. All of it. The shopping, cooking, and plating. The story behind every dish."

Jane tried to conceal her astonishment. Mrs. Hubbard had been communicating with Mia Mallett? And she'd managed to keep that a secret? Mrs. Hubbard was terrible at keeping secrets.

"She's good at that—reminding people what matters most," Jane said. "If books are the soul of Storyton Hall, then Mrs. Hubbard is its heart."

Normally, Jane would warn her head cook that a VIP wanted to visit her domain, but there was no time. She could only hope that Mrs. Hubbard wasn't in the middle of a tirade. Her staff knew that she was all bark and no bite, but Jane didn't want Mia to get the wrong impression.

Luckily, Mrs. Hubbard was giving a sous chef feedback on his sauce when her esteemed guest walked through the smaller prep kitchen into the larger kitchen.

The room was a frenzy of aromas and sounds. Steam hissed, sauces bubbled, steaks sizzled, and water gurgled as men and women in aprons chopped, fried, seared, sautéed, grilled, and shouted at one another. Servers hustled in with trays of dirty dishes and left again carrying clean trays loaded with chilled soup, shrimp cocktail, or a salad of summer greens.

Mrs. Hubbard lowered her tasting spoon and told the sous chef to add a pinch of salt. When he didn't respond, she followed his starstruck gaze and let out a squeal.

"Mia Mallett! In my kitchen? After you add that pinch of salt, Jorge, pinch my arm. I *must* be dreaming."

Mia dropped her handbag on a stool and rushed over to hug Mrs. Hubbard.

Mrs. Hubbard raised her hands in protest. "Oh, honey! I'm filthy and your outfit looks like Swiss meringue!"

Mia gave Mrs. Hubbard a quick squeeze, stepped back, and pointed at her jumpsuit. "This isn't the real me. I only look like this because four people won't let me go outside until I'm photo ready. At home, I wear sweats and T-shirts. And aprons. Not that they help. When I cook, I get food everywhere. On my shoes. In my hair. On the ceiling."

She and Mrs. Hubbard laughed.

Mia turned to Jane. "I've doubled my followers this year, which doesn't mean much to people until I explain that my followers donate to the causes I care about. So the more I have, the more we can help other people. But lately, I've been so focused on numbers that I lost touch with the chef and food blogger I used to be. Mrs. Hubbard helped me find them again."

Jane slung an arm around her head cook's shoulder. "And what wisdom did you impart, Chef Yoda?"

"I told her to make a wild, wacky, colorful cake," said Mrs. Hubbard. "A cake that a child would love. Something magical and silly. I told her to break a lot of eggs and throw the rules out the window. To forget about photos and focus on rainbows and sprinkles."

"It totally worked." Mia grinned. "I made this crazy roller-coaster cake, and it ended up being my most popular post of the year. It went viral within the hour."

Jane stared at Mia. "Wait. That's *your* cake? With the chocolate cars that go in and out of each tier? And when they get to the erupting volcano top tier, they drop down into a rock candy lake before popping back through the bottom tier again? You created that?"

Mia beamed. "Yep."

"My sons showed me a video of that cake," Jane said. "I didn't think it was real."

Mia shrugged. "Lots of people thought it was fake. And yeah, it had a few mechanical parts and battery-powered fairy lights, but 90 percent was edible. It was such a blast to bake, which is why I had to thank this lady in person." Reaching into her handbag, she pulled out a gift-wrapped object and handed it to Mrs. Hubbard. "This is for your collection."

"For the cookbook nook?" Mrs. Hubbard asked, her face shining with excitement. "Would you like to see it?"

When Mia said that she would, Mrs. Hubbard led her past the butler's pantry, walk-ins, and the staff eating area to a narrow hall. At the next intersection, she turned right, leading Mia into a narrow space containing built-in shelves, a dainty love seat upholstered in floral chintz, a side table with a lamp, and a needlepoint footstool.

This was Mrs. Hubbard's hidey-hole. When she needed a break from the chaos of the kitchens, she'd retreat to the cookbook nook. Once there, she'd put up her feet, have a cup of tea, and peruse one of her cherished cookbooks.

The space was small but cheerful. The combination of butter-yellow walls and white shelves filled with antique dishes, teapots, and books gave the room a homey feel.

"Wow," breathed Mia.

Her admiration sounded sincere, and when Mrs. Hubbard opened her gift, revealing both volumes of *Mastering the Art of French Cooking*, Jane liked Mia all the more for putting such a huge smile on Mrs. Hubbard's face.

"There's another surprise inside the first volume," Mia said.

Mrs. Hubbard looked like she might burst from happiness. "Sweet heavens! It's signed by Simone Beck *and* Julia Child! This is too much. I can't accept these just for giving you a bit of friendly advice."

Mia walked over to the shelves and carefully relocated a Wedgwood Jasperware teapot. "Looks like you have room for them right here."

Knowing it would be ungracious to protest further, Mrs. Hubbard slid the books into the space. Stepping back to admire them, she said, "Oh, my dear. I hope you can have more roller-coaster cake moments while you're at Storyton Hall."

Though her smile didn't waver, doubt flashed in Mia's eyes. "I hope so too."

As Mrs. Hubbard showed their guest her prized first-edition cookbooks, Jane noticed that Mia sparkled less brightly than she had a few minutes ago. Was she tired? Worried?

She's a beautiful billionaire. What could a woman like that have to worry about?

As Jane escorted Mia back through the kitchens, flames shot out from a sauté pan. They were gone almost as soon as they appeared, but Jane still quickened her pace. She didn't want to see any more fires today.

Does Mia know about the arson?

On the elevator to the third floor, Jane decided to broach the subject. "I don't know if you heard, but there was a fire near the tent today."

"Yeah. Ty sent me pics," Mia said, unfazed by the event. "I'm kind of relieved because he wanted to shoot the opening outside, but I don't. The winner of this competition gets a line of cookware named after them and a cookbook deal, so I want this season to open with a regular person following a recipe. A family recipe like the one I got from my nonna. That's my Italian grandma. My Thai grandma wrote her recipes on cards and added little drawings to each one. Recipes will mean more to our viewers than a staged picnic scene."

The elevator stopped, and the doors whispered open.

As Mia stepped out of the cab, Jane said, "I love your idea. You could even have a child in the kitchen. A budding young chef learning a recipe."

"From a grandparent!" Mia put her hand to her heart. "Those connections are really important. They were to me. I learned about Thai, Italian, Croatian, and French food from my grandparents. I bet every chef in this competition can name the family member who taught them about food. Well, almost every chef. There's one who only says nice things about himself."

When the door started to slide shut, Jane stuck her foot out to keep them open. If Mia disliked a chef, Jane wanted to hear about it.

She asked, "How well do you know the contestants?"

"I've met three of them before, so I know them well enough. The other three I know more by reputation. I can tell a lot about people by how they treat Bentley, my assistant. A certain chef has been super rude to her—and to me—in the past. I hope he's evolved since then." For a second, she looked concerned, but then she smiled and said, "I'd better put my party dress on."

"And I have to don my apron and figure out how to make spinach irresistible to my sons."

"Do they like spaghetti and meatballs?" Mia asked. At

Jane's nod, she went on. "Replace the meatballs with fried spinach balls. I'll text you a recipe."

By the time Jane crossed the Great Lawn and entered the former hunting lodge that was now her home, Mia had sent three recipes. In addition to the fried spinach balls, there were also recipes for crispy fried spinach and spinach dip served with carrot stars.

Her final text said, I love using dip to get kids to eat their veggies. Hide a different veggie (like a radish slice) at the bottom of the dip bowl and make your sons guess what it is. They'll be so focused on finding the mystery food that they won't notice how fast they're eating their veggies!

Jane made the spinach dip and hid an olive at the bottom of the bowl. The twins loved the game and the dip so much that they asked if they could have it again the next night.

Later, as Jane settled down on the sofa with a glass of wine and *Notes from a Young Black Chef*, the memoir she'd be discussing with her book club in a few days, she wondered how she could thank Mia for her thoughtfulness. Not only had she gotten Fitz and Hem to devour spinach, but she'd also brought joy to Mrs. Hubbard—a woman who devoted herself to others' happiness.

And then, an idea struck her. Smiling to herself, she reached for her phone.

"Your timing couldn't have been better," Edwin said by way of greeting. "I was just about to murder a *Posh Palate* contestant. Have you met the chefs?"

"I said hello to four of them when they checked in, but I was tied up when Chef Michel and Chef Pierce arrived."

"Chef Pierce." Edwin's tone was scornful. "What an insufferable cad. If he weren't your guest, I'd have tossed him out on the sidewalk before he could put his napkin on his lap. You know me, Jane. I can handle prickly customers. You can't last in the restaurant business if you get upset every time customers complain about the number of ice cubes in their water glass or the presence of bones in their Korean short rib dish, but I've never wanted to stuff a napkin down a customer's throat until tonight."

Jane took a fortifying swig of wine before asking, "Did Chef Pierce complain about your food?"

"Indirectly. He masks his insults as questions. For example, he asked one of the female chefs if she thought yellow was a good color for her. Considering she was wearing a yellow blouse, she obviously liked the shade. I bet she never wears that shirt again."

Jane drank more wine. "What else?"

"He asked Chef August if he thought the color of his skin was the main reason he'd been invited to the competition. Chef August is Black."

Jane was too shocked to reply.

"Chef August turned it around by asking Chef Pierce the same question. Instead of apologizing or backing down, the oaf launched into a monologue about the oppression of the straight white male, which I immediately interrupted by announcing the daily specials."

"I almost hate to ask, but what did Chef Pierce say to you?"

"He wanted to know if my Ethiopian spicy fish stew was flavored with cayenne pepper or berbere. He then had the gall to ask if I'd ever heard of berbere."

Since the word was unfamiliar to Jane, she said as much.

"Berbere is an Ethiopian spice," Edwin explained. "The dish wouldn't be authentic without it. Implying that I'd used a substitute was an insult, as was the implication that

I was too backwoods to know about the spice in the first place."

"I'm sorry, Edwin. He sounds like a total jerk. I feel terrible for the other chefs too. Is Chef Pierce ruining their meal?"

Edwin said, "No, thank goodness. After the entrees were served, Pierce and that Botoxed director started talking movies. That left the rest of the party free to eat, drink, and be merry. But if I want them to stay merry, I should get back out there. Otherwise, Magnus might serve Pierce a small bowl of chocolate mousse with a large dollop of cyanide. Call you later."

After wishing Edwin luck, Jane put down her phone and carried her empty wineglass to the kitchen for a refill.

As she listened to the *glug, glug* of the wine moving from the bottle to her glass, she wondered why Mia Mallett had invited such a distasteful person to be on her show. And then, she remembered what the director had said earlier that day.

"If drama doesn't happen naturally, we create it."

Had Chef Pierce been included because he was bound to irritate his rivals and shock the viewing audience? Had he been preassigned the role of villain for the sake of drama?

Jane pushed a rubber stopper into the mouth of the wine bottle and grumbled, "The only place I want drama is between the pages of a book."

And with that, she got comfortable on the sofa and tried to lose herself in one.

Chapter 3

The next morning, after waking her sons, Jane cheerfully informed them that they'd be attending a very special kind of summer school.

"School?" rasped Hem.

"In the *summer*?" Fitz shook his head in disbelief. "This is child abuse."

"Trust me, you'll love it," Jane said while parting the curtains. "For the next two weeks, Uncle Aloysius will teach you to play chess, and Aunt Octavia will introduce you to the art of photography. She's even turned a supply closet into a darkroom. You'll continue your archery and martial arts lessons, and I might need you to do a little spying too. Someone started yesterday's fire on purpose. That person could be dangerous, so keep your eyes and ears open."

The twins stopped grumbling at once. As the future Guardians of Storyton Hall, they took pride in helping their mother keep their guests, and the contents of the secret library, safe.

The priceless collection of books, scrolls, maps, documents, and other literary treasures was housed in a fireproof, temperature-controlled vault located in an attic turret. To access the secret library, Jane had to enter Aunt Octavia's closet, remove an air duct cover, and insert a key into the keyhole concealed behind the vent. By turning the key with one hand while pulling a lever with the other, Jane could activate the mechanism attached to the china cabinet in the living room. The cabinet would swing away from the wall, revealing a dark space.

After slipping into that space, Jane would ascend the spiral staircase until she came to an impenetrable steel door. That door was a Narnian portal to an array of wonders so rare and priceless that people had committed terrible atrocities in an attempt to find them.

Jane didn't want her life, or the lives of her sons, to be marked by violence. For this reason, she'd made the momentous decision to sell or donate the treasures stored in that turret. It would take years to complete this task, but eventually, the secret library would become a thing of the past.

The thought made Jane incredibly sad. After all, she was a Guardian. She'd inherited the title from Uncle Aloysius, who'd inherited it from his father, and so on. But unlike those men, Jane was also a mother—a mother who'd do anything to keep her boys safe. If that meant anonymously donating a never-before-seen Shakespeare play to the Folger Shakespeare Library or the sequel to *Jane Eyre* to the Brontë Society, then she'd do it.

Fitz and Hem might not have a secret library to protect when they were older, but they would still inherit Storyton Hall. And Jane knew, despite the state of their bedroom, that the estate would be in good hands with her sons.

Pointing at the dirty clothes on their floor, she told the twins to clean up and be downstairs in ten minutes.

Propping himself on his elbow, Hem asked, "Can we still take care of the kitchen garden?"

"We *have* to, Mom," Fitz cried before Jane could get a word in. "Mrs. Hubbard said that we did such a good job last summer that she wants to hire us again."

Jane smiled in approval. "Of course. I love how you guys take care of that garden."

Hem swung his legs over the edge of the bed. "We get to harvest all the veggies when they're ready. Mrs. Hubbard even bought special gloves for us because the cucumbers are prickly."

"And we're getting a raise." Fitz puffed out his chest with pride.

Seeing a furrow appear on his mother's brow, Hem quickly added, "Mrs. Hubbard had extra money because the TV people paid for all the rooms on the third floor, even though only five of them are staying there."

"She's saving money this week because she doesn't have to make as much food. That's why she gave us a raise," explained Fitz.

Jane nodded. "Makes sense."

"The chess and the photography stuff is cool, Mom, but we need free time too," Fitz said. "Jorge's going to teach us how to make jam. We want to sell some at the berry festival. If it's really good, the Pickled Pig might buy some too."

Jane was impressed. "A side business, eh? Are you saving up for something special?"

After exchanging a glance, the boys answered in unison, "We want to buy an Xbox."

Though Jane knew this day would come, she still felt a prick of anxiety. Would the twins stop reading once they had a game system? Would they spend less time playing outside? All of their friends had video game systems, but Jane had always hoped that her sons wouldn't develop an interest in them. However, she knew that they were dying to play a particular world-building game with their friends. Having researched the game, Jane found it highly imaginative. If her sons wanted to build cities with virtual LEGO blocks in a Dungeons and Dragons landscape, she wouldn't stop them.

"Okay," she said. "If you want to buy a game system, I'm all for it."

The boys stared at her with such openmouthed incredulity that she had to laugh. "See you downstairs in ten!" she called over her shoulder as she left the room. Behind her, Fitz and Hem released a chorus of jubilant whoops.

Jane was in high spirits when she and the twins entered Storyton Hall. In the staff corridor, they parted ways, the boys heading for the stairwell and Jane to the Daphne du Maurier Morning Room.

She'd asked the kitchen staff to set up a breakfast buffet here because the room was bright, cozy, and private. It also had an oversized fireplace, paintings of famous literary couples, and shelves stuffed with romance novels.

Today, sunlight streamed in through the picture window and glinted off the silver coffee urn and chafing dishes. The delicate floral pattern of the Royal Stafford Hedgerow perfectly complemented the flowers growing just outside the window.

The round table in the center of the room was big enough to accommodate the six chefs, Ty Scott, and Mia Mallett. Jane had been told that Mia's staff always breakfasted in their rooms.

Jane looked up to see Butterworth straightening the

throw pillows on a pink settee. As usual, he'd entered on cat feet. If she didn't know better, she'd think he teleported around Storyton Hall like a character from *Star Trek*.

With the pillows fluffed and angled to his specifications, he looked a question at Jane. "Should the servers bring the dishes now?"

Jane consulted her watch. "Yes. And while we're waiting for everyone to arrive, I want to tell you about Edwin's experience with Chef Pierce."

Butterworth's left eyebrow twitched. "I'm on tenter-hooks."

Jane had just enough time to describe Chef Pierce's behavior at the Daily Bread before a line of servers appeared with breakfast. They arranged the food on the buffet table and returned to the kitchens.

Jane placed a preprinted card in front of the corresponding dish and then stood back to admire the spread.

"Florentine frittata, bacon and gruyere frittata, sweet potato pancakes, quinoa fruit salad, Greek yogurt with ginger granola and berries, buttermilk biscuits and whole-grain croissants. And last but not least, huckleberry jam. Lovely."

Butterworth filled water glasses and placed two carafes of fresh-squeezed orange juice on the table.

"Okay," Jane said. "We're ready."

"And we're hungry!" boomed Ty Scott from the doorway. Catching sight of Butterworth, the director lowered his voice a notch. "Please tell me there's coffee."

Jane waved him over. "Come on in. I'll pour you a cup while you help yourself to the buffet."

Ty paused to address someone in the hall. "Ladies first."

As three women entered the room, Ty announced them as if they were contestants in a beauty pageant.

"Here they are. The lady chefs! Chef Saffron, Chef Alondra, and Chef Lindsay."

Jane had met the women only briefly during check-in, but it was easy to tell them apart because they looked nothing alike.

Chef Saffron's skin was the color of toasted almonds. Her lustrous black hair was pulled up in a bun, accentuating her large chandelier earrings, which were made of multicolored beads. Whenever she moved, the earrings swung back and forth, catching the light and painting tiny rainbows on her cheeks.

Her earlobes must be made of steel, Jane thought.

She asked Chef Saffron if she'd like coffee or tea before turning to greet Chef Alondra, a stocky woman with a boy cut and hazel eyes sparkling with good humor. As she reached for a pair of serving tongs, Jane noticed the tiny tattoos on her fingers. Her left hand featured a carving knife, a chef's hat, a whisk, and a ladle. On her right hand, she had a spatula, a spoon, a rolling pin, and a vegetable peeler.

Following Jane's gaze, Chef Alondra said, "After I win this competition, I'm going to add a cookbook to my right thumb."

Jane admired her confidence. "What about the left thumb?"

"I'm saving that for my Michelin Star." Chef Alondra winked and continued down the buffet line.

"Good morning." Jane smiled at the last of the female chefs.

At thirty-three, Chef Lindsay was the youngest chef in the competition. She was also the thinnest. Chefs Saffron and Alondra weren't overweight, but there was a softness to their bodies that spoke of a love of good food. Chef

Lindsay, on the other hand, was all sharp angles and severe lines. She wore her blond hair in a blunt bob with a fringe of ruler-straight bangs. Her minimalistic makeup was flawless, and her clothes were highly structured. From her starched white blouse to her dove-gray slacks, everything was perfectly tailored.

"Hi," she said to Jane. Her teeth were as white as Ty's, and Jane wondered if all the contestants were told to get their teeth bleached prior to filming.

The first male chef to join the party was Chef Pierce. Even if Jane hadn't recognized the man from his cookbook covers, she would have known him by how the female chefs reacted to his arrival. After exchanging frowns, they all became laser-focused on the buffet food.

Chef Pierce ambled over to a velvet love seat and picked up one of the throw pillows Butterworth had just straightened. "Another book room? I don't get it. Just watch the movie, people, it's always better." He tossed the pillow on a brocade wing chair and approached the buffet. "Do you gals come here to worship Jane Austen? And that prissy man-boy. What's his name? Darcy?"

"Chef—" Ty began.

Ignoring the director, Chef Pierce crept up behind Chef Saffron and moaned, "Oh, *Mister* Darcy, your huge *mansion* makes me hot, and your giant *income* gets me so randy."

Butterworth was at Chef Pierce's side in an instant. He put a hand on the chef's elbow and steered him away from Chef Saffron. "The line starts over here." After a lengthy pause, he reluctantly added, "Sir."

Chef Pierce was balding and bloated. Having seen his driver's license, Jane knew that he was in his mid-fifties, but he looked a decade older. The skin on his face was dry, wrinkled, and speckled with age spots. His neck and cheeks were ruddy, and his nose was covered in spider-shaped veins. When Jane asked if he'd like coffee or tea, Chef Pierce's mouth curved into a wolfish grin.

"Aren't you a pretty thing?" He studied Jane from head to waist and back again. "Can you rustle up a mimosa for me? If I'm going to create masterpieces in a few hours, I need my vitamin C."

Though the celebrity chef made Jane's skin crawl, she nodded at Butterworth. The butler swiftly left the room, but not before returning the throw pillow to its proper place.

"Your mimosa will be brought to your seat," Jane told Chef Pierce. "I'm Jane Steward, the manager. If you have questions or special requests, I'd be glad to address them."

"Was this your family's house?"

"It was," answered Jane.

Chef Pierce loaded his plate with several frittatas and a tower of pancakes. "That's a long way to fall. One minute your people are lord and lady of the manor. Next minute, a rotating door of strangers is eating, sleeping, and doing the nasty in your house. Me? I'd sell this pile of bricks and move into a sweet penthouse apartment."

Struggling to hide her dislike for this man, Jane said, "Our guests come to Storyton Hall because they want to escape the chaos of the modern world for a bit. They read, relax, and savor the beautiful surroundings. This room, like many of our rooms, is filled with books because our guests are book lovers. I grew up surrounded by these intelligent and sensitive people. They make Storyton Hall feel like a home."

Chef Pierce barked out a rueful laugh. "How many times have you practiced that speech, princess?"

"My name is Ms. Steward." Jane's tone was clipped. "Not pretty young thing. Not princess. Ms. Steward. Is that clear?"

Twisting his head around to face the room at large, Chef Pierce said, "We've got a live one here!"

"Give it a rest, Pierce."

A man with walnut-colored skin and a linebacker's build approached the buffet. After stopping to pull out a chair for Chef Saffron, he strode up to Jane and held out a giant hand. His honey-brown eyes shone with warmth. "I'm Chef August and I can't remember the last time I had such a good night's sleep. I feel like a king in a castle."

"That's exactly what we're going for," she said. "Would His Majesty care for coffee?"

"Yes, please. Mmmm, look at this spread." He surveyed the buffet with unabashed delight. "I could get used to other folks cooking for me."

Mia walked over to the buffet and put a hand on Chef August's massive arm. "You ready to cook your heart out today, Chef?"

Chef August swung around and grinned at Mia. "Hey! It's good to see you."

"You too. Go on and fuel up. I'll be right behind you."

Jane greeted Mia, who looked stunning in a yellow crepe-de-chine wrap dress. The two women exchanged pleasantries until Jane saw the last chef enter the room. Butterworth was right on his heels.

After serving the mimosa to Chef Pierce, Butterworth returned to his place behind the settee while Jane focused on the newcomer.

Chef Michel, a handsome man with piercing blue eyes and an aquiline nose, apologized for being late.

"Thank you for having us," he said to Jane. "Such a beautiful place. My wife would love it."

"You can always come back for a romantic getaway."

Michel passed a hand over his close-cropped hair and sighed. "She and I are overdue for one of those. Between our jobs, our two sons, and our parents, we haven't had a vacation in years. Cooking is an escape for both of us."

"Is she a chef too?"

Michel's face glowed with pride. "My Shelley is a chocolatier. A magic maker. She turns dreams into chocolate. People travel from all over to visit her shop."

"Maybe Shelley should have been on the show instead of you!" Chef Pierce called out. "Come on, Froggy. Let's get this party started."

Michel's cheeks turned red, but he didn't respond. He quietly selected his breakfast foods and joined Ty, Mia, and the other chefs at the table.

Mia gave him a few minutes to eat before tapping her spoon against her water glass. "I want to start off by thanking everyone for participating in this season's show. It's going to be our best yet, and I know our judges are super excited to taste your food. We'll see Levi and Coco later today when we film your first challenge."

Saffron raised a finger. "Are we still using the tent?"

"Yep. Ty's people covered the stained side with furniture. We're good to go."

"We're going to die out there," Chef Pierce declared.

Jane shot a nervous glance at Butterworth, but Mia laughed.

"The chances of another fire are like a billion to one. Accidents happen. On set. In kitchens. But we adjust and move on. Right, Ty?"

Ty nodded and bit into a croissant.

Jane stared at the director. *Why hasn't he told Mia the truth about the fire?*

"I'm not talking about the fire," Chef Pierce spluttered. "I'm talking about heat. It's June in Redneckville. It's already hot as hell, and you want us in chef's coats inside a tent? We're going to die. I have serious medical conditions." He reached into his shirt pocket and pulled out an orange pill bottle. "See?"

"Don't worry. The tent is air-conditioned," Mia looked at the other chefs. "Our viewers want to see the six of you sweat. But not too much."

"You want to see me sweat?" With a leering grin, Chef Pierce held out his brass room key. "I'm in room four-ten, hostess with the mostest."

Mia narrowed her eyes and said, "You signed a contract that includes a code of conduct, *Chef.* If you can't follow it, you should leave now."

Chef Pierce polished off his mimosa and pointed his glass at Mia. "You can't get rid of me, and you know it." He raised his glass high in the air and tried to get Butterworth's attention. "Can I get a refill, my good chap?"

"Cook's Pride is a generous sponsor," said Mia. "They're putting up a hundred grand in prize money and creating a cookware line named after the winner. They're also providing the daily challenge prizes. They want our show to appeal to the Hallmark Channel audience, so the rules of conduct are really important." She stared Chef Pierce down. "No more mimosas for breakfast."

"I don't care how many millions you have; you can't tell me what to drink." Chef Pierce balled his napkin and threw it on the table. "Are we done here?"

With perfect composure, Mia said, "We are. But when

we're in that tent, I *will* tell you what to do. It's my show, remember?"

Muttering obscenities, Chef Pierce got up from the table and left.

Later, Jane saw him devouring a bacon cheeseburger and fries in the Rudyard Kipling Café. Judging by the empty pint glasses on his table, he'd also polished off three beers. And even though he'd be competing in less than an hour, he ordered a fourth.

Jane considered warning Mia but suppressed the impulse. After all, Mia had chosen the contestants. She knew what she was getting with Chef Pierce.

He'll bring the drama.

By the time Jane showed up at the tent, the chef's introductions had been filmed, and Ty was prepping for the next segment. The judges, whom Jane had met earlier that morning, were seated at their table. A makeup artist, the young man with the straw fedora, was powdering Mia's cheeks and forehead.

Mrs. Hubbard waved Jane over to their assigned spot in the corner opposite the judges. Storyton Hall's head cook was giddy with excitement.

"You really don't know anything about this challenge?" she whispered to Jane.

"Nope. They're top secret. Only Mia, Ty, and certain crewmembers know the details." She gave Mrs. Hubbard a playful nudge. "What? Mia didn't tell you when you two were having those friendly talks?"

Mrs. Hubbard's apple-round cheeks turned pink. "It was just a few emails. She didn't ask me to keep them between us, but I felt I should. Most people want something from her, and I think she liked having somebody like me to talk to. Somebody without an agenda."

"Who also happens to be a wonderful listener," Jane added.

Embarrassed, Mrs. Hubbard pointed at the cupboards lining the back wall of the tent. "Look at all of the different spices, flour, sugar, and bottles of oil the chefs have at their disposal. This tent is better stocked than my kitchen."

Mia gave Ty a thumbs-up. She was ready to start filming the first challenge. With a microphone dangling over her head and a dozen lights shining in her face, she looked directly into the camera and smiled.

"Today's challenge is inspired by my childhood summers. Every Sunday, my mom would pack a picnic lunch for our family. We'd grab our library books and walk to the park. My mom always prepared our food in a special way. She'd cut sandwiches into shapes or string our grapes like a necklace. Everything she made felt magical to me. Whenever I see a library book or picnic basket, I think of my mom."

The camera panned down, focusing on Mia's hand, which rested on a stack of vintage books atop a small table covered by a gingham cloth. The table also held a picnic basket and a bouquet of sunflowers wrapped in brown paper.

"Storyton Hall is home to thousands of books. At this beautiful resort, bibliophiles can read, stroll through the gardens like Elizabeth Bennet, or dine like Jay Gatsby. In honor of our setting, all of our challenges will have a literary twist, starting with today's." Mia took a book from the stack on the table and opened it. "Ernest Hemingway was a famous American writer. He was also an outdoorsman and a food lover. For today's challenge, the judges and I would like you to create a Moveable Feast consisting of three dishes. You must pack these dishes in a picnic basket." A wicked grin appeared on Mia's face. "But there's a catch.

Everything you make—utensils, plates, *and* the picnic basket itself—must be edible. You have two hours to create your Moveable Feast, and five minutes to grab your ingredients. Ready? Your five minutes starts now."

The chefs leaped into action. Chef Pierce pushed past Chef Alondra, knocking her into Chef Michel's cooking station. When her hip collided with the counter, she winced in pain.

The camera caught the judges exchanging shocked glances.

Mrs. Hubbard whispered, "What a brute."

The chefs loaded their arms with blocks of cheese, jugs of milk, sticks of butter, and various meats from the refrigerator. After depositing supplies on their individual counters, they rushed off to collect flour, oil, fruits, vegetables, herbs, and spices from the cupboards.

Mia walked over to the male judge, Levi Anjou, and asked, "What would you make first?"

"I'd start with the picnic basket, which I'd make out of bread. If the chefs choose to do this, they'll need to make the dough and give it time to proof while they work on their three dishes."

Mia looked at Coco Kennedy, the female judge. "Edible utensils and plates would be environmentally friendly, but are they doable?"

"I think so," said Coco in a silky voice. "If it were me, I'd make crackers. Like a flatbread cracker for the plates, and a Parmesan cracker spork."

"A spork would be fun," Mia said. "Or crackers made into chopsticks."

When the cameras focused on the contestants again, Mia pointed out that most were using their stand mixers to make dough. The exceptions were Chef August and

Chef Pierce. Chef August was melting sugar in a saucepan while Chef Pierce was grilling chicken breasts.

"Looks like Chef Pierce isn't starting with his basket," Mia said.

The film crew circulated through the tent, getting footage of the chefs as they chopped, fried, baked, and assembled their dishes.

The entire process was fascinating. Jane was enthralled from the moment the contestants stormed the pantry until Mia called out, "Fifteen minutes remain in your Moveable Feast challenge!"

Her announcement was met by groans, cries of alarm, and an expletive from Chef Pierce.

As the activity at the chefs' stations intensified, the air was filled with a delightful potpourri of aromas. Jane smelled baked bread, fry oil, browned butter, and chocolate.

The buzzer sounded, and Mia told the chefs to stop working. The lights and cameras were turned off, and the chefs were given a quick break to drink water, wipe the sweat from their faces, and have their makeup retouched.

When the cameras started rolling again, the chefs were standing behind their Moveable Feasts.

Four of the six chefs had woven strips of bread dough into picnic baskets. Chef August, who was known for his incredible sugar work, had used isomalt and yellow food coloring to create a basket that looked like glass. Chef Pierce had carved a watermelon basket with scalloped edges. He'd also created a green and white pattern by cutting diagonal strips in the rind. His design was clever and charming.

As the chefs presented their meals to the judges, Jane was amazed by their skill and artistry. To her, the most appealing entrées were Chef Saffron's shrimp and mango lettuce rolls and Chef Michel's croissants stuffed with tomato, mozzarella, baby spinach, and apricot jam. Mrs. Hubbard was impressed by Chef Alondra's potato and chorizo empanadas with avocado cream as well as Chef Pierce's bourbon vanilla fruit dip.

The judges were filmed tasting every dish. When they were done, they asked the chefs to line up at the front of the tent.

Coco spoke first. "Chef Lindsay, while we loved your antipasto kebabs, your buttermilk fried chicken was too safe, and your meringues were a bit on the chewy side."

Levi turned to Chef August. "Your sugar work basket was beautiful, but your sugar toothpicks were too sharp. We asked for a utensil, not a weapon. Stuffing strawberries with white chocolate mousse was genius, and we were both impressed by your bacon gruyere tart."

Chef August thanked the judges and sagged in relief as they moved on to the next chef.

"Chef Pierce, your basket was colorful and fun," Coco began. "We loved your grilled chicken pressed sandwich and thought your truffle mayo was delicious."

Levi spread his hands. "Unfortunately, your carrot toothpicks didn't work, and we had issues with your basket. While watermelon rind is *technically* edible, we didn't *want* to eat it."

A dark look appeared in Chef Pierce's eyes. "That's why I made the fruit dip."

Coco dismissed him with a cool, "Thank you, Chef."

While the judges critiqued Chef Saffron's food, Chef Pierce took several swallows from his insulated water bottle. The anger drained from his face. After another swallow, he tucked the water bottle out of sight. His eyes were now glassy and unfocused, and he looked like he was ready to take a nap.

"I wonder what's in that bottle," Mrs. Hubbard whispered.

Jane murmured, "I'd bet my book collection that it's not water."

As soon as the judges finished their critique and returned to their seats, Mia reached into the picnic basket and withdrew a gold envelope emblazoned with the Cook's Pride logo.

"Cook's Pride came up with the perfect prize for the winner of today's challenge," she said, holding out the envelope to let Ty zoom in on the logo. "The winner of the Moveable Feast challenge will follow in Ernest Hemingway's footsteps by embarking on a luxury tour of Spain."

The chefs gasped or whistled in excitement.

"All of our chefs did an amazing job today, but there can be only one winner. The winner of today's challenge is . . ." There was a long pause, and Jane imagined a series of commercials would play before Mia finished her sentence. After several long seconds, she started again. "The winner of today's challenge is Chef Saffron."

A beaming Chef Saffron accepted congratulations from the other chefs as Mia presented her with a golden serving spoon. Having watched *Posh Palate* before, Jane knew that a golden spoon was given to the winning chef after each challenge. The chefs who won multiple spoons usually made it to the final round, so Chef Saffron already had an advantage over her competitors.

The lights and cameras were turned off, the judges left the tent, and the chefs began to pack up their tools. Chef Pierce just stood behind his station, sulking.

While Mia and Ty compared notes about the day's work,

Jane, Mrs. Hubbard, and the film crew were invited to sample the Moveable Feast food.

Jane was dying to try the fishes, but she had to see to the chefs' comfort first. Opening the tent door, she peered outside to see two cars waiting to transport the competitors back to Storyton Hall.

"Whenever you're ready, your rides are here," Jane announced to the chefs.

Looking tired and hot, they collected their knife bags and began filing out of the tent.

Chief Pierce was the last to leave. As he passed by Chef Saffron's station, he noticed the golden spoon on her worktop. Eyes glittering with malice, he picked it up and used both hands to bend it in half before dropping it into the utensil crock.

As he turned toward the exit, he met Jane's horrified gaze.

Most people, having just been caught in the act, would be embarrassed or ashamed.

Not Chef Pierce.

He blew Jane a kiss on his way out.

Seconds later, Chef Saffron darted back into the tent. When she saw the state of her gold spoon, she let out a cry. She then pressed the ruined spoon to her chest and snarled, "I'm going to kill him."

She stormed out of the tent, her face twisted with fury.

Chapter 4

With their first challenge out of the way, the chefs were free until evening. At six, they were to meet for drinks in the Ian Fleming Lounge and then attend a dinner in their honor. For the first time in Storyton Hall's history, Mrs. Hubbard wasn't preparing the meal. She'd be breaking bread with the celebrity chefs instead.

Edwin would also be joining the party. He was eager to compare notes on eclectic eateries and unforgettable dishes with Mia. He wanted to know where she'd had the creamiest gelato, ripest cherimoya fruit, or the tenderest cedar plank fish.

The final spot at the table was reserved for Eloise. She'd had boxloads of cookbooks shipped directly to Storyton Hall, and the celebrity chefs were scheduled to sign a third of the books after dinner. The signed copies would be displayed at Run for Cover, while the rest would be made available to the public an hour before the next challenge.

Eloise also planned to ask each chef to inscribe a cookbook for Mrs. Hubbard. "It'll be a thank-you from the Cover Girls," she'd told Jane several weeks ago. "For all the goodies she made for our book club this year."

"She'll love that," Jane had said, feeling a rush of affection for her generous and thoughtful friend.

Now, as she prepared a quick meal of chicken strips with a ranch panko crust and roasted green beans for the twins, Jane wished she had a new cookbook. She felt like she made the same meals all the time and desperately needed to add to her repertoire.

"It would be nice if our celebrity chefs created more recipes for busy parents," Jane said to Mia later that evening. "So many of their recipes require lots of prep time and expensive ingredients. And while French children might gobble up foie gras or omelets stuffed with caviar, my sons won't."

"You need recipes like the spinach dip I told you about."

Jane smiled. "Yes! Are there more dishes like that in your cookbook?"

"Tons. I think that's why it sells so well. The food is fun to make and fun to eat."

The two women were sitting at the bar in the Ian Fleming Lounge, waiting for their cocktails. When their pear mojitos were served, they were too full to carry, so the women took a few sips before maneuvering past the other guests to where the six chefs had commandeered a group of leather chairs in the back of the room.

"Take a load off, ladies." Chef Alondra waved at two empty chairs.

Chef Saffron passed a bowl of cocktail nuts to Mia. "How did your photoshoot go? Did you dress like a Bond girl?"

Mia's face lit up. "I did. I'm really into vintage fashion, and I wore an *amazing* Valentino off-the-shoulder feather gown. With all the wood and leather furniture in here, my red dress totally popped. Bentley will edit the pics and post one tonight."

"Is that why you dragged us to the Overlook Hotel? So you could take selfies in rooms named after dead authors?" asked Chef Pierce. When Mia ignored him, he raised his glass in salute. "At least the bartender knows what he's doing."

Chef Lindsay frowned at Chef Pierce over the rim of her wineglass. "That basil gimlet is a craft cocktail. It's not meant to be guzzled like Gatorade. Is it even safe for you to be drinking alcohol? Does it mix with those pills you showed us at breakfast?"

"It mixes just fine, Mom. I'm only taking two prescriptions. One for my I-got-no-rhythm heart, and one for my blood pressure, which is off-the-charts because my life is full of pushy women. If I wanted someone to nag me about booze, I'd call one of my ex-wives." He glowered at Chef Lindsay. "Maybe *you* should try guzzling a few protein shakes? You could use more meat on your bones. Men like soft, squeezable women."

"And women like to be treated as equals, not rolls of Charmin. I can see why you have so many ex-wives." Chef Lindsay sneered and turned away.

Chef Michel pulled his chair a little closer to Chef Pierce's. "We might be competitors in the kitchen, but we should try to get along when we're not cooking, no? Why not see this as a chance to make new friends?"

Chef Pierce snorted. "I'm not interested in bonding, and you shouldn't be either. Tell me, Frenchie. Why are you here? Why do you want to win?"

"If you can't call me by my name, I won't talk to you."

Rolling his eyes, Chef Pierce said, "Fine, fine. *Michel*. Why do you want to win?"

"I want to start a college fund for my sons. I was the first person in my family to go to college, and it took me a long time to pay off my student loans. Because of those loans, I couldn't get ahead, no matter how hard I worked, and I don't want my boys to have the same burden. I also want to give some money to my sister who lives in France."

Chef Pierce waved a meaty hand in dismissal. "You're a good guy, which is why you won't beat someone like me. I'm here because my three ex-wives have sucked me dry. I'm broke and desperate. I don't need friends. I need to win, and I'll do whatever it takes to be the last man standing."

"Like ruining Saffron's golden spoon?" asked Chef August.

Feeling Mia's eyes on him, Chef Pierce put a hand over his heart. "I just wanted to see if it was real gold. I had no idea it would bend so easily. My bad."

"You know not to touch things on another chef's station," said Mia. To Chef Saffron, she said, "I'll give you a new spoon."

Chef Saffron shook her head. "That's okay. The bent spoon will motivate me. If there's one person I'm going to beat in this competition, it's Pierce."

Jane decided to intervene before Chef Pierce ruined the entire evening. "I think Chef Michel has the right idea," she said. "You might be competing for the same prize, but you can still be friendly when the cameras are off."

Someone mumbled, "Most of us are friendly."

"You all have stressful jobs and could use a little pampering," Jane continued. "Which is why I've arranged a spa experience for you. Tomorrow, you can choose from a variety of facials or massages, and as a Walt Whitman Spa guest, you can hang out in our relaxation lounge or in our all-new steam room."

"My aching back would love that. Steam me like a dumpling!" cried Chef August.

The other chefs laughed. Even Chef Pierce.

After fielding questions about the spa, Jane led her guests to the Madame Bovary Dining Room. As the hostess escorted Mia and the chefs to their table by the window, the other diners stared at the celebrities in open admiration.

Edwin, Eloise, and Mrs. Hubbard were already seated, but Edwin jumped up to pull out chairs for Mia and Chef Lindsay. Chef Michel, who continued to impress Jane with his genteel manners, did the same for Chef Alondra and Chef Saffron.

Jane performed the introductions, and it wasn't long before Eloise and Edwin were talking to the chefs as if they were old friends.

As for Mia, she was clearly thrilled to be sitting next to Mrs. Hubbard. "You look beautiful," she told the head cook.

Compliments always flustered Mrs. Hubbard, who reddened and glanced down at her plate. But Jane could tell that she was pleased. She was even more pleased when Edwin leaned over and said, "I agree with Ms. Mallett. You look enchanting tonight."

"I guess I should take off my apron more often." Mrs. Hubbard gave Edwin a saucy wink.

Servers appeared with warm dinner rolls and several bottles of wine. As the chefs buttered bread and sipped wine, they shared their greatest kitchen triumphs and disasters with Eloise, Mrs. Hubbard, and Jane.

Edwin and Mia were too busy sharing anecdotes about street food in Bangkok to be drawn into anyone else's conversation. By the time the salad course was done, they were embroiled in a good-natured argument over whether *kua kling* was spicier than *gaeng som*.

Jane, who was seated between Chef August and Chef Michel, hoped to learn more about their lives outside the kitchen. As fathers, both men understood the challenges of running a business while maintaining a close bond with their children. Jane realized that being the executive chef of a fine-dining establishment wasn't that different from managing a five-star resort. She became so engaged in their discussion that she forgot to try her entrée.

When she finally took a bite of her coffee-rubbed grilled steak, it was barely warm. But the chimichurri sauce was so fresh and flavorful that she ate most of her steak anyway.

The stimulating conversation, delicious food, and excellent wine had Jane feeling relaxed and happy. Everyone seemed to be having a wonderful time, and for once, Chef Pierce was behaving. He was so enchanted by Eloise that he forgot to badger their server for refills on wine.

Catching Eloise's eye, Jane arched her brows as if to ask, "Are you okay?"

Her best friend responded with a brief nod. She then tucked a strand of honey hair behind her ear and smiled at Chef Pierce. Eloise's English rose skin and beguiling blue eyes were glowing. She looked as radiant as the bride she'd soon be.

The entrée plates were cleared, and Chefs Michel and August began talking about their wives. The two men exchanged first-date and wedding stories for a few minutes before Chef Michel turned to Jane and asked, "And you, Ms. Steward? Did your husband plan your honeymoon? It sounds like he's been all over the world."

"Actually, Edwin is my partner. My husband, William, passed away, and I never remarried."

Chef Michel's face went as red as a maraschino cherry. "I'm so sorry."

Jane touched his hand. "Don't be. I've been very lucky. I've had the love of two wonderful men in one lifetime. Edwin knows that William will always have a place in my heart, and my late husband would approve of Edwin because he loves me and my sons."

Chef Michel stared at the candle on the table, momentarily transfixed by the flickering flame. "My employer, Olivia Limoges, also lost her husband in a terrible tragedy. No one knew how to comfort her. Including me." He looked at Jane. "She came to Storyton Hall some time during today's challenge. She told me that her guest cottage feels like a home away from home. Thank you for letting Olivia rent that cottage. She's like a sister to me. A blunt and bossy sister, *oui*, but I love her."

"Is your boss here to make sure you win?" Chef August gave Chef Michel a playful nudge.

Chef Michel blanched. "*Mon dieu*, no! She's having writer's block and thought a change of scenery might help her break through it. If I make it to the finals, she'll come cheer me on. Otherwise, I won't see her much. She's a very private person. And she's behind deadline."

Jane didn't know much about the authoress from Oyster Bay, North Carolina, other than Eloise was a fan of her work. For this reason alone, Jane was looking forward to meeting her.

"Lemon-blueberry cheesecake parfait," the server announced as he placed a glass bowl in front of Mia.

"This place is heaven," Mia said after sampling the dessert. "I've never gone this long without checking in on social media, but it feels amazing to unplug. I should visit once a year." She smiled at Mrs. Hubbard. "And I'll bring a cookbook every time."

"Speaking of cookbooks, where should the chefs sign theirs?" Eloise asked Jane.

"I thought we'd use the break room in the kitchens."

Chef Lindsay pointed at the wine bottles in the center of the table. "Can we bring the dessert wine? It's too good to waste."

"I like the way you think." Lumbering to his feet, Chef Pierce grabbed two bottles in one hand and his glass in the other.

The chefs followed Jane to the kitchens where they thanked the staff for the excellent dinner.

Beaming with pride, Mrs. Hubbard asked the guests if they'd like to see her cookbook nook. They all said yes, which gave Jane and Eloise time to organize the books into separate piles. Edwin volunteered to help and had just finished with Chef Saffron's cookbooks when his phone buzzed.

After glancing at his screen, he put a hand on the small of Jane's back. "Magnus is in the weeds. I need to bail him out."

"Good luck," Jane said, turning to give Edwin a kiss.

"You were the most beautiful woman at the table tonight," he whispered. "As always."

Eloise put her hands on her hips and glared at her brother. "What am I? Chopped liver?"

"Hardly." Edwin grinned at Eloise. "You're more like a lemon scone. Blond, sweet, and flaky."

Edwin ducked as Eloise threw a dishrag at him.

"I don't know what you see in him," Eloise said to Jane.

Jane smiled. "My future."

The chefs began filing into the break room.

"The last time I saw such rare French porcelain, I was in a museum. That soup tureen alone!" Chef Michel whistled. "*C'est très magnifique.*"

Eloise handed him a pen and directed the other chefs to their seats.

"My parents are from India," Chef Saffron told Jane. "After immigrating to the States, it took them ten years to buy their first house. My father's boss gave them a silver tea set as a housewarming gift, and my parents treasure that set. They'd be really impressed by your silver collection."

Chef Pierce leaned against the doorframe and surveyed the crowded room. He held a wine bottle in one hand and an empty glass in the other. "I need my own space, so I'll sign in the kitchen."

Because Jane had to load her arms with a stack of his *A Man and a Pan* cookbooks, she was unable to stop Chef Pierce from plopping down on a stool at the dessert prep station. He rested his torso against the wall as if he needed it to hold him up and poured the rest of the wine into his glass.

Because Jane didn't want to interrupt the young woman plating desserts, she stood in the aisle and waited for the cook to finish piping chocolate swirls on four plates. The pastry chef then used a squeeze bottle to produce dots of raspberry sauce. By pulling a knife through the dots, she transformed them into flower petals. Finally, she slid a square of chocolate cake onto each plate, topping the squares with a mint leaf, a dollop of whipped cream, and a single raspberry.

After examining her work, she used a napkin to wipe off an errant speckle of raspberry sauce on the edge of the first plate. She was about to clean the rim of another plate when Chef Pierce's hand cupped her backside.

Wearing a lecherous smile, Chef Pierce curled his fingers and squeezed hard.

The young woman shouted and jerked to the side. In her haste to get away from Chef Pierce, she knocked a dessert plate off the counter. It hit the floor, smashing into pieces and splattering her calves with chocolate and raspberry sauce.

Jane opened her mouth to berate Chef Pierce when Mrs. Hubbard materialized with the suddenness of a fairy godmother. Except this fairy godmother wielded a cleaver.

"If you lay a hand on another Storyton Hall employee ever again, I'll carve you like a turkey." Mrs. Hubbard spoke in a low growl. "Leave my kitchens in under ten seconds, or I'll make a eunuch out of you! Ten . . . nine . . ."

Chef Pierce was gone by five.

Mrs. Hubbard put her arm around the young woman's shoulders. "Are you okay, Jessie?"

Jessie nodded. "Sorry about the plate."

"Don't you apologize," Mrs. Hubbard said. "This was *not* your fault. No one is allowed to touch you without your permission. I don't care who they are."

When the young woman didn't respond, Mrs. Hubbard looked to Jane for help.

"Why don't you and Jessie hang out in the cookbook nook for a few minutes?" Jane suggested. "After I have a quick word with Mia, I'll come check on you."

Another staff member came over to clean up the broken plate.

"Should I make them some tea?" he asked Jane.

"Irish coffee might be better. Thanks, Niko."

Jane returned to the break room and dumped Chef Pierce's cookbooks on the counter.

"Sorry, Eloise. You'll have to sell these without a signature." Jane glanced around. "Where's Mia?"

"In the cookbook nook catching up on texts," answered Chef Alondra.

Jane found Mia and Mrs. Hubbard huddled together on the love seat. There was no sign of Jessie.

"Jessie's new," Mrs. Hubbard was saying to Mia. "It's only her second week."

"Has she gone home?" Jane asked.

Mrs. Hubbard folded her arms over her chest. "She's back on the line, plating desserts. That's where she wants to be."

Jane felt a rush of admiration for the young woman. "There's no debating what needs to happen next."

"You won't have to tell Pierce to leave," Mia said. "I'll do it first thing in the morning. He's probably passed out in his room by now anyway."

Mrs. Hubbard wagged a finger at Mia. "Don't give him the news by yourself. We can all predict how he's going to take it."

"I'll have him come to my suite. That way, my staff will be there."

Jane's anger was still rising. "Why did you include someone like him? Because he'd create drama?"

"Is that what Ty said?"

"Not specifically about Chef Pierce, but he made it clear that drama hikes ratings. And since the rest of the chefs are extremely likable, I assume Chef Pierce is here to stir up strife."

Mia gazed at the colorful cookbook spines lining the shelves. "The other chefs are friendly because we just started. With every challenge, the stress increases. If you've watched the show, you know how crazy things get. Chefs play mind games with each other. They leave a freezer door open so another chef's ice cream will melt. The nicest person can turn mean."

"Jessie has nothing to do with your show." Jane's eyes flashed. "Chef Pierce's behavior will not be tolerated at Storyton Hall."

Mia stood up. "He'll be gone in the morning. That's a promise."

Jane and Mrs. Hubbard headed back to the kitchens to check on Jessie. When she assured them that she was fine and would prefer to focus on her work, Jane returned to the break room. The other chefs were gone, and Eloise had packed up the cookbooks earmarked for Run for Cover.

"What happened?" she asked. "Mrs. Hubbard looked upset."

"With good reason," Jane said. After giving Eloise a brief account of Pierce's behavior and the consequences he'd suffer as a result, she tapped her watch face. "It's been a long day. I'm ready to go home and put my pajamas on."

"Go ahead. I'm going to meet Landon out back in a few minutes."

Eloise smiled. "See you tomorrow."

As she passed under the arbor into Milton's Gardens, Jane inhaled the perfume of confederate jasmine. She walked slowly, her steps moving past rows of baby's breath and cosmos that glowed like stars. White moths flitted among the blooms. Peepers and crickets serenaded Jane with their night music, inviting her to forget about the day's trials.

Across the Great Lawn, the lights of her home shone like a beacon. Soon, she'd be in bed with her book.

Suddenly, a shadow emerged from a copse of trees on the far side of the lawn. The shadow creature had four legs and was racing straight for her.

Jane froze. She'd seen foxes on Storyton Hall's grounds. And once, a coyote. The animal bearing down on her was too big to be a fox, and only a rabid coyote would run directly at her.

With no shelter nearby, she was as defenseless as a rabbit.

"Go away!" she cried, trying to startle the creature. Fear turned her voice shrill. "*Go!*"

A whistle pierced the air, and the animal immediately veered toward the path leading to the staff cottages. And then, a ghostly figure stepped into the pool of lamplight. In her long, white dress, with her halo of fair hair, she could have been Diana, Goddess of the Hunt.

She bent down, opening her arms in welcome, and the shadow animal rushed into them. His tail wagged furiously, and he bathed her cheek with his tongue. He was no beast. He was a dog.

Seconds later, the pair left the circle of lamplight and melted into the darkness.

Jane exhaled in relief. The woman was neither a ghost nor a goddess. She was a writer named Olivia Limoges. And her companion was a black standard poodle.

I'll have to tell Ms. Limoges that her dog can't run loose like that, Jane thought as she continued walking.

She wished she could reclaim the peacefulness she'd felt in the garden, but it was gone.

At home, she reminded herself that tomorrow was a new day. She then climbed into bed and reached for her book.

* * *

Jane's bedroom was still draped in darkness when her phone rang.

She came awake with a start and squinted at the clock. A phone call before sunrise was a bad omen.

"Hello?" she croaked.

"Ms. Steward? I'm so sorry," said a man. His voice was familiar, but no name surfaced in Jane's sleep-fogged brain. "I wasn't sure who to call."

"Who is this?"

"Murray Lloyd. From the kitchens. I come in first to start the baking. But when I turned on the lights, I saw . . ." He let out a breath. "There's a man here, Ms. Steward. A dead man."

Chapter 5

Jane threw on sweatpants and a T-shirt and scribbled a note to her sons. It was four in the morning, and since she had no idea when she'd be back, she left the note next to a box of cereal. She also placed bowls, spoons, and two bananas on the counter. She couldn't predict what the day would bring, but she'd feel better knowing that Fitz and Hem had breakfast.

Outside, bright stars were pinned to a Prussian blue canvas. There was no sign of the coming dawn.

Jane crossed the dew-soaked lawn at a brisk pace, accompanied by the muted drone of insects and the faint squeak of bats on the wing.

During the night, the moon had lost its luster. A swath of diaphanous clouds made it look like a wooly yarn ball instead of a shiny coin, but it was still capable of casting eerie shadows over the garden.

Ahead, the manor house was a slumbering stone giant. No light streamed from its windows. All the curtains in the guest rooms were drawn. The public spaces were illuminated by soft energy-saving lights that seemed to emphasize the somnolent atmosphere.

Jane swatted at a veil of gnats and opened the loading dock door. It closed behind her with a bang, and her footfalls echoed on the tile floor. She felt like she was in a horror film, and she was walking straight toward danger.

In the kitchens, every light was on and the ovens were humming. The hushed voice of a man singing the blues floated through the air.

A radio sat on the prep counter near the ovens, along with the necessary ingredients and equipment for bread baking.

Murray was nowhere to be seen, and there was no sign of a dead man.

"Murray?" Jane softly called.

There was no answer.

Jane took out her phone. With her thumb hovering over the red emergency button, she entered the break room.

The lights were on here too, and Murray had brewed a pot of coffee. The glass carafe was full and hot to the touch.

Her anxiety rising, Jane selected a potential weapon— a set of poultry shears—from a utensil cylinder near the sink and yanked open the door to the walk-in fridge. Eddies of cold air rushed out, raising gooseflesh on her arms, but everything looked as it should.

She checked the dry goods pantry next. Its shelves of canned and bottled foodstuff told her nothing, so she headed for the cookbook nook.

"Ms. Steward?"

The thin whisper came from the hallway to Jane's left that led to the staff restrooms.

Jane turned to face a gray-haired man wearing an apron. He had a rolling pin in one hand and was pressing a paper towel to his mouth with the other. His skin had the weathered patina of a person who spent his free time outdoors, which is why Jane found his pallor alarming.

"Murray." She moved closer to the baker. "Are you okay?"

He nodded and lowered the paper towel. "Sorry, ma'am. I didn't think I'd be sick, but I was. I've seen my fair share of dead game up close, but this is different." Murray pointed toward the cookbook nook. "You shouldn't go in there alone. Give me a minute to get my breath back, and I'll come with you."

Taking Murray's elbow, Jane steered him to the break room. She filled a coffee cup with water and told him to drink it.

"I'll be right back. If it's as bad as you say, we'll both need something stronger than water."

"I reckon so, ma'am. I reckon so."

As Jane approached the cookbook nook, she saw what had captured Murray's attention.

It was blood.

A thin stream of it had traveled across the hallway tiles and formed a pool against the back wall.

Jane looked at the blood and tried to gather her courage. She knew she was about to see something terrible, and she was scared.

Though she had no need of a weapon, she found comfort in the feel of the poultry shears in her hand. Squeezing them so hard turned her knuckles white, and she peered into the cookbook nook.

Her gaze immediately locked on a man's body. He was on the floor, his belly and part of his face pressed to the tiles. His head was turned toward the hall so that he was staring at Jane's feet. The man's right arm was pinned under his torso while his left hand was near his chest, inches away from his motionless heart.

Jagged shards of broken porcelain surrounded his body like Artic icebergs. And like the iceberg that sank the *Titanic*, one of the shards had punctured the man's belly. The wound, which was closer to his hip than his navel, was likely the portal through which the man's life had drained.

Stepping into the room, Jane noticed a dagger-shaped piece of porcelain tucked in the curve of the man's left hand. The pointed tip was covered in dried blood, as was the dead man's palm.

"What were you doing here in the middle of the night?" Jane asked Chef Pierce. Her voice held no condemnation. Only pity.

Having seen enough, she returned to the hall and called Butterworth.

"Alert the other Fins," Jane said after she told Butterworth about Chef Pierce. "Except for Lachlan. He might be with Eloise, and I don't want to alarm her. Grab a bottle of whiskey from the lounge too, please. For medicinal purposes."

Jane hung up and went to check on Murray. When Butterworth appeared, she signaled for him to add a splash of whiskey to Murray's coffee.

"You're having one too," Butterworth told Jane. "You might think you're okay, but you're not."

Jane and Murray sipped their whiskey-laced coffee while Butterworth left to examine the cookbook nook.

"I have to call Sheriff Evans, and I imagine he'll want to speak to you," Jane said to Murray. "If you'd be more comfortable at home, I can tell him to find you there."

Murray cradled his warm mug. "I'd rather bake, Ms. Steward. It'll calm my nerves."

"I understand. When the rest of the kitchen staff arrives, please tell them we have a Rip Van Winkle in the cookbook nook. They may want to have a peek—it's natural to be curious—but I'd like you to remind them that the deceased is still our guest. I don't want gawking or gossiping."

The staff knew that Rip Van Winkle was code for an expired guest. Innocuous codes for serious situations were common practice in the hotel business. Though it was an unpleasant truth, people died in hotels all the time, and there were protocols for handling these unfortunate incidents.

Murray sat up straighter and grabbed his rolling pin. "You can count on me, ma'am."

Jane thanked him warmly, put her coffee mug in the sink, and went to join Butterworth. It wasn't long before Sinclair and Sterling appeared.

Sinclair put a hand on Jane's shoulder. "I'm sorry you had to wake up to such a grim sight, my girl."

"He has it far worse," Jane said, indicating the dead man.

Sterling held out several wrapped swabs. "I'll collect a few samples before the sheriff comes. Just in case."

Jane leaned into Sinclair, comforted by the scent of books on his clothes. "I wish his ending had been peaceful. For his sake, and for ours. Would you say a few words, Sinclair? I'm too numb to think of anything."

"Any eulogy I came up with would be colored by what I know about this man. Therefore, I'll borrow from Chaucer."

Butterworth's brow twitched. "Chaucer isn't known for his brevity."

Sinclair lowered his head and began to speak.

"'Certain, when I was born, so long ago,
Death drew the tap of life and let it flow;
And ever since the tap has done its task,
And now there's little more but an empty cask.'"

Sterling murmured, "Pretty grim farewell," and bent to collect a blood sample.

"I was inspired by that." Sinclair pointed at an empty wineglass with a ribbed stem on the fourth shelf from the floor. The glass was used only in the Madame Bovary Dining Room, which meant it was probably the same one Chef Pierce had carried from the table into the kitchens.

"Was he planning to steal a cookbook? Or one of the antiques?" mused Butterworth.

Jane studied the shelves. "The first volume of the two-volume set Mia gave to Mrs. Hubbard isn't flush with the other books. It looks like Chef Pierce was in the middle of pulling it off the shelf when . . . what? He had a heart attack? Or a stroke?"

"It's hard to say." Sterling traced a line through the air from the shelves to Chef Pierce's body. "An intense pain or the sudden inability to control his movements would explain why the dishes were swept off the shelf."

"Then what? He collapsed to the floor, falling directly on that knife-sharp piece of porcelain?" Jane stared at Chef Pierce's left hand. "Somehow, it impaled his belly, and after pulling it out, he pressed his hand to the wound. But he couldn't stop the bleeding."

Butterworth frowned. "That's a very unlikely scenario."

"The bleeding from the abdominal wound is no surprise, but the smaller cuts bled like crazy too." Sterling looked at Jane. "Did he mention any health issues in front of you?"

Recalling the breakfast in the Daphne du Maurier Drawing Room, Jane explained how Chef Pierce had brandished his pill bottle. "He said he took medicine for his heart and blood pressure."

Sterling glanced at Chef Pierce's waxen face. "He had a bad ticker and high blood pressure, and those are the health issues we know of."

Jane said, "He could also put away large amounts of food, and he drank like he was trying to quench an insatiable thirst."

"An apt description of alcoholism," said Sinclair. "The thirst is both physical and emotional." As he looked at Chef Pierce, his gaze softened. "This man's history is rife with poor choices and indecent behavior."

Sterling folded his arms. "None of this explains what he was doing here. Would he steal a book or antique at the beginning of the competition?" He pointed at a china fragment. "Is this stuff even worth the risk?"

"Before it broke into bits, that piece was a Royal Copenhagen soup tureen worth twenty thousand dollars," said Sinclair. "I also see the remains of a blue and white fish platter worth thousands of dollars."

Sterling whistled.

"The books would be easier to hide in a suitcase," said Butterworth.

The men fell quiet and Jane decided that it was time to call the sheriff's department.

The dispatch operator told Jane that because Sheriff Evans wasn't on duty until eight, Deputy Phelps would be the responding officer. Jane liked the young deputy, but she wanted Sheriff Evans to take charge of the situation. He had a shrewd mind, a calm manner, and was far more experienced than Deputy Phelps.

Jane pocketed her phone and looked at Sterling. "The cavalry's coming. After you get those samples to your lab, will you review last night's video footage? I'd like to know if Chef Pierce prowled about alone, or if he had company."

Sterling hurried off and Butterworth headed to the loading dock to meet Deputy Phelps.

Jane decided to wait in the hall, and even though Chef Pierce's glassy-eyed stare could no longer find her where she stood, Jane could still feel the dead man's presence. He'd demanded attention in life, and he was continuing to demand it in death.

As if reading Jane's mind, Sinclair said, "Chef Pierce did not go quietly into the night. He raged and he fought. The aftermath of that struggle has left an imprint."

The sounds of the kitchen staff preparing for the breakfast service drifted down the hall, and the familiar din made Jane think of Mrs. Hubbard.

"Poor Mrs. Hubbard. The cookbook nook is her special retreat. She's told me before that the pieces on the shelves are worth a small fortune, but it's not like I'd ever sell them. And though they've been in the Steward family for generations, it's Mrs. Hubbard who cherishes every platter and teapot."

"At least her cookbooks are unharmed," said Sinclair.

Jane didn't think this would be much of a consolation. She could only hope that Chef Pierce's body was removed before Mrs. Hubbard arrived to oversee the lunch service.

The crackle of a walkie-talkie drew Jane's attention to the end of the hall. She saw Deputy Phelps carrying a field kit. He wasn't alone. Sheriff Evans was right behind him.

Jane was so relieved that she almost smiled.

Sheriff Evans touched the brim of his brown hat. "Good morning, Ms. Steward."

"Sheriff. Deputy Phelps. I'm sorry to call you out this early."

Evans said, "I'd get up even earlier if it meant I could have a cup of your excellent coffee."

The sheriff knew that a guest had died, but he had no idea that the guest was a celebrity, or that his death would soon have the media descending on Storyton like a plague of locusts.

Evans studied Jane's face. "It's a bad one, isn't it?"

Jane nodded and stepped aside, giving the lawmen an unobstructed view of the blood trail. She and Sinclair hung back while Evans and Phelps entered the cookbook nook. It felt like an eternity before they reemerged wearing examination gloves and solemn expressions.

Deputy Phelps removed a stack of evidence markers from his field kit and carried them into the cookbook nook. The sight of the small, yellow signs with their black numbers filled Jane with dread.

"This isn't a clear case of death by natural causes, so we'll need to process the scene," the sheriff told Jane. "When Doc Lydgate gets here, he'll give us a better idea of what we're dealing with. In the meantime, who found your Rip Van Winkle?"

At the sheriff's behest, Jane asked Murray to step into the break room. The kitchen staff shot curious glances in his direction but continued with their work.

It didn't take long for Sheriff Evans to interview Murray, and by the time the baker was back at his station, rolling out a mound of dough, Doc Lydgate had arrived.

The village doctor was known by everyone in Storyton. His hair and beard were as white as egret feathers, and though his face was a map of wrinkles, his mind was sharp and his hands were gentle and sure.

Doc Lydgate gave Jane an affectionate pat on the arm. "I haven't examined a patient in your kitchens before, but who could blame a person for wanting to spend their final moments surrounded by such heavenly smells?"

"And our guest may have been too drunk to smell much of anything."

"I see," said the doc in a low tone. "Would you lead me to the patient, please?"

Jane admired how Doc Lydgate claimed Chef Pierce as his patient. Whether he deserved it or not, the infamous chef would be treated with dignity by those investigating his death.

Deputy Phelps had finished photographing the scene, so Jane followed the doc into the cookbook nook. She needed to hear Doc Lydgate's initial impressions because she'd soon be facing a barrage of questions, and the only people who could provide answers were in this room.

The doc looked down at the dead man's face. "It seems the gentleman liked to imbibe, judging by the broken capillaries around the nose. In addition to the expected lividity, the skin has a yellow tinge indicative of liver disease. The hypostasis on the bottom half of the face tells me that the patient died in this position, causing the remaining blood to pool in the parts of his body closest to the floor. The extreme pallor of his neck and hands is due to blood loss. The minor lacerations appear to have bled at an accelerated rate. The patient may have been taking anticoagulants. If his blood couldn't clot, the wound in his side would have been fatal. It appears that he tried to stem the flow with his hand, which speaks to the patient's desire to live."

He paused as if the gravity of this statement called for a moment of silence.

"The patient was overweight and in poor health," the doc continued. "He probably used the last of his strength removing that shard."

Jane turned to the sheriff. "Have you searched his pockets?"

"Not much on him. Just the key to his guest room and a matchbook from a bar in New York. The key was in his pocket, but the matchbook was tucked under the band of his underwear."

It took a second for Jane to digest this. "Who keeps matches in their underwear? May I see them?"

Evans nodded at Phelps, who retrieved the evidence bag from his kit. Jane examined the unremarkable matchbox before giving the sheriff a forlorn look. "Are you treating this as a crime scene?"

"We are. Storyton Hall has a history of attracting violence, and I'd rather be wrong about this situation than fail to gather the evidence when I had the chance."

Jane said, "You're right, of course. And all eyes will be on us when it gets out that one of the contestants from *Posh Palate with Mia Mallett* died after the first episode."

The sheriff's expression turned pensive. "I've never watched the show, but Deputy Phelps filled me in on the ride over. Since these chefs are competing for such a lucrative prize, it raises the question: How far will they go to win?"

Jane stared at the body in the cookbook nook—at the blood and broken china—and wished she could go back to bed and wake up to a different reality. But there was no escaping the dead man on the floor. There was no avoiding Sheriff Evans's question. And his was one of many swirling around inside Jane's head.

Why did Pierce come down here in the middle of the night?

Was he going to steal something?

Was he looking for a recipe?

Was he going to burn something with those matches?

The kitchens were the heart of Storyton Hall. Their noise, bustle, and warmth never failed to distract Jane from her worries.

Until today.

Today, death was stronger than the heat generated by the ovens or the pervasive aroma of baking bread. Today, death evoked a silence more powerful than the clamor of the cooks.

In that silence, another question formed in Jane's mind. She tried to ignore it, but it grew and grew like rising dough, refusing to be tamped down.

Was it murder?

Chapter 6

By the time Chef Pierce's body had been loaded into an ambulance, Storyton Hall was coming to life. The delivery bell rang, the noise in the kitchens escalated, and room service orders began trickling in.

Butterworth insisted on mopping the hall and cookbook nook himself. "It's easier to control the gossip if no one views the scene but us. I believe we can rely on Mr. Murray's discretion."

Sinclair offered to help with the cleaning. While the two men set about their gruesome task, Jane fetched hydrogen peroxide and baking soda to address any residual stains and called home to check on the twins.

Fitz answered the phone with a groggy, "Hey, Mom."

Jane could hear cereal hitting the bottom of a bowl. The boys were having a late breakfast.

At least someone got some rest, she thought.

"Why'd you leave so early?" asked Fitz.

"We had a Rip Van Winkle," Jane said.

After ordering his brother to switch to speaker mode, Hem said, "What happened?"

Without going into detail, Jane told her sons that the

deceased was one of the celebrity chefs. She went on to add that his passing was sure to throw the resort into chaos.

"What should we do?"

"Get dressed and report to Uncle Aloysius and Aunt Octavia. Tell them what happened and that I'll fill them in as soon as I can."

Having spoken with her sons, Jane was ready to visit Mia's suite.

"I'm heading to the third floor," she told Butterworth and Sinclair. "We're expecting a crowd of two hundred people later this morning, so if Mia decides to cancel the show, I'll need to get the word out as soon as possible. You two will have to break the news to Mrs. Hubbard, I'm afraid."

Jane hurried to her office where she ran a brush through her hair and applied a little powder and lipstick. The reflection in her compact showed a sleep-deprived woman with worried eyes.

Mia answered her door dressed in a silky white robe over cotton pajamas with a pineapple print. Her makeup-free face was as luminescent as a pearl. Her dark hair was in rollers and her room smelled of nail polish.

"This is a surprise." She smiled as she took in Jane's appearance. "Were you working out?"

Jane glanced down at her T-shirt and sweatpants and blushed. She never interacted with guests looking like this, but here she was, talking to a beautiful billionaire in the clothes she used for yard work.

"Sorry to show up without calling first, but I have bad news. May I come in?"

Mia's smile faded and she stepped aside.

The two women sat on the sofa in the living room area.

After politely refusing Mia's offer of coffee, Jane said, "Chef Pierce passed away last night."

Mia's eyes widened and she clapped her hand over her mouth.

In Jane's experience, it was best to deliver bad news quickly and in plain terms.

"A staff member found him this morning. I reported the incident to the authorities, and the sheriff and our local doctor have conducted a preliminary examination. I don't know how Chef Pierce died, and it could take hours—or days—for the medical examiner to make a ruling."

Mia stared at Jane in disbelief. "But we just saw him at dinner. He was fine. He was . . . do you think this happened because of his drinking?"

Instead of answering, Jane asked her own question. "How much do you know about the contestants' health? Do they submit a medical history or sign waivers as part of their contract?"

Sounding dazed, Mia said, "They submit health forms. Our insurance company requires them."

Jane made a mental note to ask Bentley for a copy of Chef Pierce's forms.

"And Chef Pierce's drinking? Was his excessiveness common knowledge?"

"His employees and some food critics and customers would know about it. But most people wouldn't see it as a big deal." Mia shrugged. "Lots of chefs have issues. Their jobs are super stressful, and their craft demands most of their time and energy. It's not unusual for chefs to have an addiction. Smoking, drinking, drugs—whatever keeps them cooking."

She went on to describe the punishing schedules and physical challenges faced by executive chefs. "After years of this, many chefs become sick or depressed. The burnout rate in the profession is crazy high."

"I had no idea," said Jane. "Mrs. Hubbard might yell and shout at times, but she's happiest in a kitchen."

"She definitely loves her work." Mia gazed into the middle distance. "It might not seem like it, but Chef Pierce still loved being a chef too. I wanted him on the show because I knew he'd create drama, but he's also super talented. The man was born to cook delicious food."

Mia continued to stare at nothing. She seemed miles away.

Jane wanted to give Mia a little time to process her feelings before asking how Chef Pierce's death would impact the show, so she fell silent.

The quiet was soon broken by an alert from Mia's cell phone. She glanced at the screen and said, "That's Ty. I need to tell him what happened." She started removing her curlers. "If the other chefs are okay with it, we'll stick to our schedule. Later, we'll add a dedication and a video montage of Chef Pierce's career to the end of today's episode. I think he'd like that."

Jane had expected Mia to cancel the show or, at the very least, postpone the filming. But seeing as the decision wasn't hers to make, she hid her surprise and got to her feet.

Mia dumped the rollers on the coffee table. "I think Chef Pierce would want us to keep going. He was committed to this competition."

"And the other chefs? Would you like me to give them the news?"

"No, thanks. I'll do it after breakfast," Mia said. "Ty will handle the crew."

As Jane turned to leave, she noticed a laptop on the

writing desk. The sight reminded her of Mia's online presence, and of her millions of followers. "If the chefs or crewmembers have questions, please refer them to the Storyton Sheriff's Department. Please make it very clear to everyone involved that the public should hear about Chef Pierce's passing from the sheriff's department *first*. No tweets or posts before the official statement has been released."

"Of course."

Jane left Mia's suite and rushed home to shower and change into a floral skirt and a pale blue blouse. She grabbed a banana from the fruit bowl in her kitchen and ate it as she crossed the Great Lawn for the fourth time that morning.

She'd just entered Milton's Gardens when her phone pinged with a text from Sterling, asking her to meet him in the surveillance room.

Before she could reply, Sterling sent another text. It said, Chef Pierce had a late-night visitor.

Jane changed course. Instead of stopping by the kitchens to check on Mrs. Hubbard, she headed directly for the surveillance room.

Once there, she looked at the bank of television screens and said, "Show me."

Sterling waited for her to sit down before pushing the space bar on his computer. The screen to Jane's right displayed the elevator banks on the west wing's second floor. The doors of the middle elevator slid open and Chef Pierce lurched into the hallway.

He wobbled past the vending niche, paused to rest at the housekeeping closet, and then lumbered on to his guest room.

"Your dinner party left the dining room around ten. The group went to the kitchens next. After being told to leave,

Chef Pierce went directly to the Ian Fleming Lounge. He left the lounge around eleven thirty."

"Which means he drank for another hour before turning in," Jane grumbled. "We should ask the bartenders if they saw him interacting with other guests."

Sterling jotted a note on a legal pad. "I'll see to that. The next bit of footage comes from the camera positioned over the stairwell door. I know you were against placing cameras in the guest hallways, but this might convince you that it was a good call."

Jane held her breath and waited to see Chef Pierce's visitor appear onscreen. Her gaze flicked to the timestamp. 11:59. A breath from midnight. Only a handful of seconds divided one day from the next—an end giving way to a beginning. Except for Chef Pierce. For him, it was the beginning of the end.

A young woman approached the door to his guest room. She wore yoga pants and a baggy hoodie. Her hair was rose gold.

"That's Mia's assistant, Bentley," said Jane.

Sterling pulled a face. "Like the car?"

Jane was too focused on the screen to reply.

Bentley used her fist to deliver three quick bangs to Chef Pierce's door. She waited a few seconds, and then knocked again. When there was no response, she pulled out her phone. She jabbed at the screen with her index finger and put her ear to the door.

Suddenly, she jerked backward and spoke into her phone. When she was finished, she folded her arms and glowered at the door.

It finally opened, revealing Chef Pierce in boxer shorts, tube socks, and a grungy white T-shirt that failed to cover his belly. He squinted at Bentley through half-shuttered lids and his face made it clear that he was confused by her presence.

Bentley pushed past him into the room. He turned to follow her, and the door swung shut.

"I'm glad I can't see what happened next," said Jane.

"It's not what you think," Sterling assured her. "Watch. She's about to come back out."

A few minutes later, Bentley exited the room wearing a satisfied look. Whatever her aim in visiting Chef Pierce in the dead of night, she'd achieved it.

Was this a personal errand? Or was she doing Mia's bidding?

Sterling paused the feed. "From here, the young lady goes straight back to her room. As for Chef Pierce, he dresses in the suit he wore to dinner and takes the elevator to the ground floor. He then disappears into the staff corridor. We can't track him in there, but he obviously ended up in the cookbook nook."

"Were you able to see his face once he reached the ground floor?"

"Not clearly. He seemed to be concentrating on not falling. He kept his eyes on the floor and his hand on the wall for balance. I haven't completed tests on the blood sample I collected, but I know a drunk man when I see one."

Jane frowned. "I'll have to ask Bentley about her visit. As much as I want to honor her privacy as a Storyton Hall guest, she was the last person to see him alive."

"Unless someone was waiting for him in the cookbook nook," Sterling said in a grim voice. He tapped a screen showing the view from the loading dock door. "Your friends are here."

Jane watched as four of the Cover Girls, Eloise, Betty,

Violet, and Mrs. Pratt, filed into Storyton Hall. Their arrival meant that it was almost time for the cookbook signing.

Jane jumped up. "I hope Sheriff Evans calls soon. I'll have to tell the rest of the guests about Chef Pierce, and at this point, I don't have much information to share."

In the kitchens, Jane found her friends fussing over Mrs. Hubbard, which meant she'd already told them about Chef Pierce. Jane knew she should scold her head cook for having a loose tongue, but she wouldn't.

"No, really. I'm okay," insisted Mrs. Hubbard. "My little retreat isn't ruined because a famous chef spent his final moments there, but I am upset about those lovely antiques. I was going to use some of those pieces for Ms. Octavia's eighty-fifth birthday party."

Jane exhaled in relief. Mrs. Hubbard had been spared the gory details of Chef Pierce's death.

Spotting Jane, Mrs. Hubbard pulled her in for a hug. "You poor lamb! I hear you came in before dawn. Why was Chef Pierce in the cookbook nook in the middle of the night?"

"I don't know," Jane answered truthfully.

Mrs. Hubbard tapped her temple. "I think he needed help. My cookbook collection is one-of-a-kind. There's a culinary library in that nook. Maybe he was looking for inspiration. Or a winning recipe. And before he could pick one, his heart gave out."

Betty, the proprietress of the Cheshire Cat Pub, gasped. "You mean, he was going to *cheat*? Like, he already knew about the next challenge and wanted to prepare for it?" She turned to Jane. "What's today's theme?"

"I have no idea," said Jane. "Only Mia, the director, and their support staff know."

Violet sighed dreamily. "I can't believe Mia Mallett is here. I might run a small-town salon, but I keep up with the latest beauty trends, and no one's trendier than Mia. Her posts are so positive too. Is she sweet in real life?"

Jane nodded. "She's sweet, cheerful, and easy to talk to."

"And drop-dead gorgeous," Violet added. "How can anyone who eats out all the time stay so thin? It's not fair."

Mrs. Hubbard cupped Violet's cheek. "You're perfect just as you are. And life's too short to say no to cake."

"Amen!" bellowed Mrs. Pratt. The retired schoolteacher was the senior-most member of the Cover Girls, and often, the most boisterous.

Eloise moved closer to Jane. "I'm sorry about Chef Pierce. You could have called Landon for help. I'm not moving in until after the wedding."

Mrs. Pratt shook her head in astonishment. "How can you spend a single night away from that man? Have I told you that your hunky fiancé looks like the lumberjack on the cover of my current read?"

"You've mentioned it once or twice. You should come to the store and pick up your copy of *Honor Student*. *That* cover should make you think of Roger."

"I don't need to fantasize about Roger now that he lives in Storyton. He's been very busy with the antique store and his online classes, but we have dinner together most nights. And *after* dinner, we like to—"

Jane smoothly interrupted by saying that it was time to set up the signing stations.

The Cover Girls loaded boxes of cookbooks onto hand trucks and wheeled them into the lobby. Butterworth had positioned a row of tables and chairs outside the Madame Bovary Dining Room, and the women began arranging cookbooks on every table.

"I bet you sell out of Chef Pierce's right away, seeing as he'll never sign another book," Mrs. Pratt told Eloise.

Violet looked scandalized. "Isn't that a bit insensitive?"

"I'm just stating a fact. *A Man and a Pan* is now a collector's item, and I'm putting one aside for Roger."

Eloise promised to add it to Mrs. Pratt's order and then returned to the task of distributing pens and bottles of water. When she was done, she stood back and surveyed their handiwork.

"I wish I'd brought flowers. The tables look elegant but bland."

Jane smiled. "Your wish is my command. Be right back."

Mrs. Templeton, the head housekeeper, had done a wonderful job repurposing the flowers from yesterday's challenge. She'd even put an arrangement on Jane's desk, which Jane now divided into several mason jars.

"How cute," said Violet. Suddenly, her eyes widened. "Mia's coming our way. How does my hair look? What about my face? Did I use too much shimmer powder?"

Though she didn't know shimmer powder from talcum powder, Jane told her friend that she was lovely and hurried forward to grab a private word with Mia.

"How did the chefs take the news?" she asked.

"They were pretty rattled, but we talked things out and came up with an idea," Mia said. "We've decided to cut one of the challenges and use that time to honor Chef Pierce. The finale will now have three contestants instead of two."

"I should make sure Sheriff Evans was able to inform Chef Pierce's family. We can't have the audience learning of his death before they do."

"My team took care of that. They also told Chef Pierce's ex-wives to contact the sheriff's department."

Jane hoped Chef Pierce had more in the way of family than three ex-wives. "Was there anyone else? Parents? Kids?"

"Two step kids, but they weren't close to Chef Pierce." Mia spread her hands. "His employees were his real family, which is why I called the manager. He'll tell the staff." She jerked a thumb over her shoulder. "The chefs are on their way. We need to be in the kitchens, ready to film, by eleven."

"During lunch service?" Jane was floored. "Does Mrs. Hubbard know?"

Mia grinned. "I hope so. She's participating."

Jane wanted to pepper Mia with questions, but the chefs were heading her way. She'd have to get her answers by watching, just like everyone else.

After showing the chefs to their seats, Jane introduced the Cover Girls. "These lovely ladies are here to make sure the signing event runs smoothly. Before we start, I just want to say how sorry I am about Chef Pierce."

Chef Saffron dabbed the corner of her eyes with a tissue. "Just ignore me. I cry at the drop of a hat."

Chef August patted her hand. "Me too. My wife won't go to the movies with me after we saw the one about Mister Rogers. I was blubbering so loud that the people behind us had to change seats."

The other chefs smiled and started talking about sad films. By the time the attendees began lining up to purchase cookbooks, the somber atmosphere had dissipated.

Every attendee bought a cookbook, and most bought two or three. The least popular by far was Chef Lindsay's. It was difficult to say if the customers were put off by the title, *Superior Vegan*, or by the cover photo featuring a haughty-looking Chef Lindsay holding a basket of fresh vegetables. It wasn't nearly as enticing as the other cover photos.

"I feel bad for the skinny chef," said Violet. "Which is strange because I'm usually too jealous of skinny people to feel bad for them. But I wish she'd sold more cookbooks."

Jane said, "Me too. We can't do anything about it though. The chefs need to go to the kitchens now."

Turning to the people still waiting in line, Jane announced that it was time for the day's challenge.

The attendees responded by clapping loudly while Chef Saffron bowed, Lindsay waved, and Chef Alondra let out a whoop. Chef August pumped his fist in the air and slung an arm around Chef Michel's shoulders.

"I'm coming for you, man!" he taunted.

"Today is not my day to go, *mon ami*," replied a grinning Chef Michel.

In this, Chef Michel was correct. The chefs were divided into pairs and told to prepare a three-course *To Kill a Mockingbird* lunch for two hundred. Not only did their dishes have to incorporate the Southern flavors of Harper Lee's fictional town of Maycomb, Alabama, but the main course had to include a fried food in honor of Chef Pierce. The chefs were given a pantry filled with Cook's Pride products.

The teams would have ninety minutes to create their lunch, but the first course had to be served within forty-five minutes. Each team would also be assigned a member of the Storyton Hall kitchen staff to assist with prep work.

The audience was invited to sip mimosas, sparkling mint water, or flavored iced tea while watching the chefs move around on the large projector screens at the front of the dining room.

"For a retired schoolteacher, I lead a very colorful life. I thank the stars that I live in Storyton and that I'm lucky enough to be Jane Steward's friend," Mrs. Pratt said as she accepted a mimosa from a server.

The Cover Girls raised their glasses to Jane before focusing on the screens again.

It was fascinating to see the chefs work as a team. Other than Chef Saffron and Chef Lindsay, they all seemed to be in perfect harmony. Chef Lindsay wanted to make a meatless main course. Chef Saffron agreed with the condition that their entrée would still look like something Chef Pierce would create.

"He'd never use that garnish," Chef Saffron protested when Chef Lindsay started plating.

Chef Lindsay ignored her, and when their mustard-crusted fried tofu, kale, and potato casserole went out to the dining room, each plate had a lavender sprig garnish. The two chefs argued over their dessert too. Chef Lindsay wanted to top their bourbon pound cake with caramelized walnuts while Chef Saffron argued that mascarpone whipped cream with a roasted pecan crumble would add much-needed salt to their dessert.

Finally, Chef Saffron lost her temper and yelled, "I trained as a pastry chef, remember?"

Chef Alondra and "Chef" Mrs. Hubbard created delicious dishes without a single hiccup. The Cover Girls enjoyed the ladies' pan-fried pork chops with garlic butter, whipped sour cream and chive potatoes, spicy collard greens, and Lane cake, but they had to admit that Chef Michel and Chef August made their favorite dishes.

Their "hot" fried chicken served over crackling bread "waffles" was fall-off-the bone tender. Every bite of their summer vegetable slaw was garden-fresh, and their dewberry tart—honey-vanilla custard and dewberries served in a cornbread tart—was beautiful and delectable.

When the meal was over, the diners voted on their favorite and least favorite dishes. Chef Saffron and Chef Lindsay received the fewest votes. Chef Michel's dewberry tart had wowed the crowd, and he was awarded a golden spoon and ten thousand dollars from Cook's Pride. Jane and her friends were almost moved to tears when Chef Michel announced that he'd be splitting the prize money with his teammate, Chef August.

"A kitchen bromance. I love it," sniffed Mrs. Pratt.

Mia was about to announce the name of the chef to be eliminated when a server leaned over and whispered, "Phone call for you, Ms. Steward. It's the sheriff."

Hiding a strong sense of foreboding, Jane smiled at her friends and excused herself. She picked up the lobby phone and asked the front desk clerk to connect her to Sheriff Evans. While she waited, she tried to steady her racing heart.

The sheriff didn't bother with pleasantries. "I'll be heading your way in a few minutes, but I wanted to update you first. The ME's preliminary findings indicate that Chef Pierce died of exsanguination. The puncture wound on his abdomen proved fatal, but he didn't fall on that piece. The angle of the wound tells a different story."

Jane had no other choice but to ask, "Which kind of story?"

"One that ends in murder."

Chapter 7

"How did the ME come to a conclusion so quickly?" Jane asked Sheriff Evans.

They were seated at the table in the William Faulkner Conference Room while two deputies, Phelps and Emory, stood at parade rest on either side of the cherry server.

Deputy Emory was an attractive young woman with long auburn hair and a heart-shaped face. A soft-spoken, introspective person, she spent her free time reading and painting. She'd moved to Storyton to escape the violence she'd seen as a rookie officer in a big city. It wasn't long before she learned that their little village wasn't exactly crime-free.

Amelia Emory was known for her keen powers of observation, and her presence in the conference room indicated that the sheriff planned to conduct on-site interviews.

Sheriff Evans removed his hat and placed it on the table. "Based on the ME's analysis of the wound, I can tell you that we're not looking at an accidental death."

Jane went rigid, but the sheriff didn't notice. He stood up and straightened his arm so that the pen in his hand dangled below his hip. "If I fell on a china bowl, causing it to shatter,

I might be impaled by one of the pieces. In that scenario, the piece would enter my body at a vertical angle. Like this." He jerked his pen in an upward motion toward his abdomen. "You with me so far?"

"Yes."

"Now, pretend you're stabbing me in the same place."

Jane jabbed at his belly with her pen, careful not to touch his khaki uniform shirt. As she recalled the angry, red mouth of Chef Pierce's wound, her stomach roiled.

Sheriff Evans took a firm hold of Jane's hand. "The victim's wound is horizontal, which means he was probably standing when he was stabbed. You're a strong woman, Ms. Steward, so there'd be a decent amount of force behind your thrust." He moved her hand until the point of her pen dimpled his shirt. "If your weapon penetrated deep enough, your fist might cause bruising around the cut. The skin surrounding Chef Pierce's wound was bruised."

When the sheriff released Jane, she stared down at her pen. "But if I squeezed a jagged piece of china, wouldn't it cut my palm?"

"Not if you wore gloves. We found only one set of partial prints on that shard, and they probably belong to Chef Pierce." The sheriff sat back down. "Did your security cameras pick up anything that could help identify Chef Pierce's assailant?"

Jane told the sheriff about Bentley's midnight visit.

"I was going to ask her about it after today's filming was done. I can see that I shouldn't have waited."

"Let's get her in here."

Jane sent Butterworth a text, asking him to escort Bentley to the conference room without telling her why she was being summoned. Butterworth promised to fetch the young woman right away.

When Bentley entered the conference room ten minutes later, she looked more curious than alarmed. But the moment she saw Jane and the uniformed officers, her curiosity morphed into fear.

Bentley stood in the doorway, as if poised for flight, and said, "What is this?"

Jane spoke to her in soothing tones. "Ms. Fiore, this is Sheriff Evans. He'd like a word with you about last night. Please have a seat."

Recognizing a subtle command when she heard one, Bentley sat in the chair closest to the door. Jane tried to reassure her with a smile, but Bentley averted her gaze and began gnawing at her thumbnail.

"Ms. Fiore—" the sheriff began.

"It's just Bentley, okay? Why am I here?"

Her brow was furrowed in confusion. Her eyes darted wildly, unable to settle on anything or anyone. She looked like a rabbit cornered by a skulk of foxes.

The sheriff held out his hands in a placating gesture. "As you know, Chef Pierce passed away early this morning, and it's routine for my department to investigate a death at Storyton Hall. As part of that investigation, we need to establish a record of the events leading up to the time of death. We need to talk to you because you were in Chef Pierce's guest room last night."

Bentley blanched. "How'd you know that?"

"Like most hotels, we have security cameras in our public areas," Jane answered.

"You spy on your guests?" Bentley's anxiety was increasing by the minute.

"Absolutely not," said Jane. "We don't watch the recordings unless we have to. A death means we have to."

Sheriff Evans flipped a page in his notebook to reclaim

Bentley's attention. "The footage shows you knocking on Chef Pierce's door several times. When he didn't respond, you used your phone to call him. Why was the call necessary? Was he asleep?"

Bentley smirked. "Passed out is more like it."

"But you were able to rouse him."

"Yeah, after what felt like forever. And I wish he'd had more clothes on when he opened the door. Ugh. How can people let themselves go like that?"

The sheriff pressed on. "Why did you go to his room?"

"Because Mia asked me to deliver a note, and she said that I *had* to put it *in* Chef Pierce's hand." Bentley shuddered. "Trust me. I didn't want to bang on that nasty man's door at that time of night. I was chilling in my bed, watching the *Project Runway* judges rip into a guy for making clothes out of garbage bags, when Mia showed up. When I saw the look on her face, I didn't even argue. I just did what she told me to."

"What kind of look?"

Bentley's mouth twitched in amusement. "Oh, my girl was mad. *Seriously* mad. I've been her assistant for two years, and I can tell you that Mia Mallett doesn't let things get to her. I've never met someone with so much positivity. But something got to her last night. She had a major dark cloud vibe." Suddenly realizing how this sounded, Bentley amended her answer. "She wasn't mad in a serial killer way, but I knew she needed me to come through for her."

"What did the note say?"

Bentley recoiled. "I didn't read it! First of all, it was in an envelope, but even if it wasn't, I *still* wouldn't read it. Mia trusts me. The second she doesn't, I'll lose my job."

Jane put her phone on her lap and sent a message to the Fins.

Search Chef Pierce's room for a note from Mia ASAP.
Make a list of medications. Check his phone and
other tech for clues.

"All Ms. Mallett wanted was for you to put the note in Chef Pierce's hand?" Sheriff Evans raised his brows.

Bentley sighed. "I had to watch him read it too. When he opened the door, I told him about the note, and he mumbled something about not knowing where he'd left his glasses."

Sheriff Evans made a contemplative noise. "Had you given him the note at this point?"

Bentley shook her head. "I was trying not to look at him. I looked into his room instead, but when I couldn't see his glasses anywhere, I decided to just go in and find the damn things."

"Did you?"

"Yeah. They were in the bathroom. But while I was searching for them, Chef Pierce sat in a chair and went back to sleep. I had to yell at him until he woke up. I shoved his glasses on his face and he read the note. He didn't say anything. He just closed his eyes and I left."

Sheriff Evans made an encouraging noise. "And how did you learn that Chef Pierce had passed?"

Bentley glanced at Jane. "Right after you talked to Mia, she told me what happened and asked me to call the authorities and get an official statement."

"Thank you. That's all I have for now." The sheriff turned to his deputies. "Do you have anything to ask Ms. Fiore?"

Phelps shook his head, but Emory said, "What was Chef Pierce like?"

"What do you mean?" Bentley picked at an uneven fingernail.

"What did people think of him? What kind of reputation did he have?"

Bentley waved both hands. "No. No way. I can't gossip about any of the contestants or I'll get fired. Probably sued too."

Emory tried again. "I get it. I'd never ask you to gossip. But I have no idea who this man was, so can you paint a general picture for me?"

"Look. I signed a nondisclosure saying that I won't discuss details of the show. That includes contestants. Arrest me if you want, but I can't say anything else."

Sheriff Evans told Bentley that she was free to go.

She practically ran out of the room.

The sheriff turned to Jane. "Emory and Phelps will have to search Chef Pierce's room. While they're working on that, I'd like to speak to Ms. Mallett."

"I'll ask Butterworth to find her."

Jane sent two messages. The first was a group message warning the Fins that Phelps and Emory were on their way to Chef Pierce's room. The second was to Butterworth.

Tell them I'll be waiting to let them in, replied Lachlan.

Butterworth wrote, I'll bring Ms. Mallett to you without delay.

When Mia entered the conference room, her face was flushed and beads of sweat lined her forehead. She looked like a runner at the end of a hard race.

She shook Sheriff Evans's outstretched hand with enthusiasm. "Sorry. I'm sweaty and I smell like garlic. That's the downside of hosting a cooking show." She lowered herself into a chair with a sigh. "What can I do for you, Sheriff?"

"Tell me about Chef Pierce. What was he like?"

If the request surprised Mia, she didn't let it show.

"I'd see him every year at events like the Taste of Chicago or the Food and Wine Classic in Aspen. He's a talented chef. That's why I wanted him on the show. But it wasn't the only reason. Chef Pierce wasn't good with people. Especially women. He could be rude and condescending and tended to make inappropriate comments. But he had a big personality, and big personalities create drama. In television, drama means higher ratings. Higher ratings means A-list sponsors."

"So Chef Pierce was brought on board to cook delicious food and serve a generous helping of drama on the side," the sheriff said.

"Bingo." Mia pointed at Sheriff Evans. In a more serious tone, she said, "Inviting Chef Pierce to participate was a risky move. Our sponsors want to back a wholesome show. No swearing. No clips of the chefs drinking wine after a tough day. But *Posh Palate* viewers want excitement along with heartfelt stories and footage of amazing food."

"These unsuitable remarks of Chef Pierce's. Could you give me an example?"

Mia rattled off a few. The men didn't react, but Deputy Emory winced.

The sheriff glanced at his notes. "Was Chef Pierce's inappropriate behavior ever physical?"

Spots of color bloomed on Mia's cheeks. "I wouldn't have someone like that on my show. I'd never subject other women to abuse."

"Despite knowing that Chef Pierce was verbally abusive, you believed that his bad behavior was limited to words."

Mia began to fidget with the ring on her pinkie finger. As she spun it around and around, Jane could see that the stone in its center was a tiger's eye.

"He's like the old, racist, white guy from that seventies TV show. The guy with the ugly chair."

"Archie Bunker?" Jane guessed.

Mia snapped her fingers. "That's him! He was a total jerk. He could never be on TV now. But if I had someone *like* him on my show, he'd be the person viewers love to hate. He'd make the other chefs shine brighter and be a lesson to everyone on how not to behave."

Sheriff Evans mulled this over. "Chef Pierce was your Archie Bunker. And did he stick to his role?"

"Absolutely. He insulted every chef by the end of the first day."

Jane could almost hear the sheriff's inward groan. If Chef Pierce made enemies wherever he went, finding his killer would be difficult.

"Did he insult the chefs equally or did a particular chef get more than their fair share?"

Mia folded her arms on the table and leaned forward. "What's really going on here? Am I in some sort of trouble?"

"I have questions about Chef Pierce's death. It's as simple as that." The sheriff tapped his notebook with his pen. "When I spoke with your assistant earlier, she said that you asked her to deliver a note to Chef Pierce last night. She also had to watch him read it. Is that correct?"

"Yes." Mia relaxed. "I wanted to make it crystal clear that he had to come to my suite at eight this morning. I knew he'd go ballistic when he found out he was being kicked off the show, and I wanted my staff there when he did."

"Why was he being asked to leave?"

Mia's shoulders drooped. "For being exactly what he was."

Though Mia clearly felt guilty, she still had to tell the sheriff how Chef Pierce's abuse had turned physical when he'd groped a pastry chef.

After a brief pause, she looked directly at Sheriff Evans and described the incident.

"Was Mrs. Hubbard there?" the sheriff asked Jane.

Considering Mrs. Hubbard had threatened Chef Pierce with a carving knife, Jane kept her reply short and sweet. "Yes. She told Chef Pierce he could either leave the kitchens or become a eunuch."

The corners of the sheriff's mouth twitched. Any trace of amusement vanished after Mia said that she heard about the incident minutes after it occurred.

"Then why send your assistant to Chef Pierce's room in the middle of the night? You told me earlier that you'd never subject another woman to abuse."

Mia was unruffled. "I meant what I said. Bentley's a first-degree black belt. If Chef Pierce tried anything, she'd have him begging for mercy before he knew what hit him."

This piqued the sheriff's interest. "Do all of your assistants have martial arts training?"

"No, but maybe they should." Mia laughed. "Once, I filmed Bentley smashing a hidden camera this paparazzi stalker sleazebag had attached to my gate. After we posted the video, no one tried a stunt like that again. Bentley protects my personal space. She's invaluable to me."

Mia was a beautiful, stylish, wealthy young woman who appeared to have it all, but Jane wouldn't want to be in her shoes. She'd hate the lack of privacy and having to constantly focus on her image. With fame, there seemed to be no peace.

I couldn't live in the spotlight. Not even for a billion dollars.

Sheriff Evans put down his pen. "Did you hear from your assistant after she delivered the note?"

"No. I trusted Bentley to get the job done and I expected to see Chef Pierce at eight this morning." Mia waved at Jane. "But Ms. Steward came to my suite instead."

The sheriff asked Mia if she had anything else to add, but she didn't. She was halfway to the door when she suddenly stopped and turned.

"People will say that Chef Pierce was a terrible guy, and in many ways, he was. But when he was in the kitchen, he was a better version of himself. I guess I put too much faith in that side of him. I hoped that being on the show would inspire him to change. I knew he'd misbehave in the beginning, but I believed he'd turn things around by the end. It was naïve, and I feel like what happened in the kitchen—with Jessie—is my fault."

"You're not responsible for Chef Pierce's actions," Sheriff Evans said kindly. "Never stop believing that people can change for the better. Even if they prove you wrong, don't give up on hope. The world needs more optimistic and hopeful people."

Brightening, Mia said, "That reminds me of my yearbook quote. We had to read *Moby-Dick* my senior year, and I only liked one line. It was something like, I might not know what's coming, but whatever it is, I'll go to it laughing."

And while Mia couldn't laugh, she was able to muster a smile on her way out.

* * *

Ten minutes later, Jane stood in the middle of Chef Pierce's room and wished she could light a scented candle. Or a hundred scented candles.

"How did he create this much chaos in so little time?" she muttered to Lachlan. "It smells like gym socks, a barnyard on a hot day, and something rotten."

"Like this?" Deputy Phelps pointed to a plate bearing the remains of a tuna sandwich, half a pickle, and a brown apple core.

Jane gestured at the metal dome next to the plate. "Would you put the cover back on, Deputy Phelps?"

"I can do better than that. I'll add it to the pile going to my car."

While Deputy Phelps bagged the food, Sheriff Evans carried a pile of used towels into the bathroom and dumped them in the tub. "Twelve towels. How'd he get so many?"

"Chef Pierce hung the DO NOT DISTURB sign as soon as he arrived," said Lachlan. "He wouldn't let housekeeping clean his room. He preferred to help himself to the housekeeper's cart."

Deputy Emory was seated at the desk, reading emails on a laptop, and Jane wondered if she'd found something useful.

"Were you able to crack his password?" she asked the deputy.

"I didn't have to. His phone is password-protected, but not his laptop," replied Emory. "I'm surprised because he has financial and inventory records for a place called Epitome Steak on here."

Jane peered over Emory's shoulder. "That must be his restaurant."

"Do you recognize this name?" Emory pointed to an email sent to Chef Pierce at 11:12 p.m. the previous night.

"ForkedTongue212? Sounds like a pen name," mused Jane. "Wait a second . . ."

Jane took out her phone and typed "Forked Tongue" plus the word "food" in Google's search box. The first result held the answer.

"It's Levi Anjou," she told Emory. "He's a New York–based food critic and a *Posh Palate* judge. His blog is called The Forked Tongue. Apparently, he writes harsh reviews of restaurants that fail to meet his high standards."

Deputy Emory tapped her bare ring finger. "Is he married?"

"I think so. Why?"

"Could you check?"

Again, Jane turned to the Internet for answers.

"Levi has been with his wife, Sheila, for twelve years." Jane cocked her head. "What does Mr. Anjou's marital status have to do with Chef Pierce?"

Deputy Emory shifted in her chair. "Sorry, Ms. Steward, but I need to talk to the sheriff."

She closed the laptop lid and walked into the bathroom.

Jane crossed the room to where Lachlan sat on the floor, sorting the contents of Chef Pierce's trashcan.

"Emory found something on Pierce's laptop," she whispered. "I'm going into the bathroom to distract the sheriff. While I'm in there, you need to read what's on that screen."

Lachlan pressed a plastic bag into Jane's hand. "Take this to him. It'll give us the time we need."

Jane studied the bubbly script written on the front of a blush-colored envelope. She could tell by its weight that the paper was of high quality.

"Nice job." There was no need to feign excitement as she rushed into the bathroom and said, "Lachlan found Mia's note."

Since Deputy Emory was closer, Jane passed her the bag. This strategy ensured that both officers would be preoccupied for a minute or two. But a minute was all it took for the deputy to remove the envelope from the bag, peek inside, and shake her head.

"No note."

Jane turned in the doorway and called, "Did you find a note, Lachlan?"

"Still looking," he replied.

Sheriff Evans waved his arm. "If you'd excuse us, Ms. Steward. We're done in here."

As soon as Jane stepped aside, he made a beeline for the laptop.

The sheriff stared at the email for a long moment before glancing at Jane. "It looks like I have another interview to conduct. Deputy Phelps will continue working in here, but Deputy Emory and I will need to borrow your conference room again. Would you send Mr. Anjou to us? We'll need to speak to him alone."

After giving Jane an apologetic look, Deputy Emory slipped the laptop into a large evidence bag and followed the sheriff out of the room.

The door had barely closed when Jane rounded on Lachlan. "Why is the sheriff in such a hurry to talk to Mr. Anjou?"

Lachlan peeled off his gloves. "Because the email Mr. Anjou sent Chef Pierce is basically a death threat."

Jane gaped at him. "What did it say?"

"This is a direct quote: 'I warned you, but you wouldn't listen. You thought you could outmaneuver me, you inflated pig's bladder? You're done, and everyone will be happier when you're gone.'"

The brief, biting words hung in the malodorous air, and

though Jane wished she could open a window and shove them out, she was frozen in place.

Her paralysis was broken by the sound of voices in the hallway. As Jane moved toward the door, Lachlan let his gloves fall onto the discarded remnants of another man's life.

A man no one would miss.

Chapter 8

Jane would have escorted Levi Anjou to the conference room right away, but she was unable to find him. He didn't answer his cell or guest room phone. He didn't appear on any of the security monitors, and he hadn't called for a driver to take him into the village.

With his judging duties over for the day, he could be engaged in any number of activities. But after checking the log at the recreation desk Lachlan said that Levi hadn't registered for a falconry lesson, guided hike, canoeing trip, or fishing excursion. He wasn't playing lawn tennis or relaxing in a reading room either.

Sinclair called down to the Walt Whitman Spa in case the food critic had booked a massage, but he wasn't there. Nor was he taking a dip in the Jules Verne Pool, checking out a book from the Henry James Library, or sitting in a rocking chair on the terrace. He wasn't on the pickleball court or the Lewis Carroll Croquet Lawn. He wasn't taking in the scenery from the Anne of Green Gables Gazebo or strolling through Milton's Gardens.

Seeing no other recourse, Butterworth knocked on his

guest room door. When this failed to elicit a response, Jane used her master key to gain entry.

As soon as she stepped into the room, she released the breath she'd been holding. There was no sign of violence. No dead body. No chaos. The space was clearly occupied, which meant Levi Anjou had to be around somewhere.

Butterworth opened the closet door and counted the number of shirts, suit coats, and pants hanging neatly within. He then surveyed the contents of the chest of drawers.

"Mr. Anjou has expensive taste. His clothing is of the highest quality and is hung or folded with great care."

Having caught the note of admiration in Butterworth's voice, Jane couldn't resist teasing him.

"Well, a man who folds his undershirts so meticulously can't be a murderer."

Butterworth's gaze roved over the toiletries on the bathroom counter, which had been arranged by height. The two towels hanging from the rod next to the shower were perfectly aligned, and the bathmat had been folded into a tidy rectangle.

"If you're referring to the theory that violence can be a manifestation of an obsessive-compulsive disorder, I don't believe that's what we're seeing here," said Butterworth. "Mr. Anjou is simply more fastidious than our average guest. As to his relationship with the deceased, I see nothing in this room to link the two men."

"No phone, wallet, or computer either," said Jane. "I'm not authorizing a deep search of this room or opening the wall safe unless the sheriff has a warrant. This is going to be a high-profile case and we can't afford a misstep. We shouldn't even be in here. If anyone asks, I'll say I was concerned about Mr. Anjou's welfare and came to check on him."

A glint of humor appeared in Butterworth's eyes. "Certainly."

Sheriff Evans and Deputy Emory hadn't been idle while Jane and her Fins searched for Levi Anjou. They'd rejoined Deputy Phelps and continued the task of processing Chef Pierce's room. It was almost teatime when Jane touched base with the sheriff to let him know that the food critic still hadn't surfaced.

"What about the chefs? Or Ms. Mallett? Have they seen him?"

"We only spoke to the chefs we bumped into, and they couldn't help," Jane answered. "We also asked Mia and her staff. We didn't want to raise any alarm bells, so we didn't knock on Chef Michel's or Ms. Kennedy's doors. It's possible that Mr. Anjou is out on a long walk. It's a beautiful day, and he looks like he's in excellent health."

The sheriff mumbled something to one of his deputies, and though Jane couldn't make out the words, his frustration was clear.

"We're heading back to the station. I'll call Hilltop Stables from the car. Who knows? Maybe Mr. Anjou is on a trail ride. We'll give him another hour. After that, we'll have to talk to every person connected to the show. Someone must know where he is."

"As soon as Lachlan wraps up his falconry lesson, I'll have him take a Gator out on the hiking trails."

"Good. Keep me in the loop."

Jane wanted to ask the same of him but didn't have the energy. She was running on fumes. The early morning wake-up call, the shock of encountering Chef Pierce's body, and everything that had come after was hitting her hard. What she'd give if she could just flop on a lounge chair in a quiet spot and close her eyes for a few minutes. Or an hour.

But Jane's life didn't include naps. Though she couldn't grab forty winks after lunch like her great-aunt and -uncle did, she smiled at the thought of Uncle Aloysius dozing in his office chair, his fishing hat lowered over his brow, while Aunt Octavia reclined on her living room sofa. Muffet Cat, Storyton Hall's portly tuxedo, liked to perch on Aunt Octavia's belly as she slept. His round, furry body would move up and down with the rise and fall of her breath. Hem and Fitz, who'd witnessed the napping duo many times, claimed that it was difficult to differentiate who snored loudest, the lady or her cat.

With teatime approaching, Jane knew she'd find her sons in the kitchens. Listening to them talk about chess and photography would restore some normalcy to her day.

Mrs. Hubbard was transferring a lemon Victoria sponge crowned with berries from a cake board to a porcelain plate when Jane appeared. "Your darlings are in the herb garden. Tell them their snack will be ready in ten minutes."

Jane thanked her and headed out into the harsh sunlight. She walked the short distance to a garden hemmed by a low stone wall and listened for signs of her sons.

At first, she thought Mrs. Hubbard must be mistaken. The boys couldn't be in the garden. It was far too quiet.

Then, Jane saw a movement out of the corner of her eye.

A flash of yellow turned out to be a stripe on Hem's shirt. He was lying on his stomach with a camera pressed to his right eye. In front of him, a monarch butterfly hovered above the vibrant purple corolla of a lavender plant. Beyond the lavender was a cluster of mint plants. The combination of orange, purple, and green was stunning.

Jane froze, letting Hem snap several shots until the butterfly flew off to another part of the garden.

Smiling at her son, she said, "That's going to be a beautiful photo."

"Taking pictures is the easy part," Hem said, getting to his feet. "Developing them is hard. We keep messing up."

"Mistakes are part of leaning. But you'll get it. I have faith in you." Jane glanced around. "Where's your brother?"

"On the other side of the wall, talking to the lady with the poodle."

The writer!

"Oh? Did you talk to her too?"

Hem put the lens cap on his camera and nodded. "Her dog is *awesome*. His name's Captain Haviland and he's *really* smart. Ms. Olivia said he's smarter than most people. That's what she told us to call her. She lives next to a lighthouse, and the Atlantic Ocean is right behind her house! If it's not cloudy, she can see cargo ships from her deck."

Jane laughed. "She sounds very interesting. I haven't met her yet, so will you introduce me?"

"Okay, but can it be quick? Mrs. Hubbard wanted us to check for Japanese beetles and Aunt Octavia told us to take nature shots for homework. But we're ready for a snack now."

Slinging an arm around Hem's shoulder, Jane was struck by how tall her son had gotten this year. Both boys were growing as fast as the herbs in Mrs. Hubbard's garden. Before long, they'd be eye level with Jane.

It would be many more years before they were eye level with Olivia Limoges, however. As Jane approached their writer-in-residence, she felt dwarfed by the slender, pale-haired woman with the ocean-blue eyes. Jane wasn't short, but Olivia had to be six feet tall. Her handsome features and cool poise gave her a regal air.

Her standard poodle pricked his ears at Jane's approach. Olivia put a palm to her dog's neck, conveying a message that all was well. He responded to her touch by thumping his tail against the ground, his teeth showing in a wide, canine smile.

Fitz waved at his mother. "Hey, Mom. This is Ms. Olivia."

"And Captain Haviland," added Hem.

Jane offered her hand. "I hope my boys haven't been talking your ear off."

"Not at all. We've been trading stories," Olivia said, giving Jane's hand a firm squeeze.

This earned her a point in Jane's book. She hated shaking people's fingertips or a hand that felt limp and boneless. It made for a bad first impression.

"We're going in for tea now," Hem told Olivia.

Fitz gestured at the manor house. "You should try it. It's the best part of the day."

Hem's head bobbed like a buoy in a rough sea. "Mrs. Hubbard makes the most amazing cakes, scones, cookies, and sandwiches. There's clotted cream and two kinds of homemade jam. You don't have to drink tea if you don't want to. There's lemonade and soda and other stuff too."

"Captain Haviland isn't allowed in the Agatha Christie Tea Room," Fitz added sheepishly. "But I could ask Mrs. Hubbard for a bone to give him later."

Olivia laughed. "That's really sweet, but Haviland has plenty of treats in our cottage."

After shaking the poodle's paw in farewell, the boys jogged up the gravel path.

When they were out of sight, Jane let out a sigh.

"Long day?" Olivia asked.

Jane smiled ruefully. "Is it that obvious?"

"I'm an insomniac, so I know what tired looks like." She waved an elegant arm in a wide arc. "With all this to oversee, you must have plenty to worry about."

"Some days more than others. What about you? Does your restaurant keep you up at night?"

"No. Michel has been steering that ship for years now. I'm less interested in editing menus or mingling with our customers than I once was, and he's passionate about every facet of the business. And everyone adores him. He's a gifted chef with a charming personality. I'm an eccentric heiress who only comes to town when I'm low on supplies. I spend most days reading and trying to write and a good part of my nights roaming the beach. I'm turning into one of the ghosts from local legend."

Jane didn't know how to respond to this remark. She was both intrigued and disconcerted by her unusual guest but didn't have the time or energy for a lengthy chat. She had to continue her search for Levi Anjou.

"I'm sorry I wasn't around when you checked in," Jane said. "Do you have everything you need?"

Olivia cast an affectionate glance at Haviland. His mouth was open, and his pink tongue dangled from his lower lip. "We do. The cottage is lovely, and the view from my window is spectacular. I haven't left home in ages because I didn't think I'd be happy away from the ocean, but this place has a deep-rooted sense of calm. I feel like I can breathe for the first time in ages."

"Maybe you'll start sleeping better."

"Did you see me wandering the grounds last night?" At Jane's nod, Olivia touched the thin gold band on her ring finger. "I hope you were the only one. Your guests don't need to think Storyton Hall is haunted because some woman in white took a moonlit stroll."

Sorrow darkened her blue eyes and deepened the brackets around her mouth, and Jane wondered if Oliva's writer's block had something to do with that band of gold.

"Would you like to grab a drink?" asked Jane. "I'm not sure what my schedule is tonight because I need to locate a missing guest, but—"

"Just call me when you're free." Olivia handed Jane a business card that included her cell phone number. "And if you need help finding a guest, Haviland is a certified tracker. All he needs is an item with the guest's scent—something the person wore recently. It wouldn't be easy because this place is loaded with scents, but we could give it a shot."

Jane looked at the poodle. There was an expectant gleam in his golden-brown eyes.

"It's like he understands everything you say."

"He does," Olivia said. "People often underestimate dogs' intelligence."

Jane frowned. "I don't have much experience with dogs. When I was young, my great-aunt thought I had a fur allergy, so I wasn't allowed to have a pet. I feel like I missed out."

"You'll never find a more loyal or loving companion than a dog. I wish every child would know that kind of love." Her fingers moved across the top of her poodle's head. "Who's the guest you're searching for?"

"Levi Anjou. He's one of the *Posh Palate* judges."

Olivia grunted in a very Butterworth-like manner. "I don't think you need Haviland to find him."

Jane's torpor instantly vanished. "You know where he is?"

"If I had to guess, I'd say he's with Ms. Kennedy. I saw

them this morning. Very early. Haviland and I were walking through an overgrown orchard when we stumbled on a wonderful ruin."

"That's the folly. We're restoring it later this summer."

"With that view of the lake, it's a beautiful and romantic spot. And that's where I saw Ms. Kennedy and Mr. Anjou." Olivia held out a hand. "I won't go into detail, but theirs is more than a working relationship."

"I see," Jane said. "Thanks. I owe you one."

"My drink of choice is blended scotch whiskey. The older the better. If not tonight, we'll catch up another night. You know where to find me," Olivia said as she turned away. "Captain, I'm going to investigate Mrs. Hubbard's famous desserts while you have a nap. Nothing like cake to get the ideas flowing, right?"

The poodle replied with a soft bark.

Charmed as she was by the writer and her dog, the idea of an affair between the *Posh Palate* judges had Jane's thoughts turning in a dark direction.

Both judges were married. Not separated or divorced. Married. And one, or both, had children. An affair, combined with a death threat sent to the murder victim's email address, indicated that someone else had learned of Levi Anjou's double life.

"I wonder if Coco Kennedy knows that her lover threatened Chef Pierce," Jane muttered to herself as she entered the manor house.

Moving briskly through the staff corridor, Jane popped out near the Henry James Library. Sinclair was behind his desk, helping a guest. As Jane approached, he exchanged the woman's copy of Eric Ripert's *32 Yolks* for Ruth Reichl's *Save Me the Plums*.

"Happy reading," Sinclair told her.

The woman smiled and clutched her book to her chest like a gleeful child.

"Things have gone from worse to much worse," Jane whispered to Sinclair when the woman was gone.

"In that case, we'd better go through to my office."

Sinclair cast a glance at the two patrons seated in wing chairs facing the garden. Hundreds of daylilies bloomed on the other side of the window, attracting pollen-dusted bees and swallowtail butterflies.

The readers looked perfectly content, so Sinclair unlocked the wood-paneled door that blended into the wall so well that it was almost invisible until opened. It led to a long, narrow room with rows of corkboards covered in printouts. This was where guest profiles and background checks were kept.

Once inside, Jane told Sinclair about her enlightening chat with Olivia Limoges.

"Let's take a closer look at our judges." Sinclair located the profile sheets he'd created for them. "Levi Anjou. Fifty-six. Married with an adult daughter. Ms. Kennedy is forty-eight, married, and has a son and a daughter. Both children are in college. What exactly did Ms. Limoges witness?"

"Behaviors that made it clear the judges are romantically involved. She spotted them very early this morning. At the folly."

Sinclair lowered the papers. "Chef Pierce may have tried his hand at blackmail."

"I don't want to drag the sheriff into this until I find Levi. Which means I'll have to call Ms. Kennedy's room."

She frowned. "It's times like this that I wish someone else was the manager of Storyton Hall."

"I'm sure you'd rather be on your sofa with the comforting weight of a book on your lap." He patted her arm. "I understand, my girl."

Jane took out her phone. "As much as I'd love to escape to a fictional world, Chef Pierce was my guest. Someone took his life, destroyed valuable antiques, and altered the course of the cooking competition. I want to identify this person and have them removed from Storyton Hall before more damage is done."

Sinclair remained silent as Jane dialed Coco Kennedy's room number. When no one answered, she tried the cell phone number.

Coco picked up after the fourth ring. Her hello sounded muffled.

"I'm sorry to disturb you," Jane said with saccharine sweetness. "We're trying to locate Mr. Anjou. Do you happen to know where he is?"

"Um, can I call you back? I'm in the middle of something."

Jane heard splashing sounds, and before she could respond, the call was disconnected.

"I'll have to ask Sterling to go through surveillance footage again," she told Sinclair. "If the two judges enter Ms. Kennedy's room together and stay there, I'll contact the sheriff. Would you ask Bentley for a copy of Chef Pierce's health form? I'd like to figure out if one of his medications was an anticoagulant."

Sinclair said, "Right away. And Mr. Butterworth is looking into the financial state of Chef Pierce's restaurant.

You should get some rest. Remember that tomorrow's a brand-new day."

Leaving Sinclair and the library behind, Jane climbed three flights of stairs to her great-aunt and great-uncle's apartments. After a cursory knock, she let herself in.

The living room's only occupant was Muffet Cat, and he was snoozing inside the lid of a board game box. The top had been nearly flattened by the twenty-pound cat, and Jane couldn't help but grin.

Sensing her presence, Muffet Cat cracked an eye. This sliver of green conveyed his utter and complete indignation over having his nap disturbed. With his bed of game pieces, the ill-tempered cat reminded Jane of Smaug the dragon, slumbering on a mound of treasure.

Muffled voices drifted out from Aunt Octavia's library. Jane knocked on the closed door and said, "It's me."

"Come in, my love!" Aunt Octavia called.

Jane entered the book-lined room to find the twins sitting cross-legged on the floor with notepads on their laps. Aunt Octavia stood next to a rolling corkboard covered in photographs. She held a laser pointer in one hand and a pair of brass spyglasses in the other.

"We're finishing up for the day," said Aunt Octavia. "The boys have done excellent work. You must see their prints." She beamed at Fitz and Hem. "As for you two, the scopes are yours to keep. Use them to gain a different perspective on the world. The veins on a leaf, the spots on a ladybug, the moon's craters. Look at everything and anything."

The twins thanked her and raised their spyglasses to their eyes.

"Do I look like Blackbeard?" asked Hem.

Fitz shook his head. "You don't have a beard."

Jane put a hand on her boys' shoulders. "These prints are really good. Nice work, you two. Now, are you ready to flop on your beds and read comics until supper?"

Fitz collapsed his spyglass. "We want to talk to Chef Michel before we go home. Miss Olivia said that he knows everything there is to know about jam."

Hem nodded. "When we told her that we wanted to sell our jam at the berry jubilee, she told us to talk to him. Is that okay?"

Jane held up a finger. "Sure, but mind your manners."

After promising to be polite, the twins rushed off.

Aunt Octavia sank into her reading chair. "I'm exhausted!" She gave her ottoman a pat. "Sit down, darling. You look as tired as I feel. And no wonder. I heard about the tragedy in the cookbook nook. Mrs. Hubbard told me all about it."

"Of course she did," Jane said without rancor.

Aunt Octavia shoved the laser pointer into one of the many pockets of her lime and hot pink housedress and retrieved a sugar-free butterscotch candy from another. As she unwrapped the candy, she said, "I am upset about those dishes. I hate the idea of losing relics from our family's past to an act of violence, but compared to a man's life, even a ten- or twenty-thousand-dollar piece of antique porcelain means nothing. And I'd trade all of our treasures if they could buy peace and happiness for my family." She sighed. "It's hard to be old, Jane. One's body can no longer keep up with one's mind. My greatest fear is that I'll no longer be useful to anyone."

Taking hold of her great-aunt's hand, Jane stroked the paper-thin skin. "You are the matriarch, the Queen Bee, the Lady General overseeing the troops. We'd be lost without you! You and Uncle Aloysius are both walking encyclopedias. My sons are lucky to have such brilliant tutors. Useless? Please. You're as useless as the Library of Congress."

Aunt Octavia preened. "I knew Fitz and Hem would have a knack for photography. Tell me which prints you like the most. And don't forget to look on the back of the board."

Jane examined the series of nature photos on the front of the board. Most were of flowers, but a few featured an insect or a tree.

"I like the shot of the weeping willow, and the one of the dandelion seeds lit by the sun." Jane scooted behind the board to examine the prints on the backside. These photos were taken from just outside a window or doorway, giving the observer a sense of immediate space and the space beyond.

Jane saw several interesting interpretations on the theme, but one print compelled her to draw in a sharp breath and move closer to the board.

"Which one is speaking to you?" asked Aunt Octavia.

Jane removed the print from the board and carried it to her great-aunt's chair. "This one shows a view of a secluded garden bench that can only be seen from the window nook dividing the second-story suites."

"It's such a romantic spot." Aunt Octavia looked at Jane and her smile faded. "What's wrong? Lovers have always favored that bench. Haven't you and Edwin lingered in the starlight and the perfumed air?"

Jane pointed at the couple. "*These* lovers are married. But *not* to each other."

Aunt Octavia's face fell. "Oh, no."

Pointing at Levi, Jane added, "Even worse, this gentleman sent a death threat to the chef who was killed in the cookbook nook." She dumped the pushpins in the bowl on Aunt Octavia's desk. "This might be my least favorite photograph, but the sheriff will love it."

Chapter 9

In her office, Jane scanned the photograph and sent it to the sheriff by email. Looking up from her computer screen, she saw Butterworth darkening her doorway.

"Mr. Sterling is on his way to the village to collect Mr. Anjou and Ms. Kennedy."

"From?"

Butterworth's right brow twitched. "The Daily Bread."

Jane glanced at the ceiling. "Of all the places! We've searched every nook and cranny here and—wait a minute—how did they get there? None of our drivers took them, and they didn't rent bicycles. Did they walk?"

Butterworth's mouth was pinched in disapproval. "One of our drivers took them. He didn't bat an eye upon receiving a ride request for two guests named James Beard and Julia Child. Luckily, Mr. Sterling answered the phone when Mr. Anjou called to arrange a pickup for a Mr. Robuchon and a Ms. Fanny Cradock. He knew Mr. Anjou's voice at once."

"Who's Fanny Cradock?"

"A British television cook. Her show ran for two decades." Butterworth's gaze softened. "I remember it well."

Jane stared at him in disbelief. "So the judges have been at Edwin's café this whole time?"

"A good part of it, yes. I took the liberty of phoning Mr. Alcott, and he was quick to point out that if it takes hours for two people to drink a pot of tea, they're either working on a complex mathematical problem or having a romantic assignation."

"Did the judges show how they felt about each other in front of him?"

Butterworth sniffed. "According to Mr. Alcott, they were hardly the picture of discretion. He was understandably vexed when they removed their shoes to play footsie under the table. Bare feet in a restaurant are most unsanitary. Have people lost all sense of propriety?"

"On the bright side, Mr. Anjou is no longer missing," Jane said. "I'll pass the news along to the sheriff. It's been a very long day, and I'd like to go to bed knowing that everyone is safe."

"I trust Sheriff Evans to see that order is restored."

But when Jane called the sheriff to tell him that his prime suspect had been located, he responded with a bewildering lack of urgency.

"I'm in a meeting that promises to continue well into the evening, so I'll speak with Mr. Anjou tomorrow. If you or your staff witness any suspicious behavior, contact the night sergeant. Otherwise, I'll see you in the morning."

Stunned, Jane turned to Butterworth. "I don't get it. Why should Levi Anjou be given another night to dine on our food or sleep in our bed if he had something to do with Chef Pierce's death? It isn't right."

"Perhaps not. But we should give the sheriff the benefit of the doubt. He must have a plan, and he's not obligated to share it with us."

"I wish he would. We'll probably be fielding calls and emails from the media tomorrow, which means I'd better draft a statement. As for keeping an eye on our celebrity guests, should Lachlan hang out in the surveillance room while the rest of you get some sleep?"

"We'll divide the task," said Butterworth. "None of us will rest until the killer is caught, but you should. Tomorrow is likely to be another trying day."

Jane gave him a weary smile. "A small part of me hopes the sheriff doesn't show up until after the filming. Considering the early start time, the chefs must be cooking breakfast. The filming is taking place on the grass near the terrace, and I'd love to see how the literary theme will influence the challenge."

"Just as long as it's not *Green Eggs and Ham*," grumbled Butterworth.

"Oh, no!" Jane laughed. "Don't tell me you're still haunted by that *single* taste of the twins' Dr. Seuss Day food?"

Butterworth shuddered. "That discolored lump of sludge clinging to my fork was not food. I had to replace the battery in my electric toothbrush following that culinary catastrophe."

Jane tried to suppress a giggle but failed.

"Seeing as your spirits have been restored, I'll say good night."

"Good night, my friend."

Jane sat at her desk, lost in the memory of her sons celebrating Dr. Seuss Day as first graders.

"Where has the time gone?" she murmured to herself.

Turning to face her computer, Jane prepared an email for her staff. She couldn't provide many details about Chef Pierce's death, so she simply paraphrased the statement from the sheriff's department. After adding a line expressing sympathy to Chef Pierce's friends and family, she told her staff to redirect all media inquiries to the sheriff.

With this done, she took advantage of the quiet to wonder why Sheriff Evans hadn't picked up Levi for questioning. Either he didn't consider the judge dangerous, or he didn't believe Levi was responsible for Chef Pierce's death.

Refusing to dwell on the possibility that the sheriff had no leads, Jane turned off the lights and headed for the bustle and clamor of the kitchens.

There, she found Fitz and Hem at a prep counter, ladling jam into jars while Chef Michel looked on.

"The secret to making good food comes from here." Chef Michel touched his chest. "And here." He gave them a goofy grin.

"I don't get it," said Fitz.

"You should love the food you cook, and you should have fun making it. If you cook with a happy heart, your food will taste of happiness. If you cook only for money or to impress people, your food can lose its joy. People can taste a smile in your food. If you're grumpy, your food will be heavy and dull. This jam? It will taste like you two. It will be fresh and bright as the sunshine. People will line up for miles to buy a jar."

Spotting Jane, Chef Michel cried, "Welcome to the jam factory! Your sons and I have had a wonderful time. They've made me feel less homesick." He indicated the rows of jam jars. "As you can see, they are almost ready for tomorrow's festival."

Fitz picked up a jar and handed it to Jane. "How does it smell?"

The glass was still warm to the touch. Jane inhaled

the sweet aroma of fresh berries and said, "Smells like a carefree summer."

Hem gave her a funny look. "Can you tell which berries we used?"

"Raspberries. But it's a dark shade, so I think you added blackberries too."

Fitz held up two fingers. "That's two out of three."

Jane pursed her lips. "Strawberry?"

The boys made Xs out of their arms and honked.

Chef Michel laughed. "You sound like angry geese."

"Blueberries," Hem said. "They're from over the mountain. The farmer delivered a whole bunch this morning."

Chef Michel frowned. "What does this mean? Over the mountain?"

"It's how locals refer to the world beyond our village," Jane explained. "Over the mountain is where you find strip malls, car dealerships, fast food chains, etcetera. Storyton is a small town with a slow pace, which is how we like it."

"I hope it's not slow tomorrow. Not with all this jam to sell. Right, Chefs?"

The boys cried, "Right, Chef!"

Fitz untied his apron and dropped it on the counter. "We'll print out labels after dinner. Our jam has the best name ever. Tell her, Hem."

Hem puffed out his chest and cried, "Where the Wild Berries Are!"

Jane said, "I love it. Maybe your next batch could be Huckleberry Fun."

The twins groaned while Chef Michel shook his head. "That's almost as bad as mine, and I came up with Blueberry Jam for Sal."

Jane laughed. "Okay, wild boys. You need to clean up

before you leave. Thank you, Chef Michel. It was really nice of you to help my sons."

He grinned, dimples appearing on both cheeks. "Truly, it was my pleasure."

Jane went home and put on her pajamas. She was cracking eggs into a bowl when the boys tumbled into the kitchen.

"Why are you in your pajamas?" asked Hem.

Jane poured a splash of milk in the bowl. "I'm tired because I got up so early. I'm going to pack it in after dinner. I trust you two and know you'll go to bed on time."

Fitz watched Jane mix the eggs and milk. "Are we having breakfast for dinner?"

"Yep. And if you guys want to put on your pajamas, we can eat in the living room and watch that Japanime show you like."

"*Naruto* and TV dinner? Awesome!"

The twins exchanged high-fives and thundered up the stairs.

Jane poured the egg mixture into a frying pan. As it bubbled, she thought about how most of the Storyton Hall guests would be dressing for dinner now. How many of them avoided the mirror because they didn't like what they saw in their face? Were they weighed down by guilt, sorrow, or fear? How many were thinking of Chef Pierce at this moment?

The toaster ejected two pieces of golden-brown bread, and Jane's focus returned to dinner prep.

She ate without really tasting the food and was unable to follow the plot of the animated show.

"I think my brain's shutting down."

Fitz paused the show and turned to her. "We'll clean up, Mom. You should go to bed."

Hem nodded. "Yeah, we got it. And can we have ice cream for dessert?"

"Sure. And thanks. It's nice to have two men looking after me."

As Jane headed for the stairs, Fitz asked, "Should we leave a light on for Mr. Edwin?"

"No, he'll be at the restaurant till late. Don't forget about your jam labels. Love you. Good night!"

The twins' replies were swallowed by high-pitched squeals coming from the television.

In her room, Jane quickly read through Mia's email outlining tomorrow's challenge. It was going to be an early start for everyone involved.

Jane set her alarm and then sent a group text asking the Fins to report. Sterling replied that Levi Anjou was in the Rudyard Kipling Café with Coco, Ty, and several members of the film crew. Knowing the Fins wouldn't lose sight of Chef Pierce's potential murderer, Jane wished them a good evening and turned off the light.

It was such a relief to stretch out in bed. The sheets were cool and welcoming, and Jane was grateful to lower her heavy head onto her pillow. She expected to drift off right away, but her mind refused to quiet.

In the dark, Jane questioned the morality of allowing the competition to continue after Sheriff Evans made it clear that Chef Pierce's death wasn't an accident. But she could hardly stop tomorrow's challenge without a valid reason, and she couldn't be honest with her guests without sabotaging the sheriff's investigation.

She'd have to go on playing the gracious hostess while she and the Fins watched Levi Anjou's every move.

This was her last cohesive thought before sleep claimed her.

In the morning, she didn't wake to the clanging of her alarm. Something far more pleasant eased her out of slumber. She became aware of another body next to hers. There was another source of warmth under the covers. Another rise and fall of breath. And then, there was the weight of a hand on her hip.

Edwin, came the happy thought.

As if he'd heard, Edwin pulled her body closer. He didn't move or speak. He just held her.

Jane knew that Edwin had worked until after midnight. Even though he must have been dog tired, he'd used the key Jane had given him and slipped into her bed, comforting and supporting her simply by being there. His loving embrace was exactly what Jane needed.

Until she felt a different kind of need.

Turning in the circle of Edwin's arms, Jane gave him a long, deep kiss. And for a little while, nothing existed outside their world of blankets, sheets, and pillows.

Jane had no idea how early Ty had gotten up to oversee the placement of props and equipment on the terrace and lawn, but she assumed the cup of coffee in his hand wasn't his first. Judging by his rapid speech and inability to stand still, he was on cup four or five.

When Jane asked if things were running on schedule, Ty gestured at Milton's Gardens and declared, "Everything's coming up roses." He lowered his voice to a conspiratorial whisper and said, "I hope the chefs are wearing their running shoes."

"When do they arrive?"

Ty consulted his enormous gold watch. "Any minute now. If they're all still alive, that is." Seeing Jane's mortified stare, Ty flashed her a brilliant smile. "I'm teasing! I'll miss Pierce. The guy wasn't pretty, but he made for good TV. Speaking of pretty, here comes Mia."

Mia was in a 1950s-style garden party dress. The wide skirt flounced as she led the chefs to the row of deluxe gas grills sitting on the grass bordering the terrace. After telling the chefs to look over the grills and tools at their workstations, Mia joined Ty and Jane.

"Good morning," she said. "Our crew and our chefs are ready to embrace this new day. How's my wagon, Ty?"

"It's good to go." Ty studied Mia's outfit. "You're like a younger, hipper Korean version of Mary Poppins."

"You're off by about sixty years on the dress, and I've told you a hundred times, I'm not part Korean, I'm part Thai. But I forgive you because I *love* Mary Poppins." Mia smiled at Jane. "We're ready to seat the audience."

Ty glanced skyward. "I'll do a final sound and light check. Tell Bentley to get on the walkie as soon as you're in motion."

Mia waited until Ty began talking to a cameraman before she pointed at her cell phone. "It's been blowing up since five. People want to know what happened to Chef Pierce, and the sheriff's statement doesn't say much. Is there anything I need to know?"

"If Sheriff Evans has new information, we'll find out when he gets here." Jane's gaze swept over the lawn. "Where are the judges?"

"Waiting for my signal." Mia was giddy with excitement.

"We're going to make a grand entrance. You and your family have VIP seating, so you won't miss a second of what we have planned. Enjoy!"

As soon as Mia turned and headed toward the herb garden, Ty called for all nonessential personnel to clear the set.

On the terrace, Aunt Octavia and Uncle Aloysius were holding court. All of the guests wanted to thank the octogenarians for opening up their familial home.

"My husband hasn't been this relaxed in twenty years," a woman gushed.

"And my wife keeps smiling," her spouse added. "I never knew she had dimples."

The couples laughed.

"Jane, darling!" Aunt Octavia patted the empty chair beside her. "Our ever-thoughtful Butterworth fixed us a thermos of coffee. Aloysius, would you fill our cups?"

"It would be my honor, my beautiful bride."

Uncle Aloysius poured coffee into takeout cups and then demanded a tip from Aunt Octavia in the form of a kiss.

"You rake." She pretended to be scandalized. "In front of all these people?"

"A peck on the cheek is all I ask."

Aunt Octavia bestowed a kiss on her husband's wrinkled cheek, marking his skin with a smear of fuchsia lipstick. Uncle Aloysius refused to wipe it off.

"Now all the other ladies will know I'm spoken for," he said.

This exchange made Jane smile. Her great-uncle and great-aunt had an ideal relationship. They were friends as well as lovers. They'd managed Storyton Hall together, raised Jane after her parents died, and shared an unbreakable bond that grew deeper with every passing year. Jane aspired to be just like them.

When a member of the film crew raised a sign reading QUIET, the live audience fell silent and the chefs took their places behind their prep counters. Jane perched on the edge of her seat, eagerly awaiting Mia's grand entrance.

It wasn't Mia she saw next, but a pair of horses. Their chestnut coats gleamed, and their bridles were decorated with flowers. Ribbons of green and yellow peeked through the braids in their manes and tails. The horses were pulling a farm wagon carrying Mia, Coco, and Levi. Sam Nolan of Hilltop Stables sat up front. In his denim overalls and straw hat, he looked like a character from a John Steinbeck novel.

At the entrance to Milton's Gardens, Sam told the horses to hold up. He jumped down from the wagon and offered his hand to Mia and the judges. Mia picked up a basket brimming with vegetables and smiled for the camera.

"Welcome to *Posh Palate with Mia Mallett*. We're here at Storyton Hall—heaven on earth for readers, foodies, and nature lovers. With me today are TV's favorite judges, Coco Kennedy and Levi Anjou. I'd like to thank Sam Nolan from Hilltop Stables for giving us a ride to work. Sam's horses also delivered the pantry for today's challenge, and I think they should be rewarded for their efforts."

On cue, Sam held up two carrots. A camera zoomed in on him feeding the treats to his horses. He then smiled and tipped his hat at Mia.

After waving at Sam, Mia turned back to the camera. "Behind me is a garden filled with plants and flowers of every color, shape, and fragrance. Storyton Hall grows many of its own herbs and vegetables, and guests can taste that homegrown goodness in their food. Colorful plants, sunshine, and a walled garden remind me of one of my favorite childhood books—Frances Hodgson Burnett's *The Secret Garden*."

A dozen audience members whispered, "Mine too."

Mia acknowledged the murmurs with a smile. "I love this quote from *The Secret Garden*: 'I am sure there is Magic in everything, only we have not sense enough to get hold of it and make it do things for us.'" Again, she paused. "Cooking is a form of magic. The best chefs can prepare flavorful dishes with just a few ingredients. Chefs, your Secret Garden challenge is to use the vegetables and herbs in our wagon, along with eggs and other pantry staples, to make an enchanting breakfast dish."

Jane guessed what was coming next, but she still grinned when Mia said, "Sounds pretty straightforward, right? But there's a catch."

The chefs groaned.

Mia held up her basket. "You must prepare a *vegetarian* breakfast dish, and you can only make *one* trip to the wagon. Your ingredients must fit in the basket on your prep station, so choose wisely. You have one hour to complete this challenge. Go!"

The contestants grabbed their baskets and raced for the cart. They were almost there when Chef Lindsay stumbled. She pitched forward and would have fallen on her face if Chef August hadn't caught her by the arm and hauled her upright. To show her gratitude, Chef Lindsay hung back, ensuring that Chef August reached the cart ahead of her.

"There's hope for humanity yet," Aunt Octavia whispered to Jane.

Jane couldn't believe how quickly the chefs began chopping vegetables or mixing ingredients in bowls. It would take her most of the allotted time to come up with a recipe, let alone cook it.

Crew members holding cameras and mics wound their way around the prep stations, getting footage of the chefs at work while Coco and Levi watched from the judges' table. The chefs had clearly found their rhythm, and Mia was ready to ask each of them what they planned to make.

She started with Chef Alondra. "Is that a tortilla?"

The chef nodded as she worked a green-specked ball of dough into a thin disc. "My dish is huevos rancheros with a smoky pepper salsa served with avocado, cilantro, and black beans on a spinach tortilla."

When asked if she had any concerns about time, Chef Alondra said, "No. I got this."

Chef Saffron was also rolling out balls of dough for her naan spiced with garlic and lemon. "The naan will be the side of toast for my breakfast of curry scrambled eggs served with a side of roasted potatoes, onions, and bell peppers."

Chef August wasn't as calm as his female competitors. "I'm definitely worried about time, Mia. I've made cornbread twenty ways, but I've never tried to make it in a cast-iron skillet on a grill!"

Mia said, "Tell us about your dish."

"I'm whipping up some beautifully poached eggs served with hollandaise, purple sprouting broccoli, and charred cornbread."

"So the charred part is intentional?" Mia grinned.

Chef August put a finger to his lips. "I'm not giving away my secrets."

With a laugh, Mia walked over to Chef Lindsay's station. "You almost started this challenge with a hard fall. What happened?"

Chef Lindsay shrugged. "I stumbled over a rock or something. Lucky for me, Chef August is a gentleman."

"It looked like you repaid the favor by being the last person to choose your ingredients," said Mia.

"I ended up with plenty of veggies," Chef Lindsay replied. "Being last actually helped me edit my dish. When I saw the muffin pans, I knew I wanted to make my own version of toad in the hole. Instead of toast, I'm doing a rosemary and thyme popover filled with fried egg and spinach and topped with a cherry tomato garnish."

Mia wished her luck and moved on to Chef Michel's station.

"I think I bit off more than I can chew, and I have a big mouth!" Chef Michel joked, dabbing his forehead with a towel. "My one-bowl dish is a goat cheese polenta topped with an egg and salsa verde. This will sit next to a medley of charred carrots and there'll be an herb biscotti to provide a nice crunch."

"Oh, my. How can I become a judge on this show?" Aunt Octavia whispered.

Forty-five minutes went by in a blur. With only ten minutes left to go, the chefs became manic. They groaned and shouted in frustration. They wiped their sweaty faces with towels and fearfully checked the clock on the judges' table. At the three-minute mark, they started plating their dishes.

"This is so exciting!" someone whispered behind Jane.

She had to agree. For the past hour, she'd been so focused on the competition that she hadn't studied Levi Anjou's expressions or body language for signs of a guilty conscience. As soon as the chefs started cooking, she'd forgotten about both judges.

And it wasn't Levi who finally drew her attention away from the riveting conclusion of the Secret Garden Challenge. It wasn't a person at all.

"Do you smell gas?" she asked Aunt Octavia in an urgent whisper.

Aunt Octavia frowned. "I can't tell. My allergies have been acting up."

She leaned over and whispered in her husband's ear. Uncle Aloysius took a deep inhale through his nose and nodded. He smelled it too.

"Get the guests inside. *Hurry.*" Jane jumped to her feet and took out her phone. She dictated an urgent message to the Fins as she raced down the terrace steps and over the grass to where Ty and the fire safety advisor were engaged in a heated argument.

"Two minutes!" Ty hissed, blocking the fire safety advisor's path. "The judges are tasting the dishes now. The second they're done, we'll turn off the grills."

"I'm turning it off *now!*" The man tried to push past Ty, but the director grabbed him by his neon vest and wouldn't let go.

Ty might be willing to sacrifice people's safety for the sake of television, but Jane wasn't.

With a grunt, Ty released the fire safety advisor, and the man sprinted toward the row of grills.

He was halfway there when the world exploded.

Chapter 10

There was a deafening roar and a bright ball of fire rocketed skyward.

Jane dropped to her knees but didn't cover her face. She couldn't take her eyes off the flames roiling over the top of Chef Michel's grill.

Her hypnotic state was short-lived. Concern for her guests brought her to her feet, and she hurriedly scanned the area for anyone in need of help.

Seeing the terrace, her heart lurched in relief. Aunt Octavia and Uncle Aloysius had managed to get all the audience members into the manor house. Their frightened faces stared out through the windows.

Safe.

The word sounded like an answered prayer.

Jane looked around for the chefs. All five were on the ground behind the judges' table. They appeared to be unhurt. Levi and Coco were crouched in the grass, clinging to each other. Mia and Bentley were huddled together near the judges. Mia's face was slack with shock.

One of the crewmembers started shouting. As if a spell had been broken, his colleagues sprang into action, moving cameras, lights, cables, and other equipment away from the burning grill.

A man leaned over the balcony of his second-story guest room and yelled, "Get water!"

Someone else cried, "Here's a hose!"

Jane scanned the area near the grills for the fire safety advisor. Even though he wore a bright orange vest, she couldn't see him. The smoke made it impossible.

Suddenly, the fire shifted, and Jane saw a body on the flagstones. A man's body, too close to the fire.

"*Help!*" she screamed, running toward the flames. "*I need help!*"

Assistance came from every direction.

Lachlan and Sterling rushed across the terrace. They both had market umbrellas in their arms.

Butterworth ran across the lawn, heading for the terrace steps. For a big man, he moved fast. The tails of his uniform coat flapped like wings as he raced up the steps. At the top, he bellowed at the guest holding the garden hose.

"Put that down! Spray water on this fire and you'll kill us all!"

Jane didn't spare a glance for the guest. She was completely focused on reaching the fire safety advisor.

Sensing movement out of the corner of her eye, she turned her head to see Sinclair. He pulled up alongside her, carrying a two-gallon bucket in one hand and a fire extinguisher in the other.

He thrust the extinguisher at her. "You'll spray while I dump the baking soda. It'll give Butterworth time to grab hold of Mr. Gilmore. Ready?"

The heat of the fire stung Jane's skin and acrid smoke rushed into her lungs, but she planted her feet, ripped out the extinguisher pin, and aimed.

"*Now*!" Sinclair hollered.

Jane pressed the trigger and Sinclair hurled the baking soda. The double assault of foam and white powder was too powerful for the fire, and it shrank back.

Butterworth pulled the fire safety advisor out of harm's way while Lachlan and Sterling smothered the choking flames with the umbrellas. The abrupt loss of oxygen stole the fire's potency. All it could do now was blacken the umbrella canvas with its final breaths.

Lachlan and Sterling dropped the ruined umbrellas on the flagstones, and the noxious odor of singed fabric and plastic mingled with the other malodorous fumes billowing out over the terrace.

Jane's eyes were gritty and sore, and it felt like her throat was lined with soot. As she rubbed at her eyes, a troop of bellhops and desk clerks streamed out of the manor house carrying electric fans, extension cords, and power strips. The kitchen staff was there too, distributing bottles of water and other items to everyone on the lawn.

A sous chef handed Jane water and a damp cloth for her face. She passed the cloth over her eyes and drank some water. Then, she looked for Butterworth and the fire safety advisor.

A few feet away, Sinclair was speaking to Lachlan.

"Where's Mr. Gilmore?" Jane asked.

"Mr. Butterworth took him to the closest cottage. He'll tend to him however he can until Doc Lydgate arrives."

"Ms. Limoges is there, in that cottage."

Sinclair poured some water on his handkerchief and passed it over his face. "I know, but it has a fully stocked first-aid kit, and we could hardly carry the man through the manor house."

"Of course not. I'm sorry. I'm not as clear-headed as I'd like to be."

"What would you have us do?"

The question steadied Jane. "I'd like Sterling to liaise with Chief Aroneo. You and Lachlan should take a head count. Make sure everyone's present, accounted for, and unhurt. Continue to keep an eye on Levi Anjou until Sheriff Evans arrives. He'll want me to fill him in on what happened, but that'll have to wait. Mr. Gilmore was injured trying to save us. I need to do everything I can to help him."

Jane hopped in the maintenance cart parked next to the herb garden and sped down the driveway toward the employee cottages.

As she passed her house, she felt a surge of guilt because she hadn't checked on the twins. But Edwin was there, and he wouldn't let the boys out of his sight. Fitz and Hem were probably leaning out their bedroom window right now, peering through their spyglasses with the intensity of a naval captain searching for an enemy ship.

Jane took one hand off the wheel and dictated a text to Edwin.

Gas grill exploded. One person injured. I'll call when I can.

At the little stone cottage, Jane jumped out of the golf cart, ran up the steps, and burst through the front door. "Butterworth?"

An unintelligible noise came from the bedroom and Olivia Limoges poked her head into the living room. She pointed at a bowl on the kitchen counter and said, "Can you bring that back here?"

Jane carried the bowl of water into the bedroom and set it on the nightstand.

"Mr. Butterworth went to meet the doctor," Olivia said as she submerged a piece of white cotton in the water.

Jane saw a pile of the debris on the rug. With horror, she realized that it was made of scraps of clothing. There were ribbons of neon orange, a rhombus of gray cotton, and part of a leather belt. The sight drove home the seriousness of Mr. Gilmore's injuries.

"Did Butterworth cut these off?" she asked in a hushed voice.

"Yes," Olivia replied. "He said it was crucial to remove restrictive items, elevate the burned area, and cover it with cool, moist cloths."

Jane watched Olivia dip a square of white cotton into the bowl. After wringing it out, she gingerly laid it across the blistered skin of Mr. Gilmore's chest.

"Thank you," Jane said. She wanted to say more—to praise Olivia for her willingness to help—but was suddenly overcome by emotion. A lump formed in her throat and tears threatened. It took a Herculean effort to keep them from spilling over.

Olivia laid a cloth on Mr. Gilmore's upper arm. "Was it an accident?"

Jane thought back to the moments preceding the explosion. Other than the smell of gas, everything had been going well.

"I don't know," she admitted.

"What does your gut say?"

Olivia's blue eyes were as dark and unfathomable as the Arctic Sea, but her tone was sympathetic. And though Jane had learned not to confide in strangers, she felt an inexplicable affinity to this woman.

"This is our second fire in three days. I think someone is trying to sabotage the filming."

"A propane tank explosion in the middle of a cooking competition goes beyond sabotage. So many people could have been injured. Or killed."

"One person *is* injured," Jane said. Anger pushed the tears out. "And that's one too many."

Doc Lydgate told the EMS crew that he'd stay with his patient until his care was given over to the hospital over the mountain.

"Call me as soon as you can," Jane shouted right before the ambulance doors were slammed shut.

She and Butterworth stood in the driveway and watched the ambulance disappear around the corner of the manor house. Long after the vehicle was out of sight, the shriek of its siren echoed back to them.

There was nothing Jane could do for Mr. Gilmore now other than pray, so she closed her eyes and did just that. When she was done, she opened her eyes and met Butterworth's gaze.

"Mr. Gilmore will recover," he assured Jane. "But he'll bear the scars of this day for the rest of his life."

"If Ty Scott hadn't interfered, Mr. Gilmore might have prevented the explosion. If he'd been able to shut off the gas in time, he might not be on his way to the hospital." Jane's voice crackled with anger. "But this is bigger than that imbecile director. We already had an electrical fire in the archery field. Two days later, a propane tank explodes. And sandwiched between these events was a murder. We need to understand why these things happened, and until we do, the show can't go on."

Butterworth's expression turned pensive. "Would anyone benefit from its cancelation?"

That was the million-dollar question, and Jane didn't have an answer.

"Is someone plotting against the network? Or Mia? Or are the chefs the targets?" she wondered aloud. "The fire in the field didn't seem connected to Chef Pierce's murder, but after today, I believe it must be."

Jane started walking toward the manor house. When Butterworth didn't fall into step beside her, she turned and raised her brows in question.

"I don't want to repay Ms. Limoges's kindness by leaving her cottage in disarray. When I showed up on her doorstep with Mr. Gilmore, I didn't know what to expect. Before I could explain my presence, she took in the extent of Mr. Gilmore's injuries and immediately offered her assistance. She was quite remarkable."

Jane was grateful for Olivia's help as well, but she also questioned the writer's movements. "Please thank her for me. And as remarkable as she may be, you need to find out where she was this morning."

Butterworth's mouth formed the ghost of a frown. "Understood."

Glancing at the sky, Jane saw that the smoke had dissipated. "Levi Anjou didn't cause the explosion. He was sitting too close to the grills to have taken such a risk. He might be Chef Pierce's killer, but I don't think he's the reason the fire department has been called here twice this week."

"I agree."

"We need to put our heads together," Jane continued. "Chief Aroneo and his team. Sheriff Evans and his department. And all of us." She rubbed her temples. "I thought having a TV show film at Storyton Hall would be a boon for the resort and the village, but something else has been attracted to the lights and cameras. Something sinister. And I don't have the slightest idea what it wants. That scares me. And infuriates me. I'd like to take out my frustrations by practicing my archery on that damned director."

"Your arrow would probably bounce off his hair," Butterworth quipped.

At the terrace, the firefighters had used yellow tape to create a restricted area. The chief was inside the perimeter, examining the charred remains of the grill. He spoke to one of his officers in low tones while the officer took photographs. Both men were fully engrossed in their task, and Jane chose not to interrupt them.

She entered an oddly quiet manor house, but when she ran into Sinclair in the main lobby, he quickly explained the silence.

"The audience is now in the Ian Fleming Lounge. Your great-uncle has been distributing Irish coffees, and your great-aunt has been offering comfort and reassurance. Several kitchen trolleys loaded with pastries, fruit, and sandwiches were just wheeled in. I believe the guests will have recovered from the shock by teatime."

"I hope so. What about the chefs and the rest of the TV people?"

Taking Jane by the arm, Sinclair said, "I'll tell you as we walk. With one exception, they're all decompressing in the spa's relaxation area. Mr. Anjou is not relaxing. He's in the William Faulkner Conference Room, which is why we're heading in that direction."

"Ah," said Jane. "We need to go to Narnia."

When they reached a metal cupboard resembling a

broom closet, Sinclair produced a key ring, selected a small brass key, and unlocked the door.

"Go ahead," he whispered. "I'll make sure the coast is clear before I join you."

Jane stepped into the cupboard. Pushing mops and brooms to the side, she fumbled for the hidden latch. She hooked her finger around the latch and pushed hard on the back of the cupboard. With a whisper of hinges, a slim opening was revealed. Jane slipped through the gap into a narrow space.

Storyton Hall was full of secret passageways and hidey-holes. As a boy, Uncle Aloysius had been familiar with each and every one. But after his family home was turned into a resort and he became the Guardian of the secret library, he was too busy to visit every corner of the manor house. Over time, he forgot where many of the hidden panels and secret passageways were located, and though Fitz and Hem had found a few, no one knew exactly how many were left to be rediscovered.

Jane moved forward in the darkness, using the wall as a guide. She didn't go far before she heard voices. After another twelve feet, a soft light penetrated the dark. The light, which streamed through the air return grill in the William Faulkner, meant that Jane had to be very quiet from now on.

She tiptoed until she reached the second air return grill. She could hear Sheriff Evans's voice as clearly as if they were in the same room.

"And did you meet Chef Pierce the night you had dinner at his restaurant?"

"I did," replied the voice belonging to Levi Anjou. "He came out of the kitchen to schmooze. I was told he did this every night. He made customers wait for their food while he socialized."

Jane sensed movement nearby. Sinclair brushed her arm to let her know that he was there. Though touch was their only means of communication in this space, they rarely employed it. To remain undetected, they had to be as still as stones.

On the other side of the wall, the sheriff asked Levi another question. "Was your review favorable?"

"No, it wasn't," Levi replied flatly. "The entrées looked like they'd been plated by cavemen and the meal ate too heavy."

"Was your review influenced by your interaction with Chef Pierce?"

There was a long pause before Levi said, "Maybe. I review everything about a restaurant. If a chef is loud or obnoxious, it can ruin the experience."

"Tell me *exactly* what Chef Pierce said when he came to your table."

Despite the sheriff's authoritative tone, there was a long pause before Levi complied. "This is a waste of time, but here's what happened. Chef Pierce came over to our table to say hello. My wife, Sheila, was with me. She didn't look like herself because she was wearing a wig and glasses. We both were. I have lots of disguises to keep people from recognizing me."

The sheriff made an encouraging noise.

"Sheila loved her meal and sang Chef Pierce's praises to his face. Then, she went to powder her nose. Do you know what Chef Pierce said to me after she left? He told me that my mom was a sweetie. Sheila was wearing a red wig, a clingy cocktail dress, and heels. She did *not* look like my mother. When I explained that she was my wife, Chef Pierce said, 'Ouch. Sorry, man. At least she likes steak.'"

"Was that the end of your interaction?"

"Yes. He went back to the kitchen to cook more mediocre food. We didn't stay for dessert," Levi added huffily.

A creaking noise indicated that Sheriff Evans had shifted in his chair. Jane could picture him folding his hands as he surveyed the food critic. "Was the food really mediocre, or was your opinion influenced by Chef Pierce's comment?"

"Probably both. And even though I wanted to burn him, my review gave him a huge boost. You couldn't get a table at Epitome after my piece came out." He snorted. "If I'd known that saying his restaurant was only fit for cavemen would turn it into the most popular steak house in the city, I would have chosen different words."

"I see," said the sheriff with a hint of amusement. "When did you next encounter Chef Pierce?"

Levi released another exasperated sigh. "Who knows? Napa Valley. Colorado. The usual food festival circuit. I listened to him describe his dish. That's it. We never talked."

"Until?"

"Until this show. I can't understand why Mia asked that Neanderthal to be a contestant."

The comment piqued the sheriff's interest. "Did Ms. Mallett know how you felt about Chef Pierce?"

"She read the piece I wrote on Epitome. Everyone in the biz reads my reviews," he added matter-of-factly. "Mia called to talk about the contestants. She wanted my assurance that I'd judge the chefs on their food. Nothing else. If I couldn't, I'd be replaced."

This surprised Jane. Levi had been a judge on *Posh Palate with Mia Mallett* from the beginning. Why would she cast him aside for a chef? Especially a controversial chef.

"Did that make you angry?"

"You're damn right it did. Chefs are a dime a dozen. After Mia, Coco and I are the faces of the show. We're the reason people tune in."

Levi obviously had an inflated view of his importance. The judges brought an element of sophistication to the reality show, but they didn't merit much camera time. The contestants provided the drama, emotion, and artistry.

"I assume you promised to be an unbiased judge or we wouldn't be sitting here."

Suddenly, Levi sounded defeated. "I don't want to be sitting here, but I'm relieved that everything's finally in the open. I'm tired of keeping secrets."

Sheriff Evans knew this was a pivotal moment and wisely remained silent.

As for Jane, she was sure that both men could hear the thumping of her heart right through the wall.

"Secrets are heavy," the sheriff said when Levi didn't continue. "You can stop carrying them now."

The sigh that escaped Levi was almost inaudible, but the sound signaled a release.

"I thought my review would ruin Chef Pierce's career. Because he insulted my wife, which was also an insult to me, I sent him a copy the day it published. Weeks later, he wrote to thank me for the free publicity. He also said that Sheila had been back several times with her friends and that he enjoyed her company. That email made my blood boil."

A woman asked Levi if he'd like a glass of water and he gladly accepted.

Deputy Emory's in the room.

Following a pause and the clink of glass meeting wood, Levi resumed his narrative. "That review is five years old, and so much has changed since then. For one, I started doing this show. For a few months every year, I'm away from home, taping or promoting the show. I also travel to festivals and other foodie events. In this time, Sheila and I grew apart."

The sheriff said that he was sorry to hear it.

"Three years ago, I fell in love with Coco. We've had a secret relationship, but we don't want to hide how we feel anymore. We want to be together. No matter what the cost."

Levi's words poured out, flowing like a rain-swollen river.

"We thought we were alone in that train car from DC, but we weren't. Chef Pierce saw us messing around, and while Coco was talking to the hotel driver, he told me that he had a video of us on his phone. He showed me a few seconds as proof. When I asked what it would take to delete the video, I expected him to ask for a place in the finale. But he asked for money."

"How much?"

"Fifty grand. In cash. And I had forty-eight hours to hand it over."

Someone in the room whistled.

"It was insane. I told him to jump off a bridge, but he started emailing me, saying that I'd lose my reputation and be kicked off the show if he leaked the video."

"Did you reply to these emails?"

Levi barked out a laugh. "I sure did. I called him a pig's bladder and said that everyone would be happier once he was gone."

"Because he'd be dead?"

"What? *No!*" Levi cried. "Because Coco and I planned to vote him out at the end of the second challenge. But we never got the chance."

Though Levi's explanation didn't sound rehearsed, it was too convenient for Jane's liking.

"Weren't you worried that Chef Pierce would release the video as payback?"

"Not a bit." There was an unmistakable note of triumph in Levi's voice. "If you have nothing to hide, you can't be blackmailed. That's why Coco and I decided to stop hiding. The night before we heard about Chef Pierce's death, we came clean to our spouses."

Sheriff Evans started to speak but Levi cut him off. "Everyone has secrets. But a man like Pierce? Look at his life. I bet he had tons of secrets. When he couldn't run from them anymore, they dragged him down. Straight to hell."

Chapter 11

Sheriff Evans asked a few follow-up questions about Chef Pierce until Levi made it clear that he no longer wished to cooperate. "I'm done!" he shouted. "You can talk to my lawyer from now on. He'll be working on my divorce, so he can deal with you and Sheila at the same time."

Jane was just as eager for the sheriff to terminate the interview. Her left foot had gone to sleep, and there was a tickle at the back of her throat, likely provoked by dust. She was ready to leave.

To her relief, the sheriff said, "Thank you, Mr. Anjou. You're free to go. Please don't communicate with Ms. Kennedy until after I've spoken with her."

Levi didn't respond, and the pins and needles sensation in Jane's foot intensified. She wriggled her toes and wished Levi would storm out of the room.

But he didn't move.

"My God." Levi's voice was hollow with shock. "You thought *I* had something to do with Pierce's death. I was so caught up in my own drama that it didn't hit me until now. But if Pierce *didn't* have a heart attack, how did he die?"

"I can't discuss an open investigation, Mr. Anjou. And

now that the media has arrived in Storyton, I caution you to keep any details relating to Chef Pierce's death to yourself."

Jane heard the wheels of Levi's chair roll across the carpet. "The email I sent him—taken out of context, it makes me look pretty bad. So why am I free to go?"

"Because I saw the video you and Ms. Kennedy posted. You started a livestream at eleven the night before Chef Pierce's death. You didn't stop recording until six the next morning, which gives the two of you a very public alibi."

"Saved by technology," said Levi.

Sheriff Evans grunted. "I also read the comments written by your wife and Mr. Kennedy in response to that video. You may not be guilty of a crime, Mr. Anjou, but your moral compass is definitely broken. To reveal your infidelity as you did is cowardly and dishonorable. You should be ashamed of yourself. Deputy Emory, please show this man out."

Jane heard the door open and close again.

"Should I get Ms. Kennedy?" asked Deputy Emory.

"Yes. In the meantime, I'll ask Ms. Steward to round up all the guests. I'll address them as a group."

As soon as the sound of Deputy Emory's footsteps faded, Jane stretched out her hand and tapped twice on Sinclair's arm. This was their "exit" signal.

Sinclair vanished without making a noise. Jane tried to replicate his stealth, but her left foot was still numb, and when she tried to walk, it buckled, throwing her off-balance. She thrust out a hand to keep from falling, and her palm hit the wall's dusty surface with a muted thud.

Jane froze.

The silence in the conference room was absolute. She

could sense Sheriff Evans listening and didn't dare move another centimeter.

Then, to her horror, a shape appeared on the other side of the air vent.

Was Sheriff Evans on his hands and knees, peering into her hiding place?

Jane held her breath.

The dark shape let out a low growl.

"Hello, kitty. When did you sneak in here?" the sheriff cooed as Jane tiptoed away.

Muffet Cat growled louder.

"What's up, little guy? Do you see a mouse back there?" The sheriff chuckled. "You look like you've eaten your share of mice. I bet you weigh twenty pounds. Look at that tummy. Do you like tummy rubs?"

Jane was just closing the panel at the back of the cupboard when she heard the sheriff howl in pain.

"Sheriff Evans might need stitches," she told Sinclair as they hurried down the hallway.

He opened the door to the staff corridor and held it for Jane. "Did a foul-tempered feline with sharp claws and tuna breath find his way into the conference room?"

"Yep."

Sinclair sighed. "If the sheriff's encounter with Muffet Cat was the worst thing to happen at Storyton Hall today, we'd be in good shape."

Jane hoped to reach her office without delay but was hailed by one of the front desk clerks before she made it inside. Sue, a longtime employee of Storyton Hall known for her inexhaustible optimism, was the picture of worry.

"Ms. Steward? May I have a word?"

"Come on back," Jane said, bracing herself for more bad news.

In the office, Sue and Sinclair sat in the guest chairs facing Jane's desk.

"We're being flooded with calls from the media," said Sue. "Newspapers, magazines, TV stations—you name it."

"Are they asking about Chef Pierce?"

Sue glanced at the memo pad on her lap. "A few, yes. But most of the calls are about the explosion."

Jane was horrified. "How did they find out so fast?"

"Someone posted a video of it. I don't recognize the username, but judging by the viewpoint, it's one of the film crew."

Turning to her computer, Jane searched for videos of Storyton Hall. The top result was a Hollywood gossip site. The headline on the homepage cried, "EXPLOSION ON SET OF POSH PALATE!"

Jane scanned the article. The piece was nothing but conjecture, so she clicked the video's play button.

The screen filled with images of flames and smoke, which meant that username, GoldnBears2002, started filming immediately following the initial explosion. To Jane's dismay, the footage captured all the details of the chaotic scene. For sixty seconds, she relived the terrifying experience.

As she listened to the panicked cries of the cast and crew, Jane thought of Mr. Gilmore. For a moment, she was too overcome with emotion to speak.

"I'm sorry someone did this, Ms. Steward."

Jane closed her laptop. "Thank you for telling me, Sue. I'll prepare a media statement right away."

When the door closed behind Sue, Jane passed her hands over her face. "Offering to host this show was a huge mistake," she murmured. "To these TV people, Storyton Hall is just another location. They don't value it the way our regular guests do."

Sinclair pointed at the laptop. "Whoever posted that video signed a nondisclosure agreement. Ms. Mallett should find out who they are and insist the video be taken down."

"And send GoldnBears2002 packing. Can you convey the message to her? And have Sterling close the main gates. I won't have those pushy media people stepping foot on this property."

Sinclair moved to the door. "Will you tell the other Fins about Levi Anjou?"

She nodded. "Crossing his name off the suspect list means that someone else is responsible for Chef Pierce's death. And that someone else is walking through our halls and mingling with our guests. Once again, a killer is staying at Storyton Hall."

Later, after Jane had written a short statement for the press, she tracked down Chief Aroneo. He was in the kitchens, sitting at a prep counter with Mrs. Hubbard.

As usual, Mrs. Hubbard was plying her visitor with food. Plates of ham biscuits, chopped fruit, and sugar cookies sat in front of the chief. There was also a pitcher of water and lemon slices. The lemons looked like small suns drifting through a cloudless sky.

Seeing Jane, Chief Aroneo got to his feet. "I know it doesn't look like it, but I came inside to find you."

"I'm glad. You must be hot, thirsty, and tired." Jane motioned for him to sit down. "Mrs. Hubbard, may I commandeer the break room for a bit?"

"It's all yours," she replied. "If anyone disturbs you, I'll give them dishwashing duty."

Chief Aroneo stared at her with admiration. "I should hire you to train my firefighters. They always leave their dirty plates in the sink. I keep telling them that no fairy is going to fly into the kitchen in the middle of the night, wave a magic wand, and clean up their mess."

"Could you hang a sign over the sink?" suggested Mrs. Hubbard.

"I did," the chief said. "It says, 'Clean Your Dishes! Your Mother Doesn't Work Here!'"

Mrs. Hubbard frowned. "I don't think mothers should do all the dishes either. Maybe your sign should say, 'If You Can't Wash the Dishes, Don't Eat!' If your crew doesn't listen after that, take their plates away."

The chief laughed. "Genius. I knew you'd have the answer."

Jane led Chief Aroneo into the break room and shut the door.

"Speaking of answers, do you have some for me?"

The chief's gaze swept over the room. "Do you have a piece of paper and a pen? It'll be easier for me to explain this if I can draw while I talk."

After fetching him supplies, Jane watched the chief sketch an oblong shape in the center of the paper. Next, he added a neck to the top of the oblong. Inside that neck, he drew a dial and what looked like a valve.

"This is a propane tank," he began. "The first thing I should tell you is that propane tanks rarely explode. The chance of your tank exploding is about the same as being in a plane crash. These tanks are sturdy and have built-in safety devices like floaters to prevent overfilling and a relief valve. The relief valve helps control a sudden increase of pressure, which is why an exploding tank almost never happens."

"Until today?" Jane asked.

"Even if it looked and sounded like the propane tank exploded, a propane *leak* could also cause the tank to blow."

Jane stared at him in confusion. "I don't understand the difference."

The chief started sketching another shape. "Pretend this rectangle above the tank is a gas grill. If propane leaks from the valve, a hose, or a connection for a certain length of time, it creates a hazardous scenario. Add heat to that scenario, and it becomes an emergency in the blink of an eye. Igniting a grill with a leaking propane tank, a tank with a faulty valve, or a valve that was tampered with will lead to an explosion."

"I smelled gas," Jane murmured in shame. "I should have guessed there was a leak."

Chief Aroneo gave her a stern look. "Don't put this on yourself. Other folks smelled it too, but with multiple grills going, it would have been hard to know there was excess gas in the air. I've been told that Mr. Gilmore recognized the danger but was unable to act because of the director."

"That's true. Ty blocked his path, arguing that the show was almost over. When Mr. Gilmore insisted on doing his job, Ty grabbed him. I was standing right there. Ty cost Mr. Gilmore precious seconds."

The chief dug his pen into the paper. "It's a criminal offense to hinder a firefighter on duty. If a judge decides that Mr. Gilmore's injuries are tied to the director's interference, he'll be in serious trouble."

As Jane stared at the rectangle representing the gas grill,

MURDER IN THE COOKBOOK NOOK   153

she pictured the scarlet skin on Mr. Gilmore's chest and the mound of ruined clothing on Olivia Limoges's floor.

"I don't have much sympathy for Ty Scott," she said. "My concern is for the safety of my guests. I need to know if that explosion was an accident or arson."

The chief sighed. "If we hadn't just investigated a fire in your archery field, I'd assume this was a case of negligence—that the person responsible for checking the valves, hoses, and connections on the propane tanks failed to do their job. That person would have been Mr. Gilmore, which is why I need to talk to him as soon as possible."

"What if he did his job to the letter? Then what?"

"Then someone tampered with the tank. I won't know for sure until I cart the grill and tank back to the station and examine every inch of what's left, no matter how small the pieces. But I can't move anything until I catch up with the sheriff."

There was a knock on the break room door. Mrs. Hubbard poked her head in and said, "Sheriff Evans is looking for you, Jane. Should I send him back?"

"Please."

Mrs. Hubbard reappeared with the sheriff in tow. She bustled into the room, carrying a tray of finger sandwiches, bite-sized fruit tarts, and strawberry cream scones in one hand and a pitcher of iced tea in the other.

"If you'd rather have hot tea, let me know. I'm putting the finishing touches on my Secret Garden cake for today's tea service, but I always have time to spare for Storyton's finest."

When Mrs. Hubbard turned to go, Jane wished she could follow along. She'd love to sit on a stool and watch the beloved head cook decorate her cake. But Jane knew that her only chance of regaining a sense of control was to come up with a plan, so she poured iced tea and waited for the sheriff to speak.

Evans passed a glass of tea to Chief Aroneo, "What are we looking at, Lou?"

The chief repeated everything he'd told Jane.

Sheriff Evans stroked the stubble on his chin and listened closely. When the chief was done, the sheriff said, "Someone is determined to derail this show. We're already dealing with the suspicious death of a celebrity chef. Today's incident could have led to dozens of casualties, and some of those would've included people with no ties to the show."

"The audience," said Chief Aroneo.

The sheriff nodded. "We have no leads, which means I'll have to ask for help from the TV people and the other guests." He turned to Jane. "I'd like to speak to them as a group before they encounter members of the media."

"I'll tell my staff to gather everyone in Shakespeare's Theater."

Jane sent a text to the department heads, explaining the situation. They replied within seconds, and she was humbled to work beside such capable individuals.

The sheriff put a hand on Chief Aroneo's shoulder. "You must be ready to get back to the station. What do you need from me?"

The chief tapped his drawing. "I'd like to take the tank and grill with me. I won't know if this was arson without a thorough investigation. I can share our photos of the scene with you."

"Good. Deputy Phelps examined the garage where the grills were stored. No sign of a break-in." The sheriff looked at Jane. "I need to know who had access to those grills from the time Mr. Gilmore finished his safety check to the time the chefs started using them."

Jane pictured the terrace as it had been that morning. "Everything was ready when I walked over from my house, so I don't know who moved what where. I'll ask Sterling to view the security footage, but I doubt it'll help. The terrace camera focuses on the entry door."

"Is there a camera near the garage?"

"No. That garage was used for landscaping equipment before we lent it to the film company."

The sheriff's phone buzzed, and he squinted at the text bubble on his screen. "It's Doc Lydgate. He says that Mr. Gilmore has flash burns, which are caused by gas or propane. Most of them are first-degree, but he also has superficial second-degree burns on his arms. Mr. Gilmore is awake, and his pain is being managed. He wants to thank everyone who came to his aid."

Chief Aroneo stood up. "Tell the doc that I'm coming to see Mr. Gilmore. I'll let you know if he can shed any light on what happened today."

The chief left, and Sheriff Evans helped himself to finger sandwiches. "I hope you don't mind if I eat and talk. Breakfast feels like a lifetime ago."

"Please go ahead," said Jane. "It'll make Mrs. Hubbard happy."

The sheriff devoured two sandwiches before reaching for a third. In between bites, he said, "Levi Anjou didn't kill Chef Pierce. He was with Ms. Kennedy, in her guest room, from eleven o'clock at night until six o'clock the morning Chef Pierce's body was discovered. The couple posted a video, which I didn't mention to you because I didn't know if it was genuine. It took time to be sure that it was. Mr. Anjou and Ms. Kennedy are both in the clear."

"I see."

Sheriff Evans gave her a quizzical look. "Did you know about their affair?"

"I had my suspicions. A writer named Olivia Limoges is renting one of our cottages. She was taking an early morning walk when she came across Levi and Coco at the folly. Based on what she saw, she thought they were a couple."

The sheriff wrote Olivia's name in his notepad. "Could she have entered the manor house at that time?"

"Yes. Her key opens all the doors accessible to guests. But if she had come in, Sterling would have spotted her on the security footage."

"And she has no connection to the television show?"

"Actually, she does." An image of Butterworth interrogating the writer-in-residence momentarily distracted Jane, but she cleared her head with a shake and said, "She owns a restaurant in North Carolina. Chef Michel works for her."

The sheriff sat up straighter, and there was a gleam in his eyes. He looked like a bloodhound picking up a fresh scent trail.

Jane was torn over the idea of Olivia becoming a suspect. Though she liked the writer and was grateful to her for helping Mr. Gilmore, Olivia wasn't a friend. She was a guest. A stranger.

Sheriff Evans consulted his phone. "It's about that time, isn't it?"

"Yes," Jane agreed.

She and the sheriff heard the swell of anxious chatter coming from inside Shakespeare's Theater long before they entered the room. It was only when the sheriff mounted the stage and approached the podium that people began to quiet down.

Butterworth performed a quick mic check before moving aside to join Deputies Phelps and Emory.

Stepping up to the podium, the sheriff surveyed the crowd. "Ladies and gentlemen, thank you for your cooperation. I'm Sheriff Evans. With me are Deputy Phelps and Deputy Emory. We're working in conjunction with the Storyton Fire Department to determine how this morning's fire came to pass. As many of you know, Ronald Gilmore, the fire safety advisor, was injured by the blast. He's being treated as we speak, and while I won't discuss his injuries, I can assure you that he's receiving excellent care."

A woman in the third row began to cry. Others looked at her in surprise, but the man sitting beside her put an arm around her shoulders and drew her close. The woman rested her head on the man's chest as he whispered to her and stroked her hair.

Watching the couple, Jane thought of how lucky she was to have a man who offered her unconditional love, comfort, and support. While she'd been dealing with the aftermath of the explosion, Edwin had been taking care of the twins. He'd sent Jane several texts to let her know that Fitz and Hem were safe and happily occupied.

After breakfast, Edwin had driven the boys and their jam jars to his restaurant. Edwin worked the lunch service while the twins created signage for their festival booth. After that, Edwin took them to Hilltop Stables and led them on a trail ride from the stables to Storyton Hall. The twins dismounted at the edge of the archery field while Edwin returned the horses and headed back to the village to prepare for the dinner service.

Having read Edwin's latest texts as she and Sheriff Evans walked from the kitchen to the theater, Jane expected Fitz and Hem to arrive home shortly.

They're dirty, tired, hungry, and thirsty. They should sleep well tonight, Edwin had written.

Scanning the faces of her guests, Jane wondered if they'd all sleep well that night. Would fear keep some of them awake? Or guilt? The explosion could have hurt innocent people. Uncle Aloysius and Aunt Octavia could have been killed. The thought made Jane's blood boil.

Onstage, the sheriff explained that the fire wasn't his only reason for being at Storyton Hall because his department was also investigating Chef Pierce's death. This announcement was met by gasps and exclamations of shock.

"It wasn't an accident?" someone shouted.

Before the sheriff could respond, another person yelled, "Did someone kill him?"

The sheriff held out his hands, silently demanding quiet.

Jane was surveying the faces in the crowd with such intensity that she didn't hear Sinclair sidle up beside her.

Leaning over, he whispered, "There's an urgent message on your phone."

Without a word, Jane slipped out through the staff exit and looked at her phone. She'd received a text from an unknown number.

This is Olivia Limoges. Your sons are in my cottage. Two men were harassing them. One was asking questions while the other was filming them. The men got very pushy, so I intervened. They're still outside.

After replying that she was on her way, Jane ran down the hall toward the loading dock. She didn't give a second's thought about leaving in the middle of the sheriff's address. Her role as a mother would always be more important than her role as the manager of Storyton Hall.

A pickup truck driven by one of the groundskeepers

was idling at the loading dock. The man was about to pull away when Jane shouted at him to stop.

"Can you get me to the staff cottages fast?" she said, climbing into the passenger seat. "My sons are in trouble."

The man pressed the gas pedal and the truck shot forward in a shower of gravel.

When they reached the path leading to Olivia's cottage, Jane said, "I'll get out here. I want to take these unwelcome visitors by surprise."

The groundskeeper put the truck in park, grabbed a pair of anvil loppers from behind his seat, and followed his employer.

Two men in their twenties wearing skinny jeans and faded T-shirts stood in front of the cottage. The man in a green shirt was using a phone to film a man in a blue shirt. Both men looked completely at ease, as if they had the right to be there.

Eager to show them just how wrong they were, Jane crept up behind Green Shirt. Before he had time to register her presence, Jane executed a front snap kick. Her foot struck his phone, sending it flying into the grass ten feet away.

Green Shirt shouted, "What the—?"

The rest of his sentence dissolved into a shriek as he watched the groundskeeper cut the phone in half with his loppers.

Now, Blue Shirt brandished his phone. "I'm going to live stream this. Are you ready for a lawsuit, you crazy—"

A black shape raced past Blue Shirt, and he was left gripping empty air instead of a phone.

He stared down at his hand, his face turning crimson with fury. But when he opened his mouth to vent his rage, Jane held up a finger.

"Not another word!" she commanded. Then, she pointed at Captain Haviland, who was sitting on his haunches just beyond Blue Shirt's line of vision. "You have five minutes to get off my property or that dog will remove one of your body parts. I wonder which bit he'd bite off first?"

Jane advanced on the young men. "How dare you harass my sons? How dare you *film* them? *My sons*. Who. Are. Minors. Do you know how lucky you are that a pair of phones are all you've lost? If I ever see you in Storyton again, you'll lose far more than that."

The groundskeeper opened and closed his loppers, emphasizing Jane's point.

"You'd better start running." Jane looked at her watch. "In five minutes, that dog will be coming for you. Tick tock."

The young men ran.

"I'll make sure they leave." The groundskeeper hurried off before Jane could thank him.

The door to the cottage opened. Olivia stepped out and whistled for her poodle. Captain Haviland bounded up the stairs, tail wagging, to receive praise from his owner. He then trotted into the cottage and was immediately greeted with exuberant cries of, "Good Haviland! Good dog!"

Smiling at Jane, Olivia said, "You look like you could use a drink."

Jane smiled back. "Or two. Care to join me?"

Chapter 12

Jane had never invited a guest to her home before. Then again, a guest had never stopped her sons from being harassed before.

"Can Captain Haviland come too?" pleaded Fitz.

Hem clasped his hands. "Please, Mom?"

"If it's okay with Ms. Olivia, it's okay with me."

Olivia replied that she always preferred that her best friend went wherever she went. The boys smiled and scratched behind the poodle's ears and patted him on the back.

"Can we give him a treat?" Hem asked Olivia. "For saving the day?"

Hearing the word "treat," Haviland's nose quivered and he glanced left and right, hoping something tasty was on offer.

"Why don't I bring a bag of favorites to your house and you can reward him there?" Olivia suggested.

Haviland watched her slide his chicken and apple sausage dog treats and a bottle of Chivas Regal into a padded tote. He kept his eyes trained on the bag as everyone filed out of the cottage. But the moment the boys started across the grass, calling Haviland's name as they picked up speed, the poodle forgot about the treats and looked to Olivia for permission.

She whispered, "Go on," and he was off like a shot, barking with joy as he raced alongside Fitz and Hem.

"I could use some of that energy," Jane said.

She was hot, thirsty, and emotionally drained. She needed to kick off her shoes and pour herself a generous measure of chilled prosecco.

Jane popped the cork on a fresh bottle and offered Olivia her pick of glasses. The twins washed their hands, grabbed water bottles from the fridge, and went to the living room to feed Haviland and watch an episode of their anime show.

The two women carried their drinks to the kitchen table.

Raising her stemless champagne flute, Jane said, "Thanks for looking out for my sons."

Olivia knocked her glass against Jane's and took a sip of scotch whiskey.

"I also want to thank you for helping Mr. Gilmore," Jane went on. "Are you getting any writing done in the face of all this altruism?"

Olivia laughed. "To my surprise, I am. There's freedom in anonymity. No one knows me here. Except Michel. And he's too wrapped up in this competition to give me much thought. It's oddly relaxing to be a stranger in an unfamiliar place. My words are flowing again."

Jane got up and rooted through the pantry for a suitable snack. She found a can of mixed nuts and dumped the contents into a bowl. She put the bowl and a plate of cheese straws on the table.

"What about you?" Olivia asked, reaching for the nuts.

"It must be hard to concentrate on everyday tasks after the death of a guest."

Jane took a swallow of prosecco and said, "Honestly, I should be calling the sheriff right now. I should explain why I ran off while he was speaking to a theater full of guests. And I will. Eventually." She watched the shifting bubbles in her glass. "From the moment this cooking competition started, every day's felt a hundred hours long."

Olivia rolled a macadamia nut around on her palm. "That's the ripple effect of violence. This is your resort, and you feel responsible for everyone here. If something goes wrong, you'd move mountains to make it right. But with violence, you can't really make things right. Justice is the best you can hope for."

Jane gave her a sharp look. "What makes you think I'm dealing with violence?"

"A fire close to the competition tent, the sudden death of a chef, and an explosion during a challenge can't be coincidence." Olivia traced a line in the condensation fogging her glass. "My husband was a police chief. He used to tell me about some of his cases. He knew I could listen to heartbreaking or gruesome details without falling apart, because violence has always been a part of my life."

Her admission struck a chord with Jane. "Same here. I wonder if people like us are drawn to each other."

Olivia considered this. "Perhaps. You remind me of my husband in some ways. Sawyer was fiercely loyal and protective. He died in the line of duty. He gave his life to save two women. I was one of them. Michel's pregnant wife was the other."

There was a clicking of nails on hardwood as Haviland entered the kitchen. The poodle walked over to Olivia and put his head in her lap. She stroked the back of his neck and told him that everything was okay. He stared up at her with his warm, expressive eyes until she mustered a smile for him. Only then did he lay down at her feet.

"I'm so sorry," said Jane, caught between sorrow for Olivia's loss and amazement over her connection to her dog.

"Michel and Shelley named their son after my husband. I'm the boy's godmother. They're my family, and when I learned that Michel could have died today, and that it was his grill that blew up, I got very upset." Olivia's blue eyes turned cold. "Tell me the truth. Is Michel being targeted?"

Olivia's intensity didn't bother Jane. The woman had every reason to fear for her friend's safety.

"I don't know if Chef Michel was singled out or who had the opportunity to tamper with his grill. Mr. Gilmore tested and inspected every grill right before the competition. Our fire chief went to the hospital to question him. The chief will also examine the damaged grill."

"What do you expect him to find?"

Jane answered honestly. "Evidence of arson. Chef Pierce's death was no accident. Neither was the fire in the field. Someone is desperate for the show to fail."

"Are you pulling the plug?"

"I probably have a dozen emails and voicemails reminding me of the terms of my contract with the production company. But even if I'm sued for breach of contract, the show's over."

Olivia frowned. "It's a difficult situation. If the chefs don't finish the challenges, there won't be a winner and they'll have come here for nothing. If the competition continues, someone else might die. Either way, the villain is in control."

"No matter what, everyone involved will lose something. Time, money, reputation—but it's better than risking another person's life. Only an arrest could save the competition, and Sheriff Evans isn't close to making one. He's asked the guests for their help, but I doubt that'll lead to much."

A pair of ice cubes rattled around the bottom of Olivia's glass as she turned it in her hand. "Dumas once said that all of human wisdom can be found in two words: wait and hope. I've never been good at waiting. Or banking on hope. I want the lowlife committing these crimes to face justice, so if I can help by cozying up to certain guests or using Haviland to scare off more journalists, just say the word."

"You might withdraw that offer after Sheriff Evans comes knocking," Jane said. "I inadvertently added your name to his persons-of-interest list when I told him that you saw Levi and Coco the morning of Chef Pierce's death."

"I'm not worried. After all, I survived Mr. Butterworth's interrogation," Olivia said, her eyes shining with humor.

Jane's cheeks grew warm. "I guess he wasn't very subtle."

Olivia laughed. "He tried to analyze my every blink, twitch, and pause. By the end of our conversation, he gave up on that stuff and was *almost* friendly."

"You must have made quite an impression. Butterworth is as approachable as a porcupine."

Olivia's smile lit up her face, and Jane was struck by her beauty. "The older I get, the more I'm attracted to people who are unapologetically themselves. I guess that makes me a fan of porcupines."

Haviland stood up, stretched, and padded across the room. Suddenly, his ears pricked and he glanced over his shoulder, waiting to make eye contact with Olivia. When she looked at him, he issued a muffled bark.

"You're about to have company," Olivia said.

Jane hoped not. The only person she'd be happy to see right now was Edwin, and he was working the dinner service at Daily Bread.

Excusing herself, Jane peeked out the window just as Mia Mallett pushed open the garden gate. Jane felt a surge of annoyance. The sign on her gate reading, NO ADMITTANCE PRIVATE PROPERTY, was there for a reason. Jane's home was off-limits to guests. She'd made an exception for Olivia Limoges, but Mia didn't warrant the same treatment.

Olivia shouldered her tote bag and put her glass in the sink. Jane walked her to the front door where Olivia took hold of Haviland's collar and said, "Thanks for having us over. Your home is warm and welcoming. Please call me if I can help in any way."

When Olivia opened the door, Mia started in surprise. "Ms. Limoges. What brings you here?"

"I was invited. I would never invade Ms. Steward's privacy otherwise." Olivia shot Mia a loaded look before breezing down the stairs.

Jane crossed her arms over her chest and waited for an explanation.

"I'm sorry to bother you." Mia tried to sound contrite but failed. "I've been trying to reach you for ages. None of your staff could tell me where you'd gone, so I thought I'd try you at home."

Jane glared down at Mia. "Unless you came to tell me how that propane tank exploded, whatever you have to say can wait until tomorrow. I'm not on the clock. Good night."

Mia raised both hands. "Wait! I wanted to warn you that the bigwigs from Cook's Pride are threatening legal action if the filming is delayed or canceled. The CEO is already on a plane. He'll be in Storyton tomorrow with a team of lawyers."

"You heard Sheriff Evans. The competition is on hold. Indefinitely."

"The sheriff might not realize that there've been accidents—even fatalities—on set before. Stuntmen. Actors. Crewmembers. It's awful, but it happens. That's why the sponsors don't see Chef Pierce's death as a reason to cancel. The show's a major investment for Cook's Pride. Every day we don't film, the production company loses money and Cook's Pride loses faith."

Jane listened to Mia, growing more and more angry with every word. "What about Mr. Gilmore? Or the employees of Chef Pierce's restaurant? What about their losses?"

"The Epitome employees will be fine. I already talked to my lawyers about becoming a silent investor. The restaurant will close for a full reno and the staff will have paid leave. When Epitome reopens, it'll have a fresh look, reenergized employees, and my financial backing."

Though Jane was glad to hear this, she wasn't going to let it show. She was ready to go inside and pour another glass of prosecco.

Tears glittered in Mia's eyes. "I'm sorry that Chef Pierce died, and that Mr. Gilmore was hurt. I'll make sure he gets the best possible treatment and see that he's compensated for the risk he took trying to save us. My lawyers are taking care of that too."

"There hasn't been a moment's peace since the film crew arrived," Jane said. "None of this is your fault, but it's my job to protect Storyton Hall guests, including you. Someone wants to destroy the chefs or your show— I don't know which—and that should scare you as much as it scares me."

Mia spun her tiger eye ring around and around. "I *am*

scared. And I don't want more bad things to happen, but I also don't want the chefs to have made it this far for nothing. They left their jobs and their families to compete. Even if I paid them for their time, it wouldn't make up for the exposure the show would give them. Past winners have ended up with amazing careers. They own multiple restaurants, host TV shows, become the faces on new product lines, and write bestselling cookbooks. This show will change the winner's life, but every contestant will receive offers just by appearing."

"If the show is that important to the contestants, why not film it after the sheriff's investigation is over? In another location?"

Tears rolled down Mia's shell-smooth cheeks. "No network will touch the show if we do that. It'll be finished. I can always focus on other projects, but the chefs won't get a second chance to show their talents to the world. They'll be the chefs from the canceled season, which won't be good for their reputations."

Jane felt genuinely sorry for the chefs, but she wouldn't allow the filming to continue.

Sensing defeat, Mia hung her head and said, "I'd better go. I want to talk to my team about treating the chefs to a meal in the village tomorrow. I'm hoping some good food and a walk around the berry festival will distract them from the mess we're all in."

"I'll see you there. My sons will be selling their jam at the Storyton Hall booth."

Mia smiled. "Really? That's how I got started. When I was a kid, I loaded my red wagon with jam and hit the streets. I had so many customers that I recruited my cousin to help out. Eventually, we added cookies and pound cake to the menu."

"Impressive."

"Except for the name." Mia grimaced and started fiddling with her ring again. "Mia's Munchies? My cousin teased me about it for years."

Seeing the bereft look on Mia's face, Jane said that it was a cute name for a little girl's business.

"Mom!" Fitz shouted from upstairs. "When's dinner?"

"That's my cue," said Jane.

This time, Mia didn't object. She wiped the tears from her cheeks and turned away. With her downcast gaze and sluggish movements, she seemed utterly deflated.

It hasn't been a good day for anyone, Jane thought.

In the kitchen, she examined the contents of her refrigerator and considered having cereal for dinner. But her sons deserved better. Knowing they'd help with the cooking, Jane lined up the ingredients for a quick, hearty meal.

After putting a pan of water on the cooktop to boil, she called her sons.

Fitz and Hem gave her baffled stares when they didn't see plates of food waiting to be carried to the table. What they saw instead was a box of uncooked linguini, a block of Parmesan cheese, and a bag of frozen peas on the counter.

"Are we cooking?" Hem asked.

"Put your aprons on, Chefs," Jane said. "The Steward Family restaurant is serving Italian tonight. Decide who'll cook the linguini and who'll grate the cheese. I'll pop the peas in the microwave and melt butter with garlic and parsley to mix with our pasta."

After a round of Rock, Paper, Scissors, the boys headed

to their stations. Jane showed Fitz how to use the grater and gave Hem tips on cooking pasta. Fifteen minutes later, their meal was ready.

"Thanks for helping," Jane said. "Why don't we eat in the living room? We can watch *A Series of Unfortunate Events*."

Later, after they'd eaten, Hem said, "Restaurant night is cool."

Fitz gave Jane a quick hug. "Yeah. Thanks, Mom."

And just like that, Jane felt like she could do anything. She could cook dinner. She could make her sons happy. She could handle the CEO of Cook's Pride and his team of lawyers. She could even catch a killer.

Edwin had had a late night at Daily Bread, but he still called the next morning and invited Jane and the boys for a late breakfast at the restaurant.

When they arrived, Edwin beckoned Fitz and Hem into his commercial kitchen and said, "You'll need lots of energy to sell your jam, so pile on the eggs and bacon."

Jane laughed. "No need to tell *them* twice."

"And for you, my love, I have cappuccino and a bowl with yogurt, berries, and granola."

"But first, a hug."

Jane wrapped her arms around Edwin and held him tight.

"I missed you yesterday," she whispered.

He brushed her forehead with his lips. "After today's lunch service, I'm all yours. I won't let you go through this alone. I can intimidate that pretty boy director, rub your feet, or hang out with the boys. Whatever you need."

"I don't know how I ever managed without you. What

we have isn't exactly traditional, but it works, and I love us," Jane said.

After a long and tender kiss, Edwin said, "I love us too."

Thirty minutes later, Fitz and Hem had eaten their fill and were eager to set up their jam display. They loaded their crates into a Storyton Hall pickup truck while Jane and Edwin lingered in the kitchen.

As she enjoyed her second cappuccino, Jane told Edwin about the impending arrival of the CEO and his lawyers.

"That should keep those prats from the press from bothering you," Edwin said.

"I take it you didn't enjoy having them in your restaurant last night?"

Edwin glowered. "I told Magnus that it's high time we establish our own technology restrictions. Some people have no idea how to behave in public." He gestured at the door leading to the dining room. "Our tranquil atmosphere was obliterated yesterday. Those media people had so many gadgets on their tables that I had to clear away the candles and flowers to make room for their food. They barked into their phones and shouted at each other across the room. And the more they drank, the louder they got. I felt like I was in a grade school cafeteria."

Jane sighed. "And now they're combing the village in search of a scoop. I should have worn a disguise."

"You could be the Berry Jubilee mascot. No one can tell who's inside that giant strawberry head."

"No, thanks. I'd get claustrophobic wearing that thing. I think the Hogg brothers take turns being the mascot," Jane said, referring to the three siblings who owned the village grocery store. "Last year, the boys were positive it was Rufus because he has such big feet."

Edwin carried their coffee mugs to the sink. "The

mystery of the mascot will have to take a back seat to yours. What can I do to help?"

"If Mia brings the chefs in for lunch, eavesdrop as much as you can. Other than that, let's steal an hour for ourselves this morning. I don't want to be the manager of Storyton Hall right now. I just want to be a woman named Jane who loves a man named Edwin."

Edwin bowed over her hand. "My dear lady, would you do me the greatest honor by accompanying me to the festival of the berry?"

"Only if you kiss me before we go."

With a rakish smile, Edwin pulled Jane to her feet. "I live to serve."

Later, after her sons had finished arranging their jam, Jane declared that the Storyton Hall booth was the most colorful, fun, and fragrant booth of the whole festival. In addition to her sons' jam, there were berry-scented soaps, lotions, and bath salts from the Walt Whitman Spa. Seasonal items from Storyton Hall's gift shop were also on display. These included Milton's Gardens tea towels, tote bags, notecards, and candles.

The two spa staff members operating the booth volunteered to give the twins some pointers, so Jane wished them all luck and promised to stop back in an hour.

"We might be sold out by then," Hem said.

"Fingers crossed," said Jane.

She and Edwin held hands as they joined the crowd of locals and visitors surveying the booths lining both sides of Main Street.

The festival attracted vendors from all over Virginia, North Carolina, and Tennessee. When it came to homemade jam, the twins had plenty of competition, but foodstuff weren't the only items on offer.

Artisans sold wood carvings, pottery, landscape paintings, and stained-glass suncatchers. Other vendors made items exclusively for children. One booth specialized in Berry Princess tutus and straw farmer hats while another offered hand-carved tractors and farm animals. Children lined up to have their faces painted and their hair braided. They asked for temporary tattoos and berry lemonade, hot dogs and berry cotton candy.

"Aren't you glad your sons are on the selling side of a booth today?" Edwin asked.

"I'm really proud of them, but just because they want to earn money doesn't mean they won't eat their weight in mixed berry pie, raspberry cupcakes, triple berry smoothies, blackberry ice cream, and strawberry shortcake."

Edwin shrugged. "They'll have to decide what they want more. Tasty treats or a video game system."

"I just hope they sell a few jars. I think their jam's delicious, but I'm biased."

Jane paused at the next booth to admire a teapot-shaped cutting board. It would be right at home in Mrs. Hubbard's kitchen. Then, she saw a cutting board shaped like an open book. A surname was stamped into the wood followed by the words *Our Story Began On* followed by the date.

What a perfect gift for Eloise, Jane thought.

As she looked around the booth, she saw cutting boards for all the Cover Girls. She even saw a standard poodle–shaped board that she could give Olivia Limoges as a token of gratitude.

"Are you having trouble deciding, ma'am?" the vendor asked.

Jane smiled at the young man. "I know which boards I want. I'm just not sure how to get them all to the car."

Edwin volunteered to be her packhorse, and once all

the boards were cushioned in a layer of bubble wrap and stacked in a box, he headed to where the pickup was parked. Jane thanked the vendor and exited the booth, feeling a thrill of anticipatory delight. She knew her gifts would make other people happy, and this filled Jane with joy.

Her elation vanished the moment she bumped into Sheriff Evans.

He touched the brim of his hat in greeting. "Ms. Steward, your sons are born salesmen. I stopped by the Storyton Hall booth to see you and was coaxed into trying a bite of jam. It was so good that I decided to buy a jar. Somehow, I ended up with six jars." He shook his head in wonder. "At this rate, they'll sell out by noon."

Jane apologized for rushing out of the theater the day before. "Fitz and Hem were being harassed by two journalists," she explained. "I don't know how they got on the property, but they were filming my sons and badgering them with questions."

The sheriff held up his hand. "You have nothing to apologize for. Ms. Limoges told me about the incident when I spoke with her earlier. If those young men hadn't left town yesterday, I would have invited them to spend a little time at the station."

"I'm just glad they're gone," said Jane. "Did Ms. Limoges tell you everything you wanted to know?"

"She did." The sheriff's eyes scanned the crowd. "She's still a person of interest, and I told her as much. Didn't seem to bother her one bit."

As much as Jane admired Olivia, she wanted to talk about something else. "Journalists and festivalgoers aren't the only people visiting Storyton today. Last night, Mia stopped by my house to tell me—"

She was unable to finish her sentence because Mrs.

Pratt suddenly emerged from the crowd, shouting for the sheriff.

"Thank goodness I found you!" she cried. "There's a shoplifter on the loose!"

"Something was stolen from a booth?" the sheriff asked.

Mrs. Pratt stared at him as if he'd lost his mind. "I'm not talking about a pint of berries, Sheriff! The thief took antiques. *Valuable* antiques. From Roger's shop!"

Chapter 13

Mrs. Pratt was too distraught to wait for the sheriff's reaction. Having delivered her news, she turned and pushed her way through the throng, no doubt returning to the scene of the crime.

Sheriff Evans made a quick call to his dispatch officer and followed Mrs. Pratt at a less frantic pace.

Jane scanned the sidewalk in front of the Daily Bread. She couldn't see Edwin but hurried to catch up with the sheriff anyway. Edwin would forgive her for not waiting, especially if what Mrs. Pratt said was true.

Several months ago, Roger Bachman had converted the former bicycle sales and rental store into a treasure trove of antique and vintage items. The cabinets of the Old Curiosity Shop were stuffed with intriguing curios, and his new business had become the talk of the town.

A day before his official grand opening, Roger had invited the Cover Girls to a private viewing of his new business venture. Roger, a history professor from New York, had first come to Storyton Hall for a conference. When the conference was over, he'd been very reluctant to leave. Not only had he fallen for a feisty widow named Eugenia Pratt, but he'd also become enamored of the village and its residents. Though he was now a Storyton merchant as well as Mrs. Pratt's beau, Roger still taught two online classes for NYU. Because of this, many of the locals called him Professor.

The shops in Storyton looked like cottages from the British Cotswolds. Each two-story structure had a front garden surrounded by a picket fence. A flagstone path led customers through the garden gate to a painted front door. The Old Curiosity Shop's door was Antique Gold, a shade meant in inspire visions of priceless treasure.

"How can it be closed?" a woman whined as she peered through the front window. "I see people inside."

A second woman, who'd been admiring the bee balm, yarrow, coneflowers, and wild phlox in the garden, scurried over to her companion and tugged on her sleeve. "We'd better come back later, Doris."

Seeing Jane and the sheriff pass through the garden gate, Doris was even more interested. When Sheriff Evans reached the front door, she asked, "What's going on in there?"

"That's what I'm here to find out," Sheriff Evans replied with a deferential tip of his hat.

Doris and her companion retreated to the garden bench where they settled down to watch. With their upright posture and eager expressions, they looked like dogs waiting to be thrown a bone.

Mrs. Pratt yanked the door open before the sheriff had the chance to knock.

"Roger's on the phone with his insurance company," she said, waving Jane and the sheriff inside.

Jane put a hand on her friend's arm. "Are you okay? Did you see the theft?"

Mrs. Pratt's eyes blazed, and she pointed to where a

bronze urn with a marble base sat on the counter. "I wish I had! I would have clobbered the louse with that trophy."

Sheriff Evans took out his notepad. "Do you know what was taken?"

"Yes. The shelf cards for each item were left behind. I guess the thief—or thieves—didn't need a description. They knew what they were after."

Mrs. Pratt led the sheriff to a cabinet on the far side of the shop. Roger arranged the cabinets by theme and used elegant signs to identify each theme. The sign on this cabinet was decorated with cutlery and read THE ART OF FINE DINING.

Peering through the cabinet's massive glass doors, Jane could see a glittering assortment of sterling silver, porcelain, and crystal. The lower shelves were reserved for platters, decanters, punch bowls, and flatware sets. The middle shelves were reserved for oyster, salad, dinner, and dessert plates. Teapots and teacups came next. The final shelves held an eclectic array of salt cellars, butter dishes, crumb catchers, pastry cutters, knife rests, tongs, carving sets, and other serving utensils.

"The chocolate pot was taken," said Mrs. Pratt, indicating an empty spot on the teapot shelf. "It was a lovely thing too. French sterling. Eighteenth century. Had tiny feet and a wooden handle. The entire surface was embossed with an intricate floral design. Roger priced it at a thousand dollars. That's more than fair for a piece in excellent condition. You can read the full description on the shelf card."

"How big is a chocolate pot?" asked the sheriff.

"Too big to slip in a pocket." Mrs. Pratt showed him a teapot of a similar size. "The thief must have had a bag."

Considering a festival was taking place, hundreds of

people were carrying bags at this very moment. Handbags, paper bags, reusable grocery bags, etcetera.

"What about the security cameras?" Jane asked Mrs. Pratt.

"They were on and recording, and I hope they captured the thief in action. I haven't seen the footage because Roger didn't want to play it until Sheriff Evans arrived." Mrs. Pratt tapped the curio case positioned under the window. "The other item came from here."

The sheriff leaned over the case and studied its contents. "From that space in the middle?"

"Yes. I know it looks cluttered, but Roger says there isn't much profit in pillboxes. That's why he bought a collection of unusual boxes and stuffed them all in this case. I don't remember what the stolen box looks like, but I heard Roger describe it to the insurance agent as an art nouveau pillbox with a carved fish on the lid. Like the chocolate pot, it's made of sterling silver."

Jane read the price on the tiny card. "Three hundred dollars. That means the thief stole thirteen hundred dollars in merchandise."

"Which I might be paying for out of pocket," said Roger from behind the counter. "Considering my deductible and the hoops I have to jump through to prove the value of the items, I may not file a claim."

Moving to his side, Mrs. Pratt said, "I'm sorry, my dear."

Roger gave her hand a squeeze. "This won't be the first time I'll encounter this kind of shrinkage. It happens to the most eagle-eyed shopkeepers. Or so I've heard. I just hope it doesn't happen too often."

"Has the shop been busy since you opened this morning?" Jane asked.

"It's been a madhouse," Roger said with remarkable

cheer. When it dawned on him that the chaos had likely made it easier on the thief, his face fell.

"We should focus on the sales you made and on all the new customers you added to your mailing list." Mrs. Pratt gave her beau an encouraging smile. "A bad penny always turns up, so sooner or later, the thief will be caught."

Sheriff Evans, who'd been studying the angle of the two security cameras, turned to Roger and said, "Shoplifting is unacceptable. Our business owners work too hard for people to just help themselves to the merchandise. This behavior might not be unusual in New York City, but you're a Storyton citizen now, and I'd like to find this thief. Today, if possible. Can we take a look at what your cameras caught this morning?"

Roger and the sheriff disappeared into the stockroom while Jane examined the other pill boxes, hoping to understand what was special about the one the thief had chosen.

No two boxes were alike. Like the pilfered fish-shaped box, some were made of sterling. Others were made of enamel, celluloid, or gold. Most were two inches in diameter or smaller. They were all beautiful and delicate, and Jane could easily imagine an Austen or Brontë character carrying such an item in her reticule.

Her gaze fell on a box with a mother-of-pearl bird on the lid, which sat between an enamel box featuring a hunt scene and a silver box shaped like a terrier.

"They all have animal designs," she mused aloud.

Mrs. Pratt peered down at the case. "How darling is that kitten with the pink bow?"

Jane was puzzled. "I don't get it. That Tiffany pillbox with the chick standing on the egg is three times the cost of the stolen box."

"Maybe the thief really likes fish."

"And tea." Jane said. She quickly corrected herself. "Not tea. Hot chocolate."

Moving over to the large cabinet, Jane saw that the stolen chocolate pot had been one of two. The remaining pot was porcelain. Dainty pink flowers bloomed from its base and its domed silver lid was hand-chased with floral designs. If not for its shape, one might mistake it for an antique teapot. Jane read the shelf card detailing its age, condition, and price before turning back to Mrs. Pratt.

"This chocolate pot is worth more than the one taken by the thief. And its bone handle is removable, which would have made it easier to drop into a shopping bag or oversized purse." Jane reread the shelf card belonging to the missing pot. "Both of the stolen pieces were sterling silver. Is that significant?"

Mrs. Pratt looked grim. "Only if the thief plans to melt them down."

Jane hated the thought of such lovely pieces of history being rendered into lumps of metal. "I hope that's not the case."

"Me too. If so, the thief isn't very smart. Two gold pillboxes would be worth more than the two silver pieces they took."

"Then what's special about them? One was made in France. One was made in the US. They're not from the same time period or similar in style. Chocolate and pills. I don't see a connection."

An idea started to surface in Jane's brain but darted away again like a spooked fish.

"Looks like our thief is female," Sheriff Evans announced as he and Roger emerged from the stockroom.

Mrs. Pratt gasped. "What gave her away?"

Roger laid an image printed in black-and-white on the

counter. "I don't have a color printer, so this is the best we can do. See the customer with the sunhat? We think she came in for some *freetail* therapy."

"She kept her back to the security cameras at all times," the sheriff explained. "In a crowded shop, this would go unnoticed. She didn't rush. She examined several cabinets on her way to the case on the far end. I think she went for the pillbox first. It would have been the easier item to steal. When she got to the case with the chocolate pot, she put her shopping bag on the floor. She examined several items before returning them. Or so it seemed. When she bent down to retrieve her bag, the chocolate pot might have been dropped right in. We couldn't see her hands clearly because they were hidden by the long, loose sleeves of her blouse."

"A Bohemian thief," Mrs. Pratt grumbled.

Jane studied the grainy image of the woman. Her blouse hung over her hips and completely obscured her figure. Her dark jeans were unremarkable. She was of average height. If she removed her hat and changed her top after leaving Roger's shop, she'd be impossible to pick out of a crowd.

"What about her shoes?" Jane asked.

"They don't show up."

Mrs. Pratt jabbed a finger at the front door. "Do we go out there and start pulling off sunhats? Because I'll do that in a heartbeat. You can deputize me if need be."

Sheriff Evans gave her an indulgent smile. "I admire your gumption, Mrs. Pratt, but I doubt our thief is wandering around in her current attire. In the event she *is* that foolish, my team will handle it. I've sent them copies of this image and Deputy Emory is already searching for the suspect."

Mrs. Pratt didn't care for the sheriff's answer at all. "She's one deputy! There are hundreds of people walking around. I hope you're dusting for prints."

"I will, but I don't expect to find a clear set. Mr. Bachman explained that none of the cases lining the wall are locked because he wants his customers to be free to examine any item that catches their eye. Locked cases lead to fewer sales."

"That's right," said Roger. "The most valuable things are locked up in there." He gestured at the row of waist-high showcases that divided his checkout area from the rest of the shop. "I thought it was a good system. Until today."

Jane hated the note of dejection in Roger's voice. Walking over to a cabinet filled with desk accessories, she said, "It's still a good system. Take that inkwell shaped like a boar, for example. I want to tilt back his head and see where the ink was kept. I want to have a closer look at his eyes. Are they glass? And the card says that the piece is stamped on the bottom. Wouldn't serious buyers want to turn the piece over to look at that stamp?"

"I'd rather not change my ways because of one bad apple," Roger said. "I prefer to believe that most people are honest and leave it at that."

The sheriff stepped away to call the station. Jane heard him mention a latent fingerprint kit and, in a lower voice, something like "those damn reporters." Jane would have liked to continue listening in, but Mrs. Pratt was heading for the door.

Her eyes were on Roger as she said, "I'm going to walk around the festival. There's nothing I can do here, but I can put my Sherlockian powers of observation to work out there." As she reached for the handle, she glanced back at Jane. "You coming?"

Jane started forward. "Of course."

Before she made it to the door, her phone rang.

"Eugenia," she called. "Give me a second to tell Edwin what's going on. I ran off without a word."

Mrs. Pratt unlocked the deadbolt and whipped the door open. "I'm not waiting. Every minute I waste gives the thief more time to escape."

"I'll catch up," Jane promised.

But after reading Edwin's text, Jane knew she wouldn't be keeping her promise. Instead, she swung around and shouted, "Sheriff Evans!"

The sheriff, who'd been taking photos of the display case housing the pillboxes, lowered his phone and asked, "What's happened?"

"The chefs and the judges—they're all here, at the festival. They're having another competition."

Sheriff Evans growled, "*What?*"

Jane raised her phone and pointed at the screen. "Edwin's watching it right now. Lots of people are. Including a dozen journalists. And Sheriff, Ty Scott is there too. It looks like he's now in charge of the show."

Even if Edwin hadn't told Jane where the competition was taking place, she would have known where to go.

The festival's biggest tent had always been the hub for the Berry Bake-Off. Three long tables were arranged in a U, and each table featured entries in either the Cake, Pie, or Cookie category. The festival committee judged the entries throughout the morning, and awarded red, white, and blue ribbons in the afternoon with the help of Dew Drop, the Berry Jubilee mascot.

As Jane pushed her way into the tent, she didn't see any cakes, pies, or cookies. Two of the tables held camp stoves and the third was heaped with pantry items. The camp stoves divided the table into four cooking stations, all of which were covered with soiled mixing bowls, cutting boards, and utensils.

"And that's time! Put your hands up, please!" Mia exclaimed from a raised platform at the front of the tent. "What do you think, everyone? Was that exciting, or what?"

The crowd responded with boisterous cheers.

"Let's start with Chef August, who told us that his Berry Bake-Off dessert was inspired by *The Adventures of Huckleberry Finn*. Chef? What did you make?"

Chef August let out a whistle. "I swear, I've never made a dessert that fast!" He smiled and wiped his brow. "I'm a Southern boy, so when I saw those buttermilk biscuits in the pantry, I knew I had to make a huckleberry biscuit cobbler. I balanced the sweetness by adding lime juice to the cobbler and lime zest to the crème fraiche. I know my mama would love this dish, which means I did something right."

"Berry yummy." Mia winked at the camera and stepped over to Chef Alondra's station. "Chef Alondra picked *Blueberries for Sal* as the inspiration for her bookish berry dessert. How'd it go?"

Chef Alondra looked unhappy. "I'm disappointed with my plating. I made a blueberry dump cake, but there wasn't enough time for the cake to cool before I cut it, so it's not very neat. I literally had to dump it on the plate."

Jane couldn't see Chef Alondra's dish because she was

still working her way to the front of the tent. She assumed Sheriff Evans was right behind her, so when someone grabbed her arm, she stopped and turned around.

It wasn't the sheriff but one of Mia's assistants—the young man in the fedora.

"Mia wants you to know that she didn't plan this," he said. "But puh-lease let it play out. Pretty please with a cherry on top. It's the fastest challenge we've ever filmed, and she's almost done talking to Chef Lindsay. That only leaves Chef Michel and the judging, which will take like sixty seconds, I swear."

Despite herself, Jane asked, "Where's Chef Saffron?"

"She was going to be voted out at the end of the Secret Garden challenge, but the judges were busy running from a fireball, so they had to tell her at the beginning of today's challenge. She cried a little, but she's chill now. She's sitting near the judges. But listen!" The urgency returned to his voice. "Levi and Coco have been tasting the dishes the whole time Mia's been talking to the chefs. She'll announce the winner as soon as Chef Michel finishes presenting his dish, so let her finish, okay?"

At the front of the tent, Mia was pointing to where the judges sat at a table near the podium.

"Lois Lenski's *Strawberry Girl* won the Newbery Medal in 1946," Mia said. "It was one of the first chapter books Coco Kennedy read. Chef Michel, how did the berries in this book inspire your dessert?"

"My wife's favorite dessert is fresh strawberries and cream, which is why I made Strawberries Romanoff. The cream sauce is a blend of brown sugar, sour cream, and lemon juice and I topped the cream and strawberry slices with a toasted pistachio crumble."

Mia smiled at Chef Michel. "Sounds like a berry perfect pairing for a hot summer's day."

"Are we cool?" Mia's assistant released Jane's arm.

Jane saw no point in causing a scene. Mia had already walked over to the judges' table and there was no sign of the sheriff.

Scanning the crowd, Jane finally spotted him standing next to Ty Scott.

Ty made a hurry-up gesture at Mia, and she responded by shoving the mic into Levi's hand.

"If Mia didn't plan this, then who did?" Jane hissed at the young man.

Adopting a blank expression that didn't fool Jane for a second, he said, "Honey, I do hair and makeup. That intel is way above my pay grade."

Distracted by a burst of applause, Jane glanced back at the chefs just as Chef Lindsay's face broke into a delighted smile. A moment later, Coco Kennedy mournfully announced that it was the end of the line for Chef Alondra.

"Despite the bright flavors of your dump cake, we couldn't get past the mushy consistency," Levi said. "But you're an incredible chef, and we know you'll continue to make incredible food."

After thanking Mia and the judges for the opportunity to compete, Chef Alondra exchanged hugs with the other chefs. Chef Lindsay and Chef August started crying when Chef Alondra removed her apron.

Mia thanked the audience and the festival committee. She held the mic while the lights and cameras were switched off and then said, "And now, it's time to announce the Berry Jubilee Bake-Off winners. I'm going to turn things over to your festival chairwoman, Kathy Holmes, but before I go, I want to congratulate all the home bakers.

It takes courage to let other people judge your creations, and even if you don't win today, keep making food from the heart. You'll always be a blue-ribbon winner to your family and friends."

The audience gave Mia another round of applause, and she passed the microphone to Kathy.

"Wow!" Kathy's booming voice reverberated through the tent. "Just think! We'll be able to experience this amazing event again when the next season of *Posh Palate with Mia Mallett* airs. And who knows? One day, a cook from Storyton might compete on the show!"

The crowd shouted in approval. A man whistled right in Jane's ear as she worked her way over to where Sheriff Evans stood glaring at Ty Scott.

Ty said something Jane didn't catch, but she definitely heard the sheriff's reply.

"I *will* cuff you and escort you from this tent in front of all these people. I told you to report to the station this morning. That was an order, not a request, and you ignored it." The sheriff's eyes were hard and unyielding, and when he took a step closer to Ty, the director took a step back.

"Come on, Sheriff. It's all good. We showed your town a great time. How about a little gratitude?"

Sheriff Evans signaled to someone and Deputy Phelps began heading their way.

Ty raised his hands in surrender. "Okay, okay. I'll come with you. Hey, Randy! Watch my camera. Hurry up, man!"

When Ty turned to gesture at a crewmember, he saw Jane. Believing he'd found an ally, he said, "Jane. I'm so glad you're here. You need to convince Johnny Law to let us finish what we came here to do. What's one more episode? Everything's cool. The bad streak's broken, so just let us finish and we'll get out of your hair. You get paid. A chef's dreams come true. It'll be a happy ending. Don't you book people love happy endings?"

Deputy Phelps pushed past Jane. "Excuse me, Ms. Steward," he said before clamping a hand on Ty's arm.

The sheriff took hold of Ty's other arm. "Start walking, Mr. Scott."

As she watched Ty being led out of the tent, Jane considered what to do next. She wanted to find Edwin. She wanted to check on the twins. And she also wanted to help Mrs. Pratt search for the woman in the white blouse.

At the front, Kathy was still speaking. Jane heard her say, "So without further ado, Dew Drop, our Berry Jubilee mascot, will bring in the blue ribbons!"

The mascot skipped into the tent, his strawberry-shaped head bobbing as he moved. His cartoonish face with its wide smile, blush cheeks, and round, sky-blue eyes, seemed to take in the whole crowd. Dew Drop waved a green, leaf-shaped hand as he made his way to the microphone. He stopped a few feet away from Jane to exchange high-fives with a little girl in a raspberry print dress, giving Jane a good look at the back of his T-shirt.

Unlike the front of his shirt, which spelled out his name in a curly font, the words on the back had been written in black marker. They were sloppy and uneven as if done in haste.

Perplexed, Jane muttered the message aloud, "'Cook's Pride Supports Slave Labor.'"

Dew Drop danced to the front, unaware of the murmurs of shock rippling through the crowd. People pointed at the mascot and took photos of his shirt.

And then, a voice cut through the noise. "You! Strawberry head! *Stop right there!*"

Everyone turned toward a man in a business suit. He

stood with two other men and a woman. All three wore power suits and carried briefcases.

Suddenly, a hand closed around Jane's wrist.

"Time to go," said Edwin. "There's nothing more terrifying than a quarrel of lawyers."

Right before Jane slipped out through the exit reserved for festival committee members, she glanced back at the CEO and his attorneys. All four radiated hostility. Their clenched jaws, disapproving scowls, and stiff bearing made it clear that they'd come to Storyton to pick a fight.

But whoever had written that message on Dew Drop's shirt had already landed a blow, and it was a real sucker punch.

Chapter 14

"Are the boys still at the booth?" Jane asked after they emerged into the open air.

"Yes," said Edwin. "They sold all their jam and are now peddling bath salts and soap. I've never seen such natural-born salesmen."

Jane squeezed Edwin's hand. "I want to take them home. Reporters are one thing, but a combative CEO, his lawyers, and a vandalized mascot have been added to the mix. On top of that, Mrs. Pratt's running around the festival in search of a thief."

"Was something taken from Roger's shop?"

Jane told Edwin about the robbery as they made their way to the Storyton Hall booth.

"Mrs. Pratt is wasting her time. As an expert thief, I can tell you that our lady shoplifter has either changed her clothes or is miles from Storyton by now."

Jane smirked. It had been weeks since she'd thought about Edwin's secret life as a Templar and a book thief. She'd been too happy to have him around to dwell on his previous absences. For the last two months, he hadn't disappeared in the middle of the night to fulfill a mission for his order. There were no trips abroad. No postcards from exotic locales. Instead, he'd been trying out new dishes for Daily Bread and spending all of his free time with Jane and the boys. It had been bliss.

Despite Edwin's insistence that he was a modern-day Robin Hood, Jane could never quite come to terms with the Templar practice of stealing rare books, manuscripts, or documents from an individual with the aim of returning them to their original owner. Even if the original owner was often a university, library, or museum, Jane didn't believe the Templars were truly motivated by altruism. She suspected that huge sums of money or political favors were exchanged each time a precious artifact was recovered.

Edwin wasn't motivated by money or power. It was the books he cared about, and he believed that he was reclaiming them for the good of mankind. He'd been a young man when he became a Templar and having sworn an oath to the order, he'd never break it.

As the Guardian of Storyton Hall, Jane understood the gravity of such an oath. Never in her wildest dreams did she imagine she'd fall in love with a book thief pretending to be a travel writer and restaurateur, but she had. And though Edwin's secret life made their relationship more complicated, Jane could handle complicated.

"If the boys hear about Mrs. Pratt's quest, they'll never leave," she said.

There was no sign of the twins at the Storyton Hall booth.

The spa employees were nearly out of inventory. One of the young women thanked a customer for his purchase and turned to Jane. "Fitz and Hem went off with your friend. She seemed upset, and the twins said that it was okay for them to help her because she's in your book club. That was about five minutes ago."

MURDER IN THE COOKBOOK NOOK   193

"Thank you, Ainsley. Did you see which way they went?"

The young woman pointed, and Jane and Edwin hurried off.

They maneuvered through the crowd, skirting booths of merchandise and food, while the summer sun beat down on their heads. By the time they reached the Old Curiosity Shop, beads of sweat were glistening on Jane's forehead and her shirt was sticking to her back.

Mrs. Pratt was sprawled on the bench in the front garden. Eloise was sitting next to her, fanning her face with a paperback. Fitz and Hem had retreated to the stoop where they sat with their hands on their knees, watching the two women with worried eyes.

"Eugenia!" Jane cried, alarmed by Mrs. Pratt's wilted appearance.

"She's overheated," said Eloise.

Edwin told Jane he'd be right back and ran toward Daily Bread.

Jane pointed at the closed door. "We need to get her inside."

"We can't go in because the deputies are dusting for prints." Eloise put a hand on Mrs. Pratt's shoulder. "Can you make it to the bookstore, Eugenia?"

Mrs. Pratt nodded weakly and tried to stand, but she clearly needed assistance. Jane and Eloise each took hold of one of Mrs. Pratt's arms and heaved her to her feet. Slowly, the three women proceeded to the garden gate.

Edwin intercepted them before they reached the sidewalk. After handing Eloise a bag filled with water bottles, he scooped Mrs. Pratt into his arms.

"Oh, my," she murmured.

The twins took Eloise's keys and ran ahead to unlock the bookstore, so when the hot and sweaty assemblage finally made it to Run for Cover, the door was thrown open wide.

Edwin gently deposited Mrs. Pratt in a reading chair. He pressed a bottle of water in her hands and cajoled her in taking small sips while he removed her shoes. He raised her feet on a stool and told Eloise that he was going to run a dishcloth under cold water in the kitchen.

Mrs. Pratt watched him leave the room. "Jane, you're a lucky woman. Why not be Jane to Eloise's Elizabeth Bennet? You and Eloise are like sisters, and a double wedding would be doubly romantic."

Jane touched Mrs. Pratt's cheek with the back of her hand. The skin was still too warm, but the air-conditioning would help Mrs. Pratt cool down.

"Hydrate, Eugenia. We can talk about weddings later."

"An Austenian double wedding," Mrs. Pratt said dreamily. "You could be modern Bingleys and Darcys. Two hand-some men. Two beautiful brides."

Jane tapped the water bottle. "Take a sip." When Mrs. Pratt finally obeyed, Jane smiled and said, "There were no double weddings in *Jane Eyre*. I don't think we should try to convert Eloise from a diehard Brontë fan to a diehard Austen fan two months before her wedding, do you?"

"I love Austen," Eloise objected.

Mrs. Pratt drank more water. "But Jane Eyre's wedding was interrupted by Mr. Rochester's first wife. She tore Jane's wedding veil. Does Eloise really want to model her big day on *that* ceremony?"

Eloise and Jane exchanged grins. There was nothing Mrs. Pratt liked more than romance, and since she was well enough to wax on about weddings, she was clearly feeling better.

Unaware of Mrs. Pratt's improved state, Edwin returned from the kitchen and pressed the cold cloth against her forehead.

"I was just telling Jane that you two should join Landon and Eloise at the altar."

Edwin shot a questioning look at Eloise who responded with a shrug.

"I think my lovely sister deserves her own wedding day," said Edwin. "As does my Jane. I know they're thick as thieves, but—"

"The thief!" Mrs. Pratt exclaimed. "I didn't find her. Oh, what will I tell Roger?"

"That you gave chase until you couldn't anymore. A king would trade his crown for such a faithful partner as you." Taking Mrs. Pratt's hand, Edwin used it to hold the damp cloth in place. "You should rest now. Eloise? Can we help ourselves to glasses of ice? Those water bottles aren't very cold."

"Of course. Jane. Boys. Come through to the kitchen. You close your eyes, Eugenia. I won't be a minute."

In the kitchen, Eloise filled glasses with ice and distributed them while Jane described the items stolen from Roger's shop.

"A pillbox shaped like a fish and a chocolate pot embossed with flowers? I guess the thief chose them for a reason," Eloise said.

A fish, Jane thought. *Why do I feel like that matters?*

She was unable to focus on the question because Edwin squeezed her shoulder and said, "I'll get the truck and pick you up here. There's no need for all of us to fight the crowd."

Jane wanted to see Fitz and Hem safely home as soon as possible, so she thanked Edwin and kissed his cheek.

"Can we work at your booth while we wait?" Hem asked Eloise.

"We're good at selling," Fitz added. "We sold all our jam and lots of spa stuff too. I bet we could sell all of your comics and lots of books too."

Eloise smiled. "I'm sure you could, but the Randolph kids are helping me today. They want to buy books but don't have much in their piggy banks, so I hired them to be my festival assistants. They've sold books I've had sitting around for ages. I don't know how you kids do it, but I'm impressed."

While Eloise and the twins talked about comic books and graphic novels, Jane flipped through one of the wedding magazines piled on the kitchen table. Scraps of paper protruded from each magazine, igniting Jane's curiosity. Had Eloise seen a dress she liked? A bridal bouquet or centerpiece? Had she decided where to honeymoon?

Following her best friend's gaze, Eloise said, "I wish we could sit down and talk wedding stuff. I *could* share my thoughts with Mrs. Pratt, but she keeps trying to convince me that I need a rhinestone tiara and a twenty-foot train. If she had her way, I'd be limping down the aisle in glass slippers and leaving the church in an open-top carriage drawn by a team of white horses."

Jane gave a half shrug. "That part sounds pretty cool."

"I'd probably swallow a bug as soon as the horses picked up speed. Can you imagine the photo?"

Jane could, and it made her laugh.

Eloise laughed too.

"This is what I love about you," Jane said as Edwin

opened the back door and waved for them to come out. "No matter how crazy things get, you keep me laughing."

"Speaking of funny, I ordered a book called *Fifty Shades of Chicken: A Parody in a Cookbook* for our next Cover Girls meeting. I thought I'd try the Mustard-Spanked Chicken recipe."

Eloise was probably joking, but Jane gave her a thumbs-up and hurried out to the truck.

"What was my sister talking about?" Edwin asked as they drove down the narrow lane behind the shops.

"Her plans to dominate dinner," Jane replied.

Edwin's brows rose and he quickly changed the subject. "On the way to get the truck, I heard people talking about the mascot's shirt. Any idea why?"

The glint of humor in Jane's eyes faded. "Someone wrote a message on the back of his shirt. Since the suit zips up the front, the person wearing it was probably clueless."

"What did the message say?"

Jane repeated the words verbatim.

Edwin was silent for a long time. Jane didn't like the gravity of this silence but sensed that he'd gone quiet for the boys' sake.

At home, Jane told Fitz and Hem to relax while she and Edwin unloaded the cutting boards from the truck.

"We can help," Fitz said. "We already had lunch."

Though pleased by her son's offer, Jane said, "You and your brother have done enough work for a Saturday. Why don't you read for a bit?"

"Okay, Mom."

With the twins out of earshot, Jane looked a question at Edwin.

"My job as a travel writer has served as my cover for

other kinds of work, but I always took it seriously," Edwin began. "Most of my articles have been about food. Exotic recipes, obscure eateries, and unique ingredients. Investigating the source of those ingredients often got me into trouble."

"No, not you," Jane teased.

Edwin poked her between the ribs. "These scrapes were easier to get out of than, say, being locked in a medieval dungeon, but I digress. I've looked into the mistreatment of commercial fishers, as well as agricultural, aquacultural, and factory workers. All of these people harvested or packaged food for the world's largest food companies. The list isn't that long, and Cook's Pride is one of them."

Jane drew in a breath. "Is that what the slave labor reference means?"

Edwin handed Jane two cutting boards but insisted on carrying the rest. "It's been years since I researched that company. Maybe they've cleaned up their act since then. I really hope so, Jane, because exploiting children was one of their sins."

Inside Jane's cool and quiet house, Edwin stowed the cutting boards in a closet while Jane prepared a quick lunch of turkey and cheese sandwiches, grapes, and iced tea.

In between bites of food, the couple spoke in hushed tones about the impromptu cooking challenge, the arrival of the CEO and his team of lawyers, and the message on the mascot's shirt.

"This morning was supposed to be our time to relax together, but I can't seem to get out from under the black cloud created by this TV show." Jane stared down at the remains of her sandwich. "So many bad things are connected to it. A murdered chef, an exploding grill, a competition that won't quit, stolen antiques, and a vandalized costume." She fought the tremble in her voice. "It's a summer's day. The sky is blue, and the sun is shining. But I feel like we're about to be hit with a Shakespearean-sized tempest."

Edwin took her hand. "What can you do?"

"I have to move faster than the storm moves," Jane said. "All along, I've been playing catch-up. A terrible thing happens, and I try to find out the how and why it happened. But that's not working. I need to gather all the information I can and closet myself in a room with the Fins until we fully understand the motivation behind these crimes."

"How can I help? Magnus is covering the lunch service, which means I'm at your disposal."

"I can't avoid the reporters or lawyers forever. I'll have to face them eventually. But right now, I need to learn all I can about Cook's Pride and the man who runs it."

Edwin carried their plates to the sink. "I'll clean up and brew a pot of coffee. You start digging around on your laptop."

An hour later, Jane had filled a notebook page with biographical details on Fox Watterson, the CEO of Cook's Pride. Watterson's given name was Frank, but his family started calling him Fox because of his red hair and the boyhood nickname had stuck. At seventy, what little hair remained on his round head was dyed a clownfish-orange. Watterson grew up in Chicago, and after a failed attempt as a restaurateur, began working for a major food company. Years later, Watterson started his own company and hired his two siblings, a brother and a sister, to help him run Cook's Pride. The global company was now worth billions.

"They got too big, too fast," Jane told Edwin. "They

couldn't keep tabs on all the divisions, and some of those divisions turned pretty shady."

"Like using child labor in the chocolate trade?" Edwin asked.

With a grim look, Jane pulled up the article she'd bookmarked. "I had no idea that child labor has been a part of the chocolate industry for decades. It's totally Dickensian. These kids are working for pennies on the dollar instead of going to school. Competitive pricing has led to human trafficking, which means there are children working without pay on cocoa farms all over West Africa. It breaks my heart, Edwin."

Edwin's pained expression matched her own. "It's a travesty." He pointed at her laptop. "And Cook's Pride isn't the only culprit, are they?"

"No. Half a dozen companies are guilty of these barbaric practices," Jane said. "Journalists have tried to expose the injustices and there are nonprofit agencies working toward a future where chocolate is a slave-free, child-labor-free trade, but it'll take time, money, and persistence. The major food corporations claim to be on board with eradicating child labor but use the excuse that they don't know which farms their beans come from. How can they get away with that?"

Edwin studied Jane over the rim of his coffee cup. "Are you familiar with any of the journalists accusing Cook's Pride of using child labor?"

"No, but someone in Storyton takes issue with the company's business practices. They wrote that message on Dew Drop's shirt knowing it would be seen by hundreds of people." Scooping up her phone, she said, "I really need the Fins to comb through our guests' social media pages.

I asked them to search for a connection to Chef Pierce, but we obviously need to look at all the food-related posts."

Jane was still typing when her phone rang. Seeing Sheriff Evans's name on the screen, she put the phone on speaker mode and answered the call.

"Hello, Sheriff."

"Ms. Steward, I wish we could talk in person, but I'm dealing with that delusional director. He's been in a holding cell for less than an hour, but he's acting like the Count of Monte Cristo."

Jane felt no sympathy for Ty. "Perhaps he'd rather be in a hospital. Like Mr. Gilmore."

Sheriff Evans grunted. "He *should* be there, begging for the man's forgiveness. The sad truth is that I won't be able to keep him here—not with those corporate lawyers making all kinds of threats. They're gunning for you next, but I'll delay them as long as I can."

"In return, I'll send you an urn of coffee."

"That's a fair trade." The uptick in the sheriff's voice didn't last. "I wanted to tell you about a break in Chef Pierce's case. I spoke with his GP today and was told that he refilled Chef Pierce's prescriptions the day before he left for Storyton, but there are only four rivaroxaban capsules left in the bottle. He started out with thirty."

Jane tried to recall the specifics of Chef Pierce's medications. "Were those his heart pills? The ones that acted as anticoagulants?"

"Yes. Chef Pierce took one rivaroxaban pill a day with dinner. But he had other medical issues in addition to his heart and blood pressure. He also had liver disease."

Jane blurted, "But he was still drinking."

"The ME mentioned the liver disease, but it was Pierce's

GP who told me that it was quite advanced. He thought I was calling to say that Pierce had died from liver disease, and when he heard that the cause of death was exsanguination, he got upset. With proper medical care, most people don't die of blood loss, even if they're on anticoagulants. I didn't mention the large puncture wound in Chef Pierce's side."

"Chef Pierce's killer got him to ingest the extra pills." Jane was horrified by the thought. "He was never going to leave the cookbook nook alive."

"Initially, I believed Chef Pierce and his killer had an argument," continued the sheriff. "The killer lured Chef Pierce to the cookbook nook and demanded something of him. Chef Pierce got angry, there was a scuffle, and the porcelain was broken. I envisioned the killer grabbing the biggest piece to use as a weapon. Chef Pierce either ran right into that piece, or the killer coldly plunged it into his side."

Jane gazed into the middle distance. She was no longer in her kitchen but in the cookbook nook. "Chef Pierce wasn't a small man, and I doubt he was easily intimidated. But it was the middle of the night, he'd had too much to drink, and he may have unknowingly overdosed on his heart medication. It's hard to picture Chef Pierce as a victim, but he was a victim long before he entered the cookbook nook. I don't know why he went, but that meeting was the death of him."

"Exactly." Sheriff Evans sounded relieved that they'd arrived at the same conclusion. "At first, this seemed like a crime of opportunity. But if someone tricked Chef Pierce into ingesting that medicine hours before the rendezvous in the cookbook nook, then we're looking at premeditated murder."

"Bentley. She was in his room at midnight."

The sheriff agreed that not only did he plan to speak with Bentley again, but he also wanted to interview anyone who knew Chef Pierce or had access to his room. He went on to say that there were no leads in Roger's shoplifting case, and no one had been seen tampering with the festival mascot's costume.

"I feel like I'm lost in the desert without a map or a drop of water," he said.

Jane hated to hear the frustration in the sheriff's voice. She knew how self-doubt could worm its way into a person's mind during times of stress. And Sheriff Evans was under too much stress. She wanted to tell him that she believed in him but didn't have the chance.

"I've gotta run," he said. "Chief Aroneo's on the other line. I'm sending four deputies your way. Caution your guests to remain inside Storyton Hall and its grounds. And avoid the lawyers if you can. They tend to speak in paragraphs instead of sentences. If they corner you, you're done for."

Jane wouldn't be cornered by Fox Watterson's lawyers or anyone else. She was in battle mode, and when she swept into the surveillance room ten minutes later, the Fins took one look at her face and knew that the Guardian of Storyton Hall was fired up.

"We're not leaving this room until I know everything there is to know about Bentley Fiore, Fox Watterson and his company, Mia Mallett and her crew, and the celebrity chefs. We're going to fill every piece of paper in this hotel with details on these guests until we have an answer."

Jane was too keyed up to sit, so she stood behind her chair and stared at the bank of television screens. She tracked guests from one security camera to another, manically watching their every move.

Sinclair pushed a file folder to her end of the table. "Miss Jane, we've been searching for answers all morning. And we believe we've found one."

Jane's fingers dug into the soft leather of her chair. "Go on."

Sinclair waved a hand at the folder and said, "Bentley Fiore is Chef Pierce's daughter."

Chapter 15

Jane glanced at the folder but didn't reach for it. She conjured an image of Bentley's freckled cheeks, rose-gold hair, and gymnast's build. Jane couldn't see any trace of Chef Pierce in that young, fresh-faced woman.

"His daughter? Are you sure?"

Sinclair pointed at the folder. "Chef Pierce didn't believe it either. When Ms. Fiore's mother filed for child support, he insisted on a paternity test. After the test confirmed his paternity, nothing changed in Chef Pierce's life. Ms. Fiore's mother, Cindy, refused child support in exchange for the termination of Chef Pierce's parental rights. The case isn't public record, so Sheriff Evans will need to request the files to confirm Cindy's story. She was kind enough to send me an image of the paternity test results."

Dropping into a chair, Jane said, "So you believe her."

"Based on our phone conversation and the results of that test, yes, I'm convinced."

The folder contained two printouts. One was the paternity test. The second was a photo of a young man in a chef's jacket posing next to a bar. His arm was slung around a pretty, small-framed young woman in a cocktail waitress uniform. Chef Pierce had been caught mid-laugh while the waitress's starstruck gaze was locked on the man. The bar was strewn with liquor bottles, shot glasses, and shriveled lime wedges.

"Is this Chef Pierce?" Jane was incredulous.

"A younger, slimmer, and healthier Chef Pierce. The cocktail waitress is Cindy Fiore. The photo was taken in Brooklyn, twenty-six years ago, the night Ms. Fiore and Chef Pierce met. It was their only night together. Nine months later, Bentley was born. Ms. Cindy Fiore said that she met Chef Pierce during her "wild child" phase. Owing to multiple tequila shots, she doesn't remember much about Chef Pierce other than his looks and confidence. She found him far less appealing after the birth of their daughter."

Bentley had inherited her mother's straight hair, small frame, and freckled skin. Her only similarity to Chef Pierce was the shape of her eyes.

Jane scanned the paternity test. While it certainly seemed legitimate, she wouldn't know an authentic paternity test from a fake. But if Sinclair was convinced, that was good enough for her.

"Was Bentley told that she was Chef Pierce's daughter?"

Sinclair looked pained. "Not from her mother. Cindy fabricated a tale about a handsome stranger coming into the bar and sweeping her off her feet. She told Bentley that his name was James, he spoke with a British accent, and he traveled all over the world."

"She turned Chef Pierce into 007?"

"Or a pilot for British Airways," Sterling said.

Jane closed the folder. "It must have been hard on Bentley to grow up believing her father was out there, somewhere, unaware of her existence. Did Cindy ever marry?"

"No. She confessed that her taste in men wasn't the best, which is why she didn't stay with any of them for long. She also kept her dating life separate from her home life. Luckily, her parents provided financial and emotional support. As a result, Bentley is very close to her grand-parents."

"Good." Jane's relief over learning that Bentley hadn't had a lonely and miserable childhood was short-lived. "I assume Bentley figured out that her dad wasn't a British globetrotter named James, or we wouldn't be sitting here right now."

"According to her mother, Bentley took an anthropology course her senior year in college that ignited her curiosity about her father. She repeatedly asked her mother about the night she and her father had met. The more her mother stuck to her fictitious story, the angrier Bentley became. After college, Bentley took a job in a PR firm based in LA. She rarely spoke to her mother, leaving Cindy to rely on social media for updates on her daughter. Two posts indicate that Bentley discovered her father's true identity."

Jane winced. "She must have felt so betrayed."

Sterling walked to the wall opposite Jane and pulled down a projector screen. He then dimmed the lights and hit the space bar on his laptop. He'd barely touched the keyboard when a group of thumbnail images appeared on the projector screen.

"You're looking at screenshots of Ms. Fiore's Insta-gram feed. Most of her photos are of guests from Ms. Mallett's show, or food and fashion shots. The locations are quite varied. For example, here she is, drinking Chianti in Florence."

Sterling clicked on a thumbnail, and a photo of Bentley filled the screen. She wore a white cotton dress and mirrored sunglasses. Her hair was chestnut brown—not rose gold—and a cookbook was open on the table in front of her. The tip of her index finger rested just below the underlined name of the recipe.

"That's Chef Pierce's cookbook, *A Man and a Pan*," Sterling said. "It had just been released the previous day, and I don't know how Ms. Fiore got her hands on a copy in Italy unless it was given to Ms. Mallett to review. But doesn't really matter. What matters is the name of the recipe. Can you read it?"

It took Jane a second to make out the words. "The Big Daddy Burger," she said. And then, "Oh."

"If that had been the only post featuring Chef Pierce, we could chalk it up to coincidence. But when we looked at the post announcing the names of the chefs competing in this season's *Posh Palate with Mia Mallett*, we knew coincidence wasn't a factor."

Sterling clicked on another thumbnail. This photo featured the spines of five cookbooks—all written by this season's contestants. Only Chef Pierce's book was splayed open, and Bentley stared down at a cocktail recipe called One-Night Stand. A bottle of tequila and a shot glass were also in the frame.

"When Ms. Fiore posts about cookbooks, recipes, or eateries, the tone of her captions is upbeat. And she always smiles in her posts." Sterling said. "Mr. Butterworth, what's your take on her expression in this post?"

"Her posture is rigid, and she's pressing her fingers into the book pages so hard that the skin around her nails has turned red. She's also clenching her jaw. Anger is practically seeping out of her pores. But the corners of her mouth reveal another emotion. Hurt."

"We've seen people act out of anger and hurt, and all they do is spread more hurt and anger," Jane said with a sigh in her voice. "Anything else?"

Sterling clicked another thumbnail. It was a close-up shot of a chocolate bar.

"I love chocolate as much as the next woman," Jane said. "But how is this relevant?"

After waving at Lachlan to indicate that the floor was now his, Sterling sat down.

Lachlan looked at his legal pad. "The caption from this photo reads: '*Chocolate makes everything better—unless you're a kid working on a cocoa farm in West Africa. They work all day for little or no pay. Break the cycle of child labor and abuse! Only buy fair trade chocolate!*'"

Jane pointed at the screen. "Is that a Cook's Pride chocolate bar?"

"It sure is," said Lachlan.

Sterling brought up another photo. This one, taken at a farmer's market, featured baskets of tomatoes. There were a dozen different varieties, including cherry, plum, Better Boy, Tigerella, Cherokee purple, Campari, Black Krim, and Big Beef.

"The caption for this post says, '*Who harvests your produce? Are they being paid a living wage? Why do food companies mistreat migrant and seasonal workers? For profit! Do your research before you put any of their products in your shopping cart.*'"

"I assume Cook's Pride makes tomato sauce."

"Pasta sauces, soup, marinades, salsa—you name it," said Lachlan. "Ms. Fiore didn't mention Cook's Pride in the caption, but she does in her hashtags. The company name is sandwiched between the hashtags 'migrant worker rights' and 'migrant workers matter.'"

Jane frowned. "When were these posted?"

"Within the past year," replied Lachlan.

"That's pretty brazen, considering Cook's Pride is sponsoring the show this season. Either Bentley asked Mia's permission to post this, or Mia doesn't know about the posts. Does Bentley have a large number of followers?"

Lachlan consulted his legal pad. "Twelve thousand on Instagram. She has other social media accounts as well, but they don't have as many followers and aren't updated as often. She never alludes to Chef Pierce or Cook's Pride on those accounts."

"Are there more posts like the chocolate bar and tomato post?" she asked Sterling.

"Half a dozen or so," he said.

Jane walked over to the wall switch and returned the lights to the brightest setting. She then leaned against the door and thought.

She'd sat right next to Sheriff Evans when he questioned Bentley in the conference room. Bentley, who'd visited Chef Pierce hours before his death. Bentley, who was privy to every detail of the show, including where and when each challenge would take place, the theme of each challenge, and the equipment required. She probably contacted the vendors, arranged deliveries, and took care of dozens of other things in Mia's name.

"Bentley had access to Chef Pierce's personal information," she said. "His home address, email address, cell phone number, social security number. And most importantly, his health forms."

Looking at the security screens, she was reminded of the footage showing Bentley making her way to Chef Pierce's room just shy of midnight.

"What if we couldn't find Mia's note to Chef Pierce because Bentley got rid of it? If so, how did she convince Chef Pierce to meet her in the kitchens at, what, one or two in the morning?"

Jane didn't expect the Fins to have an answer. She was thinking out loud while they listened because this process had led them to answers in the past.

Butterworth filled a glass with water. As he placed it on the table in front of Jane, he said, "When the sheriff interviewed Ms. Fiore, what was her posture like? What did she do with her hands? Did she make eye contact with you? How about Sheriff Evans? Which emotions were on display?"

Though Jane continued to stare at the monitors, she'd gone back to that moment in the William Faulkner Conference Room. Bentley sat in a chair at one end of the table, picking at a jagged thumbnail. The skin around all of her nails had been red and raw.

"She was as nervous as anyone would be when called into a room with a sheriff, two deputies, and a hotel manager," Jane began. "She had a strong reaction when she realized that our security cameras had caught her visiting Chef Pierce's room. In hindsight, I believe her response was theatrical. Bentley travels with Mia, which means she's stayed at dozens of high-end hotels. Our use of security cameras wouldn't come as a surprise. Not at a luxury resort."

Jane told the Fins how Bentley hadn't wanted to leave

her comfy bed to run an errand for Mia and how defensive she'd been when Sheriff Evans asked if she knew what Mia's note to Chef Pierce said. Jane then repeated how Bentley had described Chef Pierce's appearance.

"She became more confident as the interview progressed," Jane said. "Her tone was conversational. She stopped picking at her nails. She also shifted the emotional focus to Mia. *Mia* was the angry woman. *Mia* was so upset that Bentley felt compelled to deliver a note in the middle of the night."

"Good." Butterworth nodded in approval. "The revulsion Ms. Fiore expressed toward Chef Pierce was probably genuine. Chef Pierce was an obtuse oaf who seemed to revel in offending everyone he met. The realization that half of her genetic material came from such a man may have evoked a powerful sense of shame and loathing in Ms. Fiore."

Jane looked at the three men who, along with Uncle Aloysius, had been like fathers to her. Sinclair, Butterworth, and Sterling were men of principle. They were honest, loyal, and intelligent. They'd taught her how to drive a car, interpret Shakespeare, break a wooden board with her bare hand, embrace the beauty of other cultures, admit her mistakes, apologize gracefully, and so much more.

"I had the best surrogate fathers in the world," Jane said softly. "But Bentley? How many times did she wonder what her absent father looked like or what he did for a living? She probably fantasized about meeting him a thousand times. Did she kill him because he was the opposite of everything she'd imagined?"

Lachlan stirred in his seat. "Chef Pierce rejected her.

From the time Bentley was born, he didn't want her in his life. A parent's rejection is a wound that never truly heals."

Jane and her Fins looked at the white screen. With the lights on, the images were harder to see, but Bentley's profile photo was clear enough. Was the young, vibrant face smiling out at them the face of a killer?

"We're engaging in a great deal of conjecture," Sterling said. "What evidence points to Ms. Fiore as the killer? We need to focus on facts."

Jane liked facts. She liked organizing them into lists, graphs, and spreadsheets. Facts made her feel safe. They made life, which was often messy and unpredictable, far more manageable.

Stepping up to the whiteboard screwed into the wall behind her chair, she scooped up a marker and wrote the word EVIDENCE in the center of the board. After underlining it twice, she moved to the left-hand side of the board and added the number one.

Sterling supplied the first item for Jane's list. "We have footage of Ms. Fiore knocking on Chef Pierce's door at midnight. We saw him open the door and admit her."

Jane wrote FOOTAGE OF BENTLEY VISITING CHEF PIERCE HOURS BEFORE HIS DEATH on the board.

"Ms. Fiore had access to Chef Pierce's medical information," Butterworth said.

Sinclair waited for Jane to finish writing before adding, "And she was privy to the inner workings of the show. She probably ordered the pantry items and equipment."

Jane swung around, her eyes shining with excitement. "Including the gas grills." A thought occurred to her. "But why would she set those fires?"

"For the same reason she'd vandalize the Berry Jubilee's

mascot. To draw attention to Cook's Pride," answered Lachlan.

"A patricidal activist?" Jane chewed her lip as she mulled this over. "It's hard for me to believe that Bentley would sabotage Mia's show. Her admiration for Mia seems sincere."

Sterling shrugged. "Even if *Posh Palate* was canceled, Ms. Mallett would still have her pick of new projects. She's the girl with the Midas touch, and I'm sure she'd find a way to spin her time in Storyton to her advantage."

What Sterling said made perfect sense, but Jane was convinced that Bentley would go out of her way to protect Mia's interests.

Butterworth said, "Here's an addition for the board. I overheard two of the deputies talking about the matchbook found on Chef Pierce's body. As it happens, that matchbook is from the Brooklyn bar where Chef Pierce met a cocktail waitress named Cindy Fiore."

Jane wrote MATCHBOOK LINKING CHEF PIERCE AND BENTLEY'S MOM.

"Anything else?" she asked her Fins.

"Ms. Fiore's advanced training in martial arts might be worth noting," said Sinclair. "Her discipline is Muay Thai, a combat-oriented discipline involving stand-up strikes and clinching. Skilled Muay Thai fighters can take out an opponent with a well-aimed elbow strike or kick."

Picturing Bentley's compact, muscular frame, Jane wondered what it would be like to fight her. Jane and her sons practiced Tae Kwon Do, and while sparring was part of their training, clinching wasn't. Clinching was the act of tying up an opponent's arms, a move requiring both strength and aggression.

MARTIAL ARTS TRAINING (COMBAT-STYLE), Jane wrote on the board.

She turned back to Sinclair. "Mia told the sheriff that Bentley was a black belt, so she must be highly skilled."

"Muay Thai doesn't use belts," Sinclair said. "However, when I saw a photo on Ms. Fiore's Twitter page of a black armband tied around an impressive bicep, I researched her gym. Their students can earn armbands, which means Ms. Fiore's skills are most impressive."

Jane remembered how Sheriff Evans had used a pen to demonstrate how the jagged shard of porcelain had penetrated Chef Pierce's flesh.

"The bruise around Chef Pierce's wound indicated that he was stabbed with force," she reminded the Fins. "Bentley's strong enough to apply that kind of force."

The Fins agreed with her, so Jane added BRUISE AROUND ABDOMINAL WOUND to the board.

She surveyed what she'd written so far. "Can an arrest be made based on this list?"

"If I were Sheriff Evans, I'd want more," said Lachlan.

Butterworth held up a finger. "The question is, does Ms. Fiore want more? If her goal was to punish an absentee parent, she succeeded. If she wanted to draw attention to Cook's Pride, she has. Does this young woman have an endgame?"

A wry smile appeared on Sterling's face. "There's only one way of knowing if her agenda's complete."

"Are you suggesting we allow the finale to proceed?" Butterworth's eyes gleamed with interest.

Jane's impulse was to shoot down the idea, but she bit her tongue. The items listed on the whiteboard might place

Bentley under suspicion, but the sheriff couldn't make a murder charge stick without more proof or a confession.

"Catching a criminal in the act is risky," she said. "The *Posh Palate* finale is a live show. Our guests have paid quite a bit for the privilege of attending the two-hour event. Uncle Aloysius, Aunt Octavia, and half the Cover Girls will be there. Can we entrap Bentley while keeping anyone else from getting hurt?"

"Unless we have a better understanding of her motivation, I don't think so."

As always, Lachlan had spoken in his quiet, reserved manner. And as always, his words had a big impact.

Sinclair, who never seemed to be without a book, suddenly produced one. "Anaïs Nin, the French-born writer, was a fatherless child. In her view, a child could grow older but never die until it finds its father. Also, an absent father tends to be glorified and deified." He put his hand on the cover of the worn paperback. "According to Ms. Nin, the father had to be confronted, and, I quote, 'recognized as human, as man who created and then, by his absence, left the child fatherless and then Godless.'"

"He was confronted, all right," murmured Sterling.

Jane kept her eyes on Sinclair. "Killing Chef Pierce may have given Bentley a sense of empowerment? Like she might be deluded into believing she can do away with anyone she sees as an enemy?"

Sinclair rubbed the cover of his book. "It's my working theory."

"Okay. I want to share what we've got with Sheriff Evans," said Jane. "After dealing with Ty and the corporate attorneys, he's probably fit to be tied. Hopefully, your excellent research will help him close this case."

"No need to call him." Lachlan pointed at the monitor showing the loading dock. An SUV with the sheriff's department seal pulled into a space allocated for delivery trucks.

Butterworth stood up. "I'll make fresh coffee and a plate of nibbles." Catching sight of the sheriff's cantankerous expression, he murmured, "Forget the plate. I'll bring a whole trolley."

Chapter 16

Jane met Sheriff Evans in the lobby.

"The coffee urns have been put away, but a fresh pot will be delivered to the surveillance room."

The sheriff gave her a wan smile. "As my wife says, it feels like wine o'clock." He pointed at two wing chairs near the grandfather clock. "Can we talk there?"

Jane was about to say that she had things to show him in the surveillance room when she realized that he'd probably just come from a similar room and could use a change of scenery. The chairs he'd selected were set apart from the other conversation areas, which meant they'd have privacy while still allowing Sheriff Evans to observe the guests.

To that end, the sheriff touched the chair facing the east wing and said, "Mr. Scott is going to stroll through the front door any second now. You can avoid his smug grin by sitting here."

The sheriff made no effort to hide his feelings, but Jane's contempt for the director was much stronger. She hated the idea of Ty Scott walking around Storyton Hall with his mirrored sunglasses, gelled hair, and fake Hollywood smile while Mr. Gilmore was in a hospital bed.

"I guess the lawyers earned their money today," she grumbled.

The sheriff leaned his head back and sighed. "Oh, yes. They threatened to put my department through hell if we didn't drop the charges against Mr. Scott. They seemed surprised when I refused."

"That's ridiculous."

"*I* was surprised that Mr. Scott expected to be rescued. He told me that these attorneys have gotten him out of hot water before. I couldn't understand it. Why would a corporate legal team bail out a TV director more than once?"

It didn't make sense to Jane either. "Sounds like Ty Scott has a fairy godmother."

The sheriff snorted. "More like a doting uncle. Ty Scott is Fox Watterson's nephew, and he's spent a small fortune making his nephew's problems disappear."

Jane was still absorbing this news when the sheriff's eyes darkened and his lips compressed into a thin line. Pivoting in her seat, she saw Ty and Fox strut through the main doorway, followed by the stone-faced lawyers.

Fox paused in the threshold and turned to the bellhop holding the door. Fox mimed a drinking gesture and cast a searching glance around the lobby.

"Ty probably told his uncle that all guests receive a glass of champagne at check-in. Too bad Fox isn't a guest," Jane said, taking pleasure in the look of disappointment on Fox Watterson's face. "He can trot into the Ian Fleming Lounge and buy his own drink."

"He's rich enough to buy *all* the drinks," muttered the sheriff.

Across the room, Fox threw up his arms in exasperation

while Ty checked his hair in the massive gilt-framed mirror next to the bellhop's station. When he was done preening, Ty turned and spotted Jane and Sheriff Evans. He smiled, said something to his uncle, and pointed at Jane.

Fox dismissed his attorneys with a few words and the flick of a wrist. Jane felt sorry for them. She'd heard people tell their dogs to "sit" or "stay" with more warmth than Fox had just shown to the human beings in his employ.

I bet they'd trade places with Captain Haviland in a heartbeat, Jane thought.

Olivia Limoges was wealthy, but she didn't treat people like dirt. What was Fox Watterson's excuse?

"Ms. Steward? Fox Watterson of Cook's Pride." He held out his hand. "Nice place. My nephew's show is going to make it *very* popular."

Ignoring Fox's hand, Jane said, "We're having a private conversation, so if you—"

"Not much privacy in a hotel lobby," interrupted Fox. "I just came over to tell you that there *will* be a finale, and it'll happen tomorrow. Ty will be directing as planned." He clapped his nephew on the back. "And I'm going to stay to make sure the show finishes and to present the winner with his or her prize."

Jane arched her brows. "Have you found suitable accommodations?"

Fox smirked. "They're not exactly close, but yes. Come on, Ty, we'll let them get back to their *private* conversation."

Ty smiled at Jane and saluted the sheriff and trailed off after his uncle.

"If I had the authority to shut down the show, I would," the sheriff said.

Jane hated the note of defeat in his voice. Had she known the true cost of hosting *Posh Palate with Mia Mallett*, she would have put their proposal in the shredder.

Because of that show, a man lost his life. Another man had been burned. Mrs. Hubbard's cookbook nook had become a crime scene. Antique porcelain, passed down by generations of Stewards, had been broken beyond repair. Roger's shop had been burglarized. And to top it all off, the sheriff believed that he'd failed the citizens of Storyton.

Jane understood how he felt. How often had she re-played the events of the past few days and wondered what more she could have done to protect her guests?

Protect them by planning for the next disaster, a niggling voice whispered.

"The show has to go on," she told Evans. "Not because they say so, but because the finale might be our only chance of catching Chef Pierce's killer."

"I don't follow."

In a hushed voice, Jane said, "There's another familial twist you need to know about, but I can't tell you here. Let's move to the surveillance room."

Sheriff Evans stood up and grabbed his hat. "At least there'll be coffee."

Jane smiled warmly at him. "You work tirelessly to keep our town safe. You deserve more than coffee, which is why Butterworth has a food trolley waiting for you."

At this, the sheriff brightened. "The good man knows how much I love Mrs. Hubbard's bacon rolls. Two or three of those, and I'll be a new man." He waved his hat at the other end of the lobby. "Lead on, Ms. Steward. I'm ready to hear your twisted tale."

* * *

When Jane got home that evening, she didn't have time to clean the house before book club. She had to settle for stashing clutter out of sight and wiping off the dining room table.

Luckily, the boys were having a sleepover with Uncle Aloysius and Aunt Octavia. This was a book club night tradition. While Jane socialized with her friends, Uncle Aloysius and Aunt Octavia shared stories and laughter with the twins.

Jane loved that her sons would have a mental scrapbook filled with memories of nights like tonight. She knew that when the twins were older, they'd see a fishing hat, a chess set, or a model train and think of Uncle Aloysius. And they'd forever associate dresses with wild patterns, vintage cameras, hard candy, and the scent of rosewater with Aunt Octavia. They'd remember the hours they'd spent with their relatives as some of the best of their lives. Jane wished those hours would never run out. She wished they could go on loving one another ad infinitum.

Jane was carrying a pile of comic books to her sons' room when a familiar voice called from downstairs. "It's me! I just wanted you to know that I was here."

A few minutes later, Jane entered the kitchen to find Eloise arranging wildflowers in a jug.

Jane took in her gleaming countertops. "Did you clean?"

"A few sprays here and there. Which plates do you want to use?"

"Forget the plates," Jane said. "Let's open a bottle of wine instead. I have so much to tell you."

Eloise laughed. "Why do you think I *really* came early? I'll open the wine. You get changed."

Jane took a quick shower and pulled on a loose-fitting cotton sundress. She gathered her hair into a messy bun, ignoring those strands still clinging to her damp cheeks. She decided not to bother with makeup. It was too hot, and the Cover Girls were her closest friends. They wouldn't care if she wore blush or mascara. They'd just see Jane, their tired, hungry, book-loving friend.

Their friend with the dry lips, Jane thought, searching her bathroom drawer for the moisturizing lipstick she bought at Storyton Pharmacy a few weeks ago. She'd liked the floral design on its packaging and that the name of the peachy-pink hue was Steel Magnolia. Jane supposed every Southern woman liked to think of herself as a steel magnolia, and she was no exception.

"Nice lipstick," Eloise told Jane. She then pointed at the glass of white wine on the island. "That's yours. I'll pour mine after I get Betty's dish in the oven. She can't make it tonight."

Reaching for her wineglass, Jane asked, "What happened?"

"Bob dropped a beer keg on his foot this afternoon. He kept complaining about the pain, so Betty took him to Doc Lydgate. The doc told Bob to elevate his foot for the rest of the day, which means Betty has to work. But she said that nothing would keep her from coming to the finale tomorrow."

Jane poured wine for Eloise. "And with everything she has going on, she still made a dish to share? That woman is amazing."

The theme for tonight's meeting was chef memoirs. Each Cover Girl had selected a chef, read his or her memoir, and prepared one of their dishes. Eloise had volunteered to coordinate the menu.

"Otherwise, we'll end up with five desserts," she'd said.

Though Jane was fond of dessert, she was excited to try new savory dishes. And when she read Betty's note describing her version of Anthony Bourdain's Gratin Dauphinois, Jane knew that tonight's meal would be unforgettable.

"Think of a toast while I fire up the grill," Eloise said.

Just then, the doorbell rang, and the rest of the Cover Girls spilled into her house. They swooped into Jane's kitchen like birds seeking a place to land, filling the space with movement, sound, and color.

After depositing a pitcher of iced tea on the island, Violet gave Jane a hug. "Aren't you a picture of summertime?"

"Not compared to that pitcher of tea. What's in it?"

"Lemon juice, Bacardi, a little sugar, and mint leaves. It's Emeril Lagasse's Lemony Spiked Sweet Tea. His *Essential Emeril* isn't classified as a memoir, but it's the most personal cookbook I've ever read." Violet's expression turned dreamy. "Someday, I'll eat at one of his restaurants."

"Yes, you will," Jane said before turning to greet Mabel, the owner of La Grande Dame Clothing Boutique. "We missed you this week."

"I had a ball shopping for new fabric, but that drive to Atlanta gets longer and longer every year." Mabel removed the plastic wrap from a platter of sliced tomatoes. "I'm *so* happy to be sleeping in my own bed again. You know you're old when you start traveling with your own pillow and coffeemaker."

Jane placed a set of serving tongs next to Mabel's platter. She'd made Nigel Slater's Tomato Salad with Coriander Mayonnaise after reading the memoir *Toast*.

"Grill's ready," Eloise told Jane as she grabbed a covered baking dish from the counter and scurried back outside. She was preparing tonight's entrée, Eddie Huang's Cherry Cola Hanger Steak.

Not only had Eloise loved Huang's memoir, *Fresh Off the Boat*, but she'd also binge-watched the television series. Last week, Jane had overheard Lachlan telling Sterling that he didn't understand why Eloise found the sitcom so entertaining.

"I just sit there and listen to her laugh. That's all the entertainment I need," he'd said.

Since Jane's shrimp only needed a few minutes on the grill, she arranged plates, napkins, and flatware at one end of the center island and lined up tumblers for Violet's spiked tea. She then carried her shrimp skewers outside. Her recipe, Suya, was an adaptation of Nigerian street food by Kwame Onwuachi. Jane had read Onwuachi's book, *Notes from a Young Black Chef: A Memoir*, in two nights and couldn't wait to serve one of his dishes to her friends.

Jane placed her skewers on the grill.

As they began to cook, steam rose into the air. Eloise inhaled a plume and her eyes widened. "They smell spicy!"

"The rub has ground peanuts, ginger, bouillon, and lots of cayenne pepper," Jane said, There was a sizzling noise and flames flared around Eloise's steak. Jane took a step back to avoid the heat.

Eloise put a hand on Jane's arm. "I can cook your skewers. You don't need to be out here with the grill and the flames and all that."

"I'm okay," Jane said. "If I just concentrate on food and my friends, the bad stuff fades away."

"That almost sounds like a toast."

Jane took the shrimp off the grill and carried it to the

kitchen. A few minutes later, Eloise came in with the hanger steak.

"Landon Lachlan is a lucky man," said Mrs. Pratt. "Not only is his future wife lovely, kind, and smart, but she can cook a mean steak too."

Eloise blushed with pleasure. "Tell Jane about your dessert, Eugenia."

Mrs. Pratt was more than happy to oblige. "I read Ruth Reichl's *My Kitchen Year: 136 Recipes That Saved My Life*, which is part memoir, part cookbook. Eloise already knows this, but I was so moved by Ms. Reichl's story of how food and cooking helped her recover from a major setback that I immediately ordered *Save Me the Plums*. Her voice is relatable. So are her recipes. For example, I wanted to make her Nectarine Galette, but nectarines aren't in season. But her recipe called for any unripe stone fruit, which meant I could use peaches. My peaches were so unripe that the twins could have played catch with them."

The women laughed.

"How's Roger doing?" Jane asked.

Mrs. Pratt shook her head in bewilderment. "He's taking the robbery in stride. I'd be furious—I *am* furious—but he prefers to focus on the sales he made and the new people he met. And guess what? Your resident writer was one of these new people. I wasn't in the shop when she came in, but Roger said that she knows a lot about antiques. She offered to put him in touch with a friend who owns an antique shop in Oyster Bay. Her friend will introduce Roger to auctioneers and pickers. Roger is thrilled to bits."

Jane smiled. "My impression is that Olivia Limoges is a very generous person."

"I hope she drops by the bookshop soon. I'm dying to meet her," Eloise said.

Violet glanced from Eloise to Jane. "Will she be at the finale?"

"Yes," said Jane. "I'm glad you brought that up, Vi, because I need to talk to all of you about tomorrow." She gestured at the colorful array of food on her kitchen island. "But first, we eat! Mabel? May I pour you some tea?"

"Please, and thank you. I can't wait to try these beautiful dishes," Mabel exclaimed.

Eloise put a spoonful of Betty's creamy, cheesy potatoes on her plate. "I hate that Betty's missing this. We should pack up the leftovers for her and Bob."

The other Cover Girls were quick to agree.

As the women filled their plates with tomato salad, grilled shrimp, potatoes au gratin, and cherry cola hanger steak, they listed all the things they needed to tell Phoebe and Anna when they returned to Storyton.

Over dinner, the friends savored the delicious food and talked about cookbooks, recipes, and kitchen disasters. These stories grew more elaborate as the meal progressed, and by the time they put down their utensils, the room had grown warm with laughter.

"Violet, just how much Bacardi is in this tea?" Mabel asked.

"I did exactly what Emeril told me to," insisted Violet. "Should I make more?"

Though Jane hated to put a damper on the mood, she said, "I need to talk to everyone about tomorrow, and if I have one more glass of that tea, I'll be under the table. Why don't I brew some coffee?"

In the kitchen, the Cover Girls moved with practiced efficiency. Mabel packed the leftovers, Eloise loaded the dishwasher, Mrs. Pratt dished out servings of her peach galette, Jane started the coffeemaker, and Violet set out cream and sugar.

As was their custom, the women had coffee and dessert in Jane's living room.

"How did you make unripe fruit taste like the freshest peaches I've ever had?" Violet asked Mrs. Pratt.

Mrs. Pratt feigned humility. "I just followed Ruth Reichl's recipe."

Eloise used her fork to point at her plate. "It looks like a simple, rustic dessert, but it tastes like sugared sunshine. You added that magic, Eugenia."

"She's right," Jane said. "The cook makes the recipe. Look at Mrs. Hubbard. Her food is full of love. She's been such an important part of my life, which is why I was so taken with the idea of having famous chefs visit Storyton Hall. I liked the thought of my friends, family, and guests watching that kind of magic happen. The money wasn't too shabby either, but that wasn't what inspired me. I was inspired by the Storyton Hall kitchens. It's not just the amazing food. It's the energy. The marriage of art and chemistry. The passion of the cooks. The way they create from the heart."

Eloise squeezed Jane's hand. "We wanted to experience all of that too. What happened to Chef Pierce isn't your fault. People are unpredictable. There's no telling how your guests will behave."

"If someone gets hurt tomorrow, it'll be entirely my fault." Jane set her dessert plate aside. "Originally, there were supposed to be two challenges. The third contestant is meant to be eliminated at the end of a quick challenge in the morning, but that's been nixed. Now, all three chefs will compete in front of a live audience. Everyone here bought tickets for that event, but if you're up for it, I'd like you to be much closer to the action."

Mrs. Pratt shimmied with glee. "*I* like being close to the action."

"Hear me out, Eugenia. This could be dangerous," Jane warned.

Mabel raised a hand. "Hold up. I heard about Chef Pierce, the fires, and the message on Dew Drop's costume, but isn't the sheriff's department handling the investigation?"

"Yes. The problem is, there isn't enough evidence to make a murder charge stick, or to convince the killer that it's in her best interest to confess. If we can't help Sheriff Evans find that evidence before the chefs and the TV people leave two days from now, then the woman who killed Chef Pierce may never answer for her crime."

Violet looked shocked. "Woman?"

"Settle in," said Jane. "I'm going to tell you a story about a young woman who went down the wrong road. She can't be allowed to continue on this path, no matter how sorry we might feel for the little girl she once was."

Jane picked up her coffee cup, intending to take a quick sip before continuing. The cup was halfway to her mouth when the doorbell rang.

"I'll see who it is," said Eloise, jumping up from her chair.

Half a minute passed, and the Cover Girls waited in silence.

When Eloise didn't come back, they started exchanging nervous glances.

"I'll go see what's going on," Jane said.

In the hall, she opened the front door to discover Eloise and Olivia Limoges on the stoop, chatting away like old friends.

Eloise gave a guilty start. "Were you waiting for me?"

Olivia showed Jane the bottle in her right hand. "I came by to give you this, but when Eloise mentioned Run for Cover, I couldn't help talking shop with her. I'm sorry."

Jane sensed the other Cover Girls behind her.

"Is that the writer?" whispered Violet.

"We should invite her in," hissed Mrs. Pratt.

Jane hesitated. She wanted to end the evening by asking her friends to help her catch a killer. If Olivia Limoges joined them, Jane would have to include her in the plans.

She decided to let instinct be her guide.

"Please come in and meet my friends. We have coffee and dessert, and I'm about to tell a very interesting story."

Olivia pressed the bottle of prosecco into Jane's hands and smiled. "I don't want to intrude, but I do love a good story. And I have a feeling that yours is worth hearing."

Chapter 17

Aunt Octavia was in the lobby, dressed in her Sunday finery. As usual, she was waiting for Jane and the boys to arrive. And as usual, they were late.

Hearing the impatient beat of Aunt Octavia's cane, Jane rushed over and apologized for being late. Her great-aunt didn't respond, and her mouth was set in a deep frown. When hugs from the twins failed to dislodge the frown, Jane knew they weren't the only ones in the doghouse.

"Where's Uncle Aloysius?"

"Fishing." Aunt Octavia injected the word with venom. "*Apparently*, he feels closer to the Lord out on the lake than he does at church. *Apparently*, the way folks cough, blow their noses, rustle candy wrappers, and sing off-key is distracting. What a load of horse manure."

Jane couldn't remember a time when Uncle Aloysius hadn't attended church service with her great-aunt. In such a small village, his absence would be noted, and Jane suspected that Aunt Octavia was more concerned about making excuses for her husband than his level of piety.

"Can we go fishing too?" Hem asked.

Fitz nudged his brother. "*No*. The Robersons and Hofers are paying us for their jam today, remember?"

Aunt Octavia lumbered to her feet and pointed the tip of her cane at Hem. "I thought you liked your Sunday school teacher?"

"We do," said Hem. "But we like hanging out with Uncle Aloysius more."

Ignoring the look of warning on his mother's face, Fitz said, "And we like his stories better than our teacher's. Uncle Aloysius is twice as old as Mrs. Carver, so he's twice as smart."

"Like you," Fitz added for good measure.

Aunt Octavia's expression softened, and Jane suggested they get going before they missed the opening hymn. Fitz and Hem helped Aunt Octavia into the back of Sterling's favorite car, a fully restored 1970 Rolls-Royce Silver Shadow, and played a round of Rock, Paper, Scissors to see who got to sit up front.

Jane slid behind the wheel and was about to shut the door when a hand shot out, grabbing hold of the frame, and Sterling bent close to Jane.

In a hushed, but urgent tone, he said, "I'm sorry to keep you, but I just got a call from Mr. Lachlan that you might want to hear. Another driver can take your family to church, and I'll run you over after we talk if you still want to go."

"Oh, for Pete's sake. It's Sunday morning. Can't this wait?" Aunt Octavia griped from the back seat.

Jane looked at her through the rearview mirror. "With all that's happened lately, I can't take any chances. If I don't make it to the service, would you say a prayer for everyone's safety? Especially during tonight's finale?"

Seeing the worry in Jane's eyes, Aunt Octavia gave her

shoulder an affectionate pat and said, "Of course, dear girl."

Jane switched places with the driver and waved to her family as the elegant Rolls eased forward. The boys waved back while Aunt Octavia blew her a kiss.

"I might be forgiven, but I'm not sure about Uncle Aloysius," Jane told Sterling. "He chose to fish instead of going to church with Aunt Octavia,"

Sterling said, "Your great-uncle is the reason I'm here. He sent me to find you."

Jane's stomach lurched. "Is he okay?"

"He's fine. Mr. Lachlan was surveying the trails around the lake when Mr. Aloysius hailed him over. He found something in the tall grass at the lake's edge—something valuable—and asked Mr. Lachlan to take it to Mr. Sinclair. Should we meet him in the library?"

"Are you going to tell me what this mysterious object is?"

After making sure no one else was around, Sterling said, "A teapot. An antique teapot. Like the ones in the cook-book nook."

Jane groaned. "No, no, no. Mrs. Hubbard and Aunt Octavia will have matching conniptions if a piece from that collection has been stolen."

A few minutes later, Lachlan entered the Henry James Library cradling an object wrapped in a cotton blanket. Jane and the other Fins stood in a loose circle around Sinclair's desk and watched as Lachlan put the bundle down and stepped back. He nodded at Jane, and she carefully unwrapped the teapot.

The light danced over the pot's silver surface, and Jane said, "It's not a teapot. It's a chocolate pot."

Jane remembered how Mrs. Pratt had said, "It was a lovely thing. French sterling. Eighteenth century. Had tiny feet and a wooden handle. The whole piece was embossed with an intricate floral design."

"I think this belongs to Roger Bachman," Jane told the Fins.

Sterling frowned. "Why would the thief toss it in the grass by the lake?"

"Perhaps it was supposed to land in the water," said Butterworth. "We should look for the pillbox in the same area."

Sinclair picked up the chocolate pot and examined it from top to bottom before setting it down again. "A few dents. Nothing that can't be fixed. But why risk stealing a treasure only to throw it away like a piece of trash?"

"I don't know a thing about antiques. What was special about the pillbox?" asked Lachlan.

"It was shaped like a fish," said Sterling. "Maybe the thief is bonkers and decided that a fish-shaped box belonged in a lake. Mr. Aloysius might reel it in one day."

Butterworth's withering look would have silenced another man, but Sterling was immune to the butler's glare.

"All I'm saying is that the chocolate pot was probably in the grass because the thief lacked the arm to get it in the lake."

Lachlan nodded at Sterling. "I saw the spot. It was very close to the edge of the lake. One big rain and this pot would have been a goner."

"Sleeping with the fishes," Sterling said, directing his remark at Butterworth.

Jane didn't hear Butterworth's reply. She'd gone back in time to that terrible morning in the cookbook nook when she'd had her first glimpse of Chef Pierce's body. In her mind's eye, she saw the blood on the floor and the fragments of broken pottery. She saw the dagger-like shard resting in Chef Pierce's palm.

"Fish," she murmured, gazing into the middle distance. "And chocolate."

Suddenly, her eyes lit up. "Of the three pieces of porcelain broken the night Chef Pierce was killed, one was a fish platter and one was a Limoges cup. Sinclair, you thought it was a teacup until you checked our inventory records. But it was a chocolate cup."

"That's right." Sinclair said. "Go on."

"Bentley broke those pieces on purpose. She *wanted* us to notice them. She was trying to send a message about the food industry—Cook's Pride in particular. She posted about the chocolate trade on social media. And fish?" Here, Jane paused. "Edwin mentioned something about aquaculture practices and the mistreatment of fishermen, but I don't know how that relates to this case."

Butterworth cleared his throat. "Ms. Fiore may not be our only suspect. Mr. Sinclair, would you be so kind as to lock the door? I'd rather not be interrupted just now."

Jane's mouth went dry as Sinclair walked to the door and turned the skeleton key until there was an audible click.

Butterworth waited until his colleague rejoined the circle before continuing. "Per your request, Ms. Jane, we've been examining our guests' social media accounts. The exercise has me fearing for the future of mankind, but I digress. We each had a list of guests to research. One of the guests on my list was Ms. Olivia Limoges."

"Olivia doesn't strike me as someone who'd devote much time to social media posts," Jane blurted, feeling an irrational desire to forestall Butterworth.

"In that, you are correct. A virtual assistant runs her

website and handles inquiries about her work. I admit to being somewhat beguiled by Ms. Limoges, and when sleep failed to claim me last night, I found myself at the computer, gazing into her past." Butterworth pulled a piece of paper from his pocket and offered it to Jane. "The man in the grainy photo is Ms. Limoges's father. He was a fisherman, from a long line of fishermen. He was lost at sea when she was a child."

Studying the weather-beaten face and hostile gaze of the man holding a ship's wheel, Jane couldn't see Olivia in his features, but she'd undoubtedly inherited his toughness and resilience. As a fisherman, he must have possessed both of those qualities in spades.

"Two questions," said Jane. "Was her father's death an accident? And did he work for a food company?"

"His cause of death was never determined, but there were rumors of alcohol abuse." A line appeared between Butterworth's brows. "Ms. Limoges has never spoken of her father on record, but she has a history of supporting coastal fishing families whenever bureaucracy threatens their livelihood. One need only read her short story about a shrimp boat captain to know where her sympathies lie."

Jane splayed her hands. "Olivia has a strong opinion about the fishing industry. I imagine she has strong opinions about lots of things. How does this make her a suspect?"

"I believe she told you that her husband was killed in the line of duty."

"Yes." Jane's voice was grave. "He saved Olivia and Chef Michel's wife that day."

Butterworth inclined his head. "Ms. Limoges and Chef Michel were close before this tragedy, but afterward, Chef Michel and his family looked out for Ms. Limoges."

"Which brings us to my research," Sinclair said. "Chef Michel was on my list, and he made for fascinating reading. He grew up in a small town north of Paris, learned cooking techniques from his parents and grandparents, and as a young man, emigrated to the States to run a restaurant in Las Vegas. I saw no red flags in the chef's past. It wasn't until I began scouring his social media pages that I discovered a possible connection to this investigation."

Sinclair reached into his linen suit coat and withdrew a piece of paper. He handed it to Jane, and she looked at a printout showing a collage of images. All the images featured a young woman with high cheek bones, wide eyes framed with long lashes, and a brilliant smile. Her hairstyle changed from photo to photo, as did her makeup and earrings, but her dazzling smile never altered.

Jane didn't want to hear a sad story about this woman. She wanted her to be alive and well, smiling that radiant smile. She said, "Who is she?"

"Chef Michel's sister," said Sinclair. "His mother and father became foster parents after he started university. Their second foster child, Kisi, was born in Ghana. She was very young when her biological parents died. Eventually, Chef Michel's parents adopted Kisi. She lives in Paris and works for an international labor rights group. Children in cocoa-growing communities are her main focus."

"Wait. Isn't Chef Michel's wife a chocolatier?"

"She is. She also shares Kisi's posts, especially if they point a finger at food companies for turning a blind eye to unethical practices in the chocolate trade."

Jane's heart sank. She'd heard the devotion in Olivia's voice when she spoke of Chef Michel, his wife, and his two sons. She'd said they were her family. Jane knew the lengths a woman would go to for her family. And yet she couldn't see how committing murder and arson would benefit Olivia or Chef Michel.

"If these crimes are meant to raise awareness about human rights violations, the killer must attract media attention. Lots of it." Jane glanced around the circle of Fins. "What if the purpose behind these acts was getting Fox Watterson to come to Storyton? The cameras hadn't started rolling before the show became a target. The fire near the tent was no accident, nor was it very dramatic, but it was the first in a series of incidents that eventually forced us to cancel the filming." Jane put Kisi's printout next to the image of Olivia's father. "Who benefits from the downfall of Cook's Pride? Or Fox Watterson?"

Lachlan's gaze fell on the chocolate pot. "Has Ms. Limoges been to Roger's shop?"

"Yes." Jane repeated what Mrs. Pratt had told her about Olivia's visit.

"I don't care if Ms. Limoges was at the scene of every crime," said Sterling. "Unless she and Ms. Fiore were working together, I don't see how she'd coerce Chef Pierce into meeting her in the cookbook nook in the middle of the night."

"What about the grill?" asked Lachlan. "According to the sheriff, Chief Aroneo found evidence showing that someone tampered with the valve. Why would Ms. Limoges put Chef Michel at risk by messing with one of the grills? Especially since the grills were haphazardly assigned to each chef."

Butterworth grunted. "Let's leave the ladies be for now and concentrate on Mr. Watterson. If the killer's goal was to draw him here, then we need to understand his importance.

Cook's Pride isn't the only food company guilty of mistreating workers, so why single out their CEO?"

The hour Jane and Edwin had spent researching Fox Watterson had only scratched the surface. If she wanted to get a feel for this man, she needed to sit down with him. To break bread and split a bottle of wine with him. To learn about his world, she'd invite him into hers.

"Gentlemen, I'm going to ask Mr. Watterson to have lunch with me. An intimate meal in my great-aunt and -uncle's apartments would be just the thing."

Sinclair responded with an impish grin. "Where could you find a server adept at interpreting body language?"

Jane ran a finger down the soft fabric of Sinclair's suit sleeve. "The same place I'd find a sharp-dressed man to cozy up to Mia's hair and makeup artist. Ply him with strong drinks and see what he knows about Bentley."

As Sinclair cast a longing gaze at the stack of books waiting to be shelved, Butterworth's mouth formed the ghost of a smile.

The clock on the mantel in Aunt Octavia's sitting room was a breath from striking one when Fox Watterson knocked on the apartment door.

After inviting the gentleman inside, Butterworth introduced Fox to Uncle Aloysius and Aunt Octavia.

Uncle Aloysius had changed out of his fishing gear into a seersucker suit. Fox wore a pale blue poplin suit and carried a bouquet of roses, which he presented to Aunt Octavia.

"How thoughtful! No one has ever given me flowers to match my dress before." Aunt Octavia waved at the round table in the middle of the room. "Make yourself at home. I'll just put these in water."

Jane thanked Fox for coming, and she and the two men sat down.

Uncle Aloysius complimented Fox on his suit. Fox, in turn, praised Storyton Hall.

"I usually prefer modern architecture. I like walls of windows, sharp angles, and sleek design, but there's a dignity about this place. It feels solid. Dependable."

"What you sense is history," said Uncle Aloysius. "Generations of Stewards have lived in this house. It holds our stories in its rafters, our laughter in its worn stairs, and our memories are lodged in all the spaces in between. I used to tell Jane that the creaks she heard in the middle of the night were the voices of her relatives. Not ghosts but guardians."

Aunt Octavia returned. The roses were now in a silver vase, which she placed on a side table. "They'll keep me company while I read. Butterworth? We can start now."

Butterworth served watermelon, feta, and mint salad, and as everyone picked up their forks, the conversation naturally turned to food. When Jane asked Fox if he'd always wanted to work in the food industry, he spoke openly about his decision to leave a promising career at a rival food company to start his own.

The salad plates were cleared, the red snapper with herb butter entrée was served, and the conversation between the four diners flowed with ease. At this point, Jane decided that the ice had been suitably broken.

Looking at Fox, she said, "You're probably wondering if I had an ulterior motive in asking you to lunch today, and I admit that I did."

"If you're going to ask me to cancel the show—"

"I'm not," interrupted Jane. "I'll do all I can to make sure tonight's finale goes off without a hitch."

Fox relaxed. "That's good to hear."

"However, I'm still deeply concerned about the safety of my guests. Including you, Mr. Watterson. You might not be a registered guest, but you'll be sitting with the rest of the audience tonight. And I believe that the terrible things we've experienced over the past few days—from murder to arson—happened for one reason."

Fox stopped eating. "Which is?"

"Someone wanted to lure you to Storyton."

Fox laughed. He glanced at Uncle Aloysius and Aunt Octavia to see if they shared in the joke, but their solemn expressions caused the laughter to die in his throat. He turned back to Jane. "You're serious."

"Mr. Watterson—"

"No more of that, please. Call me Fox."

Though Jane preferred to remain on formal terms with this man, she needed him to confide in her, and addressing him by his first name seemed like a good way to build trust. "Okay, Fox. Let me tell you where I'm coming from. The person who killed Chef Pierce also tampered with the propane tank and wrote the message about Cook's Pride on the mascot's shirt. At first, my staff and I thought Chef Pierce was the only target. Then, we believed someone wanted to shut down the show. But after seeing the message on the mascot—on the day you showed up in Storyton—we began to ask ourselves if what the killer wanted most was you."

The notion didn't disturb Fox one bit. "Do you know how many threats I get a year? Hundreds. By snail mail. By email. To my face. It comes with the territory. No CEO of a company as big as mine makes it six months without a threat from a former employee, a disgruntled consumer, and lots of other people."

"What about activists?" asked Aunt Octavia.

Jane wanted to high-five her great-aunt. She and Uncle Aloysius knew the hours leading up to the finale were speeding by and would do anything to help Jane put an end to the turmoil that had accompanied *Posh Palate with Mia Mallett.*

Fox shrugged. "Sure. Activists too."

"We're keeping an eye on two guests who may be strongly opposed to some of your company's business practices," Jane explained. "To be clear, I'm not accusing Cook's Pride of anything, but the practices in question involve workers in the chocolate and fishing industries."

Jane didn't need to be an expert in body language to know that when Fox pushed his plate away and folded his hands in his lap, he was signaling that not only was he finished with his meal, but he didn't want to continue the discussion.

Butterworth cleared the remnants of the main course and retreated, allowing Fox time to formulate a reply.

"There will always be people who take issue with how we do business. When complaints are valid, we strive to make changes. But no international corporation of our size is perfect."

Fox raised his napkin as if he meant to deposit it on the table, indicating that their lunch was over. Luckily, Butterworth deposited a fruit and cheese board in the center of the table and asked for coffee orders before the napkin left Fox's hand. Jane and Aunt Octavia requested coffee with cream, while Uncle Aloysius opted for a digestif.

"Care to join me?" he asked Fox. "I have an apple brandy that really hits the spot on a hot, heavy day like this one."

Fox shrugged. "Why not?"

"I'm sorry," Jane said to Fox. "I don't mean to dampen the mood. Please believe me when I say that this is coming from a place of concern."

"Which I appreciate. But after the finale, I'm gone. I can take care of myself for the eight hours."

Butterworth placed brandy glasses on the table and Jane waited until he'd poured an inch of liquor into each glass before saying, "Just one more question before I drop the subject. Did you sponsor the show because your nephew is the director?"

Fox swirled the brandy around in his glass. "Ty's my sister's boy. When my sister told me that she was paying to send Ty to film school, I told her she might as well dump her money in the river. I never thought he'd amount to anything, but he proved me wrong when he landed this directing gig. So when he asked me to sponsor the show this season, I said yes. After my marketing team gave the green light, that is."

"Didn't your sister want to see her son in action?" Aunt Octavia asked. "I would have been bursting with pride if one of my brood became the director of such a famous show."

"Oh, Rosemary doesn't fly. She hasn't stepped foot on a plane in twenty years. She'd like this place, though. Calls herself an armchair traveler because she spends her free time reading."

Uncle Aloysius raised his glass. "To family."

He and Fox knocked rims and drank. While the men analyzed the brandy, Jane sipped her coffee and tried to think. Fox's siblings helped him run Cook's Pride. Was there any animosity between them, or were they all one, big, happy family?

Fox finished his brandy and surveyed his hosts. "I came here expecting a battle royale. Instead, I've had an excellent meal with fine company. Thank you. If you're ever out my way, I'd love to repay the favor."

Seeing that the meal had reached an end, Jane got to her feet. "I'll walk you to the lobby."

In the elevator, she tried to learn more about how Fox felt toward Ty or his siblings, but his answers weren't useful.

"Do you or your sister worry about him getting hurt? As the director, he's right in the middle of all the action, and there've been two fires and a murder over the past few days."

Fox shrugged. "Ty can look after himself. He might be half Scott, but he's also half Watterson. And Wattersons are bold."

In the lobby, Fox asked for permission to look around before returning to his hotel. Jane gave it, and they went their separate ways.

Fox turned toward the terrace while Jane went straight to the surveillance room. She watched Fox walk across the terrace, heading for Milton's Gardens. She also saw Olivia Limoges exit the gardens. As usual, Captain Haviland was glued to her heel. As usual, he wasn't leashed.

If Olivia and Haviland continued on their current course, they'd run right into Fox Watterson.

Jane was annoyed. She'd told Olivia Limoges that her poodle couldn't run free around other guests. And here he was, obediently stuck to Olivia's side, but still unleashed.

On the monitor, Fox froze. And then, without warning, he scooped something off the ground and hurled it at Olivia.

There was a streak of black on the video screen as

Haviland darted forward and collided with Fox. The poodle knocked Fox to the grass and pinned him in place with his front paws while flashing his teeth.

"Don't do it!" Jane cried.

As if he'd heard her plea, Haviland's ears pricked. A second later, he turned and trotted back to Olivia.

Jane rushed out of the surveillance room. In the staff corridor, she ran through the dim passageways, drawing concerned looks from her employees as they pressed against the rough stone walls to make way for her.

She was breathing hard when she burst out onto the terrace, but she hadn't moved fast enough.

Fox, Olivia, and Captain Haviland had disappeared.

Chapter 18

Jane didn't see Olivia Limoges again until minutes before Butterworth opened the doors to Shakespeare's Theater. Even with all the members of the live audience clustered outside the theater, Olivia stood out. Her height and her corona of light blond hair made her easy to spot.

Tonight, she wore a sleeveless cobalt top over white slacks and a necklace of silver beads. Though she didn't appear to notice the admiring glances of the other guests, she met Jane's gaze right away.

Stepping out of line, Olivia joined Jane by the massive lobby fireplace.

"You and I look like summer skies," she said. "You're the blue of a morning sky, and I'm the blue of a twilight sky."

Jane wore a pale blue wrap dress because it flattered her figure and allowed her to move. Her strappy sandals would be a hindrance should she have to chase a criminal, but she could hardly wear her beloved Chuck Taylors to such a prestigious event.

"I stopped by your cottage an hour ago, but you must have been out," Jane said. "Did you get my messages?"

"Yes, but not until fifteen minutes ago." Olivia's cobalt

shirt gave her eyes an electric blue cast. "I'm sorry you couldn't reach me. I invited Michel over for tea and turned my phone off while he was there. Of course, I forgot to turn it back on. Anyway, Michel wanted me to tell you that he's in."

Jane wanted to express her gratitude, but she needed to be clear on another matter first. "The encounter between you and Fox Watterson at the entrance to Milton's Gardens—what happened?"

Olivia blinked in surprise. "That was *Watterson*? The photos on the company literature have obviously been doctored. That Fox Watterson looks twenty years younger and has a full head of hair." She gave a tiny shake of her head. "What happened is this: Fox doesn't like dogs. He took it as a personal affront that Haviland wasn't leashed. He had a right to be upset, so I apologized. I also explained that while I forgot to pack a leash, Haviland would stick to my ankle like glue. Nothing I said appeased the man. He called me several names I won't repeat. His hostile tone and aggressive body language quickly escalated the situation. I warned him to stop before Haviland saw him as a threat."

"He didn't listen."

Anger sparked in Olivia's eyes. "Listen? He threw a rock at me like some playground bully, I told Haviland to take him down. Haviland trained alongside a police dog. He knows how to knock a person off their feet. Fox Watterson was never in danger, but I wasn't going to let him pick up another rock." Olivia gave Jane a quizzical look. "Has he lodged a complaint?"

"No. I wanted to know if this was the first encounter between you two, or one of many. I'm taking a big risk trusting you."

"I understand," Olivia said. "I own a restaurant, which means I know that Fox Watterson is the CEO of Cook's Pride, but we never met until today. I want to help you, Jane. I want to help Michel. I want to do what I used to do when my husband was alive."

Jane softened her gaze. "Which was?"

"Find the truth." Olivia moved a step closer to Jane. "I owe you. Because of you and your cottage, I've found my voice again. I'm brimming with words and ideas. You had my loyalty the moment my fingers started flying over the keyboard."

Olivia held up a hand to keep Jane from congratulating her. "I was really touched when you invited me to join your book club meeting. Those women are more than friends. They're sisters, cheerleaders, confidantes, and sugar enablers. I used to have friends like that, and I didn't realize how much I miss them until last night."

Jane squeezed Olivia's forearm. "You and I are going to be friends. But right now, we have places to be and people to watch."

When Olivia raised her chin in a show of determination, she looked like the goddess of the hunt—just as she had the night Jane first saw her. She laid a hand on Jane's shoulder as if bestowing a boon and whispered, "Let slip the dogs of war, Jane Steward."

The last of the guests waiting to enter the theater moved through the double doors. Butterworth nodded politely as they passed, but when Olivia approached, he offered his arm.

As Jane ducked into the staff corridor, she wondered if it had been a trick of the light, or if Butterworth had smiled at a guest.

Olivia has charmed us all, Jane thought. *If we're wrong about her, we're doomed.*

In the kitchens, the finalists were buttoning up their double-breasted jackets and unrolling their knife bags. Jane's friends placed water bottles at three prep stations. In their server's uniforms, with their hair pulled back into tight buns, they fit right in.

"My dogs of war," Jane murmured when Eloise gave her a thumbs-up.

Eloise and Violet had paired with Lachlan and Sterling to work as kitchen helpers. It was their job to supply each chef with the tools they required. The kitchen helpers would also remove dirty bowls and pans from the workstations, but only when the cameras weren't pointed in their direction.

The rest of the Fins and Cover Girls were also given assignments.

From his position at the front of the kitchen, Sinclair would monitor the film crew. As soon as the audience was seated, Butterworth was to report to the kitchen to watch Bentley's every move. Mabel, Mrs. Pratt, and Betty were to look for any suspicious activity among the audience members.

Olivia had already played her part. She'd asked Chef Michel to make a very difficult choice. When she'd said, "he's in," back in the lobby, she was telling Jane that Chef Michel had agreed to forgo his chance to win money and prestige for a greater prize: justice.

Knowing her plan couldn't have succeeded without his help, Jane tried to catch Chef Michel's eye. She wanted to convey her gratitude with a nod and a smile, but he was too busy organizing his station to notice her.

If we make it through the next two hours, I'll find a way

to thank him, Jane thought as she headed over to where Mia sat on a stool, surrounded by her assistants. Dylan fiddled with her hair, a young woman applied powder to her nose, and Bentley adjusted the tiny microphone attached to the collar of her dress.

Jane took in the ivory lace dress with its satin sash and tea-length skirt.

"You're gorgeous," she told Mia. "If I wore that, I'd look like Miss Havisham, but you're the picture of vintage glam."

"Did you hear that, guys and dolls? She said Miss Havisham!" Mia beamed at Jane. "That's exactly what I was going for. This dress is from Coco Chanel's bridal collection. Oh, speaking of collections, I have something to show you."

Mia told her assistants she was taking a breather and led Jane to a prep counter where several objects were covered in a white bedsheet.

"Can you guess what's under here?" Mia asked, bouncing on the balls of her feet like a kid waiting for the ice cream truck to come to a full stop.

Jane had no idea. "Does it have anything to do with the finale?"

Still bouncing, Mia shook her head. "Not at all. This is my way of apologizing to you and your family. My show is supposed to be a positive experience. It's supposed to give chefs the chance to show off their skills and create amazing food. But this season's been a disaster, and I'm sorry that my show brought such negative energy to your beautiful resort." She gathered a corner of the sheet in her small hand. "This doesn't make up for the bad things, but it was the only thing I could fix."

She carefully removed the sheet and tossed it aside. Her

assistants, who'd been scurrying around and chattering like squirrels, silently waited for Jane to react.

All Jane could do was stare. Her brain couldn't compute what her eyes were telling her. It wasn't possible. There was no way anyone, not even an influential billionaire, could have replaced the pieces from the cookbook nook. They were antiques. And in the case of the soup tureen, rare antiques.

Jane picked up the fish platter. She felt its heft, saw the crazing in the glaze, and turned it over to examine the maker's stamp. She was no expert, but she knew a reproduction when she saw one. This platter had the weight and patina of age.

"How did you manage this?" she asked.

Mia's smile was luminous. "I have connections. And I know these pieces haven't been passed down through your family, but Mrs. Hubbard can still have that special party for your great-aunt."

"This is incredibly generous," Jane said. "Does Mrs. Hubbard know?"

"Not yet." The light in Mia's eyes dimmed. "I can't erase what happened there, but I hope this helps."

"Thank you, I—" Jane began.

Mia flung her arms around Jane and whispered, "Thank *you* for making tonight possible," Stepping back, she waved at her assistants. "Final touches. We have five minutes."

Jane hoped to get a read on Bentley, but she was ticking items off a checklist. Nothing about her behavior raised a red flag. She seemed entirely focused on the task at hand.

"Five minutes, people!" Ty shouted through a bullhorn. "Chefs! Go to the marked spot at your stations and hold still while Mia does her intro. Everyone else should clear the set!"

Just then, Mrs. Hubbard walked out of the pantry into the kitchen. As she caught sight of the treasures on the counter, her hand flew to her mouth, and a squeak escaped from between her fingers. "How? Where?"

Jane put a steadying hand on Mrs. Hubbard's back. "Mia replaced everything that was broken. I'm glad you got to see this, but I'm going to grab Eloise and Violet and move this stuff before the craziness starts."

"That Mia," Mrs. Hubbard murmured, shaking her head in awe. "What a gem,"

As if she'd heard, Mia glanced in their direction. Mrs. Hubbard blew her a kiss and Mia mimicked the gesture.

"Four minutes!"

"Oh, I'm a bundle of nerves!" Mrs. Hubbard scurried off while Jane, Eloise, and Violet moved the treasures to the break room. Jane returned to her assigned place seconds before Ty called for quiet on the set. Then, he pointed at Mia. She walked to the center of the kitchen, pasted on a smile, and began to talk.

"Welcome to the finale of *Posh Palate with Mia Mallett*! Tonight, one of our three chefs—that's right, I said *three*—will walk away with the golden ladle. Cook's Pride, our generous sponsor, is sweetening the pot with a cookbook deal and a line of cookware named after the winner. Pretty posh, right?"

Mia paused to let the cameras catch the chefs' reactions. Several seconds later, a member of the film crew held up a cardboard stop sign, and the room went quiet again.

"This season, our show filmed on location at Storyton Hall, Virginia, an amazing resort catering to book, food, and nature lovers. The gorgeous reading rooms filled with beautiful books inspired the literary themes of our episodes and turned our chefs into culinary storytellers. It's my privilege to introduce you to our three finalists."

The feed switched to the camera focused on the work-stations. After congratulating Chefs August, Lindsay, and Michel for making it to the finale, Mia recited a brief biography of each chef.

Turning back to the main camera, she said, "Charles Dickens wrote, 'It was the best of times. It was the worst of times.' That quote summarizes this season. When one of our talented contestants, Chef Pierce, suddenly passed away, the loss touched us all. But we kept going because we knew Chef Pierce would want his colleagues to keep competing. They rose to the occasion and created some amazing dishes. Levi and Coco? Would you agree?"

The judges weren't in the kitchen. They were seated at a table in the Rudyard Kipling Café, alone except for members of the film crew. While Levi and Coco reviewed their favorite dishes from each chef, Jane watched Mia's assistants.

All four held clipboards and were laser-focused on the papers attached to those clipboards. Occasionally, they'd glance at their smartwatches before consulting the papers again. They stood, shoulder to shoulder, waiting for a break in the action. There was nothing sinister about the young assistants, Bentley included.

The light on the camera facing Mia turned red and she smiled.

"The chefs were told the theme of their final challenge a few hours ago. Now, it's your turn." Moving over to a round table holding a bounty of food that included a roast turkey, puddings, cakes, rolls, fruit, and more, she picked up the book sitting on a silver charger. "We couldn't end

our bookish cook-off without a celebration feast, and my
favorite literary feast is from *A Christmas Carol* by Charles
Dickens. I love the Cratchits. They're a reminder of how important family is to all of us. And I love how Ebenezer
Scrooge starts the book as a villain but ends up as a hero.
He brings gifts to the Cratchits, and they all sit down to
celebrate food, family, and their blessings."

There was a hitch to Mia's voice as she spoke this line,
and Jane wondered if Mia missed her family. With her
work and travel schedule, she might not see the people she
loved as often as she'd like. Even with the constant presence
of her entourage, she might still feel lonely.

Jane, who'd spent every Christmas celebrating with her
family and friends, knew how lucky she was to have them
all so close. They were always available, always willing to
give her support. They were supporting her right now.
There were Fins and Cover Girls in the kitchens, Uncle
Aloysius and Aunt Octavia sat with the other Cover Girls
in the theater, and Edwin was at Jane's house, cooking with
Fitz and Hem.

"You can't have a feast without a variety of dishes," Mia
continued. "Our chefs were given a list of every food mentioned in *A Christmas Carol*, and their dishes will feature
one of these foods. Since we haven't given them much
time, we thought they could use a helping hand. Chefs?
Would you each pick a golden spoon from the crock to see
who your sous chef will be for your final challenge?"

Chef August and Chef Michel hung back, graciously
allowing Chef Lindsay to choose first. She pulled a spoon
from the crock and cried, "Chef Alondra!"

Chef Alondra ran into the room and the two women embraced.

Chef Michel and Chef August pulled the remaining spoons out of the crock.

"Yessss!" shouted Chef August. "Chef Saffron!"

Chef Saffron rushed into the kitchen and Chef August lifted her up in his massive arms as if she were a bag of flour.

"I'm so glad to be on your team!" she said when he put her down.

"Me too." Chef August gave her a fist bump.

There was a dramatic pause as the cameras focused on Chef Michel. Raising his golden spoon in the air like Lady Liberty's torch, he said, "I am the luckiest man in this room because *my* partner is Chef Hubbard!"

Mrs. Hubbard trotted in wearing chef's whites and a wide smile. After waving at Jane and the Cover Girls, she and Chef Michel kissed each other on both cheeks.

"Chef Hubbard runs the kitchens here at Storyton Hall," Mia explained. "Not only is she a veteran cook, but she also knows how to infuse her food with the flavors of home. We're grateful to her for stepping into what's bound to be a super-exciting role."

Mrs. Hubbard gave a little bow. She then straightened and tugged the ends of her floral neckerchief. She looked antsy and eager, like the twins when Jane asked if they'd like to ride to the village for ice cream.

Mia turned to face the contestants. "Chefs. The time has come. You may now start preparing your Christmas Carol Feast!"

The chefs flew into action, racing to collect ingredients

from the pantry and walk-in fridge. With all the cameras tracking the movements of the chefs, Mia was free to sit down and be ministered to by her assistants. Three of them surveyed her clothes, hair, and makeup while Bentley read from the notes on her clipboard. Sidling closer to the group, Jane listened to Bentley review the upcoming sequence of events. She kept glancing from her clipboard to Mia's face, clearly hoping for a response, but Mia didn't seem to be paying attention.

And then, the cameras focused on the short hallway leading from the kitchen to the break room. Levi and Coco strolled into the kitchen, looking nothing like they had in the Rudyard Kipling Café.

"No way!" cried Chef Saffron as she took in the judges' Victorian garb. Levi wore a formal suit, complete with waistcoat and top hat. Coco was resplendent in a green silk gown trimmed with lace.

Stopping in front of Chef August's station, Levi said, "Tell me about your feast."

"My feast is a Southern Christmas. It's my mama's food influenced by Charles Dickens. I'm making spinach with apples and walnuts, fried oysters, Cajun baked chicken, hash brown soufflé, and a cranberry-orange sponge cake with Grand Marnier glaze."

"We can't wait to try the finished products. Carry on, good sir." Coco curtsied before moving to Chef Lindsay's station.

Chef Lindsay's angular face was already pink with exertion. She gave the judges a tight smile and answered their question before they had the chance to ask it. "I'm going to lighten up the traditional Dickensian feast by giving it an infusion of California freshness. Root veggie mince pie, potato stacks with garlic and thyme, tenderloin with wine and chestnuts, herb pudding, and a lemon and cardamom Twelfth Night cake."

Chef Lindsay picked up her knife and was poised to continue chopping potatoes, but Levi wasn't going to let her return to work just yet. "How concerned are you about time?"

"I'm very concerned," said Chef Lindsay. "But I'm also grateful that Chef Alondra is here to help me create the most important meal of my life."

Satisfied, the judges wished her luck and continued on to Chef Michel's station.

"Your outfits are *très magnifique*." Chef Michel brushed off his white jacket. "If I had known the occasion was this formal, I would have worn my black coat."

Coco laughed. "We'll be too focused on your food to notice what you're wearing. So tell us. Will your dishes feature French cuisine?"

Chef Michel smiled. "My feast will take you on a trip around the world. French food is spectacular, *bien sûr*, but when you combine the foods and flavors from other cultures—that's when a dish is transformed from delicious to unforgettable."

Levi rubbed his palms together. "An international feast. Good thing I have my passport. Tell us about your dishes."

"Tonight we're making spicy Thai grilled oysters with bird's eye chilis served with a side of Asian pear slaw, pan-seared foie gras, lamb and spinach Wellington, and onion bhaji Yorkshire pudding. For dessert, we have African chocolate pudding with chestnut whipped cream. That one's for my sister, Kisi, whom I carry here."

Chef Michel laid his palm over his heart, and Mrs. Hubbard dabbed at her eyes with the corner of her apron. Jane glanced over at Bentley. The young woman was holding her clipboard against her chest and staring fixedly at Mia. She looked nervous, as if she didn't know what Mia would do next.

But Mia wasn't doing anything. She was frozen in grief. The furrows on her forehead, her downturned mouth, and her wet eyes marked a pain that was too powerful to be sympathy. Chef Michel's remark about his sister had triggered something in Mia. To Jane, that something looked like loss.

And then, Dylan handed Mia a wad of tissues. She wiped her cheeks, blew her nose, and quickly rearranged her expression. She gave her assistant a self-deprecating smile as he bent to repair her makeup.

Across the room, the judges wished Chef Michel well and let him get on with his work.

For the next hour, Mia and the two judges took turns checking in with the chefs. Jane was so riveted by the displays of culinary prowess that she had to remind herself to keep an eye on Bentley.

The anxiety Bentley had exhibited after Chef Michel's short speech was gone. She'd relaxed her death grip on her clipboard and seemed more interested in exchanging whispered comments with her coworkers than watching the action in the kitchen.

When the countdown clock read thirty minutes, Jane stepped out of the room to call Edwin.

"We're down to the last half hour," she told him.

"Ned's here," Edwin said, referring to the bellhop who often watched the twins. "The boys started *Jumanji* after dinner, so Ned can just turn off the TV when it's done and send the boys to bed. Has anything unusual happened?"

Jane hesitated. "Nothing specific, but I'm getting a

something wicked this way comes vibe. From where, I don't know."

"Your disadvantage is that you don't know what's coming," Edwin said. "But my love, your advantage is that you're surrounded by people who are looking, listening, and waiting to leap to your defense. Including me. See you in five minutes."

Next, Jane read all the recent texts from the Fins. All was quiet in Storyton Hall. There'd been no surprise visitors and no guests wandered the grounds. A few members of the audience had left the theater to use the restroom, but most stayed in their seats, snacking on nuts, popcorn, fruit, cheese, and candy.

The Cover Girls reported that they were having a grand time and all was as it should be in the theater.

Satisfied, Jane returned to the hallway to find Mia's assistants helping her into a beautiful Victorian taffeta gown. The garnet hue highlighted Mia's creamy skin and dark hair, and the hoop skirt and lightly boned blouse accentuated Mia's narrow waist and slim frame.

Jane said, "You're a vision in scarlet."

"Thanks." Mia ran her hands over the soft folds covering her hips. "The cousin I told you about? The one who helped me sell my food when we were kids? He was born on a Sunday. In Thailand, that's a day for wearing red."

"Seven minutes," Bentley said, glancing from Jane to Mia. Bentley looked nervous again, and Jane noticed that Mia was turning her tiger eye ring around and around, just as she had the evening she showed up unannounced at Jane's house.

Mia gave Jane an apologetic smile. "Sorry, but I have to stand still and be quiet or they won't finish my hair and makeup in time."

Having been politely dismissed, Jane returned to the steamy, motion-filled kitchen.

"How can they pull this off? They're down to the last few minutes," Eloise whispered to Jane. "Oh, Edwin's here. I didn't see him come in."

Jane spotted her man standing next to Lachlan on the far side of the room. He looked devilishly handsome in a light blue dress shirt and camel slacks. Mia's assistants were openly admiring him, as were several members of the film crew.

Edwin smiled at Jane, and the warmth of his smile made her light up like a star. The show's final minute was ticking down, and her body hummed with adrenaline. She was ready to spring into action. But first, a winner had to be declared.

Levi and Coco were no longer in the kitchen. They'd returned to the Rudyard Kipling Café to taste the chefs' savory dishes. The three feasts were laid out on separate tables, with space reserved for the desserts.

As soon as Mia called, "Time!" the desserts were carried off to the café.

Mia entered the frame as the chefs were exchanging hugs and high-fives.

"This has to be the friendliest competition I've ever seen," Jane whispered to Eloise.

After briefly asking the chefs about the highs and lows of the final challenge, Mia said, "I can't wait to see the finished feasts! And as Charles Dickens said, 'The pain of parting is nothing to the joy of meeting again.' So let's joyfully meet with our judges!"

When the show aired, the action would pick up in the Rudyard Kipling Café without delay. In real time, the film crew relocated to the café while the chefs drank water, used the restroom, and washed the sweat from their faces. After changing into clean white coats, they hurried to the café and took up their places behind their feast table.

Butterworth escorted Fox Watterson to his seat of honor at the judges' table and a member of the film crew called for silence on the set.

Ty yelled, "Action!" and the cameras started rolling. Jane wasn't listening when Mia introduced Fox Watterson or thanked Cook's Pride. Jane's focus was on locating Bentley.

Moving on cat feet, Jane edged around lighting and stepped over extension cords. She saw three of Mia's assistants leaning on the bar, but Bentley wasn't with them.

She wasn't anywhere.

Jane went cold with dread. Had the killer just escaped? Or was she somewhere inside Storyton Hall, preparing to execute a finale of her own?

When her phone vibrated in her pocket, Jane grabbed for it with trembling hands. She read the text from Lachlan and went limp with relief.

We have her in the break room.

Suddenly, Edwin was at Jane's side. He slid an arm around her waist, leaned in close, and whispered, "Are you okay?"

She turned and threw her arms around him. "The Fins have her." She sighed into his neck. "Everything's okay."

Chapter 19

As much as Jane wanted to join Lachlan, she couldn't leave the café just yet. Olivia had talked Chef Michel into throwing away a potential victory, but with Bentley out of the picture, his sacrifice was no longer necessary. Jane knew that she had to convey that message to him.

After whispering her intentions to Edwin, Jane crept closer to the three tables where the chefs waited for the judges' verdict.

Levi and Coco got to their feet and moved to the front of their table. With Fox trailing along, they walked over to Chef Lindsay's table.

"Chef Lindsay, you put a fresh twist on your Christmas Carol Feast," Coco said. She held the golden ladle, which Chef Lindsay stared at with unconcealed desire. "We loved your creativity. We also admire the way you incorporate local and seasonal ingredients into your dishes. Unfortunately, the tenderloin was overcooked, and there was too much cardamom in the cake. You're an amazing chef, but I'm sorry to say that your feast didn't win the golden ladle."

Chef Lindsay's voice wavered, but she still managed

to thank the judges, Mia, and Cook's Pride. As soon as the cameras stopped pointing at her, Chef Lindsay began to weep. Chef Alondra rushed to her colleague's side to comfort her.

A few feet away, Fox and the judges stood between Chef August's and Chef Michel's tables.

"This is it." Mia shook her fist in excitement. "One of these gentlemen is about to become this season's Posh Chef. Coco and Levi, was it a tough decision?"

"Incredibly tough," said Levi. "Chefs, we were impressed by many of your dishes. Chef August, your Cajun chicken was perfectly tender and packed with flavor."

"And I wanted to lick the Grand Marnier glaze right off my plate. If I need to make a fruitcake in the future, I want to use your recipe."

Chef August spread his hands in a gesture of giving. "It's yours."

Coco turned to Chef Michel. "When you told us what you planned to cook, I was a little worried. You were using flavor combinations that I didn't think would work. Lamb Wellington and an Indian-inspired Yorkshire Pudding? I never tried anything like that, but you transformed that dish from delicious to unforgettable."

Levi pointed at a platter on the table. "To me, those Thai grilled oysters were the star of the show. The heat from the chilis was offset by the pear slaw, and there were so many layers of flavor in that dish. Mia tried it too, and it was so good that it made her cry."

The camera panned to Mia and she gave Levi a sheepish smile.

"If Coco wanted to drink Chef August's Grand Marnier glaze with a straw, then I wanted to take your chocolate cake back to my room and eat the whole thing in private,"

Levi continued. "I'm not a dessert guy, but that cake was fantastically rich *and* light as air at the same time."

Chef Michel dipped his chin. "Thank you. I'm honored."

By this point, Jane had moved into Chef Michel's line of vision. She waved, hoping he'd notice her, but his eyes were locked on the judges.

"As close as you both came to culinary perfection, there were a few flaws," said Coco. "Chef August, your spinach with apples and walnuts lacked a wow factor."

"And while Coco loved your hash brown soufflé, I wanted more crunch."

Coco looked at Chef Michel. "Levi and I weren't on the same page when it came to your foie gras. He was a fan, but I thought it ate heavy."

Chef Michel bowed in apology. When he straightened, Jane raised her right arm and waved. Again, she failed to get his attention.

"I'm glad I'm just the host!" Mia laughed. After miming wiping sweat from her forehead, she took a deep breath and slowly let it out. "Levi. Coco. It's obvious that you had a difficult choice to make, but the time has come. Please tell us the name of the winning chef."

Jane's adrenaline turned to panic, and she waved both arms, crossing them over her head as she bounced up and down on the balls of her feet. When Chef Michel finally looked at her, she shook her head and mouthed, "Don't do it."

She couldn't tell if he understood. The lights were shining in his eyes, and he was seconds away from learning if he'd earned the victory he'd worked so hard to achieve.

Levi and Coco took a step back, and Fox Watterson moved into the camera frame.

Accepting the golden ladle from Coco, Fox grinned and

said, "Before I announce the winner of *Posh Palate with Mia Mallett*, I'd like to introduce everyone to the woman who runs this incredible resort. Ms. Jane Steward, please join us."

The request caught Jane by surprise. She didn't want to be filmed. She didn't want to be on the show—not even for a minute. But since joining Fox meant she'd also be close to Chef Michel, Jane stepped into the spotlight.

"Thank you for hosting our talented chefs, Ms. Steward, and for the hospitality we've been shown by everyone at Storyton Hall." Fox smiled at Jane as if she was his favorite person on earth. "And now, Cook's Pride would like to congratulate Chef Michel of Oyster Bay, North Carolina. You are our Posh Chef."

Color rushed into Chef Michel's face, and he smiled so widely that the people on the far side of the room could see his dimples.

As the café erupted in whistles, cheers, and applause, Jane turned to Chef Michel as if she were congratulating him and said, "We don't need the teatime plan anymore—this is your win and you should accept it."

Chef Michel nodded just as Chef August enfolded him in a bear hug. The two men embraced, rocking side to side and showering compliments on each other.

Jane heard someone say, "I love their bromance!"

When they finally separated, the men used their coat sleeves to wipe away tears.

"Chef Michel, I believe this is yours." Fox held out the golden ladle.

Chef Michel stared at the trophy with longing but made no move to take it. Instead, he dropped his hands to his side and said, "I want to thank the judges for this incredible honor. I've worked in many kitchens, but I've never met a group of chefs who cook with as much heart as the ones I've met on this show. Chefs, it has been a privilege to share a kitchen with you."

Fox shot Mia a puzzled glance, but her gaze was locked on Chef Michel.

And why wouldn't it be? Jane thought. *This is drama. This is great TV.*

Still, it seemed like Chef Michel was going ahead with the plan, even though it was no longer necessary. If so, he was about to throw away a cookbook deal, a boatload of money, and his reputation.

Jane didn't realize that she'd been shaking her head until Chef Michel winked at her.

As he turned back to Fox, his smile vanished. "Mr. Watterson, my adopted sister is called Kisi. She was born in Ghana. Her parents sent her away because they didn't want her working ten-hour days on a cocoa farm. They died when she was seven. She's a woman now—a woman who gives all she has trying to protect the rights of these children. Until the world's largest food companies, Cook's Pride included, join in this effort, I cannot accept this prize. I will step aside so that you can present it to Chef August."

Fox was dumbfounded. For a moment he just stood there, gawking. He looked from Chef Michel to the judges, but they'd been shocked into silence. With no other choice before him, Fox offered the golden ladle to Chef August.

Chef August elbowed Chef Michel. "Come on, man! What are doing? You can't be serious."

"I told you about Kisi. I know you understand, my friend."

Throwing his arms up in the air, Chef August cried, "*I* can't take it either! What's happening to those kids hurts me deep in here." He pounded his chest.

"If you don't take that trophy, I will," threatened Chef Lindsay.

Jane expected Mia to intervene, but her face had gone slack and there was a faraway look in her eyes. Her cheeks were streaked with mascara tracks, and she was turning her tiger's eye ring around and around.

What made her cry? Jane wondered.

Had it been the embrace between the two male chefs? Chef Michel's speech about his sister? The raw emotion in Chef August's voice?

Suddenly, a thought struck Jane with the force of a fist slamming into her stomach.

Mia had nearly cried twice tonight. She'd teared up when Chef Michel mentioned his sister while describing his dishes and again, when she tasted the Thai oysters.

Oysters and cocoa farms.

Fish and chocolate.

Jane's head spun.

What if the note Bentley delivered to Chef Pierce had read exactly as Mia described? What if it contained an ultimatum as well as instructions to meet her in the cookbook nook? What if Mia had killed Chef Pierce? What if the wrong woman had been arrested for murder?

"Why would she sabotage her own show?" Jane whispered to herself.

She couldn't think. The lights were too bright. The room was too hot. There were too many people crowding around her.

Watching Mia play with her ring tickled Jane's memory. There'd been something significant in Mia's story about selling baked goods from her red wagon. Something about her cousin. But what?

Fox thrust the golden ladle into Chef August's hand.

"Congratulations, Chef! I look forward to working with you. We're going to design a terrific cookware line that everyone, from professional chef to beginner cook, will want in their kitchens. Chef August Cookware. Has a great ring to it, doesn't it, Mia?"

Snapping out of her stupor, Mia pasted on her red-carpet smile. "It sure does, Fox. Congratulations, Chef August."

Ignoring the chef's protests, Mia took a step away from him and faced the camera. "Wow, this has been a finale to top all *Posh Palate with Mia Mallett* finales."

As she spoke, several things happened around her. A shell-shocked Chef August retreated behind the feast tables. The golden ladle hung from his hand, looking less like a trophy and more like a piece of trash he was eager to throw away. Chef Michel also backed away, which left Mia, Jane, and Fox alone in the spotlight.

"We've never had a chef turn down the golden ladle and all that comes with it before," Mia went on. "I mean, wow. People can really surprise you."

Jane wasn't focusing on Mia's words. Her attention was zeroed in on Mia's hand, which had slipped into a pocket sewn into the folds of her gown's voluminous skirt. The muscles in her arm tightened as she grabbed the object and slowly withdrew it from her pocket.

Mia's small fingers curled around the grip of a palm-sized pistol. Her eyes had lost their animated sparkle. Now, they were flat and cold.

Acting on impulse, Jane jumped in front of Fox, shoving him backward just as Mia lunged at him, gun raised. The barrel dug into the tender skin of Jane's neck, and she went rigid.

"Damn," Mia said. "I don't know why you did that, but I can't let you go now."

Jane's mouth went dry. Her limbs felt boneless.

"I know," she whispered faintly.

Mia jerked her chin at Fox. "Why would you sacrifice yourself for *him*?"

"This is my house. Everyone under its roof is under my protection, including you."

Edwin eased into Jane's line of sight, and she sensed movement all around her. The Fins were probably motioning for the chefs and judges to get away from the two women.

"Don't you move, Fox," Mia commanded. "*You* don't get to slink off. You need to listen to me, so grab a chair and sit." She waited for Fox to comply before turning her face into the lights again. "Keep the cameras rolling, Ty. You're about to get some Emmy-worthy footage."

Ty gave her a thumbs-up, clearly thrilled by the dramatic unscripted event.

"Ty—" Fox began.

"No!" Mia shouted. "You don't get to talk. Just sit and listen." Twisting her head from one side to another, she added, "If anyone moves or tries to interfere, I'll shoot this woman. I'll shoot her because my message is more important than her life."

Jane decided her best bet was to act like an ally instead of a victim. "Please. Do what Ms. Mallett says."

The pressure of the gun barrel eased a bit. It still rested against Jane's neck but was no longer digging into her flesh.

"Tell your story," Jane said.

Mia responded to the encouragement. "My genes are like the spices in a Moroccan market, and my relatives are just as colorful. They come from many different cultures, and I inherited parts of all of them. Growing up, I tasted recipes passed down through my European, Latino, and Asian family members. My life was full of stories and amazing food. I didn't have brothers or sisters, but I wasn't missing anything because I had Sud."

To Jane's ear, the name sounded like *suea*.

"Notice how I raised my voice at the end of Sud's name?" Mia asked. "If you drop your voice, it becomes a totally different word. I used the Thai word for 'tiger.'"

Jane thought of Mia's tiger eye ring.

"Sud was my bestie, my brother from another mother, my other half. We did everything together. His mom was my mom's cousin, and our apartments were right next to each other. Sud and I rigged this pulley system between our windows, and whenever one of us was told to go to our room, the other person would send a treat over. Notes or candy or library books." To Jane, she said, "*Magic Tree House* and *Goosebumps* were our faves."

"Not *Captain Underpants*?" Jane quipped. It was a lame attempt at comradery, but it was all she could come up with.

Mia's eyes widened. "I forgot about those! Sud was a huge fan. He used to draw the captain during class. With our principal's face." She laughed. "That was Sud. He was fun and silly and he could always make me laugh. And he wasn't scared of *anything*. He was short and skinny like me, but he never got bullied. He'd start shouting in Thai and make a crazy face, and the bullies would back off."

Love for her cousin softened Mia's features and added a musical quality to her voice. She couldn't reach into her memories without seeing her cousin. Sud had been Mia's person, but somehow, he'd been taken from her. Jane knew this without Mia having to say it. She would have known without a gun to her neck. There was the tiger eye ring. The way Mia teared up whenever the chefs talked about their family. The way she'd spoken of the cousin who'd gone into business with her when they were children.

"I'm so sorry," Jane blurted.

Mia was taken aback by this unexpected display of sympathy, but she recovered quickly.

"Me too. Because this is the sad part of the story. Sud's grandparents, who lived in Thailand, lost everything they owned in a landslide. Sud and I had just graduated high school, and we both earned full rides to a good college. College was the plan until Sud decided to spend the summer working in Thailand. He wanted to help his grandparents get back on their feet."

Behind Mia, Lachlan took out his phone, glanced at the screen, and whispered something to Edwin. Edwin made hand gestures at Jane, telling her to keep Mia talking. The Fins had a plan, and if Jane gave them a little more time, they'd save her life.

"Did he find a job?" she asked Mia.

"He was in his grandparents' village, which is on the Thai-Cambodian border, for two whole days before he was approached by a guy looking for men to work on a fishing trawler. He gave Sud an advance for signing a contract to work the whole summer." Mia's face crumpled. "Poor Sud. He jumped at the chance to sign his own death sentence."

For a second, Jane forgot about the gun in Mia's hand. All she saw was a young woman in terrible pain. Mia had cultivated an image of a woman who had it all. She was beautiful, rich, and successful. But that was just a façade. The real Mia Mallett was a heartbroken girl who'd never recovered from losing the person she loved most.

"Sud was hired by a fishing syndicate that recruits men and young boys by promising them a little money up front and way more later. The men sign a contract designed to keep them working almost twenty hours a day, seven days a week. They can't stop until they repay the recruiter's fees, but they can't pay! The fees are too high, so the men work until they get sick or die! They're kept at sea or on a remote island with no hope of escape. Most of them don't come back. Ever! Survivors talk about dead workers being tossed overboard like trash. It's slavery, and you knew about it, Fox. You knew and turned a blind eye!"

Jane wished she could see Fox's reaction. Had his face clouded with guilt, or gone ashen with horror?

Behind her, Fox said, "With all due respect, Ms. Mallett, Cook's Pride is a global—"

"Don't you dare feed me that line!" Mia shrieked. "Your company is big. You can't know everything that goes on in the chain of supply, blah, blah, blah. But you knew what your fish suppliers were doing. You knew about the human trafficking just like you knew about the kids working the cocoa farms. Multiple humanitarian organizations have contacted you about these travesties. *You*. Fox Watterson. The heads of your UK and Australian divisions told you when their countries passed their Modern Slavery acts, but you figured a way around the new regulations."

Fox made spluttering noises.

"You told everyone not to worry because your divisions in other countries would make sure Cook's Pride continued with business as usual." Mia's jaw tightened in anger. "Profits before people, right, Fox?"

"You have no proof," argued Fox.

"But I do." Mia smiled at the camera. "Ladies and gents, the man behind the camera is Ty Scott. Ty is Fox's nephew. And Ty's mom is the COO of Cook's Pride. She brings her work home all the time. And she keeps lots of files in her home office. Lots."

Jane sensed that Mia was nearing the end of her speech. She needed to stall for more time, and the only way to do that was to give Mia a reason to keep talking.

"Killing this man won't ease your pain. It won't ease the pain of all the other families whose loved ones were tricked into slavery," Jane said. "You're a powerful woman. Use your platform to incite change. Tell your three million followers what happened to your cousin and ask them to take action."

Mia glared at Jane. "I've donated millions to put an end to human trafficking. I've backed politicians who didn't keep their word. I've paid journalists to investigate. I funded two documentaries! People don't want a lifestyle influencer to turn political! They want me to wear pretty clothes, have flawless skin, and post pics of amazing food that I can't eat because I'm always on a diet."

The frustration in Mia's voice was sincere, but Jane still felt like the younger woman was making excuses.

"What good can you do from prison?"

Tapping her temple, Mia said, "That's how I can do the *most* good. If I shoot his sorry ass, the story will go viral. Billionaire babe takes revenge on crooked CEO. It'll be everywhere. Ty can sell this footage and make his mark as a director. I'll give interviews. I'll write a tell-all. It won't mention the trendiest sushi bars or the most exclusive resort in the Maldives. It'll be about Sud. It'll be about the heinous crimes happening *right this second*."

Mia spoke the truth. She could shine a global spotlight on human trafficking by becoming a different kind of media sensation. She'd be a household name, and the cause that meant more to her than her freedom would finally get the attention it deserved.

"I know you want to help people, but murder is never the answer." Jane's panic was rising. "You're not a killer. You're a good person who misses her best friend. You've outed Fox and his company. Cook's Pride will have to make changes or face massive boycotts by its consumers."

"That's not enough. Unless I put a bullet in him, the story will be dead in a few days."

Jane couldn't think of anything else to say. She glanced over at where Edwin had been standing, but he was gone.

"You're not a killer," Jane insisted. "You make roller-coaster cakes. You taught me to hide an olive in my sons' veggie dip. You replaced our antiques. You bought those cookbooks for Mrs. Hubbard. That's who you are. Your cousin would be proud of you."

Mia's arm trembled, and an inch of space appeared between the gun barrel and Jane's neck. Tears raced down Mia's cheeks.

"I never got to say good-bye."

"I'm so sorry. It still hurts because you loved him so much. I promise to help you find a way to honor his memory."

Mia thrust out her chin and her arm went stiff. "This is bigger than me and Sud now. Get out of the way, Jane. It's him I want, but if you don't move, I'll shoot you instead."

Jane didn't budge. "Chef Pierce's death didn't save anyone. Mr. Gilmore's burns didn't save anyone. Why would shooting one of us change a thing?"

"Chef Pierce?" Mia was momentarily confused, but then, her anger flared. "Stop talking. *Now.* Ty? It's time to wrap this finale!"

Blood roared in Jane's ears. She'd failed to get Mia to stand down. She was out of time. If she didn't move aside, she'd die.

Her breathing grew shallow as Sinclair's lessons on disarming an armed assailant ran through her mind. She only knew how to deal with an assailant who'd approached from the front or from behind, not the side.

There was nothing she could do to save herself other than pray for a distraction.

Her desperate gaze swept from left to right, but the lights were too bright. She could see only haloed outlines and ghost-like shadows.

And then, without warning, all the lights went out.

Chapter 20

"I would have passed out," Anna said, handing Jane one end of a paper teacup garland. "But not you. I bet you kicked the gun away or tackled Mia, and by the time the lights came back on, you had everything in hand."

"Not quite," scoffed Jane.

She taped the garland to the crown molding and climbed down the ladder. Anna followed Jane to the opposite side of the dining room and waited for her to ascend the ladder before handing her the other end of the garland.

The Cover Girls were getting ready for Eloise's surprise bridal shower. Weeks ago, after a flurry of group texts, they'd decided on Literary Weddings as the theme. It perfectly complemented Landon Lachlan's *Jane Eyre*–inspired proposal and gave the women a chance to celebrate their favorite literary romances.

Jane had taken all the paintings off her dining room wall and was now hanging the framed artwork she and her friends had made. Each piece featured a romantic quote from one of the Cover Girls' favorite novels. After printing the quotes on thick cardstock, the women had decorated the margins with hand-painted flowers. The overall effect was charming.

It had been easy for Jane to pick a novel because *Jane Eyre* was Eloise's favorite, and they both loved the line, "Wherever you are is my home."

Betty hung Mrs. Pratt's quote. A voracious reader of romances, she'd had a tough time choosing just one but finally decided on a quote from Diana Gabaldon's Outlander series.

"'And when my body shall cease, my soul will still be yours,'" Betty read the line out loud. "If that isn't romantic, I don't know what is."

Phoebe, who was hanging her *Pride and Prejudice* print with its "I never wish to be parted from you from this day on" quote, groaned in exasperation.

"Jane! Tell us what happened next," she cried. "Anna and I missed *everything*, so don't get distracted!"

Jane laughed. "Sorry, my mind's all over the place. Anyway, I wasn't the hero of the hour. Mabel was. She'll explain while I grab the centerpiece from the kitchen."

Mabel stopped arranging Linzer tarts on a plate long enough to wave a dismissive hand. "I didn't save the day, either. That honor goes to the men in Jane's life."

Betty grabbed Violet's arm and said, "We'll get the centerpiece, Jane. You and Mabel tell the story of how the lights went out."

Jane shook out her lace tablecloth, and Phoebe helped her spread it over the table. As she smoothed out wrinkles in the cloth, Jane said, "As you know, Mabel spent part of the week at a trade show in Atlanta. One of the things she was most excited about was a panel on modern knitwear. Take it from here, Mabel."

"For years, I've made scarves, hats, and mittens to sell

at the shop, but I've been dying to shake things up," Mabel said. "The panel was supposed to showcase articulated pullovers, metallic tank tops, cocktail dresses, and funky tunics—the kinds of hip knits I want to make."

Mrs. Pratt left the room to retrieve the platter of heart-shaped finger sandwiches just as Betty and Violet reappeared, carrying the centerpiece. The vase was actually a stack of resin books with ivory covers. Jane had filled the hollowed out stack with baby's breath, blush-colored roses, and flowers made from book pages. She'd then woven a tiny strand of battery-powered lights through the arrangement.

"Fit for a fairy queen," Jane said, placing tea light candles around the centerpiece.

Sensing Phoebe's impatience, Mabel resumed her narrative. "The panel was great, but some of the audience members weren't. A group of women in the next row spent the whole time looking at their phones and talking. They didn't even try to whisper, and just when I was about to give them a piece of my mind, the Wi-Fi crashed. You should have seen those girls! They actually left the panel to find out why their phones had no bars."

"Even though Mabel wanted to strangle them, those tech-obsessed ladies showed her how to stop Mia," said Jane. "Mia was going to shoot Fox Watterson while the cameras were rolling. Without those cameras, there was no reason to go ahead with her plan."

"Because she wanted attention?" asked Phoebe.

"Yes, but not for herself. She wanted the save people, which was noble. If a few lives were lost in the process, that was okay with her, which wasn't noble." Jane put an arm around Mabel. "In the end, no one was hurt because this amazing woman remembered what had happened when the Wi-Fi crashed."

Not one to stay quiet for long, Mrs. Pratt hijacked the narrative. "Mabel charged out of Shakespeare's Theater! You should have seen how fast she moved. She was a woman on a mission. And her mission was to find someone to cut the power."

"That someone was Sterling. He listened to Mabel's idea, kissed her on the lips, and sprinted off." Betty grinned. "Eugenia and I saw it all. Mabel went a little weak in the knees."

Mabel fanned herself with a package of doilies. "It was a mighty fine kiss."

The Cover Girls whooped and whistled.

Anna put out serving utensils for the spinach salad, quiche, and sliced fruit platter. She then stared at Jane. "So everything went dark. And there you were, inches away from a woman threatening to kill you. How did you know what to do?"

"I didn't. I froze," Jane confessed. "After being blinded by those high-powered lights, the darkness was a shock. I couldn't process it. Not quickly, anyhow."

While Jane talked, Violet, Betty, and Mrs. Pratt set the table. White plates were topped with blush-colored napkins that Violet had cleverly folded into bows. She'd secured the center of each bow with a strand of faux pearls and a sprig of baby's breath.

"It was Sinclair's voice that got me moving," Jane continued. "When we practice Tae Kwon Do hand strikes, he always yells, 'Faster, faster.' Hearing that made me snap to attention."

Phoebe and Anna exchanged wide-eyed looks.

"I was too close to Mia to kick the gun out of her hand.

And if I used a hand strike on Mia's arm or wrist, the gun might go off. Since I had no idea where the bullet would go, I couldn't take the risk."

"Go on," whispered Anna.

"The only thing within reach was a chair. The chairs in the Rudyard Kipling are too heavy for me to pick up. But they also have substantial thick green cushions. That's what I threw at Mia." Jane smiled wryly. "Only I didn't hit her. I hit Edwin."

"You didn't," cried Phoebe.

"I did. He'd crept up to Mia from behind. Lachlan approached from the front. He was too far away to reach Mia, so Edwin grabbed her arm and forced her to aim the gun at the ceiling." Jane's eyes shone with pride. "A second later, the cushion smacked into him. and he shouted at me."

Mrs. Pratt bounced on the balls of her feet. "I love this part."

Anna gripped the back of a chair. "What'd he say?"

"'I'm trying to save you, woman!'"

Everyone laughed.

"If Edwin had a British accent, he'd be a modern Mr. Darcy," sighed Mrs. Pratt.

"Edwin called for lights, and as if someone had flipped a switch, Butterworth, Sinclair, and Lachlan were pointing flashlights at Mia's face. She was completely disoriented, and Edwin had no trouble wresting her gun away. At that point, she just sagged. Sinclair pushed a chair under her bum just in time. She dropped into it and wouldn't look at anyone."

Phoebe studied Jane's face. "I can understand feeling sorry for her after what happened to her cousin, but she was going to shoot a man—or you—in cold blood."

"That was her plan, but I don't believe she was capable

of pulling the trigger. She was frustrated and furious and deeply sad, and those feelings led her to terrible decisions. In the end, I think the Mia Mallett who creates fun food, cherishes her family, and is generous and kind would have prevailed."

"I guess we'll never know what she would have done and thank goodness for that." Betty glanced around the room. "Where are we putting the cakes?"

Jane taped a paper teacup garland to the sideboard. "Let's move the hall table in here."

"I'll get it," volunteered Mabel. "Can you bring in a cake, Vi?"

Anna taped the other end of the garland and looked a question a Jane. "Why *wouldn't* Mia pull the trigger? Didn't she kill a chef and start two fires?" She jerked her head in Mrs. Pratt's direction. "And steal from Roger?"

"Mia's assistant, Bentley, did those things," Mrs. Pratt explained. "The murdered chef was her father. They didn't know each other because Chef Pierce didn't want to be in Bentley's life. When she became an adult, Bentley wanted to know her dad's identity. She found out and decided to confront him."

Betty said, "Which wasn't hard to do. She just needed to convince Mia to have him on the show. He needed money to keep his restaurant from closing, so he jumped at the chance."

Violet appeared with the cake, and everyone stared at it in silent admiration.

Mrs. Hubbard had truly outdone herself. The cake was a stack of three books with ivory, gold, and pale pink covers. Titles marched along each book spine, forming the phrase *And They Lived Happily Ever After*. A white teapot with gold hearts crowned the book stack.

"It's almost too beautiful to eat. Almost." Phoebe turned to Betty. "You painted a pretty clear picture of Chef Pierce on our way here. How did Bentley feel when she learned that this awful guy was her dad?"

Jane said, "Ashamed. Disgusted. Angry. According to Sheriff Evans, Bentley wanted to test Chef Pierce. She'd tell him that she was his daughter and see how he responded to the news. If she didn't like his response, she'd kill him."

"Whoa," Phoebe mumbled.

"She went to his guest room in the middle of the night to deliver a note from her boss, which allowed her to put a bunch of his heart pills into his glass of wine."

Anna made a time-out gesture. "I thought she stabbed him with a piece of broken china."

"His heart pills were anticoagulants—they prevent the blood from clotting," Mrs. Pratt explained. "Bentley wanted to give him a little cut and then let his medication take care of the rest. She didn't realize that the medicine wouldn't kick in for another few hours. But it didn't matter because she stabbed him with force. It wasn't a little cut."

"When did she tell him that she was his daughter?" Phoebe wanted to know.

"In his room," Jane said. "By then, he'd downed a bottle or two of wine. He was pretty drunk when Bentley handed him a matchbook from the bar where Chef Pierce and her mother met. She also showed him an image of the paternity test, which she had on her phone." Jane shook her head. "He didn't seem to care. He claimed to have no memory of Bentley's mother. Then, he told Bentley that if it was money she was after, she shouldn't have chosen a career as Mia's . . . female dog."

Anna gasped. "*No!*"

"That poor girl," said Phoebe. "I'm not condoning Bentley's actions, but I can see how being spoken to like that—by her father—could break something open in her."

Jane nodded. "He failed her test, and she decided to go through with her plan to kill him."

"How did she get him to the cookbook nook?" asked Anna.

"By telling him that he could avoid getting kicked out of the competition if he made Mrs. Hubbard a recipe from her favorite cookbook," Jane said. "If he did exactly what Bentley said, Mrs. Hubbard would convince Mia to let him stay. Chef Pierce didn't want to cook. He was drunk and tired. He told Bentley to find the recipe online, but she explained that the cookbook was vintage, and his only choice was to borrow it from the cookbook nook and have the dish waiting in the kitchens for Mrs. Hubbard to see."

Mabel pursed her lips. "The girl thought she had it all covered. She tore up the note she was supposed to deliver to Chef Pierce and flushed the pieces down the toilet. And she used a jammer on the cameras on her hall, which is how she got to the cookbook nook undetected."

Anna's eyes glittered with interest. "I learned about jammers in one of my pharmacy school classes. They can temporarily disrupt the signal from the camera. Everything looks like it's working, but the footage doesn't get updated."

"We found the device in her room," Jane said. "She only needed to use it on her floor. After that, she took the stairs to hallways meant for staff use. We don't have cameras in any of those spaces."

Mrs. Pratt pointed at her wristwatch. "Time's marching on, ladies. We should finish up. Betty and I will assemble the gift cake. Where do you want it, Jane?"

"On the kitchen table. We'll give it to her after we've had the real cake."

For their group gift, the Cover Girls decided to build a cake using a white Dutch oven as the bottom tier, a set of mixing bowls as the middle tier, and rolled tea towels as the final tier. The cake topper would be a bouquet of kitchen utensils including spatulas, spoons, tongs, a whisk, and a pie server. The Dutch oven concealed another surprise: a box of recipe cards containing the Cover Girls' favorite recipes.

With the gift cake assembled, the only thing left to do was pop the quiche in the oven. Violet saw to this while Anna and Phoebe perched on stools at the kitchen island and waited for Jane to finish her story. The other Cover Girls sat at the table or leaned against the cabinets, ready to add their two cents if necessary.

"Desperate to stay in the competition, Chef Pierce met Bentley in the cookbook nook." Jane held up her blue dish-washing gloves and gave them a shake. "She wore a black hoodie and a pair of skin-tone colored gloves. Chef Pierce hadn't noticed them back in his room, but he'd sobered up a bit since then, and the gloves must have made him nervous. Nervous enough to take something out of his pocket and shove it down the back of his pants."

"The matchbook?" guessed Phoebe.

Mrs. Pratt pointed at her. "Yes! It was his way of identifying the person he'd met in the cookbook nook. His daughter. A woman with murder in her eyes."

The room went quiet as the women imagined the sheer terror of coming face-to-face with a killer.

"Don't go into details, Jane," Betty pleaded. "Not now. We should focus on Eloise."

Knowing Betty was right, Jane said, "Here's the short

version. After Chef Pierce hid the matchbook, Bentley pushed the dishes off the shelf. They shattered. Pieces flew everywhere. Chef Pierce reacted by calling Bentley names that no man should use on any woman, let alone his daughter. He also said that she was as deranged and low-class as her mother. Bentley picked up a piece of porcelain and told Chef Pierce to stop talking. That's when he charged at her. Bentley pivoted and stabbed him in one fluid motion. She was agile and strong. He was slow and clumsy."

"With those anticoagulants in his system, he was a goner," said Anna.

Jane quickly explained that two pieces of porcelain in the cookbook nook and the items stolen from the Old Curiosity Shop had either a fish or chocolate motif in common. Bentley had cased the antique shop the previous day when she and Ty had come to Storyton to coerce Kathy, the chair of the Berry Jubilee, to grant them the use of the main tent. It hadn't been hard to do. Ty had turned on the charm, written a generous check, and promised to mention the festival on the show.

Mia was kept in the dark about the surprise challenge until she arrived at the festival with the cast. Of course, her assistants knew what was happening. They'd done her hair, makeup, and selected her outfit. And when she found out what was happening, she saw no point in canceling.

Bentley had taken care of every detail. She'd come up with the theme and bought food from the Pickled Pig and camp stoves from Storyton Outfitters. Once the competition started, she put on a sunhat, wedge sandals, and a billowy blouse, and pilfered the chocolate pot and pillbox from Roger's shop. After dumping her shirt, shoes, and hat in a trash can, she cut through the small tent where committee members sold raffle tickets and collected booth rental.

The tent was empty, and when Bentley saw Dew Drop's costume draped over a chair, she grabbed a permanent marker and scrawled a message on the back. The costume zips up the front, so no one noticed the message until Dew Drop skipped into the main tent.

Phoebe frowned. "Why take the risk? She'd committed murder for crying out loud. Why add shoplifting and costume defacement to her list of crimes?"

"Sheriff Evans asked her the same thing. At first, Bentley said that she wanted to shine a spotlight on Cook's Pride and their unethical treatment of workers. But the sheriff pressed her until she admitted that she was in love with Mia. She'd spent years preparing to be Mia's ideal assistant—just to get close to her. She succeeded, but her obsession continued to grow. She would have done anything to win Mia's approval. Anything. Including murder."

"Did Mia know about Bentley's plans?"

Jane sighed. "She swears she didn't. But when she heard about Chef Pierce's death, she immediately suspected Bentley. Mia sent Bentley to Chef Pierce's room in the middle of the night and feared that her assistant was the last person to see Chef Pierce before his death. She also worried that Bentley had punished Chef Pierce for assaulting another woman. Bentley was enraged when she heard how he'd groped a pastry chef in the kitchens."

"Why didn't Mia say something?"

"Bentley acted so normal the next day that Mia brushed aside her suspicions. She certainly didn't suspect her of causing the propane tank fire. It was only when she saw the message on the mascot that she wondered if she knew her assistant at all. She confronted Bentley later that day."

Mrs. Pratt pointed at the clock. "It's time."

Jane made a shooing motion. "Come on, girls! We need to hide!"

The Cover Girls stepped into closets, dropped down behind the sofa, or went halfway up the stairs leading to the second floor.

A few minutes later, they heard Edwin call out, "Hello? Anyone here?" Receiving no reply, he said, "I'll look in the kitchen. Can you check the coffee table?"

The Cover Girls heard Eloise say, "I don't see you leaving your keys there, but okay."

As soon as Eloise entered the living room, Mabel, Mrs. Pratt, Betty, Phoebe, Violet, Anna, and Jane emerged from their hiding places with shouts of, "Surprise!"

Eloise shrieked. She stood stock-still in the middle of the living room and put her hand over her heart. "I think I just aged ten years!" she panted. "What are you crazy women up to?"

Jane hurried over to her best friend and placed a wedding veil attached to a rhinestone tiara on her head. "There. You now have a tiara, just as Eugenia suggested. Welcome to your shower, beautiful bride-to-be."

Color rushed into Eloise's cheeks. "Really? I thought my big brother was taking me to lunch. Edwin! Was that story about the keys a total lie?"

Edwin appeared in the living room doorway. One end of a wooden spoon touched the tip of his nose while the other end pointed at the closet. "Call me Pinocchio." He then bowed gallantly, told the ladies to have fun, and left.

"Eloise? Would you like a drink?" asked Betty.

"Yes, Betty, I *would* like a drink!" Eloise nodded so emphatically that her tiara almost fell off. She grabbed hold of it and laughed.

The party was off to a merry start.

Jane and Betty opened bottles of prosecco while the rest of the Cover Girls led Eloise to the dining room.

"This is incredible!" Eloise exclaimed as she took in the food and decorations. "I'm the luckiest woman in the world. Not because I'm getting married, but because you're my friends."

Violet raised her glass. "I think that qualifies as a toast."

The women touched rims and sipped the bright, fruity sparkling wine.

"I have a toast too," said Jane. "To paraphrase Rumi: We love our friend Eloise, with neither our hearts nor our minds. Hearts may stop. Minds can forget. We love her with our souls. Souls never stop or forget."

There wasn't a dry eye in the room as the women raised their glasses to Eloise once more.

Mrs. Pratt dabbed her cheeks with a tissue and said, "No more toasts. Let's eat."

Over lunch, Eloise was asked to match her friends to the correct book quote. Because she knew everyone's reading taste, she nearly aced the challenge. Her only mistake was mixing up Phoebe's and Betty's quotes.

Phoebe grinned at Betty. "You're my reading twin. If you fall for a book, I know I will too."

After discussing their current reads, Eloise told her friends about the new releases she'd received in her last shipment.

"The cookbooks sold out in two days, so the display window is now full of beach reads."

Eloise talked about the summer's most anticipated books while Jane began collecting empty plates. Anna and Phoebe jumped up to help.

In the kitchen, Anna washed dishes and Phoebe dried

them. Jane started the coffeemaker and put the clean dishes away in the cupboard.

"Is this your wedding china, Jane?" Anna asked, gesturing at a luncheon plate.

"We didn't register for any. Aunt Octavia gave me this set when I moved back home. The pattern is called Lady Jane."

Phoebe ran a towel across the plate, which had a blue border with flowers and gilding to the top edge. "Was Aunt Octavia upset about the pieces Bentley broke?"

"Mrs. Hubbard took it the hardest, but to everyone's surprise, Mia presented me with replacement pieces on the final day of filming." Jane shook her head. "She has so many good qualities. It's a weird thing to say, considering she threatened to kill me, but she's an incredibly generous person. She pumped money into Chef Pierce's restaurant, spent a fortune replacing our antiques, and gave Mr. Gilmore a huge check because she felt terrible about what happened to him."

"Mr. Gilmore? Was he the man who was burned?"

Jane put the plate on the top of the stack. "Yes. He was posing as a fire safety advisor."

Anna dipped a plate in soapy water. "Posing? Why?"

"For money. Mr. Gilmore is really an actor named Charlie Smail. Bentley hired him to create an on-set disaster. The propane tank he tampered with was *supposed* to explode when the chefs were running to the wagon to get their ingredients, but the gas didn't leak out fast enough. Mr. Smail researched his role, but gas leaks aren't an exact science." Jane watched coffee dribble into the carafe. "He messed up the fire in the archery field too. It was supposed to burn the tent to the ground. Both disasters were meant to go viral. Bentley believed that such negative attention would lure Fox Watterson to Storyton."

"So Mia could murder him on camera? Because she blamed him for her cousin's death?" Phoebe asked.

"Bentley knew that Mia wanted to send a message too loud to be ignored," Jane said. "Fox knew all about the barbaric treatment of fishermen. He received documents from the Australian division of Cook's Pride detailing just how bad it was. But Fox turned a blind eye to the suffering of countless boys and men to protect his bottom line. That's why Mia hated him. She was willing to throw away everything she'd built to save others from her cousin's fate."

Phoebe passed her the last plate. "I know what she did was wrong, but I understand why she did it."

"Me too," said Anna. "What'll happen to her?"

Jane poured the coffee into a silver pot and loaded a sugar bowl and a creamer of milk onto a tray. "Last I heard, her lawyers and the district attorney were working on a deal. Mia will probably plead guilty to the lesser charges. She didn't actually hurt anyone, but the gun was hers and it wasn't in her pocket during the finale by accident. If she serves any time, it'll be nothing compared to Bentley's sentence."

Anna sighed. "She's so young, and her life is basically over."

"Mia will do what she can for her. She's covering the legal fees for Bentley, Ty, and Mr. Smail. Mia told Sheriff Evans that she feels responsible for Bentley's actions. If she hadn't talked about getting even with Fox Watterson, Bentley wouldn't have worked so tirelessly to give her what she wanted. Mia knew Bentley would go out of her way to please her, but she never imagined she'd take things this far."

Anna picked up the stack of dessert plates on the counter. "And the footage from that night? Will people be able to watch it?"

"Ty's cameras were seized as evidence. Unless someone on the film crew recorded the events on their phone, the most dramatic part of the finale will never air."

"I think we're ready for the finale of this party," Phoebe said.

Anna grinned. "Coffee, cake, and a gift for our lovely bride-to-be is all the drama we need."

Jane carried the tray to the dining room. She poured coffee for her friends while Betty sliced and served the cake.

After the women finished their dessert, Mrs. Pratt cleared a space on the table and Jane presented Eloise with their group gift.

"Alfred Hitchcock said that 'happiness is a small house with a big kitchen.'" Jane waved her arm, indicating all the Cover Girls. "We hope that you and Landon will always have a kitchen filled with delicious food, lively conversation, and endless happiness."

Her eyes glistening with tears, Eloise glanced around at her friends. "I'm going to buy a big farm table so we can sit together, just like this, and talk about everything and anything. We'll eat, drink, and be content. Cover Girls forever."

She put her hand in the middle of the table. The other women stacked their hands over hers and repeated, "Cover Girls forever."

It was moments like these that allowed Jane to recover from the tumultuous experience of having a television show film at Storyton Hall. The new memories that Jane made with the Cover Girls, Aunt Octavia and

Uncle Aloysius, the twins, and Edwin contained more than enough love and light to chase away the shadows cast by *Posh Palate with Mia Mallett.*

And whenever Jane needed a reminder of all that was right in the world, she'd stop by the kitchens and watch Mrs. Hubbard and her staff work their magic.

It was in the kitchens that Jane felt the heartbeat of Storyton Hall. As she sat at a prep counter, cradling a cup of tea, she could hear the pulse of the house. Its steady rhythm was like a song, echoing deep in her soul. It was a song of belonging. The warm and unwavering lullaby of home.

Epilogue

The Posh Palate scandal didn't keep guests from flocking to Storyton Hall. People called morning till night, hoping to book a room.

"I'll stay in a shed. A barn. A broom closet. Just as long as I'm on the property," one man pleaded.

The reservations email address was flooded with similar requests. People offered to pay double or triple the going rate. They promised to write stellar reviews on their blogs and social media pages. A few creative souls even used literary quotes to prove how much they wanted to spend a single night at Storyton Hall.

Over and over, the front desk clerks explained that there was no availability until September, which tended to provoke a fresh round of cajoling, whining, and attempted bribery.

To save her staff from having to repeat themselves, Jane recorded a message on the reservation line.

"Are all these inquiries from journalists?" a clerk asked Jane.

"That, or fans of Ms. Mallett. Apparently, they'll do

anything to see the Rudyard Kipling Café. Sterling caught a young man climbing the front gates last night, and Lachlan encountered a couple on motorbikes taking photos of the archery field. Another woman offered a thousand dollars for sixty seconds in the cookbook nook, and a young man pretended he was applying for a job as a dishwasher, but Mrs. Hubbard saw through him five minutes into the interview.

The clerk pointed at her computer. "Things *were* calming down for a bit, but we've had so many reservation requests today that our system might crash. I've never seen anything like it."

Jane, who'd just refilled her coffee cup from the urn in the lobby, frowned. "I'd better take a look online."

As she sat down at her desk, her phone rang. Seeing Eloise's name on the screen, Jane picked up.

"Wow, wow, wow!" she cried. "Are you watching the news?"

"No. What's going on?"

Eloise exhaled. "Someone leaked the finale footage. *All* of it. I watched it, but it made me feel sick. Seeing that gun pressed against your neck—it was awful. I don't know how you stayed so calm."

"I wasn't calm. I was stalling for time." After a pause, Jane added, "Instinct made me jump in front of Fox Watterson. I'd invited him to Storyton Hall, so he was my guest, and I've always been concerned about the safety of my guests. But my top priority should be my sons. What would have happened to Fitz and Hem if I'd been killed?"

Eloise let out a small cry. "Let's not go there, please. You're fine, and your sons are proud of their brave mom. I'm proud to be your friend."

Jane didn't reply because her attention had been caught by a headline on the BBC News site. It read, BILLIONAIRE TV HOST WILLING TO KILL TO PUT AN END TO HUMAN RIGHTS VIOLATIONS.

Below the headline was a video. The frame was frozen on Mia's face, which was contorted in pain. The article took up half the page.

"Who leaked the video?" she asked.

"Someone identifying as GoldnBears2012 sold it to TMZ. An anonymous source claims that GoldnBears2012 is Mia's hair and makeup guru. He graduated from the University of California, Berkeley, in 2012, and Berkeley's athletic teams are called the Golden Bears. No one else involved with the show went to Berkeley."

"Whoa," Jane breathed.

"Yeah. Whoa," Eloise agreed. "And as much as I want to forget about that night, I'm kind of happy that it was leaked. If the bad things that happened here bring about positive change, we can focus on that, and not on how scared we were. If everyone starts talking about the mistreatment of workers and how major food companies exploit these people, I believe things will improve."

Jane opened a new browser window and visited the online version of a major newspaper. She repeated this action three times. Every site featured a story about Mia and a link to the video showing the unscripted ending of the finale. Jane was pleased to see that all the articles included reactions from officials at the International Labour Organization.

"She did it," Jane murmured. "She wanted to shine a spotlight on injustice, and the light is shining."

"People are coming forward to tell their stories. Fisher-

men, cocoa farmers, migrant workers, and many more."
Eloise was silent for a moment before she said, "I hope
someone tells Mia."

Jane had no doubt that Mia already knew. "Remember,
she was sent to a country club prison. With all of her
money, she can afford things most inmates never could. I
doubt she'll be incarcerated for more than a few months.
By this time next year, her tell-all book will be in your
shop."

When Eloise spoke next, her voice was steely. "No, it
won't. I know you have a soft spot for Mia. You feel sorry
for Bentley. But people can't go around committing murder
to ease their pain or anyone else's. You might be able to
forgive Mia, but I watched her point a gun at you, and I
can't forgive her for that."

The force of Eloise's anger gave Jane pause. "You're
right. Both women crossed lines they shouldn't have
crossed."

"You need to get to a TV, pronto. Chef August is giving
an interview when this series of commercials is over. If
they *ever* end." Eloise told Jane which station to tune to
and hung up.

In the surveillance room, Jane listened as a pair of
newscasters talked about the *Posh Palate with Mia Mallett*
contestants.

"Usually, a reality show has to air before the cast becomes famous, but that's not the case with these five
chefs," the anchorwoman said. "They're now household
names after a leaked video revealed how the show's finale
nearly turned deadly."

"Representatives from Cook's Pride declined to comment. However, we were able to secure an interview with

Chef August. He's joining us now, from his home. Good morning, Chef."

Chef August's face appeared in a rectangular box onscreen. He smiled and said, "Good morning, Brett. Leslie."

Brett dove right in. "So, Chef, are your friends and family reeling after the release of the finale video?"

Chef August shrugged. "I told my wife about it the night it happened. She's my rock, and I needed to hear her voice. I was pretty shaken after what went down. All the people who matter to me knew before the video came out. They didn't like seeing it, but they're okay."

"Did anything change for you professionally after the filming ended?" Leslie asked.

"Not really. I'm still making amazing food at my restaurant, and I'm working on recipes for a new cookbook. All the chefs from this season are creating this cookbook together. We're really excited about it."

Chef August seemed genuinely happy, and Jane hoped all the chefs were in a similar state. They'd faced death and danger, and now deserved a lifetime of success and peace.

Brett raised his brows. "So you're in touch with the other chefs? Can you tell us how they're doing?"

"Everyone's fine. Chefs are a tough lot. Gotta be. If we couldn't handle pressure, he wouldn't have gotten this far." He chuckled. "My man, Chef Michel, is doing what I'm doing. Cooking at his bistro and loving on his wife and kids. We'll be friends until we're old men, and if nothing else came out of the show, that would be more than good enough for me."

"Is Chef Lindsay involved with the cookbook too?" asked Leslie.

"Of course."

Brett frowned. "Even after she said that she'd take the golden ladle if you didn't?"

Chef August waved this off. "She didn't mean anything by it. She just said that because she was stressed out. It had been an intense couple of days, and she just wanted it all to be over. We all felt that way."

"What happened to the hundred-thousand-dollar prize money?" Leslie's eyes gleamed.

"Cook's Pride split it five ways. We all got checks, and we all sent every cent to the organization where Chef Michel's sister, Kisi, works. We were never going to touch that money, and we felt good knowing it could help other people."

A photo of Kisi appeared on the screen along with the name and URL of the organization she worked for in Paris. Jane's heart swelled. The more media attention the organization received, the more people would support it through donations and letters to politicians.

Brett thanked Chef August and promised to share more revelations on the *Posh Palate* scandal after the commercial break. Jane switched to another channel. Three women were seated behind a table. They all held copies of Mia's cookbook and described Mia's behavior at the finale as "deplorable" and "shocking." Another channel was airing a recorded interview of a Thai fisherman who'd escaped from a situation exactly like Sud's.

"We barely had enough food to survive," he said. "We worked ten, twelve hours a day. If we were sick, we had to work. If we were hungry, we had to work. No one could leave. I got away by swimming to a small island in the middle of the night. I was barely alive when a local fisherman found me, but I got away. So many others don't."

When the newscaster asked if he had a message for Mia Mallett, the man's eyes filled with tears and he pressed his hands together. He said something in Thai, and though Jane couldn't understand the words, the man's expression of gratitude was unmistakable.

Channel after channel, people were talking about Mia, Bentley, the chefs, workers' rights, Fox Watterson, Cook's Pride, Storyton Hall, and herself.

There was a knock on the door and Sterling entered the room. "The phones are lighting up like Christmas trees. Everyone wants to interview our fearless leader."

"I'll have to talk to one of them, or this will never stop."

She decided to call the station that had interviewed Chef August, and within the hour, she was on the phone with Leslie and Brett. Jane had rejected a Skype interview. One viral video of her was enough.

She answered questions about the show, the cast and crew, and Storyton Hall. She refused to discuss the particulars of the crimes and suggested that all members of the media contact the Storyton Sheriff's Department for that information. Jane also took the opportunity to announce that the resort was booked through mid-September and that anyone interested in photos of the terrace, archery fields, or Rudyard Kipling Café would find them on Storyton Hall's website.

"What about the room where Chef Pierce was killed?" asked Brett.

"I won't disrespect Chef Pierce's memory by posting photos of the cookbook nook. That area is accessible to our staff only. It's completely off-limits to the public. No exceptions."

At this point, Leslie gave Jane an opportunity to tell viewers about Storyton Hall.

"Our resort caters to readers," Jane said warmly. "Our reading rooms and libraries are brimming with books of every genre. We also have a world-class spa, incredible food, and a long list of outdoor activities from fishing to falconry. People come to Storyton Hall to relax. They come for peace, beauty, luxury, and places to curl up and read. That's what we offer."

Leslie smiled wistfully. "Sign me up. I love to read, but I can't seem to settle down long enough to finish a chapter. I don't know how to relax anymore."

"Sounds like you need a Storyton Hall getaway," said Jane.

And with that, the interview was over. Jane received many more interview requests that day, but she politely refused them all.

"I have no desire to become a celebrity," she told a pushy producer after the woman called for what felt like the twentieth time. "I want to put the whole experience behind me. Please don't call again. I won't change my mind."

By the time she walked across the Great Lawn and pushed open her garden gate that evening, she was bone-tired. But she immediately brightened when she saw Edwin sitting on her front steps.

He stood, kissed her hello, and said, "Kick off your shoes."

"Why?"

"I'm taking you to an exclusive restaurant, and there are no shoes allowed."

Jane grinned. "I like the sound of this place."

Leaving her shoes on the stoop, she took Edwin's outstretched hand. When he led her around the corner of the house to the patio, Jane let out a gasp of surprise.

Her patio table, draped in a colorful botanical cloth, was

set with melamine plates and several lanterns. Strands of string lights ran from the house to wooden poles buried in the mulch at the edge of the patio. An outdoor rug covered the weathered bricks and Edwin had loaded a bar cart with a selection of glasses, drink mixes, liquor bottles, and an ice bucket. Another new addition was an outdoor sideboard, which held a row of covered dishes.

"When did you do this?" Jane asked.

Edwin escorted her to the table. "Today. The boys helped. They'll be out in a bit, but I thought you could use a drink and a few minutes of quiet first."

"No. *First*, I need to tell you how much I love you."

Jane put her arms around Edwin and kissed him. She then rested her head on his shoulder, breathing him in. He removed the clip securing her hair and she sighed in contentment as his fingers moved through her loose locks. Under the twinkling string lights, with fireflies winking at her from the bushes, Jane's worries floated away.

Later, after a round of mojitos, the boys joined them for a casual charcuterie supper. As they ate, Fitz and Hem asked if Jane and Edwin felt like playing a game.

"Your mom had a long day, so it's up to her," Edwin said.

Jane smiled at her sons. "I'll play anything but Monopoly. It took us a week to finish our last game."

The four of them carried the dinner things inside and cleaned up the kitchen. Jane wanted to change into shorts and a T-shirt while Fitz and Hem picked a board game, so she grabbed her shoes from the front stoop before going upstairs.

Yesterday's mail, which Jane hadn't time to examine, sat on the hall table. The letter on the top of the pile caught her eye. Because she so rarely received handwritten letters, she leaned over to examine the return address. The letter was from Olivia Limoges.

In her room, Jane changed quickly. She was eager to read Olivia's note before the twins set up a board game. The first few lines made her smile, but by the end, she was frowning in confusion.

"We're ready, Mom!" Hem shouted.

Edwin was in the kitchen, filling a pitcher with ice water, when Jane entered the room.

"I got a letter from Olivia Limoges," she said, waving it in the air.

Edwin dropped lemon and lime slices into the pitcher. "How is she?"

"Great. She finished her book. She says she wouldn't have written it at all if she hadn't come to Storyton, and she wanted to thank me for getting her through an acute case of writer's block. She enclosed a gift certificate for a bed-and-breakfast in Oyster Bay. She said there's a seaside cottage on the property that would be perfect for the two of us. And Chef Michel wants to cook us a special dinner too."

Edwin was delighted. "Should I start packing?"

Jane laughed. "This *would* be a good time to run away, but we should wait until after Eloise's wedding."

"But you definitely want to go?"

Jane kissed him tenderly and said, "On a romantic get-away? You bet I do. The twins will be fine without me for a few days. So will Storyton Hall. I love the idea of holing up in a cottage by the sea with you."

"I'm going to tell Eloise to order lots of copies of Olivia's new book," Edwin said. "She made my day."

Jane shook the letter again. "She sent the boys a surprise gift too. It's supposed to arrive early tomorrow morning.

Here's the strange part. She asked me to remember what I told her about my childhood when I see the gift."

"What did you tell her?"

"That my parents died when I was very young. How lucky I was to have Aunt Octavia and Uncle Aloysius. I'm sure there was more, but I can't remember all the details."

Edwin put a hand on her waist. "I guess we'll find out tomorrow."

When the doorbell rang at seven thirty the next morning, Jane let out a groan. It was a Monday, but she'd taken the day off and didn't want to get out of bed.

Beside her, Edwin stirred.

Determined to let him rest, Jane slipped out of bed, grabbed her bathrobe, and hurried downstairs.

Thankfully, Jane was able to open the door before the young man standing on her welcome mat could ring the bell again.

"Hi, I'm Zeke from Coastal Carriers." He smiled cheerfully. "I have a delivery for Fitz and Hem Steward."

Jane looked over his shoulder, expecting to see some sort of box, but the young man only had a clipboard. "Sorry, ma'am, but my instructions are to deliver the package to Misters Fitz and Hem. I'm not allowed to give it to anyone else."

"Can you tell me if it's from Olivia Limoges? Of Oyster Bay?"

"Yes, ma'am. It is."

Stifling a yawn, Jane said, "Give me a moment, and I'll get Fitz and Hem. Would you like some water or juice? I haven't made coffee yet."

"No, thank you, ma'am. I'll just stand here and admire the view."

Energized by curiosity, Jane bounded up the stairs to the twins' room and shook them awake.

"Miss Olivia sent you a present," she told them. "The deliveryman has to give it to you, so hop to it! He's waiting at the front door."

The boys sprang out of bed and raced out of the room. Jane followed at a much slower pace.

In the hall, the front door stood open. There was no sign of Zeke or her sons. Hearing voices from the patio, Jane cut through the kitchen and stepped outside in time to see Zeke remove the sheet covering a large wire cage. She saw her sons' faces fill with wonder and joy as they beheld the puppies inside the cage.

The puppies had black coats, white bibs, and white paws. They whined and yipped in excitement as Fitz and Hem dropped to their knees and stuck their fingers in the cage.

"They're ours?" Fitz asked Zeke.

Unable to tear his eyes away from the puppies, Hem whispered, "Are we dreaming?"

Jane was too stunned to move. As she leaned against the doorframe, she suddenly remembered telling Olivia that she'd never had a childhood pet and that she felt like she'd missed out on the experience. Olivia didn't want Fitz and Hem to miss out. She wanted them to know the unconditional love of a dog. And not just any dog. A standard poodle.

Two *standard poodles*, Jane thought, trying to process the enormity of this moment.

Jane knelt down next to her sons and reached into the cage. Her fingers were immediately covered in puppy kisses.

She gazed into their wide eyes, watched their little tails wag furiously, and laughed with glee.

"Can we keep them?" Fitz pleaded.

"Please, oh, please, oh please," Hem begged.

Jane smiled at her sons. "I guess we're a family of six now."

Fitz and Hem threw their arms around their mother and kissed her cheeks. The puppies yipped louder, Fitz and Hem whooped with happiness, and Jane kept laughing.

Before he left, Zeke gave Jane a book on raising poodles. Inside the front cover, Olivia had written, "Groucho Marx knew what mattered in life. He wanted a comfortable couch, a dog, and a good book. You now have everything that matters."

Jane couldn't have agreed more.

Don't miss the latest in the Secret, Book & Scone Society series from Ellery Adams . . .

INK AND SHADOWS

In the new mystery from *New York Times* bestselling author Ellery Adams, controversy erupts in Miracle Springs, North Carolina, when the owner of the local bookstore tries to play peacekeeper—but winds up playing detective instead . . .

Nora Pennington is known for her window displays, and as Halloween approaches, she decides to showcase fictional heroines like Roald Dahl's Matilda and Madeline Miller's Circe. A family-values group disapproves of the magical themes, and wastes no time launching a modern-day witch hunt. Suddenly, former friends and customers are targeting not only Nora and Miracle Books, but a new shopkeeper, Celeste, who's been selling CBD oil products.

Nora and her friends in the Secret, Book & Scone Society are doing their best to put an end to the strife—but then someone puts an end to a life. Though the death is declared an accident, the ruling can't explain the old book page covered with strange symbols and disturbing drawings left under Nora's doormat, a postcard from an anonymous stalker, or multiple cases of vandalism.

The only hope is that Nora can be a heroine herself and lead the Secret, Book & Scone Society in a successful investigation—before more bodies turn up and the secrets from Celeste's past come back to haunt them all . . .

Available from Kensington Publishing Corp.
wherever books are sold

Read on for a preview!

Chapter 1

O' What may man within him hide, though angel on the outward side!

—William Shakespeare

Nora Pennington stood on the sidewalk, frowning. Most people wouldn't understand her reaction to the bookshop's window display. The window was full of cute plush toys inspired by children's book characters. With the help of parachutes made from autumn leaves, Curious George, Olivia, the Very Hungry Caterpillar, Babar the Elephant, Peter Rabbit, Pete the Cat, Paddington Bear, Clifford the Big Red Dog, Winnie-the-Pooh, Arthur, Frog and Toad, Fantastic Mr. Fox, Maisie, and the Pigeon floated in a bright blue sky. All the animals were aiming for the same landing zone: a giant book. The book glowed, illuminating the fur of the closest parachuters, and its open pages were covered with letters made of rainbow glitter.

At the top of the window, a biplane piloted by Stuart Little trailed a yellow banner with the words FALL INTO A GOOD BOOK!

That August, the window had drawn smiles from locals and visitors to Miracle Springs, North Carolina. Then, September came, but summer wouldn't let go. It was as hot and humid on the first day of school as it had been on the Fourth of July. Plants wilted. People drooped. The whole town was sunbaked and dry. It was hard to believe that October was right around the corner.

Autumn's refusal to kick summer to the curb had gotten under everyone's skin, including Nora's. She stood outside, shading her eyes from the sun's glare, and tried to imagine a festive fall scene in her display window. But nothing was coming to her. It was too hot to think.

"Are you channeling the Grouchy Ladybug?" asked Sheldon Vega.

Nora's friend and employee pointed at her ALL THE COOL KIDS ARE READING T-shirt, which happened to be red.

"I'm pensive," she said. "More Harriet the Spy than grumpy insect."

Stroking his silver goatee, Sheldon looked at the window. "This display let our customers hang on to that summer freedom vibe while also giving them hope that they'll still have time to read in between soccer games, PTA meetings, back-to-school nights, and the *zillions* of fall festivals I saw listed in the paper. You people are festival addicts."

Nora laughed. "I had the same reaction when I first moved here. When I saw the festival calendar, I thought it was some kind of a joke. Molasses, Railroad, Guinea, Folk, Irish, Scottish Games, Greek, Clay, Cherokee, Zombie, and Mountain Bike Festivals. I'm a *big* fan of all of them. You know why? They draw *big* crowds. And a portion of those crowds find their way to Miracle Springs. From now until New Year's is our money-making season, and I'm hoping it's a banner one. I'd like to put something away for a rainy day."

Sheldon nodded. "My nest egg could definitely use a little more yellow in its yolk."

"Then we need to pick up the pace, starting with this window. Our next display needs to be less cutesy and more compelling."

"We raised the bar too high these past few months," said Sheldon. "We became the Fifth Avenue department store at Christmastime—full of magic and wonder and sugarplums. This month, our sugarplums were a little flat." He tugged at the ends of his peach and purple bowtie. "Happens to the best of us."

Nora smiled. Sheldon had that effect on her. Though he'd been working at the bookshop for only five months, she didn't know how she'd ever managed without him. He had a profound love of reading, an excellent eye for design, and he made the world's best coffee.

Sheldon Vega had inherited his love of reading and his ability to put people at ease from his Jewish mother. His self-assurance and passion for good food came from his Cuban father. Sheldon was in his sixties and looked like Don Johnson's character in *Django Unchained*. He had a penchant for sweater vests, Nutella on toast, and bear hugs. He suffered from chronic pain, which caused him to be absent or late to work. Nora had liked him from the moment they'd met.

"Lots of shops have their Halloween displays up," Nora went on. "It's one of the things I hate about retail. We always have to jump the gun on holidays. Valentine candy hits the shelves January first. And on February fifteenth, out comes the chocolate bunnies and jellybeans."

Sheldon shuddered. "And those revolting marshmallow chicks."

Nora turned to him. "So what should we do? Hang up

ghosts and goblins even though it feels like we're a desert planet from *Dune*?"

"Ghosts and goblins. Dracula and Frankenstein. Do they really have a wow factor?" Sheldon pursed his lips. "These stuffed paratroopers failed. They didn't lure people inside. We need to do better."

"True," said Nora. "But in our defense, September is all about back-to-school. I've talked to a few of the moms about their schedules, and it stressed me out just listening to them. They're driving kids here and there, working all kinds of hours, hitting the gym, stocking the fridge, prepping meals, balancing the books, and keeping everyone in their house happy. I've been shoving copies of *Mrs. Everything* into their hands and wishing I could afford to give away a spa voucher with every purchase."

Sheldon held up a finger. "Hey, now. You might be onto something with this. Today's women are women of power. Gifted, talented, and driven women. Magical women. Why not fill the window with women like that?"

"I'm picturing the Hocus Pocus witches around a cauldron," Nora said in a dreamy voice. "The cauldron's rimmed with salt because the witches are brewing margaritas. It's their ghouls' night out. Get it?"

"The UV rays must be getting to her," Sheldon mumbled to himself. "Witches? Sure. It's Halloween, after all. But not the hags with hairy warts and pointy hats. Beautiful witches. Multigenerational. Culturally diverse. What if they brew books in their cauldron? Stories about powerful females?"

Nora was instantly caught up by the idea. "Yes! We could display book covers featuring powerful women. Lady Macbeth. Medusa."

"Elphaba, Alina Starkov, Matilda."

"Medea." Nora could see books flying out of the cauldron. Books with cardboard wings and paper bodies. Colorful, glossy, magical books.

"Don't forget Hermione Granger," Sheldon added. "We can't have a power coven without her."

The two friends became more and more animated as they discussed materials, lighting, and other design elements.

Suddenly, Nora noticed the time.

"We'd better get ready to open. Even though it feels like the first circle of Dante's Inferno outside, people will still want coffee."

"That's because it's my coffee," Sheldon said. "I'll get my elixir going and pull some titles. We'll have a window's worth of fierce females by lunchtime."

Sheldon opened the front door to the noisy jangle of vintage sleigh bells. They hung from a hook on the back of the door, signaling the arrival or departure of customers—a useful alarm in a rabbit warren of a bookshop.

Useful or not, Sheldon hated them. "One of these days, I'm going to stuff those bells with bubble gum. Or plaster of paris."

Nora was about to reply when a woman's scream pierced the morning air.

The scream had come from up the street. Somewhere close.

It was just past nine on a muggy Tuesday, and downtown Miracle Springs was quiet. Kids were in school. Working professionals were in their air-conditioned offices. The shops on Main Street were either already open or preparing to open at ten. There was light foot traffic on the sidewalks and across the street in the park, but it didn't look like anyone else had heard the scream.

Nora believed the sound had come from the town's

newest business. The insurance agency that used to occupy the space had relocated to a newer office building with ample parking, and Nora expected someone to grab the prime retail space right away. After it sat empty for months, she learned that the lease was for the entire building, including the storefront and the two-bedroom apartment above it.

But all that was about to change. Two days ago, Nora had been walking back to the bookshop from the Gingerbread House when she'd noticed a purple awning over the entrance to the former insurance agency. A young man was on a ladder, wiping fingerprints from the dark purple letters he'd just applied to the front door. The letters spelled SOOTHE.

Soothe was a block and a half away, and the scream had come from that direction. Nora didn't hesitate. She took off running.

Nora ran until she came up behind a woman who was hunched over a large object on the sidewalk. The woman had a slim frame, long, gray hair mottled with brown, and freckled skin. She passed her hands over the object and let out a soft moan.

Nora took a few more steps and the source of the woman's distress was revealed. It was a life-sized sculpture of a robed figure.

Squatting next to the woman, Nora looked her up and down. "Are you hurt?"

"I'm sorry," the woman said without taking her eyes off the sculpture. "I shouldn't have screamed like that. She's broken. But it's okay. Broken things are still beautiful."

Nora glanced at the pair of workmen standing under the purple awning.

"We've moved lots of heavy stuff, and nothing like this ever happened before." The younger workman, who wore jeans and a sweat-stained RC Cola T-shirt, sounded spooked.

The older man had a bearlike build and a gruff voice. "I tied that knot myself. The rope slipped like it was covered in butter."

He made the sign of the cross, and Nora's gaze shifted back to the sculpture.

It was an angel. A winged angel.

Her right wing was intact, but there was a patch of rough marble where its left wing had been. As Nora stared at the wounded angel, she involuntarily brought her hand to her own shoulder. She could feel her burn scars through her thin shirt. The angel's scar reminded her of lunar rock. It was nothing like hers, which looked like jellyfish and small octopi, forever suspended in an aquarium of skin.

She heard someone breathing hard behind her and glanced up to see Sheldon offering his hand to the woman.

"I don't usually pant like a golden retriever when I meet people, and if I help you up, I promise not to lick you."

The woman gave him a grateful smile and took his hand. When she and Nora were both on their feet, she introduced herself as Celeste Leopold. "This is my store. Mine and my daughter's. Bren's inside and probably has no clue what just happened to Juliana."

"Is that the angel's name?" Nora asked.

Celeste cocked her head. "Angel, saint, healer, cunning woman. She's had many titles."

Nora and Sheldon introduced themselves and told Celeste about Miracle Books. By this time, the workmen had picked up the angel's detached wing.

"Where do you want this, ma'am?" asked the older man.

"Put it in the window, please." Celeste said. Her tone was surprisingly light considering how upset she'd just been. "I'll use it as a display. There aren't any mistakes in art. Only marvelous new creations."

As the men carried the wing inside, Sheldon mopped his brow with a handkerchief. He was still breathing heavily.

"Go back to the shop and put your feet up," Nora whispered to him. "You're as white as that angel."

Sheldon bobbed his head at Celeste. "Excuse me, neighbor, but when my skin goes from Greek god bronze to blanched almond, it's my cue to leave. I hope the rest of your move is uneventful."

While Celeste thanked Sheldon for his concern, Nora stared down at the angel.

The hair that framed her face was wavy and fell all the way to the embroidered belt at her waist. Attached to the belt was a thick chain. The chain reached the hem of the woman's floor-length skirts, and the last link was broken. The angel's hands were cupped, and the stalk of a leafy plant was tucked under her left arm. Though she reminded Nora of the statues in European church naves, there was something modern about the woman's expression.

She isn't humble.

The angel's gaze was direct. Unflinching. Her chin was raised. Was she confident? Or defiant?

"Does Juliana have a story?" she asked Celeste.

The question clearly pleased Celeste. "She sure does. It's my story too. And my daughter's." Her face glowed with pride. "For many generations, the women in my family have been called Juliana. Sometimes, as a first name. Sometimes, as a middle name. That's how important she is to us. She and I are centuries apart, but we share the same passion. She devoted her life to healing, and almost all of her descendants have followed in her footsteps."

The workmen reappeared on the sidewalk with more rope. They eyed the sculpture warily before winding rope around her torso.

"What's with the chain?" one of them asked.

There was a far-off look in Celeste's blue eyes. "Some say she was chained to a devil. Others say it was a dragon. Since I sculpted her, I decided to set her free."

The younger workman frowned. "Why not just get rid of the chain?"

Celeste glanced at Nora before answering, "Because once you've danced with a devil—or been burned by dragon fire—you don't ever want to go near those things again. The chains are there as reminders."

"I'd rather tie a string around my finger," the man said. A movement in the window directly above the store's entrance caught Nora's attention. Shielding her eyes against the sun's glare, she looked up and saw a milk-pale face and dark eyes peering down at her. The ghostlike vision drew a finger across its throat before smiling in delight.

Suddenly, Nora's burn scars began to tingle. The sensation started on the back of her hand and traveled up her arm to her neck. It crept over her cheek and forehead, even though a plastic surgeon had erased those scars over a year ago.

"I'd better go," Nora stammered to Celeste. "Good luck with everything."

She shot a glance at the second-story window, but no one was there.

Nora turned and started walking fast, eager to get back to Miracle Books. Her skin was still tingling like crazy.

Must be prickly heat.

At the end of the block, the tingling turned to itching. Nora put her hand to her forehead. Her hairline was damp. She needed to get out of the sun. She'd left her hat inside the shop and though she always wore sunscreen, she probably needed to reapply it.

As she paused under the welcome shade of the hardware store awning, the itching stopped. She now felt the weight of eyes on her back.

Was Celeste watching her?

Or the person who'd made the throat-cutting gesture? The tickly feeling of being watched stayed with Nora until she entered the bookstore.

"And you said *I* was pale," Sheldon cried from behind the espresso machine. "The ghost emoji on my phone is tanner than you. Sit down. I'll get you water."

Five minutes and a glass of water later, Nora was herself again.

"That was weird—for both of us to get overheated like that," she said. "At nine thirty in the morning?"

"Not really. I skipped breakfast and you went on a hike before work. I need food and you need fluids. Doctor Vega is in the house."

Nora waved a hand, dismissing the subject. "Is the paper back there? I think I saw a short piece about Soothe on the front page."

With the paper in hand, Sheldon sat down in the purple chair opposite Nora's mustard-colored velour chair. Three other mismatched chairs formed a circle around a glass coffee table. This was the readers' circle, the most popular place in the shop.

"All right, children, are you ready for storytime?" Sheldon cleared his throat and began to read. "'The Greene Building has a new tenant. Ms. Celeste Leopold has signed a three-year lease on the retail space and two-bedroom apartment. Ms. Leopold's boutique, Soothe, an eclectic mix of merchandise meant to reduce stress and take the sting out of chronic pain, will open in late September. Soothe will also stock organic food and drinks in the form of CBD comfort muffins and anti-inflammatory teas.'"

Nora gaped. "Comfort muffins? I wonder if Hester knows about this."

"Knows about what?"

Hester Winthrop, owner of the Gingerbread House Bakery and a member of Nora's book club, the Secret, Book & Scone Society, came around the corner of the Fiction section carrying a large bakery box. Inside were puff pastries shaped like open books. The scent of buttery dough wafted through the air, mingling with the aroma of fresh coffee. Nora couldn't imagine a more heavenly smell.

Sheldon took the box from Hester and carried it into the ticket agent's office. "We were just reading about our new neighbor."

Hester's face lit up. "I saw movers at the purple awning. What kind of store is it?"

Nora pointed at the paper. "Read the article on the bottom of the front page."

"I don't have time. I—"

"You need to read it."

Hester's apple print apron was dusted with flour and

cinnamon, so she grabbed the paper and read the article where she stood. When she reached the final sentence, her eyes widened in shock.

"*Comfort* muffins?" Her voice was shrill. "What the hell?"

Sheldon slung an arm around Hester's shoulder. "Celeste probably doesn't know about your comfort scones. She hasn't even moved in, and we're already getting mad at her." He looked at Nora. "Why don't we invite her over for coffee and a chat? We'll tell her about Hester's scones and suggest an alternative name for her baked goods. Mellow muffins?"

Hester smiled. "That's pretty good. But are CBD muffins even legal?"

"Yep," Sheldon replied. "I use CBD oil all the time. Lots of people do. I wouldn't worry about a few muffins, sweet girl. Your food is enchanted. You have lines out the door every day."

"You're right. Besides, this town needs more female business owners. I should do what I can to support Celeste. Let me know when you ask her for coffee, Nora. I'd like to be there."

As Nora hurried to finish her opening tasks before the clock struck ten, all thoughts of Celeste Leopold were pushed aside. After the shop was ready and Nora had greeted her first customer of the day, she began gathering titles for the new window display.

A woman picked up the copy of *Alchemy and Meggy Swann* from the top of Nora's pile and examined the back cover.

"I love historical fiction," she said to Nora. "Do you think my granddaughter would like it? She's in the sixth grade."

"She's the perfect age for Karen Cushman. Does she like historical novels?"

The woman looked aggrieved. "Not really. She's what you'd call a reluctant reader."

"Hm. Maybe she just hasn't met the right book. What are her interests?"

"Well, the last time I saw her, she told me about a paper she'd written on gender equality. Her teacher was very impressed. And she marched in a parade last year."

Nora smiled and touched the cover of the book in the woman's hand. "Meggy, the main character, travels to London to work for her alchemist father. However, she is turned down because she's not male. This is a story of a young woman fighting for her future. I have a feeling your granddaughter will cheer on Meggy Swann."

Though the woman thanked Nora, she didn't look happy. "It's hard to connect with my grandkids. I don't get their technology. I don't know what they're talking about most of the time. Are there books that can explain these things to me?"

"Probably, but I don't think you need them. Why don't you and your granddaughter read this book at the same time? Maybe you could meet somewhere special to talk about it? That would be a pretty cool way to connect."

The woman loved the idea. "I'm going to write a note on the title page. And buy us matching bookmarks too. I thought I saw some . . ."

Nora pointed her toward the bookmark spinner and returned to her stack. Now that she'd sold her only copies of *Alchemy and Meggy Swann*, she'd have to find a middle-grade replacement for the window. Luckily, she had another Cushman novel, *The Midwife's Apprentice*, on the shelf. While she was in the children's section, she also grabbed *Ella Enchanted, Malala's Magic Pencil, The Witch of Blackbird Pond, Matilda,* and Neil Gaiman's *Coraline.*

After bagging the grandmother's purchases and telling her to come back soon, Nora perused the stack of YA titles Sheldon had selected for the window display.

"Every book has a feisty female on the cover," he said as Nora looked at copies of *Throne of Glass, Labyrinth Lost, Children of Blood and Bone,* and *Uprooted.*

Nora nodded in approval. "These books paint a picture of strong, determined, powerful women of all ages. Magical women. We can add *Wicked* to the pile, but not *A Discovery of Witches* or *Practical Magic.* There are no women on those covers. Let's find a few more adult titles."

In between helping customers, Nora pulled copies of *The Mists of Avalon* and Paulo Coelho's *The Witch of Portobello,* and Sheldon added Alice Hoffman's *The Dovekeepers* and Isabel Allende's *The House of Spirits* to the pile.

Later, while Nora was reviewing their final selections, a young woman with pale skin, purple-tipped black hair, black clothing, and a sullen expression approached the counter.

"This is from my mom," she said, dumping a paper bag on top of *The House of Spirits.* "For checking on her this morning."

Nora took in the young woman's nose ring, eyebrow piercings, Metallica T-shirt, and knee-high combat boots. "You must be Bren. I'm Nora."

Bren pointed at the empty space above Nora's pinkie knuckle. "She said you'd been in a fire. How'd it happen? Did you start it?"

But Nora wasn't listening. She'd just recognized Bren's

face. "You were in the upstairs window—when the angel fell—I saw you."

"I *know*. Wasn't it awesome?" Her smile didn't reach her eyes. "I mean, who wants to be an angel? They don't have any fun."

She walked over to the bookmark spinner. Using her middle finger, she spun it once. Twice. Three times. The bookmarks lifted into the air.

Sheldon stepped out from behind the North Carolina Authors section just in time to see Bren whip the front door open, creating a riot of noise from the sleigh bells. She left the shop without a backward glance.

"What's in the bag?" Sheldon asked. "A hand grenade?"

Nora peeked inside. "Two chocolate muffins. Do you want one?"

Sheldon curled his lip. "If that girl does *Like Water for Chocolate* baking, those muffins will taste like angst and hostility."

Picking up a muffin, Nora gave it a tentative sniff. "It's a gift. I should try it, at least."

Sheldon watched with interest as Nora broke off a piece and popped it into her mouth. His interest was even more piqued when she immediately spit the piece back into the bag.

"It's that bad?" he asked. "Should I feed it to the pigeons during my lunch break?"

Nora shoved the bag into the trash can under the register. "I won't be held responsible for the deaths of innocent animals."

Sheldon picked up the single bookmark that had fallen off the spinner and handed it to Nora.

"Why do I feel like things are about to get interesting around here?"

A customer entered and he and Sheldon disappeared into the stacks.

Nora didn't even notice them. She was too busy staring at a photograph of a stained-glass window. The figure in the center of the window was an angel.

As she held the bookmark, Nora's uneasiness from that morning returned. Angels were supposed to be symbols of light and protection.

But there was another kind of angel. The fallen kind.

The ones who became devils.